The Unlikely Master Genius

The Unlikely Master Genius

The St. Brendan Series

Volume One

CARLA KELLY

CAMEL PRESS

Seattle, WA

Cover design by Sabrina Sun

The Unlikely Master Genius
Copyright © 2018 by Carla Kelly

ISBN: 978-1-60381-683-0 (Trade Paper)
ISBN: 978-1-60381-684-7 (eBook)

Library of Congress Control Number: 2017959752

Printed in Canada

To Heather Brown Moore,
who asked me to write a short story,
which led to this book.
I owe you, Heather.
To Euclid, too, of course.

Books by Carla Kelly

Fiction

Daughter of Fortune
Summer Campaign
Miss Chartley's Guided Tour
Marian's Christmas Wish
Mrs. McVinnie's London Season
Libby's London Merchant
Miss Grimsley's Oxford Career
Miss Billings Treads the Boards
Mrs. Drew Plays Her Hand
Reforming Lord Ragsdale
Miss Whittier Makes a List
The Lady's Companion
With This Ring
Miss Milton Speaks Her Mind
One Good Turn
The Wedding Journey
Here's to the Ladies: Stories of the Frontier Army
Beau Crusoe
Marrying the Captain
The Surgeon's Lady
Marrying the Royal Marine
The Admiral's Penniless Bride
Borrowed Light
Enduring Light
Coming Home for Christmas: The Holiday Stories
Marriage of Mercy
My Loving Vigil Keeping
Her Hesitant Heart
Safe Passage
The Double Cross
Marco and the Devil's Bargain
Paloma and the Horse Traders
Season's Regency Greetings
Regency Christmas Gifts
The Wedding Ring Quest
Softly Falling
Doing No Harm
Courting Carrie in Wonderland
The Star in the Meadow
One Step Enough

Non-Fiction

On the Upper Missouri: The Journal of Rudolph Friedrich Kurz (editor)
Louis Dace Letellier: Adventures on the Upper Missouri (editor)
Fort Buford: Sentinel at the Confluence
Stop Me If You've Read This One

But Love is a durable fire
In the mind ever burning
Never sick, never old, never dead
From itself, never turning.

Sir Walter Raleigh, "Walsinghame"

Chapter One

❧

TWENTY-ONE YEARS AFTER HIS first classroom flogging in a Dumfries, Scotland, workhouse, Sailing Master Able Six had forgotten neither the pain, nor the surprise.

He was five years old, ragged and hungry like all the other boys. There were workhouse girls, but he never saw them in a classroom. Girls mattered for naught beyond kitchen duties, sewing and ironing, and probably jollying the workhouse master, likely against their will.

From the perspective of two decades, Able suspected that the teacher who had seemed so old then hadn't been much beyond his twenties, if that. More specifically, Able remembered the pointer he carried and tapped in his hand, the gesture both mesmerizing and menacing.

But what was Able to do? The teacher had written the sentence, "Thou shalt not bear false witness," on the blackboard, a mere bit of black paint over rough boards.

Young Able had flinched along with other pupils each time the teacher slammed his pointer against each word on the blackboard. In terror, poor Jedediah Winkum had pissed in his pants and sat in misery throughout the classroom ordeal. Maybe what he smelled was more than piss; who could tell? They all stank.

The boy directly in front of Able had fidgeted, or scratched, or held his mouth wrong, or done something to attract the teacher's attention. The master pounced on the unsuspecting child, a boy with not much wit to begin with, even though he must have been two or three years Able's senior.

"Read this sentence, bastard," the master demanded. He pushed his pointer under the unfortunate child's chin and raised his head. "Stand ye up!"

The boy did as ordered, shaking visibly. He stared at the words, shook his head, and the pointer slammed down on his shoulder. The boy cried out as he sank to his knees.

When the teacher raised the pointer again for another blow, some power he did not understand made Able Six leap to his feet. "Thou shalt not bear false witness," he sang out at the top of his voice.

A blow to his ribs knocked the wind from him. Able wavered, but righted himself, an ability that would serve him well in the coming years on pitching, yawing ships.

Able should never have looked in the teacher's eyes. He was used to disgust and neglect and being called a bastard, even though at the time he wasn't certain what it meant. What glared back at him was hatred. Not too many years later, Able came to understand that the hatred was likely directed inward rather than at the five-year-old staring back with a grave expression.

Standing there, the focus of a miserable man's undivided attention, Able gathered he had committed another sin: he knew too much.

"Ye can't read yet, bastard," the man said, his voice neutral in that danger zone of bullies. The teacher's sad eyes flicked across a row of cowering older boys in the front row. "Which one of ye told him? Trying to make a fool of me?"

Already in pain, already terrified, Able saw no need to involve others. They probably all knew what the sentence said, but were wiser than he, because they remained silent. How did he know how people learned anything? He was but five.

"No one told me, sir," Able said.

"Impossible!" The brute slammed down the pointer again and Able gasped in agony. "You've only been in this class two days."

Able put up his hands to protect his face as the pointer whisked down once more. Years later in the fleet, a ship's surgeon had remarked on Able's forearm, which was slightly crooked. "Master, you had an early injury, didn't you?"

"It works fine," was all Able said, still unwilling to discuss the event that changed his life. How could a surgeon, a well-educated man, understand that a child could look at letters and know what they meant?

He had fainted from the pain and woke up in his bed in the room he shared with twenty-five other bastards, foundlings plucked from church steps, hedgerows, and noisome rooming houses in Scotland's southern districts. Someone with more sympathy than skill stuck a piece of wood next to his forearm and wrapped it with a few twists of a stinking sheet. He lay there, stunned by what had taken place, only to be scolded by the boys around him, demanding that he not say one more word, even if he could read.

"Don't be smart," one of the older boys warned, a boy Able looked up to because he sometimes shared bits of food finessed from the kitchen where he washed dishes. It was a plum job, one the other lads envied. "We'll all get in trouble."

"I thought everyone could read it," Able had whispered.

He heard that infernal pointer whistling down even now, as he lay wide awake in his comfortable room in the vicarage of St. Matthew's Parish. The unfailing clock in his remarkable brain told him it was thirty minutes past midnight, and he faced a busy day of travel from rural Devonshire to Portsmouth on the mail coach.

Time to sleep, if he could. He had no trouble redirecting the chaos of his brain to a more recent memory, when Meridee Bonfort kissed him while her sister's back was turned and wished him a shy goodnight.

He smiled in the dark, wondering if Meridee tossed and turned as he did. He knew the answer to such a simple question, so he sat up, looking around for his trousers. In his stocking feet, Able crept down a flight of stairs and tapped on Meridee's door.

She opened it so promptly that Able knew she had not been asleep, either. She gratified him with a kiss, and then another. She gently rubbed her cheek to his as he held her close, then supplied her own admonition, far more pleasant than anything he had heard in his nine years in the workhouse.

"Master Six, two more weeks," she whispered in his ear as she stood on tiptoe and he generously held her up a little higher. "Last Sunday's banns and two more Sundays. Go back upstairs."

He had only known this woman for a month, this darling who was going to become his wife, even though he was a sailing master too young to have any prize money yet, thrust ashore on half pay because of the damned Treaty of Amiens. As much as he wanted her, he wasn't planning any stress on her virginity. That would wait, because he understood rules. That had been another hard-earned workhouse lesson.

Still, a man could try for sympathy. "I'm afraid," he said, because it was true.

For several years after his encounter with that classroom sadist, Able Six had not looked anyone in the eye. Once in the fleet, the bosun's mate had taken him aside and declared, "I see real promise in you, lad, but you need to look at people addressing you."

"Sir, that earned me beatings," he replied, because Able Six never forgot a single event.

"I was a workhouse brat, too," the bosun's mate informed him. "You can practice by looking *me* in the eye."

And so he looked in Meridee Bonfort's lovely eyes. "Aye, lass, I am afraid."

To his relief, she took his hand, tugged him into her room, and closed the door. He hadn't been there before so he glanced around and saw her travel trunk open. She had only just returned from Portsmouth herself.

"You're certain the headmaster at St. Brendan's will see me as an answer to prayer? I'd be lying if I told you I had no doubts, " he confessed.

He felt as alone as any man in the universe who realizes he will soon be supporting another creature in this harsh world. "I'm on half pay. What am I *doing*?"

"Marrying me," she said calmly and kissed him.

He had kissed other women in bedrooms before. Christ's bones, he had done more than that in back alleys just off wharfs, moments after leaving a frigate, hull-barnacled and back from a two-year voyage. Meridee Bonfort was different, so he gave her a clinical kiss and held her off by the shoulders.

She appraised him, and to his continued amazement, seemed not to find him wanting, even though it hadn't been much of a kiss. Her hands went to his face.

"What you're doing is taking the mail coach to Portsmouth in the morning, where you will meet with Captain Hallowell and accompany him to St. Brendan's School," she said. "You know how to teach young lads."

Doubting Thomas, get thee behind me, he thought. "I have been instructing two well-behaved pupils in a vicarage—why, mercy, this one," he reminded her with a smile. "Meri, I *know* workhouse brats. They are cut from different cloth."

"Precisely," she said, apparently unwilling to even consider that if he failed to impress the headmaster, there was no way he could afford the upkeep of a wife. As it was, the pennies for an outside seat on a mail coach were going to tax his purse to its skinny limits.

"You will know what to do, Master Six," Meridee said.

She spoke with the same sincerity he had heard in her voice from their first conversation. He felt sudden awe at the bedrock certainty she meant every word. "Where you doubt, my love, I will supply twice the confidence." She touched his face again. "When I have doubts, you can do the same for me."

"Aye, lass," he told her, feeling better. "Give me another cuddle and I'll go back to bed."

She held him close, her arms tight around him, this gentleman's daughter who saw something in him to love, even once she understood his special gift. If he found himself with a free moment in Portsmouth, he would write a letter to Lieutenant Caldwell, comrade from the frigate now in ordinary, waiting out a doomed peace treaty. Caldwell had informed him of a temporary position teaching two sons of a country vicar too busy during Christmastide to continue their lessons. Able should thank him.

He had another question for this lovely lady in his arms. "Meridee," he said, holding her off because it seemed safer, "how in the world did you figure out my secret?"

"I watched your eyes in my brother-in-law's study," she said. "You weren't looking at him. You were scanning every single title in the bookcase behind him. You did it in under five seconds."

"I can't help myself. You know that," he said. "But *why* were you looking at my eyes?"

She laughed softly, the kind of intimate laugh reserved for bedrooms, which was precisely where they were. *I am an idiot*, he thought, mildly put out with himself. *The door, Durable Six, the door. Head toward it. Two more weeks and she's yours, provided you do not make a fool of yourself in Portsmouth.*

"Able, you're the handsomest man I ever saw," she told him simply. "I couldn't help watching your face."

"I think my mother's name was Mary. I have no idea who my father was," he reminded her. "Was he from Greece or Italy? Spain or God-help-us France? One thing more: why doesn't this bother you? Meri, I'm a bastard. You know that."

Undeterred, she walked him to the door. "I am your keeper, Master Six. Captain Hallowell told me so. Goodnight."

Chapter Two

❧

WAS THERE ANY PLACE colder than the top of a mail coach in December? Thank God he had not pawned his boat cloak, no matter how desperate he was for the few coins it would bring. Able hunkered down to endure, something he was good at.

He touched the ragged copy of Euclid's *Elements* in his pocket, knowing that if the cold overwhelmed him, he could warm himself by reciting a random proposition and devising mental exercises. Shivering inside—never a good sign—he tried it now.

Despite the cold that clawed at his temples, he relaxed as Euclid's grand work unrolled in his mind like a scroll. Ah, Prop Eight: *If two triangles have two sides equal to two sides respectively, and have also the base equal to the base, they will have the angles equal which are contained by the equal straight lines.*

How could a man not feel better, with Euclid on his mind? They were friends of long standing. He saw the diagrams clearly in that mind's eye Shakespeare wrote of in *Hamlet*, Act I, Scene 2. Once he considered all the geometric angles, Able started at the beginning of *Hamlet* and thought his way through the play as the mail coach trundled toward Portsmouth.

By the time his brain brought down the curtain on *Hamlet* with the arrival of Fortinbras, prince of Norway, the mail coach stopped for victuals. Able ate inside the coach, since Meridee had kindly packed him a lunch.

He wasn't alone. An angular lady, sharp-chinned and all elbows, ate her own lunch on the seat across from him. A sociable man, Able wanted to speak to her, rather than eat in silence rendered embarrassing because they were both too poor to eat in the public house. With no introduction, he maintained his silence. Each tried to ignore the other.

He eyed her skimpy meal, grateful Meridee Bonfort was concerned for his welfare. He polished off two boiled eggs and one sandwich thick with meat and cheese, a feast compared to the lady's one carrot and single cracker with a nearly invisible skiff of butter.

He had another sandwich, but could not eat it, not with the lady eyeing it when she thought he wasn't watching. Her silent desperation reminded him forcefully that being poor in England was much harder on women.

Are you a man or a mouse, Durable Six? he asked himself. He cleared his throat. She glanced up, and the hope in her eyes nearly broke his heart.

"Miss, we have not been introduced, but this extra sandwich is too much. I know it won't keep. Would you ...."

She blushed but did not look away. "I would, sir."

"There's this egg," Able added, encouraged. "Take it, please."

She did, with no hesitation. Looking into the canvas bag Meridee had packed for him, he was happy to see some sort of bread pudding, the substantial kind that would help keep out the cold when he climbed back on top of the mail coach. He munched on the tasty thing, trying not to listen to the small sounds of appreciation coming from the unlucky lady, heading somewhere alone.

Meri, I promise you will never be alone and hungry, if you hitch your wagon to my decidedly ramshackle horse, he thought. *We'll manage somehow.*

The lady cleared her throat. "I am Miss Mercer," she said, even if there had been no real introduction. "I am going to an estate near Sidmouth to become a governess."

Fair enough. "I am Sailing Master Six, hoping for a teaching position at a boys' school in Portsmouth. Pleased to make your acquaintance."

He watched a cloud fall over her face. Perhaps he shouldn't have spoken. A governess might think she outranked a sailing master. She surprised him.

"Master Six, my brother served the guns on the *Triumph* at Camperdown," she said. He saw the pride in her eyes, as well as sorrow.

"Captain Essington's ship," he said. "They fought well. I was on the *Powerful*." Should he ask? "Where is he now?"

"It was his last fight," Miss Mercer said softly.

"I'm sorry, Miss Mercer," he replied. "These are trying times."

"They are," she agreed, and pulled her threadbare dignity in the form of a cloak tighter about her.

He was spared thinking of something else to say as the more fortunate riders left the public house, ready to journey on. He nodded to Miss Mercer and climbed up to his cold seat. When the coach stopped at Sidmouth, she waved to him.

He waved back, watching her struggle with a valise against the winter wind. He didn't see a vehicle waiting for her so he turned away, much as he might turn away from an abandoned pup when he could offer no help. He could do nothing for Miss Mercer except resolve to manage his life so Meri never had to resort to the half-life of a governess. Meri might call herself his keeper, but in Sidmouth he decided that he was hers, too.

Euclid didn't tempt him then; neither did Shakespeare. Until they stopped for the night in Poole, he warmed himself by thinking of all the ways he loved Meridee Bonfort, a charming spinster of one month's acquaintance. Funny how a man could bumble along, never considering there might someone waiting just for him.

In his line of work, wives were a luxury. War and more war poured out by an upstart Corsican had effectively shunted aside typical avenues of sociality that often led to matrimony, people being what they were. In the fo'c's'le and later the wardroom, he had listened to the complaints of fellow seamen, grousing because life at sea was no way to meet anyone of the fair sex, let alone contemplate the future.

He had another strike against him, one that came with having been born in a back alley in Dumfries, Scotland, and then abandoned and found, nearly frozen, on the steps of St. David's Church. He had risen to the top of his profession as a sailing master at the unheard of age of twenty-two. That could have assured him the respectable hand of a shopkeeper's daughter, or even the offspring of another warrant officer like himself, but it would never happen because he was still a bastard, worlds without end, amen.

He had met a charming miss in Plymouth two years ago before his last voyage, the eldest daughter of the harbormaster. He could tell she was interested in him at least superficially, because he knew what he looked like in a mirror—the olive skin, pleasing features, and full head of curly black hair.

Then came the moment of truth. She had earlier accepted his birth in Dumfries, then naturally wanted to know more about his family. Should he have lied? He did not, and a few minutes later, found himself outside.

Meridee Bonfort was different. For some unknown reason, perhaps because she knew he was only going to stay long enough to instruct her nephews, she had asked about his name first, never having seen Abel spelled Able.

Knowing he had nothing to lose, he had explained he was named Durable because he hadn't died from exposure on those stone steps in February, and Six because he was the sixth foundling entered on the rolls of Dumfries Workhouse in 1776. The only expression that had registered on Meridee's pretty face was interest.

THAT NIGHT HE SHARED a stranger's bed in Poole's least-favored inn. The man snored and reeked of garlic, but otherwise posed no threat. Able thought about sharing a bed with Meridee, which meant getting up and walking around the small room, training his mind to Euclid and Proposition Nine. He laughed out loud at Prop Nine, which did look a bit phallic. He mentally rehearsed all the propositions, wondering about Euclid.

Portsmouth hove into view through a squall. As a port, it had none of the raffish charm of Plymouth; even its nickname of Pompey had no inherent meaning, as seemingly unplanned as a bastard child. Able sniffed the air, happy to be back in the land of tar and new rope, mingled with dried or drying herring. Under all was the tang of brine and stink of low tide.

He tried to see it through Meridee's eyes and felt doubt creep aboard his heart. Portsmouth was no place for a gently reared lady. Still, she had seen it herself only a few days ago, with no apparent complaint.

He caught his duffel tossed down to him, grateful he had packed his best uniform, sober black with gilt buttons and nothing more, because Admiralty had yet to assign sailing masters a uniform. He could wear it to St. Brendan's, then on his wedding day.

Thanks to the noxious Peace of Amiens, he was the only man at Gunwharf shouldering a duffel. He looked toward the harbor, where few frigates rode at anchor, sails furled, and in some cases, sails gone. He shook his head to see the prison hulks against the horizon, carrying their suffering cargos of Frenchmen not yet repatriated, or maybe forgotten. Who knew?

He was glad enough to leave the docks and walk to Water Street, with its tidy homes belonging to merchants grown rich from victualing vessels and post captains home from the sea.

Able took a deep breath and another as he raised his hand to the brass knocker at 63 Water Street, the residence of Captain Benjamin Hallowell, Yankee captain admitted to Vice Admiral Sir Horatio Nelson's select Band of Brothers for his tenacity at Aboukir Bay three years ago.

He must have been expected, because the captain's butler didn't bat an eye to see a shabby sailor needing a haircut asking for his master.

"This way, sir," the butler said, and made his majestic way to the bookroom. "Please be seated. I'll take your … your …."

"Duffel," Able supplied, and handed over the sorry thing.

Too nervous to sit, Able stared at the three filled-to-overflowing bookcases for fifteen seconds, memorizing titles.

The door opened. "You can take one or two books to bed tonight, if you've a mind to read, Master Six."

Able turned around with a smile that faded as he stared in open-mouthed wonder at the black eye of epic proportions his lovely Meridee had planted on Captain Hallowell. She had confessed her impulsive right jab to Able before he left for Portsmouth, blaming it on her irritation that the captain seemed less than helpful when she had visited earlier to plead Able's case.

He saluted his captain, appalled at the carnage one fierce woman could inflict, then grateful right down to his holey stockings that she was on his side, ready to fight his battle with him. Tears welled in his eyes at the thought.

He had known Benjamin Hallowell for years, one of the two commanders who winkled out his great secret, the one that set him apart in ways that even his lower-than-low birth could never have done. He knew Captain Hallowell as a stalwart man who never backed down from a fight, even when the prospect of success or survival was nil.

He gazed in silence at a black eye turning green, and decided Meridee Bonfort could hold her own in Portsmouth.

"A piece of advice, Master Six," the good man said, extending his hand. "Whatever you do, never underestimate Miss Bonfort. It might be your last conscious thought."

Chapter Three

❧

"BELVEDERE, HERE HE IS, a bit older, but probably not any wiser," Captain Hallowell said as he indicated Able standing in the doorway to the drawing room that afternoon. "How could he be wiser than he is now? Wasn't it you, my fine fellow, who swore to me that if Master Six had lived four hundred years ago, he'd have been burnt at the stake?"

Oh Lord, Able thought. *For my sins ....*

He glanced at Captain Sir Belvedere St. Anthony in his wheeled chair, entire right leg gone. He wished, not for the first time, that Sir B's surgeon, a competent fellow, hadn't been so overwhelmed by wounded at the Battle of the Nile. Of course, Sir B hadn't helped his own cause by waving his surgeon on to more seriously wounded sailors, all rank aside. But that was Captain Sir Belvedere St. Anthony, the enigma of the fleet.

"I did indeed say that," Sir B replied. "Ben, you should have seen this handsome scamp years before Camperdown when I caught him lying on the operating table, reading."

"My skinny bum ached for weeks, after my surprise landing on that deck," Able said. The only way to survive Sir B's wit was to equal it.

"What I did discover was that he had done his work and was allowed to read, although at lightning speed," Sir B said. " 'Pon my word, I've never seen pages turn so fast."

He gestured them both farther into the drawing room, but Captain Hallowell held up his hand. "You two may reminisce on your own time." He nodded toward Able. "If we are not on the road to Surrey within the hour, Mrs. Hallowell will give me what for."

He reached into his inside coat pocket and pulled out a sheet of paper folded twice. "Hand this to Mrs. Fillion at the Drake after your wedding and strive to make your new bride forget she's marrying a Navy man. That's an order."

Able took the paper and opened it. "Sir, it's too much," he began and tried to hand it back.

Captain Hallowell would have none of it. "Two nights at the Drake with a compliant woman on her back? What is the Navy coming to? On the contrary, Master Six, it's scarcely enough, considering what you did for my nephew. Sir B, do your best with this genius of ours."

"We'll manage, Ben. Good Christmas to you."

"I recall your good work for me," Sir B said after Captain Hallowell showed himself out. "I hadn't heard about Cape St. Vincent. You amputated Ben's nephew's leg, after the surgeon died?"

Able found it vexing to remember every detail of Cape St. Vincent, to hear the moans and pleadings of the wounded, and the listing of the ship in critical need of its own emergency treatment. After Surgeon Sproul died when a Spanish ball pierced the HMS Captain below the water line, two of the other loblolly boys carefully placed Nathaniel Hallowell on the bloody operating table and looked around, wondering who might operate. The pharmacist's mate had drawn himself into a tearful ball.

Able had watched Sproul perform numerous amputations. With no hesitation, Able had stepped up to the table and cut off the young man's leg.

"Aye, Sir B," he replied, embarrassed.

"Why so modest? I have seen your ability."

"I believe you spotted it first, Captain," Able said.

"Wise of me, don't you know? Pour us some smuggler's sherry."

Able did as asked, shoving the sickbay scenes to the back of his mind and substituting lazy days on a ship calmed in the South Pacific.

"Let us move smartly along now. I've taken an interest in St. Brendan's," Sir B said after a sip and a smack. "Damned good stuff! When my footman admitted Aloysius Bonfort himself, and a pretty miss clutching his hand, I knew this was going to be good."

"Miss Bonfort can be tenacious, or so I have discovered," Able said.

"Tenacious doesn't begin to frame the matter," Sir B said. "Her eyes were fierce to look at, and yet there was such hope in them." He leaned forward. "I could tell after only a few sentences that you had found your keeper, Master Six."

"You're the one who told me I needed a keeper," Able reminded him.

"So you do. Sir Horatio Nelson himself showed up here bare minutes later, summoned by our redoubtable Yankee captain, I don't doubt. So glad he was in port."

"I trust Mer … Miss Bonfort was suitably impressed, to see the great man."

Sir B took another sip and smiled at the memory. "She took it all in stride. Your lady told us why you needed to be teaching a classroom of masters-in-training, rather than running one quarterdeck. I'll never forget her! 'Sirs,' said she, looking so lovely, 'just think: with masters well-trained as only Able Six can do, you'll reap the benefits for years.' What could we say?" he concluded, then made Able laugh. "No one wanted a facer such as Miss Bonfort had planted on Ben Hallowell. I rest my case. Are you in, lad?"

"I am, Sir B," Able replied. He finished his sherry. "Now I have to convince a headmaster, I imagine."

"You do, but you come highly recommended," Sir B replied. "Let us visit St. Brendan's School of Incorrigibles. Is it cold outside?"

"There's a stiff wind from the west by northwest at about ten knots," Able said.

"Be more specific, Master Six."

With a grin, Able told him the degrees and minutes.

"That's better! Can't have you losing your grip." Sir B rang a copper bell at his elbow. "I directed Gervaise to summon my coachman. There you are, Gervaise."

Without a word, Able took the captain's boat cloak from the valet and slung it around Sir B's too-thin shoulders, then put on his own. With a pang, he remembered Sir B as a robust man. This thin fellow with the sallow skin still looked burnt to the socket, and the Nile was five years ago.

"You're worried about me, Master Six, I can tell," Sir B commented as his valet, a sturdy fellow by necessity, opened the door on wind and rain.

"Aye, sir," Able said, knowing better than to play the fool with this sharply intelligent man. "I'd like to see you on a quarterdeck again."

"Some things are not meant to be," Sir B replied.

"Perhaps, sir, but I can wish it."

He stood back while Gervaise wheeled his former captain and current mentor to the carriage and lifted the frail man into the vehicle. Able seated himself next to the commander whose opinion he valued, and who seemed interested, who knows why, in furthering his own modest career. "Thank you for what you are trying to do for me."

The melancholy left Sir B's face. "Your almost-wife is a persuasive lady," he said. "I think we all fell a little bit in love with her as she stated your case." He laughed softly. "She reminded me a bit of Shakespeare's Portia in *The Merchant of Venice*."

Able knew what was coming. It was the same test administered years ago when Captain St. Anthony had loaned him Shakespeare's Folio and told him to begin anywhere. "Act Four Scene One: 'The quality of mercy is not strained,' " Able quoted, enjoying the memory of Portia pleading Bassanio's cause, as

Meridee had pleaded his. "'It droppeth as the gentle rain from heaven upon the place beneath. It is twice blest: It blesseth him that gives and him that takes.' More, Sir B?"

"We could go through all the plays, could we not?"

"We could," Able agreed. "I remember an evening in the dog latitudes doing precisely that."

"You never faltered, and I realized the Royal Navy had someone special on board. Miss Bonfort seems to know how to use your mind to best advantage."

"She's bright, and for some reason unknown, she loves me," Able said simply. "Here's one for her, sir, the last verse of 'Walsinghame,' by poor, headless Sir Walter Raleigh: 'But true love is a durable fire, in the mind ever burning; never sick, never old, never dead, from itself never turning.' "

Sir B sat in silence, looking out the window. "I haven't thought of that one in years. Did I quiz you on it?" he asked finally.

"Aye, sir. You know I am Durable."

"Master Durable Six, you'll evermore be the only man entered on Admiralty rolls with such an outlandish name." The captain sighed. "I'd forgotten how lovely that poem is. 'Never sick, never old, never dead ....' Able, don't waste a moment."

Since Sir B was silent, wrapped in a cloak of melancholy, Able absorbed the route, taking in the mansions that gradually yielded to merchants' houses. The closer they came to the mighty wharfs of Portsmouth harbor, the meaner the houses. He wracked his super-agile brain to remember St. Brendan's, but nothing came to mind, which meant he had never seen or even heard of it. The scroll of his brain had stopped at a blank space.

He glanced at Captain St. Anthony, hesitant to speak, until he saw his mentor turn his way, as if giving him permission for conversation.

"I confess I have never heard of St. Brendan's School," he said. "I know well who St. Brendan is, but ...."

"Patron saint of sailors like you and me, lad." Sir B gestured to a narrow street but a block from Gunwharf, where ships headed for dry dock deposited their cannon in neat rows. "We'll wind down here into the oldest part of Pompey. It was a monastery at one time, who knows how long ago. After Henry the Eighth worked his cruel will on the Catholic Church, the monastery sat idle for centuries." He chuckled. "The street is called Saint's Way, far more holy than Portsmouth warrants, I vow."

Able held the carriage door while Gervaise efficiently moved his master into his wheeled chair again. He turned his collar up against the chill wind that blew toward revolutionary Europe, as Sir B told his coachman to wait.

"Hopefully, the old priss won't be set upon by roving gangs of hungry seamen," Sir B joked. "Ring the bell, Master Six. Your life is about to change."

Chapter Four

◆∞◆

"IT ALREADY HAS, SIR," Able said, amused, intimidated, unnerved, and
wishing Meridee were tucked close beside him. He needed his keeper.

"It will change some more."

Able steeled himself for whatever lay on the other side of the door, hoping
it wouldn't remind him of his nine awful years in the Dumfries Workhouse,
where boys were beaten for nothing except that they were illegitimate, smelly,
hungry, and there.

He received his first surprise as the door was slowly opened by a little
fellow, putting all his puny muscle into the effort.

Bright, inquiring eyes looked into his. A quick glance, that blink of
information that told him everything at once, took in a child dressed soberly
in black, reminding Able of his own Royal Navy quasi-uniform. Black buttons
substituted for gilt ones, and he saw a wonderful crest on the left breast: St.
Brendan the Navigator, cradling a small ship of medieval origin in his arms.

The lad's shoes were sturdy and he wore black stockings. Able couldn't
recall stockings during his Dumfries years. He received his first pair in the
fleet, and remembered staring at them, wondering briefly if they were for his
hands.

The boy's hair was cut close to his head, and he looked as tidy as a pin.
He held the door open wider, and gestured them in with a bit of a flourish.
There was nothing ground down or hangdog in his expression, so Able Six
took heart.

"We have come to speak with Headmaster Thaddeus Croker," Sir B said.
"He is expecting us."

"Follow me, sirs," the little fellow said, turning smartly and striding down
the chilly corridor, confident, apparently, that they would follow.

"He'll command a quarterdeck someday," Sir B commented with a smile of his own, as Gervaise whizzed him along. "Answering the door is probably a prized duty here. What was your favorite task in the workhouse?"

"Staying alive," Able whispered, unwilling for the child to hear him. He heard Sir B's sharp intake of breath and wondered briefly what privileged people like Captain St. Anthony really knew of workhouses. "We fought over kitchen cleanup. Potato peelings were worth their weight in gold."

"Good God," Sir B murmured.

"You asked, Captain," Able said, amused.

Able gazed around the narrow hall. To his surprise, he saw battle flags, one from the *Haarlem*, sunk at Camperdown; another from the *Serieuse*, battered to death at the Battle of the Nile. And there was the *Salvador del Mundo's* ripped flag, captured at Cape St. Vincent.

Able turned in a slow circle, seeing other enemy flags, probably from smaller ship-to-ship engagements across all the oceans, seas, inlets, and bays throughout their world at war. Some he knew personally; others were the stuff of legend.

"Who … who is behind this school?" Able asked, when they stopped at a heavily carved door, probably the office of the monastery's abbot in years gone by.

"I have no idea. All I know is that St. Brendan's School for … for … guttersnipes, thieves, and workhouse bastards has been here for three years." He shrugged.

They waited silently as their escort knocked on the door.

"Come in," they heard and entered a room lined with books and papers stacked on benches and a window seat.

"That will be all, Mr. Wolf. Close the door behind you."

"Aye, Headmaster Croker."

The headmaster stood with his back to the door, staring out the window, hand behind his back, rocking on his heels. He was dressed in black like his students. A tall man, he seemed even taller because of leanness bordering on emaciation.

"Join me, gentlemen," he said in a voice that carried.

Gervaise moved Sir B into position. Able clasped his hands behind him too, ready to admire the view as well. For all that his squadron frequently docked in Plymouth or Torquay, Able's familiarity with Portsmouth stretched back to his earliest days in the fleet. He knew the harbor, with its broad anchorage, the narrow streets hazardous to a man's health from too much grog, diseased whores, and cutpurses. Bustling, busy, raffish Pompey.

"Try the view from this window, Master Six," the headmaster said. "I do enjoy a corner office."

Able looked down at a surprisingly tidy expanse of grass, where boys dressed in black walked. They were orderly and neat, much as their little escort. A ship's bell rang and the boys moved faster. Must be time for class.

Interested, he watched them hurry inside, then turned his attention to a silted-in, stone-lined retaining pond or tidal basin. A relic from earlier days, it must have been a sheltered spot for small boats to tie in, letting monks off at the monastery. Unused for years, perhaps centuries, it had been gathering garbage up to and perhaps including dead dogs, and maybe unwary mariners. It looked to be about eight feet deep, give or take a few inches. *What I could do with that*, he thought, as ideas scrolled through his mind and lodged there. The usual background noise in his skull grew louder, as though trying to jealously clamor for his attention.

The headmaster watched him with a slight smile. "Introduce yourself, young man."

Able felt his face grown warm. *You're off to a good start for employment, dunce*, he scolded himself. He bowed. "Sailing Master Able Six. I'm here about a job."

To his surprise, the headmaster and Captain Sir Belvedere St. Anthony glanced at each other and laughed. "You haven't heard a word I've been saying, have you?"

Embarrassed, Able shook his head and felt himself transported years and miles back to Dumfries. "I beg your pardon, sir. That stone basin had my full attention." *And everything else in my brain*, he added to himself, *but you needn't know that.*

"I thought it might, Master Six. I wanted you to see it." The headmaster returned Able's bow with a nod. "I am Thaddeus Croker. Do have a seat."

Able sat, feeling inadequate, out of his league, silly for making plans about a filthy pond when he was no more than a few shillings from complete poverty. Good God, and getting married in two weeks to a woman he could not live without. Both men were looking at him expectantly, but he had no idea what they wanted.

His equilibrium returned. He crossed his legs and leaned back, in control of himself again because he was a man with ideas. "I would clean that pond, sir, fill it to three feet of water and do two things right away." He took a deep breath. "I doubt there is a boy in this school who can swim. They need to learn."

"You know as well as I do, Master Six, that sailors are superstitious about learning to swim," Sir B said. "Tempt the devil, eh?"

"I could care less, sir," Able said, mincing not a single word. "They'll be of more use to the fleet if they don't drown on their first encounter with the enemy." He stretched his legs out, comfortable with the conversation. "I recall swimming to a bomb kedge in Copenhagen with an auger. Two holes and down it went."

"He did, Thad," Sir B said, his smile broad. "Swims like a fish."

"But we're at peace," the headmaster protested.

"Four months more, sir, give or take a little," Able said decisively. "First Consul Bonaparte wants this world, but by God, we shan't hand it to him on a silver salver. Not while I breathe."

He spoke quietly. When he held her close and kissed Meridee yesterday, she had whispered in his ear for him to go all out and take no prisoners in Portsmouth. *My keeper tells me so*, he thought, and felt her calming influence.

"What is the other thing, Master Six? You mentioned two things," Thaddeus Croker asked.

"It's more than two, I reckon," he continued, on terra firma now. "My lads and I would build small boats or platforms and sail them on that pond. It would be easy enough to ruffle the waters and see the effect of wind and current on a brisk day."

"Upon my word, it sounds like play to me, Master Six," Thaddeus Croker said.

"It *is* play," Able replied, remembering in time to be patient with slower minds. "Physics and hydraulics are fun. We will learn to arrange ballast and cargo in our little boats. Later, I'll add water to our inland sea until it's eight feet deep. They'll learn to swim with clothes and shoes on." He smiled at the men watching him so intently. "You need to produce well-prepared sailors. That is my aim."

"Mine, too." Thaddeus Croker slapped his knees and stood up. "Come along. Let's see how you teach."

Chapter Five

❦

"THE STUDENTS ARE HOUSED in two large rooms," Thaddeus Croker said as they moved along the corridor, "the younger in one room, the older in the other. We have twelve now in the upper grade and only nine left in the lower."

"Why the difference, sir?" Able asked.

"An excellent reason," the headmaster replied. "Since they have been here, those three were claimed by close relatives."

"They are most fortunate, indeed," Able replied, wondering at such good luck. In his years in Dumfries Workhouse, no one had ever claimed anyone. "And these remaining lads, do they have their own beds? Enough blankets?"

"They do. You've seen the uniform, Master Six. Much like yours," Thaddeus said. "They are fed and warm." He sighed. "They're used to nothing, but some still languish."

"Do they know you care about them?" Able asked.

"Too much caring might overwhelm them and produce an effect opposite from what we intend, in the school trying to turn wharf rats into masters," the headmaster said, after evident thought.

Able stopped. "You can't care for them too much, with all due respect."

"Scholarly minds would argue with you, Master Six," the headmaster said.

"They are wrong," Able said simply. He mentally slapped his forehead, hoping he hadn't ruined all his chances before he even saw the boys. "I'd have given the earth for kindness." He started walking again. "I am twenty-six. Not until three weeks and five days ago did a woman put her arms around me."

"Come now, Master Six," Sir B chided. "You've been abroad in the world."

"For lust and money, sir. Not for love."

"You're blunt, but I understand you," the headmaster said.

They turned a corner to the eastern wing of the monastery and went up a flight of steps rendered uneven by the passage of many feet over the space of centuries. Able sniffed the fragrance of food cooking, and hoped he would be invited to eat. He had just enough money to get him back to Plymouth and Meridee, with nothing left over for frills, such as food.

With no knock or any fanfare, the headmaster opened the door. Twelve pairs of eyes turned their way. The teacher's disapproving gaze was already fixed upon the three men who had invaded his classroom.

Interested, Able looked around, impressed with several windows facing the wharf. That the beautiful casement windows had survived centuries of wear and tear in a tough town was ample testimony either to luck, or a special blessing from St. Brendan himself.

He saw tidy rows of books on two shelves, and a table with a globe. The logs in the fireplace gave off a cheerful glow, if not much heat, because the master's desk was plunked right in front of it. *Share and share alike, Master Whoever*, he thought, unimpressed.

The master was a youngish fellow wearing a black university gown. He held a long pointer, which he tapped against the palm of his hand. Able watched the students' eyes follow the motion, which told him all he needed to know about the method of classroom management.

"This is Master Blake, who instructs in English and history," the headmaster said. "The curriculum includes mathematics, Master Blake's subjects, and what we call natural science—alas, void of instruction. It is difficult to find teachers wishing to live in this part of Portsmouth. Sailing Master Fletcher also comes in occasionally to teach the use of a sextant to the older class."

He indicated Master Blake, who executed a small bow. From his smirk, Able knew that he had already been discussed at St. Brendan's, and probably found wanting in some way. It wouldn't be the first time someone had underestimated him, and Able knew it wouldn't be the last.

"Master Blake, let us turn the class over to Master Six here."

"Yes, let us see what he can do," the teacher said, as he handed Able his pointer.

Eyes on the boys again, Able took the pointer. As one, the students watched the stick in his hand and his heart broke a little. *Meridee, I don't know if you would approve of me*, he thought, then cracked the stick over his leg.

The boys gasped and Master Blake exclaimed, "How dare you?"

Able glanced at the headmaster, who had started in surprise, too, but recovered quicker, a smile lurking around the corners of his mouth. Captain Sir Belvedere St. Anthony's eyes registered approval and he nodded.

Able looked from the two pieces of the pointer to the boys, who seemed as one to relax. "Which of you lads is a fast runner? Anyone here ever need to show a clean pair of heels to run from a beadle or a magistrate?"

He eyed them. A hand went up slowly, then another. "You two, front and center."

They stood before Able and he recognized their type, boys up for a spree and willing to skirt the edge of discipline. They were the kind of lads who, if well-trained, would someday be capable of quick decisions and vast courage. He recognized himself.

"I want you to run down the stairs as fast as may be, and position yourselves on each side of this window. Not too close, mind, because it is never my intention to skewer young boys. How could I explain that to the Navy Board?"

The students chuckled and loosened up further. Able held up his hand and the room became instantly silent.

"When you are in place, I will drop these two unequal pieces of this damned pointer at the same time," Able said. "I want you to watch closely and tell me which piece hits the ground first. Handsomely, now!"

The two boys dashed out and clattered down the stairs. Able gestured for the other students to come close to the window. The headmaster and Sir B came too, while the teacher sulked against the wall.

Bang went the door downstairs. Able rested his arms on the ledge of the open window. "Ready, lads?" he called.

"Aye, sir," came the answer.

Able dropped the two pieces. He glanced at the boys on either side of him, pleased to see he had their total attention. One little fellow already had a frown on his face. He opened his mouth as though a question had already formed in his brain.

"Run back upstairs with the pointer," Able called. He closed the window against December chill.

"Well?" he asked, when the boys burst into the room again. They gave Master Blake a wide berth and handed the pointer pieces to Able.

"They landed at the same time, sir," one boy said.

"Why?" asked the student Able had observed at the window. "The bigger piece should fall faster, sir. Shouldn't it? It's heavier."

"Do you others think so?" Able asked. He saw what he expected to see: affirmation, negation, and puzzled expressions.

"Please sir, why?" asked the same student.

"The better question is how, rather than why," Able said.

"Lord help us," Master Blake muttered. "What is the difference?"

"Night and day, Master Blake. I will explain it to you sometime," Able said, and saw in an instant he had made an enemy, if the pointer hadn't been enough of a felony. "In a few weeks, God willing, we will rummage around in Sir Isaac Newton's brain and see what he thinks," Able said. *Provided I haven't fouled my anchor here*, he thought as he quietly set the useless pointer pieces on the master's desk. *In for a penny, in for a pound.*

He sat on the desk. From the horrified expressions on young faces, he quickly gathered that Master Blake had never done anything so vulgar.

"How many of you can swim?" he asked.

No one raised a hand, which did not surprise Able. What workhouse boy was ever given useful training? He waited. A hand went up slowly.

"Yes, Mister … Mister …. What is your name?"

"Jimmy Bawn," he said promptly. "I've heard it's bad luck to swim. The ocean is unforgiving."

"Aye, it is, Mister Bawn," Able replied. "Let us say your ship is shot to pieces and dismasted and you are drifting toward a lee shore. Wouldn't it be nice to know how to swim that little distance and live to fight another day?"

He watched the boys nod in agreement, their eyes serious.

"We'll learn to swim, because it's smarter than drowning. We'll also become acquainted with Sir Isaac Newton, and another chap named Galileo Galilei," Able assured them. "Tell me something about yourselves. Are you from workhouses? Did you live on the streets?"

He didn't think they would admit to such misery. He also knew it was his turn to tell them about himself, and in the telling, build a bond that must grow strong, if they were to feel safe to learn in an unsafe world.

"My name is Durable Six," he said, and saw the smiles they could not hide. "A ridiculous name, eh? Go ahead and laugh. You have my permission."

Some of them chuckled.

"I'll tell you how I got my name. I was found naked and newly born on church steps in Dumfries, Scotland, in February of 1776," he said. Some of them nodded. "I was the sixth bastard admitted to the Dumfries Workhouse since the start of the new year. The workhouse master waited for me to die— we'll agree I had a rough start—but when I didn't, he declared me Durable and named me Durable Six. My friends call me Able. You will call me Master Six, because I am a sailing master in the Royal Navy."

He watched some of them mouth his name. "Are any of you numbered?"

Two hands went up, the students more confident now, because he was one of them. He gestured for them to stand, well-acquainted with their wary expressions. *Almost as if you are wondering when the other shoe will drop and you will be back in the workhouse*, he thought with sympathy. *Not on my watch. Never.*

"You, sir?"

"William Eight, Master Six. Someone had pinned the name William to me blanket."

"A blanket and a name? Someone cared for you, then," Able replied, thinking of the baby on the church steps, hair still wet from birth and starting to freeze. "Consider yourself lucky, Will. Stand here beside me. And you, sir?"

"Billie Two." He grinned.

"Excellent! Stand here just so, and I will stand between you. What do we have here? You there."

Another boy stood, the same child who had questioned why, when the sticks fell. "We have eight and six and two."

"Subtract us. Use your fingers." Able heard a grumble from Master Blake. "Yes, your fingers, if you need to. Why not?"

"We take the six from the eight and have two," another lad said from the back of the room. "And if we add you, sir, and Billie, we'll have Will Eight."

"Indeed. Impressive. Suppose you subtract Billie Two from me? What then?"

"Four, sir."

"And if we add me and Billie Two?"

"Eight, sir."

"And then subtract us from Will Eight?"

"Zero, sir," said Will Eight. "Gor! Think of the combinations!" Frightened, he looked down. "I spoke out of turn."

"No one speaks out of turn in my classroom," Able said. "Blurt out answers any time."

"But this is *my* classroom, Six," Master Blake said, deliberately not using his title. "You are wasting my time."

The headmaster gestured to Able and he realized he had taken precisely twenty-eight minutes of someone else's classroom instruction. And broken his pointer, too. The word "Failure" grew to enormous size on the unscrolling sheet of paper that was his brain. It even began to blink.

As he passed Master Blake, the teacher muttered, "You owe me a pointer."

"I owe you nothing," Able snapped back. "Boys don't learn through fear."

He left the room, head high, amazed at himself and nearly looking around for Meridee Bonfort, so badly did he need her to tell him if he had made a fool of himself, or if perhaps he had succeeded.

Silent, he walked between Sir B and Thaddeus Croker down the hall and back into the headmaster's office.

"Sit yourselves, gentlemen," Croker said. He moved a few papers on top of his desk and handed one to Able. "This, Master Six, is a contract with St. Brendan the Navigator School." He pointed. "That is your annual salary, which you will receive monthly in twelve portions. You've probably already read the entire thing, if I can believe Miss Bonfort and Captain Hallowell, who visited me last week."

"Aye, I have," he replied, knowing they would never understand the blink that registered every word immediately in his brain. "There is a house, and a cook and maid."

"The house is situated directly across the road from St. Brendan's. It is already furnished. In two weeks, there will be food in the pantry, and fuel for the fireplaces. Do come and teach with us, Master Six."

Captain St. Anthony raised his hand. "I have been directed to inform you that you will remain on the rolls of the Royal Navy. Should national emergency decree it, you can still be summoned to the fleet. What say you?"

For some reason, the Lord Omnipotent had finally seen fit to smile upon one of the least of his earthly sons. Able could barely breathe as his brain seemed to race around in his skull, shouting and clicking its heels together, and pinging off cranial craters. He could actually wed Meridee Bonfort and teach boys much like himself to become useful masters in His Majesty's Royal Navy. What more could a man wish?

"Aye," he said simply.

Chapter Six

❦

O N THE DAY ABLE Six was supposed to arrive from Portsmouth, Meridee insisted on taking the gig to Plymouth, accompanied by eight-year-old Gerald, her nephew who had drawn the long straw. James had gone away to sulk, muttering something about the unfairness of life.

"I'll miss you, Aunt Meri," Gerald had told her while they waited in the tea room next to the less genteel Davy Jones Inn, where the mail coach stopped. "May I call him Uncle Able in a few weeks?"

"He'll be delighted, I am certain," Meri assured the little boy. "You and James will be his only nephews that he knows of. Would you like another cinnamon bun?"

Of course he would. While Gerald ate with relish, Meridee Bonfort considered the events that had taken her to this point in her previously placid life.

She was no fool. When her father ran out of income, which meant no dowry for her, she accepted the fact and went to live with her dear Amanda Ripley, older sister and vicar's wife. She resigned herself to spinsterhood because she wasn't a woman to waste time mourning what would never be.

Then Sailing Master Durable Six had moved into her orbit and everything changed. She had never met anyone like him, and soon knew there *were* no men like him, at least not since Sir Isaac Newton. By the world's standards, he had nothing to recommend him beyond a brain so exceptional that there were no words to describe it. He was illegitimate, poor, and down on his luck because France, Spain, and England declared a shaky peace and his ship was superfluous. He came to teach her nephews until after Christmas, when the boys' father had more free time again. That was it; that was all.

The irony that a man of some ambition might prefer war to peace wasn't lost on her. The lover in her demanded that she help him. The realist in her knew perfectly well that if he did not succeed in Portsmouth, he would have to return to sea when the treaty ended, as he assured her it would. By going to Portsmouth first and pleading his case before an amazing group of seafarers, she had done all she could. It lay with Able Six to finish the matter, and return home employed. And so she waited. With some trepidation, to be sure, but also hope.

He did not disappoint. When they heard the coachman blowing on his yard of tin, she leaped to her feet and stood under the tearoom's sheltering eave, because rain still thundered down.

She scanned the coach roof for Able Six, dismayed to not see him sitting there as he had sat on the outbound trip, to save a few pennies. She started breathing again when the door opened, and Able was the first man out. He paused to hand down two ladies who looked perfectly capable of leaving a mail coach unassisted, but were obviously charmed by the curly-haired man in black who had good manners.

He handily caught his duffel that the coachman threw down, and hurried the few yards to the tearoom, where he set it down and grabbed her in a close embrace.

"We're in, Meri," he whispered in her ear. "I've a contract in my pocket and the key to our house."

She hugged him back then kissed him soundly, not caring for a minute that one of her brother-in-law's parishioners stood in the tearoom doorway. Meridee knew the woman would tell her friends that Miss Bonfort, a most respectable spinster, had slid socially and didn't care who saw her kissing a remarkably handsome man, who, if rumor had it, was an unemployed bastard.

"Master Six, you're getting wet," Gerald announced. "Step inside, both of you."

"Master Ripley, you are wiser than we are," Able said.

He was hungry for more than cinnamon buns, so Meridee ordered a meat and cheese sandwich to accompany them, plus tea.

"When I didn't see you, I was afraid," she said, after the servant left with the order.

"No fears. I spent a night with your Uncle Aloysius. How useful of you to have an uncle who heads the victualing department in Portsmouth. He insisted on paying for an inside seat for my return trip." He touched her cheek. "Said he didn't want me to ruin a good wedding by contracting pneumonia. By the way, he insists on walking you down the aisle."

"What a dear man," she replied.

"There's more to it." He took his wallet from inside his uniform coat and opened it. "Look here. He gave me—us—fifty pounds."

"How kind, but why?"

"He thought you might ask. He called it many back payments for being a niece who should have had a dowry like her sisters. Hey now, no tears. He thought you might do that too." He gave her his handkerchief. He lowered his voice. "Frankly, I'm grateful you didn't have a dowry, or I'd not have stood a chance."

"Give yourself credit, Able," she whispered, her lips close to his ear. "You're still the handsomest man I ever gawked over."

He gave a totally phony sigh. "Miss Bonfort, you are an easy mark, if a man's looks paralyze you from wiser decisions."

"You have winkled out my sordid secret," she teased back. "Show me your contract."

He spread it out on the table. "A house, a cook, a maid," she said. She looked closer. "You will be teaching mathematics and everything left over from the usual courses? Isn't that odd?"

"*I'm* odd," he admitted. "The headmaster is giving me a free hand to teach the calculus, if I decide a student is up to it, or ... or ... swimming, or natural science, or how wind blows a ship around. There will probably even be a contest in how to stack blocks like ballast on a floating platform and see which sinks the fastest. Whatever the moment calls for." He shook his head. "I never expected this."

He seemed almost puzzled by such carte blanche, which made her bless someone's amazing wisdom in understanding this dear man's astounding mind. "I will never be able to keep up with you," she said.

"Believe me, I do not want this ... odd affliction, for so it seems, at times. All I ask is that you love me."

She smiled at his simple mandate. "I already do."

"Then I'll give you this." He took a sheet of paper folded and sealed from that same pocket. "This is *your* contract, if you're willing. It's your decision, not mine."

A question in her eyes, she opened the paper and read of her own appointment as house mother to four of the youngest students at St. Brendan's, if she should wish it.

She read of Headmaster Thaddeus Croker's interest in seeing to the nurture of lads of age six and seven, who had never known the delights of a mother to care for them, and who seemed a bit more adrift than the other students.

If you wish to help them, make them part of your own little family, yours and Master Six's, she read silently. She blushed at the paragraph stating this would not begin until some few weeks after their wedding, so she and the master could settle into marriage without children underfoot. *Master Six so stipulated, and I agree,* she read.

"Twelve pounds?" she asked in amazement. "A pound a month for doing what I would happily do for free? I like little boys."

"And a big one of twenty-six?" he joked.

"Even better," she said, too shy to look at him.

"Good answer, Miss Bonfort. I thought you might feel that way about the boys, but I did not mention it to Headmaster Croker," Able said. "This income will be yours entirely."

"Ours," she said firmly.

"Yours," he repeated, equally firm. "Every woman needs her own money."

"This one doesn't," she told him, her shyness gone. "My salary will go into our common pot. I know enough about little boys to suspect I will earn every penny."

"No doubt," he told her. "Equal partners in everything?"

"Everything," she repeated. "I insist. I will promise to obey you in our wedding vows, but I warn you, Master Six, I have my opinions."

Gerald spoke up, surprising Meridee, who had forgotten his presence. "She has decided opinions."

"I'm shocked," Able said with a straight face.

"I thought I should tell you," Gerald said seriously, then grinned. "But sir, she's a game goer. Of all my aunts, and I have many, she's the most fun."

"That's what I thought, Gerald."

With an arch glance at her that nearly rendered Meridee incapable of one more second of rectitude, Able reached in his pocket and took out a coin. "Take this to the ostler next door and have him bring 'round your aunt's gig."

After Gerald darted off, Able took a glance around then kissed her hand. "I could have bought a slave woman in Marrakesh, had I wanted someone to obey me. I could have bought two. Not interested."

"We're venturing into something new," she said finally. "Marriage, most certainly, but this school too, this unusual, strange, unheard-of school." She had to say it. "I hope you have no regrets with either."

"Not one."

Chapter Seven

◈

THEY WERE MARRIED ON Christmas Eve, 1802. Able had already suggested they forgo a ring, even though they had a cushion now in Uncle Aloysius's gift, and the twenty pounds Amanda gave her, whispering that Mama had pledged it to her youngest daughter, if she ever married.

"Someday there will be a ring, my love, but I feel the need for caution," Able told her. "Suppose I discover in Portsmouth that you have a predilection for faro and lose it all in a gaming hell? Pompey has many."

"Knothead," she said, but nodded in agreement. She was frugal in her ways too.

The issue resolved itself after she went to the room she now shared with two nieces who had arrived with their parents, ready to celebrate Aunt Meridee's wedding to a seafaring man. She had tucked the little ones into the trundle bed when she heard a familiar two taps followed by one tap.

She couldn't help the flutter in her stomach, thinking how little sleep she planned to get the following night.

"My, but that night cap is fetching," Able said when she opened the door and glared at him. "If looks could slay …."

He pulled her into the corridor. "My heart is racing," he teased. "I've never seen a lovelier nightgown."

"I'll wager you have," she teased back.

"Hold out your hand," he ordered.

She stared at the gold ring he set in her palm. She admired the delicate tracery, wondering how her man had come by such magnificence. "Where in the world—"

"Captain and Mrs. Hallowell sent it over from the inn in Pomfrey," he said. "They just arrived. Here is the note."

She handed back the exquisite ring and took the note. " 'To Master Six,' she read out loud. 'I have carried around this bauble for years. If you don't think me presumptuous, put it on your wife's finger. Years ago, I took it off a dead Barbary pirate. I trust she is not squeamish. Sincerely, Benjamin Hallowell.' "

"Are you squeamish?" Able asked. "If you're not, hold out your finger."

Meridee, you already know this is no ordinary marriage, she told herself. *Do you need more proof?* She held out her hand.

Able slipped the ring on her finger. He laughed as it spun around. "I'll wrap thread around it until a jeweler can size it."

Meridee tipped her finger down into his palm, where the ring dropped, kissed him, then went back into her room. She stood by the door until she heard him walk away.

Too restless to sleep, she took the pillow from her bed, grabbed up a blanket and made herself comfortable in the window seat. She looked around her room, her refuge for the last six years since her mother's death, after being told by her sisters, but kindly, that there could be no husband because she had no marriage portion. Papa's money was gone.

Six years had been sufficient time to master the hard lesson, as she observed the spinsters in her brother-in-law's parish. Some had withered and others had prospered. Clear-headed, Meridee chose to emulate the unmarried ladies who took restoratives to sick neighbors, tended other people's gardens, and sewed clothing for the parish poor, all the while grateful she had a place to live.

Then came Able, walking to Pomfrey from Plymouth to take up a temporary position as tutor to her nephews. Meridee couldn't discern the moment when she decided no other man in the world would do for her. Since she had never expected a husband, the notion must have crept up on her like a gray cat dimly seen through fog, suddenly there.

She blushed to think of seeing Captain Hallowell tomorrow, since she had blacked the man's eye barely two weeks ago, driven beyond rational thought when he told her there was no way he could keep Master Six from seagoing duty, once the Treaty ended. She had lashed out because it was obvious to her that her man with the prodigious brain could prove far more valuable by educating others with skills that would make them useful immediately in the fleet.

Meridee saw St. Brendan's for the miracle it was. The general hardness of life assured her such opportunities were providential enough to fall under the label of God's work. She thanked the Almighty and watched the moon glide across a familiar landscape she was soon to leave behind. In the vicarage of Pomfrey, she had learned patience, and how to wait upon the Lord.

Meridee rested her chin on her up-drawn knees, thinking of earlier tonight, when four of her five sisters—Abigail lived in Canada—had crowded in this room, locked the door against children, and given their youngest sister marital advice. None of them told her what she really wanted to know, and she was too shy to ask.

Amanda, who knew her best, had come the closest. As the sisters left the room, Amanda lingered behind. She touched Meridee's cheek and whispered, "I suspect Master Six will know precisely what you need. Trust him."

Meridee knew good advice when she heard it. Now was the time to act. When all was silent in the household, she padded on bare feet up the stairs. Careful to avoid the squeaky boards, she went silently up to the chamber closest to the eaves. She knew he wasn't asleep.

"I wondered when you'd come knocking," he said and tugged her inside. "Cold feet?"

She looked down at her toes. In a fit of methodical preparation, she had already packed her bedroom slippers. "Not this kind," she said, "at least not in the length of time I am going to spend in here, Able."

He picked her up and sat with her on his bed. "Now your toes are off the bare wood. What can I do for you?"

"Answer one question," she said, grateful the room was dark, because her face flamed.

"Fire at will, Miss Bonfort," he said. "Before you begin, let me state I will be gentle tomorrow night."

"I already know that," she told him, which meant he held her closer and muttered something about barely deserving such trust.

"Then what, madam?"

"A simple question." She took a deep breath. "Am I going to enjoy this, too? I dearly love to have fun."

"I do not doubt for a second divided into one hundred equal parts that you will enjoy anything more," he said. "I cannot claim more prowess than any man, I suppose, but I know what I'm doing." He stood up with her in his arms and walked to the door, which she reached over and opened. He deposited her in the hall. "Go to bed, Mrs. Five and a Half."

Who could not sleep well after that?

IF THE SUCCESS OF a wedding can be gauged by the number in attendance, then the marriage of Miss Meridee Bonfort, spinster, to Sailing Master Durable Six, Royal Navy, was the event of the year in Pomfrey, Devon.

Dressed sensibly in dark-green wool, with Amanda Ripley's borrowed knitted collar, a brand-new winter bonnet, and the lace handkerchief her departed mother had carried, plus a sixpence in her shoe and blue garters, Meridee Bonfort became Mrs. Durable Six.

A gaggle of nieces had preceded her down the aisle, tossing Christmas ivy at random. She clung to the arm of Uncle Aloysius Bonfort, suffering in a tighter neck cloth than she suspected he usually tied, but beaming down on her. To her amusement, he strutted as he took his time getting her down the aisle, savoring the moment. She happily let him. It was a short aisle in a small church, and Able didn't appear inclined to leave it without her.

Meridee looked around the congregation, delighted to notice what close attention the women were paying to her almost-husband. She had no doubts that the stories of his supremely inappropriate birth and upbringing had circulated industriously. So, apparently, had the news of his undeniable good looks. From the top of his curly black hair, meandering down past a handsomely straight nose and high cheekbones, to lips that thankfully just skirted on being Scottish, Master Six was a wonder to behold, and Meridee knew it.

Why stop there? The man of acutely low parentage carried himself impeccably, with wide shoulders sloping toward a narrow waist and down long legs. Meridee Bonfort thought him a masterpiece. She had never been to Greece, of course, but Papa had possessed a book with a series of splendid paintings of Greek statues, some with fig leaves, some without. She had caught her older sisters giggling over it one afternoon when they knew Papa was gone. They slammed the book shut and wouldn't let her look. She had waited until they were gone to get her own glimpse of masculine perfection. Whether Able Six fit *that* mold, a few hours from now would serve to enlighten her. She did not think he would disappoint.

She nearly gasped to see an amazing red waistcoat of Oriental design, instead of his usual plain vest. There was even a lacy frill at his throat, provided, Able had told her in a note sent 'round that morning, by none other than Captain Sir Belvedere St. Anthony. Meridee dared any groom to appear more splendid.

She could barely bring herself to look at Captain Hallowell, who had consented to serve as his former sailing master's best man. When she did, she saw a smile aimed specifically at her, his black eye scarcely noticeable now. And Lord, he *winked* at her.

Uncle Aloysius handed her off to Able, and then it was time to pay serious attention to her brother-in-law, as he married them.

Before she could do that, there was the smallest tug on her hand from the man holding it, the one about to assume her care. He was a man with nothing to recommend him except a brain probably more liability than asset at times, and a heart she suspected was his mind's equal.

She tugged back and looked at him, then away, because there were tears in his lovely brown eyes. While John Ripley waited with a smile on his face, Able

Six, the man with the made-up name, leaned close to her and whispered, "You are my everything. I need nothing more."

Oh dear. That warranted another glance and the sight of the most reassuring husband a woman could ask for, a man so capable she could follow him anywhere with good conscience.

The vicar cleared his throat. " 'Dearly beloved, we are gathered together ....'

Meridee listened with her whole heart to every word her brother-in-law spoke, holding tight to the hand of the man she adored. Each glorious sentence sank into her mind and heart, driving out any bitterness she might have admitted to earlier—only under duress—that she had not found a husband sooner because of life's circumstances. She dismissed those moments joyfully, grateful to be twenty-four, unencumbered, and marrying a man worth waiting for.

She smiled at Able's firm responses, and heard low laughter from some in the congregation who hadn't suspected that a man who looked like a Greek god would sound like a Dumfries Scot. *If you think that is the only thing strange about this man, you have no idea,* she thought.

Then came the moment when John Ripley asked for the ring and Able handed him the glorious bit of gold filigree taken from a Barbary pirate, carefully wrapped on one side with enough thread to keep it on her finger. John set the amazing bauble on the Book of Common Prayer he held. He looked down at it for a long moment, and Meridee heard his sigh, and his whisper, "Beloved sister, we'll miss you."

"And I, you," she mouthed.

He handed the ring back to Able, who took it and faced Meridee. He slid the ring gently onto her finger and held it there. "'With this ring I thee wed, with my body I thee worship, and with all my worldly goods....'"

That phrase brought smiles to the three of them. Were there two poorer people in England? "'... all my worldly goods I thee endow. In the name of the Father, and of the Son, and of the Holy Ghost. Amen.'"

Chapter Eight

⧬

"ARE YOU HAVING FUN, Mrs. Six?"

God Almighty, *he* was. Able Six raised his head a little from the pillow they shared, even though the bed came with two. He knew right where she was, tucked against him with one bare leg thrown over his body, but he craved the unbelievable luxury of looking down to see her hair spread out on his chest.

He fingered her curls, alive again to the pleasure of burying his face in them last night when he took her so easily to a generally successful conclusion of their first lovemaking. One would think Mrs. Six had been waiting a little impatiently for a lucky husband to come along and do precisely that.

He tapped on her head. She swatted at his hand, barely awake. Apparently he had not married a lark.

"Merry Christmas, Mrs. Six," he told her as she raised her head and glared at him. "My, that is not the look I anticipated."

Her eyes softened at that, and she kissed his chest. He put both hands on her head and began a slow massage. He discovered a few minutes later that she was far livelier at the crack of dawn than he had reckoned.

Satisfied, he flopped back down on the mattress, wondering how he had managed to reach the ripe age of twenty-six without a wife. More specifically, since he was a man who dealt in specifics, how he had managed without *this* wife.

"You realize this is habit-forming," he told her, when she returned to bed after a wash and brought along a damp cloth for him.

She threw back her head and laughed, then smothered his face in the wet rag, straddling him in fun now, which led to a bit of a tussle that she won, because he felt far too complacent to put up a struggle.

"If you expect to be rescued, you have to scream louder than that," she said and sat back on him.

"Help," he whispered, which led to another assault with the cloth and more giggles from his unrepentant darling. Still laughing, she collapsed on his chest and stayed there until her breathing became deep and regular. The room was cool, so he pulled a blanket over them and let her sleep, worn out like a pup after rambunctious play.

To be fair, neither of them had slept much last night. He thought about her initial reticence, abandoned soon enough because he knew as much about female anatomy as any surgeon in the fleet. Once the *Triumph*'s surgeon understood his rare loblolly boy, pointed out by Captain Sir Belvedere St. Anthony, he turned over his medical texts with the admonition to read them only in spare moments.

The man had been astounded, and at first disbelieving, when Able returned them two days later. He had hollered at Able, who stood there and took the abuse. Amused, Captain St. Anthony suggested the surgeon give Able Six an oral exam, which turned the ship's doctor into a believer in genius. "He knows it all," the surgeon had said that evening in the officers' wardroom. "What alchemy is this?"

"The Isaac Newton sort. He's a bona fide polymath," Captain St. Anthony had replied, or at least so he had reported the next day as Able emptied urinals over the side of the *Triumph*, becalmed west of the Azores.

Female anatomy. Shooting stars. Maritime knots. Celestial navigation. Pi. Under the pleasant weight of his wife, Able rested his arms on the curve of her back, briefly running through the vertebrae and touching her coccyx. He couldn't resist stroking the smoothness of her hips, which made her sigh and murmur something. He concluded that Meridee Six knew what she liked already. He slept, his mind peaceful.

Meridee was still asleep when he woke. Carefully he edged out from under her and sat up, hungry and wondering what was available in mid-afternoon. At least the church bells had quit their thundering. He dressed and looked down at Meridee Six, his wife, his lover, his keeper. He said a silent prayer to the god of all those noisy bells and let himself out into the hallway.

Per Captain Hallowell's thoughtful instructions, the proprietor had isolated them on the top floor. Able already knew this floor was famous for the privacy it offered when ships and their officers came into Plymouth and their wives had no inclination to wait until the men came home.

And lately, at least until the Treaty of Amiens, there had been little free time for officers to leave Plymouth and go home, not even to remind themselves how people not associated with the Royal Navy lived.

The matter of wives readily available at the Drake had never affected

Able Six. He had been happy enough to wave off husbands from the frigate swinging on its anchor in the harbor and remain aboard to see to last-minute details. He had no one eager to see his wind-scoured, thirsty carcass.

Thanks to his wife's masterful efforts to find him a position highly suited to his unique talents, the most strenuous part of his working day would be crossing Saint's Way, the quiet street between St. Brendan the Navigator School to his house. He already knew Meri would be waiting for his return.

He went down two flights and peeked in the dining room. Empty. He wondered if he and Meridee were the hotel's only Christmas guests. Following the "nothing ventured, nothing gained" principle that kept life interesting, he went to the kitchen, where the redoubtable Mrs. Fillion hummed and stirred a pot.

"Master Six, I wondered if anyone was alive upstairs," she said as she moved the pot off the hob. "Can I interest you in something hearty that will increase your stamina? It has oysters."

That was Mrs. Fillion. No point in blushing. He laughed—he knew there was nothing wrong with his stamina—and went to the cupboard for a bowl. She filled it and sat him down at the kitchen table, joining him with a cup of tea for herself and coffee for him. Amazing how the woman remembered her guests' favorites.

He ate with relish, considering that his last meal had been wedding cake and wassail. When he finished, she filled his bowl again. After that went down slower, he sat back and answered her questions about St. Brendan's, realizing as he did so how little he really knew about the place, beyond that someone in the government or Admiralty had enough pull and interest in helping workhouse vermin.

"Twenty-one little students is all we have," he told her. "The youngest looks to be not more than seven or eight. The oldest is maybe thirteen, and probably headed to the fleet this spring. Some are small. I know they have been underfed."

She sighed at that, and asked if he wanted another bowl of stew. He gave a regretful shake of his head.

"When I ran away from the workhouse at nine, I actually grew taller on shipboard fare," he said. "I wasn't alone in that. Workhouse brats grow in the fleet."

They sat in pleasant silence. He knew Mrs. Fillion had started at the Drake as a scullery maid years ago. She had probably grown taller on kitchen fare, herself.

After their quiet conversation, he accepted a bowl of stew for Meridee and went upstairs, where his wife lay snuggled on his side of the bed, looking as contented as a cat in a patch of sunlight when he woke her.

She left not a drop of stew and polished off the buttered bread with masterful aplomb. Finally she sat cross-legged with her nightgown around her knees, which afforded him quite a view.

The nightgown came off soon enough, once the bowl was on the floor, and Able shed his clothes in record time. Later, the Sixes settled into what he knew was going to be a lifetime of comfortable post-coital conversation, that delicious, satisfying chat that must be one of the delights of married life. He had something to tell her. She knew him pretty well now, and didn't think she would consider him certifiable.

Pillowing herself in the hollow of his shoulder, she laid her cheek against his chest. He breathed deep of her personal fragrance, enjoying a whiff of lavender too.

"I have an early memory, Mrs. Six, quite an early one."

"Say on, Master Six," she replied. He felt her eyelashes open and close against his chest, and settled himself lower.

"It was dark and sleeting," he began. He closed his eyes and felt the chill all over again, he who was destined never to forget a thing. "Someone was breathing loud and groaning. I remember being cold, and even getting stiff. I cried." He was silent, wondering if he should be telling her this so soon. "Will *you* believe this, Meri?"

She had put her hand over his eyes, so he knew they were moving under his closed lids. She took her hand away and tucked it against his neck. "You know I believe you."

"I felt someone's hand on my stomach, and then my head, which was wet. A woman said, '*Grá mo chroí*.' The next thing I remember is an old man wrapping me in a brown shawl or cape and carrying me inside a church. I smelled incense."

He heard Meri's sharp intake of breath. "Heavens! How could you possibly remember …" she stopped. "Able, I must learn to never be surprised at what you tell me."

"Wise of you," he said. "When I was six, a laddie from the country came to the workhouse. He spoke only Gaelic, so I taught him English. When he knew enough, I asked him what *Grá mo chroí* meant. "

Her hand gently covered his eyes again. Through the roaring in his ears, he heard her tell him to slow his breathing. He did as she said, but she kept her hand over his eyes.

" 'Love of my heart,' he told me." Able took a deep breath, "Meri, she loved me."

She took away her hand and he felt her tears on his chest. "Meri, it's fine. *I'm* fine. I've never told another soul this before, but I think you needed to know."

She sat up and looked him in the eyes. "There's more. I see it in your face."

"You have your own gift," he said, pleased. "All I had was a prayer book inscribed with 'Mary.' I don't know if that was her name, or if she stole it from someone named Mary. I still have it. It's in the bottom of my duffel over there. I never go anywhere without that prayer book."

She got up, pulled on her nightgown, and rummaged through his battered duffel that had traveled all over the world. He smiled to see her barefoot, disheveled, and utterly adorable. She pulled out the book and opened it to the first page. Sniffing and wiping her eyes, she held the book tenderly to her breast. *How did I get so fortunate?* he asked himself, entranced with marriage and a woman like Meridee Six.

She came back to bed and sat high on his hip, which made him laugh. "We had a cat like you on one of my frigates," he told her as she slid down the mound of his hip and plopped in front of him. "He'd flop down wherever he felt like it."

Meridee pointed to the number under Mary's name, a question in her eyes. He took the book from her and closed it. "Someone made certain the prayer book remained with me. It was my only possession. Her numbered wooden grave marker was 134."

How tender his wife was. She made an inadvertent sound that was a cross between a groan and a sharp exhalation of breath.

She curled up beside him. "We could take some of Uncle Aloysius's money and get her a proper stone."

"I already did, Meri," he said, his fingers gentle in her hair. "I haven't been a full-fledged sailing master too long, but I took what little prize money I earned for a ship sold for salvage and used it. When I could arrange leave, I went north to Dumfries, and had a stone cutter chisel 'Mary' and then '134' under it. I'm proud of that granite marker, Meri. I'll take you there someday."

She kissed his palm. "You are a good son," she whispered.

Might as well dump it all on her. "Maybe I'm not so good," he confessed. "Before I left Dumfries to return to Portsmouth, I paid a visit to the workhouse."

"I hope you gave the master a generous portion of your mind," Meridee declared.

"I wanted to thrash him as he used to thrash me. Damn my eyes, I couldn't. After all, I had survived and ended up someplace better. *He* was still in the workhouse. Still a bully too, I have no doubt. Why would he change?" He blew out a deep breath. "I stood in the doorway, pointed my finger at him and said 'Shame on you!' Can't blame him for laughing."

Meridee sat up, her expression militant now. "I'd have ... I'd have ...."

"Given him a black eye?" he teased, then grabbed her hands. He easily turned her on her back and sat on her this time. "Woman, are you going to fight all my battles?"

"If I can," she replied, her eyes dark, intense, and close to his face. She tugged up her nightgown. "But right now, I don't feel like fighting."

"I don't, either," he said, and kissed her.

Chapter Nine

⚬⚬⚬

LORD HAVE MERCY, THE *uses of a husband*, Meridee Six thought, as they left Plymouth two days later, bound for Portsmouth, and both of them scared to death, if two clammy hands hanging onto each other was any indication.

Or maybe hers was the only clammy hand. She glanced at Able and found him looking back, with considerable glee in his eyes.

"Aren't you afraid?" she asked, wondering about her man.

"Not a whit. I'll tell you what does frighten me: a rogue high wind in a storm when my ship is trying to claw out of a trough. What frightens you?"

"How can I even admit what scares me, after your observation?" she asked, wanting to feel grumpy, but having a hard time.

He raised her hand to his lips and kissed it, which did amazing things south of her stomach. *Gadfreys*, here they were on the mail coach and he was giving her impish ideas.

"Meri, we've led different lives up to this point," he told her. "Fear is fear and I understand it. Say on."

She whispered her fears to him about finding a cook and setting up housekeeping in a place of some ill repute. He proved quite willing to soothe her in public fashion by pulling her closer. *Oh, capable man*, she thought, and leaned into his protection. *How do I love thee?*

When it was his turn to doubt, as Portsmouth drew closer, she reminded him how well he taught her nephews in the vicarage, and how she knew he would be more useful as an instructor training other sailing masters than as a single master.

"I do confess some uneasiness," he said. "You saw how I taught your nephews. We sat on the floor and played jackstraws, and broke them and counted fractions." He sighed, as if wondering what to do with himself. "I am no ordinary teacher."

That is the understatement of the century, she thought, jollied out of her own doubts. "That's why the headmaster wants you, and what is he called … the man with all those names?"

"Captain Sir Belvedere St. Anthony?" he said with a smile now.

"Do you actually call him all that?"

"No. We'd have been thrust upon many a lee shore, if the helmsman had to spit out that name at a moment's notice. He's Sir B. And yes, I think that's why they want me." He sat back, resting her hand on his thigh. "I think it's the spur-of-the-moment bits of knowledge the men in charge want, plus real training in navigation."

"Whatever it is, you're equal to it," she said. She patted his thigh and he chuckled. "I suspect you're good at everything."

"We had a jolly this time morning, didn't we, Mrs. Six?" he teased, his voice low, and his eyes on the clergyman sitting opposite them and giving them both *The Look*. "You seemed to be highly involved," he whispered.

Meridee felt her face grow warm. She hadn't meant to make so much noise. At least there wouldn't be little boys in their new house right away. "You know I was," she whispered back. "My goodness, Master Six."

She moved her hand farther away from his thigh, which kept the grin on his face. The clergyman wisely looked down at the Bible in his lap. "We've inspired him," Able the Incorrigible whispered. "He turned to the Song of Solomon."

"Able!" She lowered her voice. "It doesn't make any difference if you read upside down or right side up, does it?"

"No."

"You probably even know the chapter and verse and what it says," she said, wondering if she would ever come to understand his brain.

"Aye, miss. Something about the whiteness of my lover's thighs, if memory serves me," her husband said. "Chapter three verse fifteen, give or take."

"Give or take," Meridee scoffed. "Precisely fifteen, and you know it."

"I do," he replied seriously. "The wonder is that you don't look askance at my strangeness. I can say and think what I wish, and you will not step away because you do not understand me."

What could she say to that? Meridee rested her head against his shoulder as equal measures of love and relief flooded through her. No one else might understand Able Six, but she knew she had married the most capable man on earth.

She turned to look into his eyes, saying nothing—not because she had nothing to say, but because they had an audience. "What I do not understand, I accept," she told him quietly, not surprised to see tears well in his lovely

Greek, French, Italian, or maybe Spanish eyes. She leaned into his shoulder and slept, worn out from the last two days.

Plymouth to Portsmouth was completely possible in a one long day, but not at the end of December, apparently. Snow mingled with rain meant a night at an inn, which brought no complaints from Meridee. She wanted to love her husband, and neither of them wasted a minute in doing precisely that.

More practiced now, Meridee settled into the rhythm of love. Equally pleasurable was to simply lie beside her remarkable husband, spent, his arm under her head and gently clasping her shoulder in a manner both endearing and possessive.

Drowsy, she listened to him tell her about years at sea, and battles, and his own confusion to find ways to communicate who he was and what he could do to much smaller minds.

"I owe an enormous debt to Sir B," he told her.

"What did he do, my love?"

"I told you about my encounter with the ship's surgeon," he said with a laugh. "A few days after I read all the books on surgery and pharmacopeia, Captain St. Anthony sat me down in the officers' wardroom and made me describe my life."

"Did that frighten you?" She asked, wide awake.

"A little," he admitted. "I knew I dared not trust anyone in the workhouse. I was four and whipped for stealing a book from the classroom where I was supposed to pick up trash and sweep."

"You were reading at four?" she asked, still amazed at him.

"Earlier, actually," he said apologetically. Some part of him still seemed startled at himself. "Three. Remember that prayer book belonging to Mary?"

She nodded, and kissed his chest because his hand had tightened around her shoulder.

"I usually kept it under my pillow. One morning I was really hungry. I opened it to distract myself, and stared at what I didn't even know were words. They turned into sentences. I understood them."

She knew without any light in the room that his eyes were closed and moving fast behind his eyelids. She put her hand up and covered them, until she felt him relax.

"Thank you, Meri. Heavens, how have I managed without you?"

"And I, you," she said.

"In my naïveté—I was three years old—I read out loud to the matron. She pinched me hard, and told me to say nothing because I was obviously bewitched."

"Oh, husband," Meridee said.

"I didn't say anything, but I started reading everything I could lay my hands on." He chuckled. "When books started to disappear, no one suspected me. Reading became an amazing distraction from hunger. Mrs. Six, don't sigh so loud. Obviously I survived with my faculties intact, and other useful things."

She laughed at that. "Especially other useful things. My goodness, I daren't tell my sisters how much I've learned in the last few days."

"You're a quick study, Mrs. Six," he teased. He turned serious. "It's a been a lifetime of furtive learning, a lot of thinking and wondering whom I could trust. Bless Sir B for understanding I was different. He let me read every book, manual, and chart on his frigate. When his injuries grounded him, he handed me off to Captain Hallowell, with his own instructions, I am certain."

"I am still chagrined at striking that man, but he tried me to the bone, Able," she said. "Don't laugh."

"I wish I could have seen the look on his face," Able the Incorrigible said.

"I am relieved you didn't," Meridee scolded. "I had his full attention." She thought a moment about the experience she preferred never to recall. "He said something I believe I understand now. '*Bravissima*,' he said. 'Success.' "

"No surprise to me. When he gave me this ring for you, he told me how certain he was that I finally had myself a keeper," Able assured her. "Everything I do now, I do for you and with you."

She kissed him once and then twice and then they moved quickly on to more serious endeavors.

In late afternoon, Meridee took her second look at that huge port of the Royal Navy. "My brother-in-law's parting words to me were to be careful in this city of sin and great wickedness," she told Able.

"His parting words to me were to keep you safe," Able replied. "He doesn't really trust the Royal Navy." He laughed at that, a most knowing laugh, to Meridee's ears. "There's more vice available here than anywhere outside of Macao."

The mail coach let them off close to Gunwharf, where vessels unshipped their cannon before they went into dry dock for repairs, or into ordinary. While Meridee stood by their luggage, Able procured a carter to follow them to Saint Brendan's. He secured a hackney and helped her in.

In giving directions to the jarvey, he patiently explained, "Aye, St. Brendan's does exist. Listen to my directions. It's on Saint's Way, a forgotten street. It's a quiet place for serious instruction."

"What do you know about St. Brendan's?" Meridee said.

"Little more than you. You were here first," he reminded her. "I suspect that although no one wants to admit it, Trinity House plays some role here. Captain Hallowell told you that Trinity furnishes navigational certification to merchant mariners, as well as some sailing masters. I never went that route, but it's a worthy one. I strongly suspect Trinity has fingers in other pies that we ordinary mortals know nothing of."

You have never been an ordinary mortal, Meridee thought. She tucked her arm through his, smiling to herself at the proprietary glance he gave her. She was beginning to understand this husband of hers. If ever a woman had a protector, she did. And if ever a genius had a keeper, he did. What more could two people ask?

"Here we are," he said soon. "Look directly across the street to our home, Meri." She heard all the emotion in his voice.

It was a large stone house of two stories, intimidating in its size, though squashed between two similar buildings. *Here I will live and make a home for my beloved, extraordinary husband,* she thought, humbled. *We will probably have our children here.* She dabbed at her eyes, then darted a glance at her husband, who was doing the same thing.

"We are two sillies," she said.

"Without a doubt." He took her hands in his. "Meridee Six, the time for backing out is long past. Let me help you down."

Only a few minutes were needed to empty the cart that followed them. She stood beside their paltry possessions, looking at the quiet street wrapped in post-Christmas stillness. For a tiny moment, she wished herself back in the Devonshire countryside, where a glance out any window showed open fields. Gone were the days when she would feel free to roam, usually accompanied by her nephews. Portsmouth was probably noisy during the day, flaunting its rollicking reputation as England's largest Royal Navy port. Besides, she was a matron now, with more on her mind than country gambols.

After the carter carried their belongings closer to the front step, he tipped his hat to her and wished her well. What was it about her small size and youth that brought out the concern of others?

"Be careful, miss," the carter said, then smiled, showing the presence of few teeth. "All the same, welcome to Pompey."

"Thank you," she told him, and walked up the steps, her husband beside her now.

As she watched, Able took the key from his pocket and stared at it a moment, almost as if he could not believe even now that he had a house, he who had started life with demerits not of his choosing.

"Key in lock," she teased, which made him grin at her like a boy.

"Key in lock," he teased back. "I turn now."

So it was they were both laughing when he picked her up and carried her over the threshold. Once inside, he gave her a little toss, which made her shriek and tighten her grip on his neck. In turn, he made a gargling sound. She kissed his cheek; he kissed her back, set her down and held her close.

They stood that way for a long moment, until he reached back with his foot and closed the heavy door. They still clung to each other, two sillies embarking on life's further adventures as man and wife.

"It's getting dark," he said into her neck.

"Open your eyes," she replied. "Must I do all the thinking?"

He laughed at that. "I'll tell you right away, Mrs. Six, that you are in complete charge of all domestic matters in this house, including household financials. Arithmetic gives me the shivers. I'll stick to the calculus. This house is your domain."

"This *home*," she amended, which made Master Six take a deep breath.

"It's getting dark. As master of the Six Fleet, I'll go find a lamp."

He let go of her, patted her hip, and went in search of a lamp. Meridee stood by the door, feeling surprisingly shy. *How did I ever get so lucky* alternated with, *I'm in charge.* Her practical nature took over quickly—all she really wanted was to crawl into bed with Master Six and jolly him a bit.

She looked around, startled by a knock low down on the front door. Curious, she opened it and felt her heart turn over.

There stood a small boy dressed in what she already knew was the uniform of a student at St. Brendan's, sober black like her husband wore, but with a stitched-on crest of St. Brendan himself, holding a boat. Next to him stood an older student.

"Welcome to our home," she said. "I am Mrs. Six. Please come in."

As they entered, she thought of another workhouse boy, one bewildered and frightened at his strangeness in a place where a child had no hope, unless he found it within himself. These two lads were tidy and looked well-fed. She saw curiosity on their faces, but mingled with wariness—the workhouse look she sometimes saw on her husband's face.

"Your names, please?" she asked.

"Jamie McGregor," the older boy announced. "I am in my third year." She heard the pride in his voice. "I will be at sea soon."

"Welcome. And *your* name?" she asked the younger one, kneeling down to be on his level.

"David Ten," he told her.

She couldn't help her sudden intake of breath, then felt a firm hand on her shoulder. Her husband helped her to stand.

"Are you our welcoming committee?" Able asked. "Classes starts soon, I believe, promptly at two bells in the forenoon watch."

David Ten nodded, then ducked his head, as Jamie McGregor cleared his throat and gave him a pointed look. "I mean, 'Aye, Master!' " David took a step forward. "Will we learn great things, sir?"

"The greatest," her husband said. "I promise."

David glanced at the older student beside him. Through a film of tears, Meridee saw sudden fear in the younger boy's eyes. She watched him swallow that fear, and she saw a different kind of greatness take its place.

David took another step forward, just a small step that made her touch his shoulder. A wary look, and then he relaxed visibly. "Jamie says no one will be beaten in your class if they don't have a right answer."

Meridee leaned back against her husband and felt his involuntary shudder. She took his hand, because she was his keeper.

"No one will be beaten in my classes," Master Able Six said. "Anything else, lads?"

"Nay, sir," Jamie said. "He's new. That's all he wanted to know."

Meridee could tell David Ten had more questions. "Yes?" she prompted.

"Headmaster Croker said I was to be one of your particular boys over here," he said. "I am wondering …." He stopped and looked at Jamie, who shook his head—a small gesture, the kind a lad makes who has served his own time in a workhouse and doesn't want to be obvious.

"Are you wondering where you will be slinging your hammock?" Able asked.

"Aye, sir," David replied, his voice no bigger than a whisper.

Able turned to Meridee. "What say we look upstairs and find out?"

"Aye, sir," Meridee said promptly, which meant three men in uniform nodded their approval. "If there are spiders in the rooms, I will count on you all to protect me. I mean it."

Jamie grinned, but David nodded, all seriousness.

Able led the way, holding his lamp high, throwing strange shadows against the stone walls. *Who lived here?* Meridee wondered as she took Able's free hand. *Were they happy? I intend to be happy.* She kissed his hand impulsively, and she heard a small sound deep in his throat.

The first chamber was empty. David peered inside. "No spiders," he reported.

The next room contained a handsome bed, already made, with two chairs, a chest at the foot of the bed, and a door probably leading to a dressing room. *This is our room. We're probably going to make some babies in here,* Meridee thought, then blushed, even though she knew she hadn't spoken out loud.

"Check for spiders, men," Able ordered. "If Mrs. Six sees spiders, I might not be able to coax her in to it."

The students did as he commanded and looked around. "No spiders, Master Six," Jamie announced.

"That's a relief," Able said. "As you were, men."

"Sir, you might need to find a stepstool for Mrs. Six," Jamie said. "She's short."

"You're right, McGregor. I shouldn't just fling her up there."

The students giggled, reminding Meridee that they were little boys, even though destined for the fleet in a few years. "No flinging," she said firmly, despite the fact that Durable Six was quite capable of flinging her anywhere. "I have my standards, where flinging is concerned."

They moved into the hall and opened the door on two more empty rooms. The first chamber on the other side of the hall showed a pleasant room with two smaller beds, chairs, and desks. David Ten forgot himself and tugged at her skirt. She looked down and saw the question in his eyes.

"I believe this will be your room in two weeks," she told him, and he nodded.

The next chamber showed a nearly identical amount of furniture. The room beyond was empty, so they trooped downstairs. Jamie McGregor went to the door and David Ten followed more slowly. Meridee knew he wanted to stay right there. She thought again of another workhouse boy who never knew the delight of a mother reading to him, or singing to him, or making certain the coverlet was snug around his neck. She silently thanked the Lord God Almighty for the resilience of little children and vowed to be a mother to all of her St. Brendan's lodgers.

Able opened the door. Jamie McGregor touched his finger to his forehead. "Class in a week then, Master Six?"

"Aye, lad. A week, and then every day after, excepting Sunday, until you go to sea."

Chapter Ten

❦

"WHAT TIME IS TWO bells in the forenoon watch, Master Six?" Meridee asked the next morning, after more important matters had been dealt with, including the location and reapplication of her nightgown, because the room was cold. She snuggled closer to her favorite warm body.

"Nine in the morning," he told her. "Day after tomorrow, my carcass will report to Headmaster Croker. I will probably have a stupid grin on my face from a surfeit of loving that seems to be my lot in life."

"Will people know what we've been doing?" Meridee asked.

Her husband laughed loud and long. "It doesn't show on your face, Meri. I doubt Headmaster Croker will leer at us. Shall we find out?" he asked, and flung back the covers, dragging her after him.

She decided there must be a law against a husband looking so magnificent and wearing nothing but a smile. Able *did* compare most favorably to those Greek statues in her father's book. He ruined the effect by scratching his backside and wandering into the dressing room, to return wearing a ragged robe.

"Theodore Croker informed me that we were to report to the dining hall for our meals until our cook comes on board. I am hungry, Mrs. Six."

She dressed and went downstairs, wondering how to turn a centuries-old heap into a home, especially on a slender budget. Her optimism grew as she came into the kitchen, where her husband had found some ship's crackers and dubious-looking cheese. He handed her a slice of cheese on the end of his knife. "It's not too hard."

It was too hard, but she rolled it around in her mouth to soften it. She sat next to him, leaned into his comforting bulk, and surveyed the kitchen. The medieval fireplace she had been dreading was instead a modern Rumford. The pots and pans hanging on hooks close to it appeared to be new. Someone had made a serious effort to turn this kitchen into a place where edible food could be prepared and served. All she needed was a cook and a maid of all work.

Dressing for breakfast across the street presented no difficulties, beyond Master Six insinuating his hands inside her gown when she asked him to button her up the back. "Durable Six, we're going to be late for breakfast," she said firmly.

He took his hands out and buttoned her dress. "It begins," he said to no one in particular. "I am Durable Six when I am in trouble?"

She turned around, pulled him close, and kissed him.

"I'm not in trouble?" he asked, his arms tight around her.

"Not yet. I have every hope for you."

"I am relieved," he declared. "I have many schemes that involve you. Mrs. Six, let us go to breakfast."

To her surprise, there wasn't any more traffic this morning than there had been at dusk yesterday. She looked up and down the quiet street. "It's almost as though no one even knows St. Brendan's exists," she marveled.

"That may have been one of the reasons our patron, whoever he is, chose this place," Able replied. "He apparently wanted a quiet, out-of-the-way place to prepare young men for the fleet. A place with no distractions and few temptations." He patted her hip. "I may be the only one at St. Brendan's with distractions."

"Master Six, can I not take you *anywhere*?"

"I'll behave. Perhaps. In we go, Meri."

She paused inside the door and sniffed the air, pleasantly surprised to smell rye bread and the tang of dried herring. They followed two older boys in uniform, who looked back at them. One of them waited for the Sixes to join him.

"You were in Master Blake's history class, weren't you?" Able asked. "Your name is Daniel Renfrew."

The boy in question stared. "Master, how on earth did you remember my name?"

He probably saw your name on a scrap of paper. Upside down. Written in invisible ink, Meridee thought in delight.

"When I entered the room, your instructor had just said your name in exasperation because you did not know who won the War of the Roses," Able reminded him. "I trust you remember it now."

Renfrew nodded. "You recited a quatrain, sir. How can I forget it?"

"Easiest way to learn things. Are we headed in the right direction for breakfast?"

"Aye, sir, and ... and Mrs. Six," the student said. "This way."

He opened a heavily carved door and gestured them in. Meridee took a step back, shy to see twenty-one boys staring back at her, plus servants and the man she remembered as Headmaster Thaddeus Croker.

Able pushed her forward gently. The headmaster rose and took her by the hand. He raised his other hand for silence in an already silent room.

"Lads, may I present Master Six, St. Brendan's newest instructor, and his charming wife, Mrs. Six."

The students were of all sizes, dressed alike. Most had dark hair cut short, some with olive skin similar to her husband's, and others with the light tones and red hair of the British Isles. *I will probably come to know you all*, she thought, as she inclined her head toward them.

Croker ushered her toward the head table and indicated two chairs. "Do join us, please," he said. "I believe there will be a cook coming your way today or tomorrow. Until then, you are most cordially welcome here."

Able pulled her chair out for her and she sat down. The plates and cups were of tin, with a serviette for her lap. The cleanliness of the table met with her approval, as did the little dish of reconstituted apples beside each plate and thick slices of rye bread. There were boiled eggs with the heat still rising from them, and porridge waiting to be passed.

Headmaster Croker cleared his throat. "Now, my lads, we will pray."

His blessing on the food was short. "Lord of battle, Lord who calms the seas, bless this food for our use and our service to the nation, amen."

Meridee smiled to herself, thinking of the occasionally long-winded prayers her brother-in-law inflicted on his offspring, boys the same age as these seated before her. This was better. She was no lover of cold food.

Meridee waited for the headmaster to pick up his spoon and begin so they could all eat, but he wasn't through.

"What will it be this morning?" he asked.

Several hands went up. Croker pointed to a small fellow, who stood up at attention. "Please, sir, 'Heart of Oak.' "

"Very well. Lasenby, give us a note."

From another table came Lasenby's note. The benches scraped back as twenty-one boys leaped to their feet. "First table, what say you begin this time?" Croker asked.

The words rang to the beams above. " 'Come, cheer up, my lads, 'tis to glory we steer, To add something more to this wonderful year. To honor we call you as freeman not slaves, For who are so free as the sons of the waves?' "

She felt her heart grow tender at the words sung by workhouse bastards, her husband among them, who must have felt more like slaves, surviving by sheer will. Able had already reduced her to tears with a few of his own memories, but these boys wanted her sympathy no more than he did, she was certain. They sang with gusto, pride on their faces.

Everyone joined in the rousing chorus. *Should I?* Meridee asked herself as her husband started to sing. *Certainly I should.* She took her own deep breath and came in a few words later. " '... Jolly tars are our men, We always are ready; steady boys, steady! We'll fight and we'll conquer again and again.' "

Two more verses followed. Able took her hand and pressed it to his heart, the heart that had beat in rhythm pressed against hers only a few hours ago. She watched the young faces before her, feeling a sudden dread at the sharp reminder that the purpose of this school was to train them for the fleet, war, and possible death.

Have I the courage for such a place as this? she asked herself. *God alone knows. Time will tell if I have a heart of oak.*

Chapter Eleven

❧

H E HAD MARRIED A game goer. Able watched as Meridee took a bite of what he told her was burgoo, and recoiled.

"My stars, but this is sweet," she whispered to him. "Burgoo?"

"Porridge to you," he said. "Cookie makes great pots of it before we sail into battle and he has to douse the fire in the galley. The sweeter the better. Have a boiled egg, dear heart."

Dear Heart grinned at him, looking nearly as young as the lads who ate and watched her covertly. "I crack it on the table?"

"No frills here, Mrs. Six," he assured her. "Headmaster, the rye bread is an unexpected touch."

"A baker on the next street has discovered us," Croker said, as he applied a dab of jam. "We even had white rolls for Christmas Day. The lads were fair amazed."

"Over something so simple," his wife said. Able heard the marvel in her voice.

"You cannot fathom how such a kindness tallies into hearts like theirs," Able replied, then amended, "like mine. I'd have given the earth for plum jam, any small sign someone knew I was in a terrible place and cared even slightly."

"You'll have plum jam and more," he thought he heard her say, but she had turned her face into his sleeve.

"I already do," he said. "Thank you." He took another spoonful of burgoo, hard to swallow around the boulder in his throat.

He gazed at the boys in their two rows perpendicular to the head table. Some of them, probably the newest arrivals, ate the way he used to eat, hunched furtively over their burgoo, packing it in as fast as possible, fearful someone might kype it. He recognized others eating slowly as they could, wanting it to last because they knew there would be nothing before evening. Able's experience taught him it was one way or the other.

He turned his attention to the older table. These boys took more time. As they chatted with each other, they passed the rye bread up and down the table. The jam went around too, no one snatching more than his share, because they already knew what the younger boys didn't—there would be more.

He watched in appreciation as one of the serving women walked down the row between the two tables, a light hand on one young boy's shoulder when he tried to grab all the rolls, a word (he hoped) of encouragement in another lad's ear when he just sat there, too stunned to eat. She moved on.

Meri sat up straight. He felt the tension in her arm before she moved slightly away. Watching her face, he tensed himself, because every emotion of hers seemed to be registering in him, as well. Was this another facet of his weird mental acuity?

She turned to face him and he saw resolution in her eyes. "I'm going to be on the employment roll soon?" she asked.

"Two weeks or so. I believe it's negotiable."

"I'm starting early."

Admiration for his wife grew even greater as she walked to the little boy who sat there staring at his food. With a minimum of fuss, the student next to him moved over and Meridee sat beside him. With no hesitation, her hand went to his back, and then to his neck. She pulled him close and let him sob into her breast.

In another moment Able heard her humming to him. He smiled when he realized it was the chorus to "Heart of Oak." In no time, all the boys at the table were singing, too, this time softly and slowly, as though England's most rousing Navy ditty had turned into a lullaby.

When they finished, they looked at each other and laughed. Talk resumed, the bread went around again, and the little fellow picked up his spoon. Meridee sat with him until he finished his burgoo. She buttered rye bread for him, which threatened to bring on more tears. He knew from hard experience that no one ever saw butter in a workhouse, but the now-fortunate child had the kindest woman in England—no, in Newton's clockwork universe—seated beside him. She took a bite, and he took a bite. And another. His smile could have lit up the room.

"Master Able?"

"Yes, Headmaster?"

"I thought only you were going to be St. Brendan's *summum bonum*."

"An honest mistake, sir."

Headmaster and master smiled at each other in perfect charity.

When breakfast finished, the lad on Meri's other side helped the boy take his dishes to the rolling table where the matron stood. Meridee watched a moment more, then rejoined him at the head table.

The headmaster took her hand. "Mrs. Six, you have a fine instinct."

"I like children," she said simply.

Croker gestured toward the door. "The boys have their assignments for the morning. We're doing some general tidying around the place. An institution as old at St. Brendan's never lacks for corners, sills, and closets where grime lurks. Come with me, both of you."

Able pulled his wife close in the hall and kissed her cheek, to the amusement of two boys already poking at lurking grime.

"Master Six, you're supposed to set a sterling example for the lads at St. Brendan's," Meri told him. "Kissing me can't be approved in any contract devised by the hand of man."

"I contend we two are the best example anyone could ask for, Mrs. Six," he replied, completely unrepentant.

"You're hopeless of remedy, you know," she said as they went into the headmaster office.

"Alas," was the best he could summon on short notice. He could explain tonight that workhouse boys needed to know how real people behaved, and not the frail women who abandoned them, the ogres who ruined them, or the sanctimonious who judged them. He reconsidered; Meri needed no explanation. She knew.

They sat in high-backed chairs in front of the headmaster's desk. He spread out four sheets of paper and picked up the first one. "David Ten, whom I believe you have already met," Croker said. "He's one of our numbered boys, Master Six, as you have obviously divined."

"He paid us a visit. He worries about being beaten if he cannot furnish a right answer," Meridee said.

Croker steepled his fingers together. "I cannot guarantee that in other classes."

"Master Blake has another stick to replace the one I broke?" Able asked.

"He seems to think no one will learn without it."

"Is he a good teacher, otherwise?" Able asked.

"I thought he was, until I watched you teach," Croker said. "Now I have my doubts."

Able knew it was not his prerogative to criticize the instructors. "How did you choose the students?"

"The teacher at St. Pancras Workhouse told me David is relentlessly curious, and he wasn't pleased."

"Curiosity can drive an uncreative instructor mad, when he has thirty lads crammed into one room," Able said. "Let's put David's skill to good use."

"Mrs. Six, to answer your question, I sent out inquiries to workhouses in England and Scotland, requesting them to let us know of intelligent, curious, imaginative, resilient lads for a special school." The headmaster made a face. "I heard from few. Are you surprised, Master Six?"

"Not at all," Able said. "For the most part, workhouse teachers have no imagination of their own. The resentment is high in such places, and it creates bullies. Where it does not create bullies, you will find men of moral superiority who think infants are responsible for their parents' sins. I confess to being surprised you found any teachers willing to help you."

"They're rare," Croker admitted. He eyed Able shrewdly. "You are a man of firm opinion."

"I am an observer by nature," Able replied. "My observations propelled me off to sea at nine. If I wanted to survive, I had no choice."

"How *did* you find your pupils?" Meridee asked.

Able smiled inside. Trust Meri to persist with her original line of reasoning until she was satisfied. She was not a woman easily distracted.

"I started asking workhouse teachers about restless pupils, argumentative, endless questioners—students they would happily discharge."

"You had to sort through a lot of chaff, I suspect," Able commented, thinking of the criminals-in-the-making in Dumfries Workhouse.

"Indeed. Some were rascals I wouldn't have taken if the king himself had recommended them. That's how I found the jewels in the midden." He sat back in triumph. "I have assembled leaders, scholars, seekers, number-lovers, all with a goodly dose of rascality and shrewdness."

"They are survivors," Able said. "I recognize them."

Croker held up another paper and slid it toward them. "I see that Mrs. Six wishes me to get to the point."

"Sir, I—"

"Quite all right, my dear. I tend to wander from the subject. Nick. My dear, he's the lad you so kindly tended during breakfast. He is new to us. He showed up at a workhouse in Northumberland, the one name pinned to his shirt. Poor lad, he was shivering so much I thought he would overset himself."

"He is here because—"

"He loves to read." He shook his head. "He also does not trust a single living soul on the planet. Who would, with parents who abandoned him?"

Another paper came across the desk. "Stephen Hoyt, the son of two thieves transported to New South Wales. He's a runner."

"How are we to keep him here?" Meridee asked.

"Plain and simple: you will earn your one pound a month, my dear. I cannot answer your question."

"I will make the Six home so pleasant that no one wants to bolt," she said.

I wouldn't bolt, Able thought. *As it is, I must be pried from bed with a lever.*

"Last and most certainly not least, I give you John Mark, a son of a girl who, as far as we know, was snatched and passed around a foc's'le for nine horrible months, then dumped on Gunwharf to die. None of those barbarians let on they had her on board, and she was used terribly. The teacher in his workhouse called John Mark tenacious, and if I may, durable." He sighed. "Those animals had even …." He stopped. "No more."

Able heard a small sound, and took Meri's hand. "Life is no picnic on the docks and in the belly of ships."

"Were those men punished?" she asked, her voice small.

Croker ran his hand across his eyes. "Not enough. I believe they were lashed and separated to other ships, at least."

"I hope they all died miserably," she said, her voice trembling with anger.

"I, too." Croker spread his hands on his desk. "There you have it—four boys with no advantages except that now they are in a safe place where they will be trained, and in your home, cared for."

"I'll do my best," Meri said.

"I do not doubt that for a minute, Mrs. Six," Croker said as he stood up. "When you go across the street, you will find my own housemaid waiting for you. Put her to work today. You'll have some household assistance of a more permanent nature soon. Not much gets done in the week between Christmas and New Year's."

A great deal got done in our case, Able thought. *I've never been happier.*

"See your lady home and return to me. I'll spell out your own duties, and see how hard we can work *you,* short of mutiny."

Chapter Twelve

❧

"**I** HAVE LIVED A cloistered existence," was Meri's comment as she let go of his arm, once they crossed the street, and nodded to the maid waiting at their door.

"Please never resent me for dragging you into this life," he said, voicing his only fear. "I never used to fear anything. Now I fear that."

Bless her sweet heart, Meri kissed him, evidently forgetting the maid only a few steps behind her. His hand on her lovely throat, he kissed her back.

Another quick kiss and she turned around to see the maid. Meri's laugh was so contagious that the maid smiled. "I am so discreet! You are Headmaster Croker's maid?"

Meri dipped a playful curtsey to her lord and master, unlocked the door, and ushered the maid inside. Able went back to the school, pleased that his wife of recent tenure hadn't run back to Devonshire. A man could count his blessings.

A smile on his own face, Theodore Croker had apparently watched the whole trip across the street, the kiss, and the laughter. Able wondered if he should apologize for his bold behavior, but decided against it. After all, Portsmouth wasn't a city known for its rectitude or the quality of its citizens.

"She's a charming lady," the headmaster said, admiration evident in his voice.

He pointed toward the hall with classrooms. "We'll begin this new term on January second. Third door on the right, Master Able."

His corner classroom overlooked the Solent, with its anchored warships and the distant line of prison hulks. There was a desk, battered but serviceable, a filled bookcase, and twelve desks and chairs. A globe tilting at an angle on its base and a chalkboard completed the room's entire furnishing.

"We're a bare-bones academic institution," Croker said. "Our patrons are sincere in their determination to help our wharf rats and misbegotten urchins, but not everyone looks with favor on the poor, deserving or otherwise."

"These patrons … might I know them?"

"*I* don't even know them," Croker said, with mild exasperation. "The whole school is kept quiet, as if people in power are ashamed of it." He shrugged. "P'raps they are. For myself, I have never understood the point in condemning children who had no say in their birth."

"Refreshing of you."

"There aren't many as enlightened as I am," Croker replied, with some spirit.

"How were you declared headmaster here?" Able asked, considering himself chastened for his sarcasm. His amazing brain recalled years of slights, abuse, and scorn.

"I'll spare you the gory details, but I was teaching some gutter rats right here at my own expense. Simple things like arithmetic and letters. Captain Sir Belvedere St. Anthony found out. There seems to be a prodigiously effective word-of-mouth channel among sailors."

"Prodigious," Able echoed. "Why were you doing this in the first place?"

A shadow of great melancholy passed over the headmaster's countenance. "Penance, Master Six, and I'll say no more about it." Again the hand across his eyes, as though he saw something he could not dismiss. "I was invited to Admiralty House, quizzed a bit about my interest in teaching young boys of low or less-than-low birth, and installed in this place officially. This is our third year."

"Any of your pupils in the fleet yet?" Able asked. He knew better than to pry further into a man's life.

"This spring will see the first of the lot," Croker said. "All twelve of my upper class have stayed and succeeded, which still surprises me. I was certain we would lose a few. It's not an easy course."

"When your alternatives are a return to the workhouse or life on the street, St. Brendan's is highly attractive."

"Hadn't thought of it like that."

"Few do."

"I have already mentioned the three fortunate lads who were taken from here earlier by relatives," Croker said. "I will find more lads."

"It's a rare thing when anyone seeks out a workhouse child," Able said. "In fact, I have never heard of it."

"Really?" Croker spent a moment in thought. "That is one area where Master Blake shines. He went out of his way to find relatives."

I wouldn't have credited Blake with that much interest, Able thought. *Howsoever, Meridee would scold me soundly if I ragged on about Master Blake.*

"Perhaps I should give him the benefit of the doubt, Headmaster Croker."

"P'raps you should. Call me Thaddeus, when we are private," the headmaster said, and dismissed more comment on the matter of Master Blake. "I would like you to teach the younger boys mathematics, at least at first. Acquaint them with numbers in a way that will not terrify them. I wonder: in exchange for this admittedly slow going for someone of your ability, could I tempt you with the calculus for one or two of the older lads?"

"With pleasure. Headma … Thaddeus. We could meet daily wherever you say." He looked around at his bare classroom. "How do you aim to use me in the afternoons?"

"This is where I intend to veer from a rigid schedule," Theodore Croker said. He walked to the window. "We have before us a world reluctantly at peace. How much longer do you give the Treaty of Amiens?"

"A wild guess? Four months at most. Better weather returns by May. I know Whitehall doesn't wish to give up Malta, as stipulated by the treaty."

"In light of this, I propose a course I will loosely call Seamanship. Teach them what they need to know to survive in the fleet. It is ambitious to make miniature sailing masters of them, but I would like you to try." He waited barely a second. "How will you begin, Master Six?"

Able pointed to the window close to the building's corner. He looked down at the debris-filled stone basin. He had seen one like this in Livorno, Italy, with hot sun turning the basin into a shallow pool where toy boats bobbed about.

"They're going to learn to swim. I'll start with a depth of three feet, maybe less, so they can master floating."

"You had mentioned that. In superstitious minds, does not learning to swim tempt Neptune to sink ships?"

"Have you ever seen a man drown? I have. He doesn't struggle. He tips his head back then silently slides underwater. God, what a waste," Able said softly. "I predict the renewed war will not stop until one of us is bled dry. If something as simple as swimming helps our side, I am for it."

"Very well, master. Sir B told me you have a gift for going right to the meat of an argument."

Able nodded in agreement. "I will not be on the side bled dry."

"Once they have learned to float?"

"We'll add more water and they will learn to swim."

"It's devilish cold water right now, master," Thaddeus said, but with a smile now, as if pleased to play devil's advocate.

"Unless they are sailing in the South Pacific, the water is always cold," Able replied. "I'll know when to reel them in. I suspect Meri will be standing by with towels and admonition, if I fail to notice cyanotic lips."

"You'll enlist your long-suffering wife?" Theodore joked.

"I know Meri Six," Able said. "It will be her idea. You should see her with her nephews. She likes taking care of the little boys." *Big ones even more*, he thought, and felt his face grow warm.

"Very well, let us assume they can swim like otters now. What then?"

"I'll return the basin to water shallow enough to stand in and we'll build little boats."

"Is this play or work?"

"How about work disguised as play?" Able questioned in turn. "I'll teach them how to balance small loads on their little ships to keep them in trim, one of the most critical duties of a sailing master."

His mind raced along at its usual breakneck speed, so he forced himself to speak slowly, aware no one thought as he did. "If the weather is too inclement—I'm no monster—we'll come up here and practice keeping the ship's log, which as you know, is another duty of the sailing master."

Thaddeus bowed elaborately, but Able noticed no condescension or mockery in the gesture. The headmaster appeared genuinely appreciative.

"How will you clean out this … this midden?"

"With shovels and little boys," Able said. "With your permission, I'll call for volunteers tomorrow after breakfast."

"They've been informed that the days this week are for their own purposes, before we plunge into another rigorous term. We know when to let up, and now is the time."

"If no one volunteers, I'll begin myself," Able said. "Do you ever wager, sir?"

"No! You plan to make this irresistible, somehow? You're going to clean out a disgusting basin full of God knows what and have the lads lining up to help?"

Able smiled. "I think they will. Will you secure a cart of some sort and several rakes and shovels by tomorrow morning?" They stood in the classroom doorway now. "Tell me where we can dump the trash."

Thaddeus stopped, unmindful of the students in the hall, some sweeping, some sitting on the benches reading, others doing nothing, all watchful. "Does nothing daunt you, Master Six?"

"Durability is my legacy and my name, Headmaster Croker," he said most formally. "No man is dauntless, I suppose, but I come close."

Able looked around him at the boys in the hall, lads like himself. He gazed into their eyes and understood the need to be in this place at this time. They seemed to understand that he knew them.

"We have work to do." Able Six knew he was a cynical man. Where was this great lump in his throat coming from? "We must find the greatness within, during this time of national emergency."

"It will be a hard task, perhaps a thankless one," Croker commented. "Obviously *you* found greatness."

"To a point, sir. I can rise no higher in the fleet because I am still a workhouse bastard." He stopped. "Now I would like to … to think a bit, with your permission."

The headmaster gave him a nod, which looked surprisingly deferential to Able, who knew he would never get used to such … such what? He didn't know the word. Acclaim was too strong. Admiration came closer, but still wasn't right. Better leave it alone. A man can't know every word.

He closed the door behind him in his classroom, and gave a sigh of profound satisfaction. He stared down at the debris-filled basin, thinking of the lessons to be learned there.

He left the corner view and walked to the other windows, opening one to see the home he now shared with the woman who, along with several ship captains, saw his greatness, or whatever it was.

As much as they laughed about his need for a keeper, it was true. A man could have no better advocate. Put her in the form of a wife, something he never thought to acquire, and a man could ask for no more.

The wind blew cold off the Solent, but he breathed in deeply, knowing he would miss the free range of a ship at sea, but aware this was his domain now, here and across the street, where another kind of destiny, the loving and gentle sort, awaited him.

Chapter Thirteen

❦

B Y THE TIME AFTERNOON shadows began to lengthen, Meridee knew their house was one step closer to a home.

She looked around the sitting room with real pride, amazed at how the simple lace table covers she had squirreled away years ago turned austerity into near luxury. It was the home of her own she had wanted for years.

She had spent the day working alongside Sadie, the maid Thaddeus Croker had so kindly loaned to her. The first course of action had been to assure Sadie that she was used to turning a hand in the vicarage, and she wouldn't stand by idle. That bit of awkwardness put aside, they scrubbed floors, washed windows, and rearranged items in the kitchen.

Luncheon had been kindly delivered to them from St. Brendan's: meat pies and potatoes, washed down with actual grog. Sadie laughed at Meridee's wary expression as she sniffed the cup.

"Aye, ma'am, rum and water, but I assure you the cook at St. Brendan's leans heavily on the water spigot for the boys."

Dessert was petits fours, which made Meridee stare again. "One of the bakers nearby heard about St. Brendan's," the maid explained, as she picked up a delectable morsel robed in chocolate with a candied cherry on top. "He's embarrassed if we exclaim over him, but he likes to surprise the headmaster with seasonal delicacies."

"What does Mrs. Croker say about all this?" Meridee asked, after polishing off the other chocolate petit four. She eyed the one with candied lemon peel on top and picked it up.

"There is no Mrs. Croker," Sadie said with a shake of her head. "Rumors say she suffered some preventable illness, but the master was too busy to see to her comfort before she died."

"Heavens, recently?" Meridee set down the pastry, which had lost its appeal.

"Years ago, long before I came into employment. He never speaks of it."

Meridee tried to imagine a husband too busy to care for wife, and couldn't. She remembered her own mother agonizing over Papa as he declined and faded away, despite all anyone could do. She knew Able would never neglect her welfare, and she knew it worked both ways.

She picked up the petit four again and ate it thoughtfully, savoring the lemony tang and the smooth icing, still getting used to the idea of marriage and wondering who to ask if she ever had any questions. She smiled to herself, knowing the only person she ever needed to ask was the man who shared her bed.

It was a beguiling thought, which she carried with her as they prepared the rooms where four boys would take up residence soon enough—sheets and blankets tucked, pillows fluffed. Sadie found rugs for the boys' rooms and one for Meridee's room, which they tugged upstairs after a thorough beating in the backyard.

When they finished and the chairs were back in place in front of the fireplace, Sadie gazed around like God on the sixth day and pronounced their efforts excellent. "You'll be warm and cozy here, Mrs. Six," she said. "There is even room over there for a cradle."

Meridee blushed, even though Sadie hadn't said anything she hadn't already been thinking for the past tumultuous week. The words were matter-of-fact and woman to woman. Something about the saying of them out loud settled around Meridee's heart. This was her life now. If matters moved ahead as they did every day for thousands of women like her throughout the British Isles, there would be babies and more challenges and heartache mingled with laughter, because that was how life ran through a person's mortal span.

She spent a quiet moment gazing out the bedroom window to St. Brendan's School across the road, and the watery Solent beyond. She reached the pleasant conclusion that her role was to provide the daily, mundane routines of life that a man would want, be he ordinary or exceptional.

Before she left for the night, Sadie fetched a pot of soup from the school. "The headmaster eats most of his meals with the boys, but you and Master Six might enjoy a quiet dinner together," she said, setting the pot on the hob.

"My goodness, what is it?" she asked, as she lifted the lid and sniffed the combination of exotic spices, mixed into a hash of what looked like well-done potatoes and leeks, plus meat she had no previous acquaintance with. She wanted to poke it suspiciously with a fork, but that didn't seem polite, not after Sadie had gone to so much trouble to help her today.

"Lobscouse," the maid announced. "A particularly fine one, I might add."

"Is it a sailor's delicacy?" Meridee asked, hoping her question sounded innocent, rather than wary.

"I suppose you could say so," Sadie replied, after some consideration. "Tars have a tendency to put a little of this and that into a pot and hope for the best." She held out a waxed paper packet of what looked like cornmeal. "Cookie already ground up the ship's biscuit. You can add it just before you serve it."

Might as well expose her ignorance. "Is a lobscouse some sort of fish?"

Sadie whooped with laughter. "Mercy, no!" she said, her eyes lively with merriment. "Someone must have named it that for want of a better idea. It's corned beef that comes out of a keg long at sea. That's why there are so many spices. Cloves, cardamom, allspice, and nutmeg."

"I am dubious," Meridee admitted, unwilling to poison her husband of a mere week. "A very long time in a keg?"

"Since we're in Pompey, it's fresh corned beef, or as near as. Your man will love it."

Will I? Meridee asked herself. She walked Sadie to the front door, grateful for her help, but unwilling to be left alone with lobscouse. "Should I serve something else with it?"

"Bread would be good," the maid said. "I'm heading home, which isn't far from a bakery. Get your cloak and hat."

Meridee grabbed up her cloak, reticule, and winter bonnet. Dusk came quickly as they hurried along. "I won't have to walk too far back alone?" she asked, trying to sound adult and casual.

"Two blocks is all," Sadie said. "Mind your step. Haven't seen a street sweeper in ages."

There was no point in telling the maid that she had never walked alone to little Pomfrey without someone accompanying her, even if it was only her nephews. She didn't think Sadie would understand.

It was two long blocks, past warehouses where workers were shrugging into overcoats and leaving. Others hurried along, heads down, as a raw wind whipped along, making Meridee clutch her cloak tighter.

They passed a lamp lighter. Perched there on his ladder, he must have said something impudent to Sadie, who responded with salty language. "Maybe we shouldn't ..." Meridee began, as Sadie grabbed her arm and tugged her into a brightly lit bakery.

"What does Master Six like?" Sadie asked.

"Rye bread, ship's biscuit, and brown bread," Meridee replied. She looked for white bread and saw none, but there, nestled in the corner, were a half-dozen petits fours. "And all those petits fours," she said, pointing to them. "Yes, that will do."

"Show me your money first, miss," the baker said, which told Meridee worlds about his usual customers.

She already knew better than to open her reticule wide. She took out a handful of coins and put them on the high counter. The baker nodded and smiled at her. "A lady of quality in here?" he asked, but his tone was kinder, now that he knew she had money.

"She's the wife of Master Six, St. Brendan's new instructor," Sadie said. "No cheek now. She's quality, like you said."

The baker scowled at Sadie, who glared back. "Don't let him cheat you, Mrs. Six," she said, loud enough to be overheard. "You'll be fine. I'll be on my way."

Meridee resisted the urge to beg her to walk her at least halfway back home. *I've done a foolish thing*, she thought, but smiled instead. "Thank you for your help today, Sadie."

With a wave of her hand, Sadie hurried into the increasing gloom. Meridee turned back to the counter. Might as well show a brave face. "Here's my basket. I'd like one rye, one brown bread, a dozen ship's biscuits, and those petits fours." She knew her lot in life now was to cajole tradesmen. "I had some earlier that you must have given to Headmaster Croker at St. Brendan's."

It was the right comment. The baker nodded and dipped his head in what Meridee might have called shyness in someone younger and more sensitive-looking. She reconsidered. He was obviously an artist, no matter his floury apron and red face.

He filled her basket, took some of the coins on the counter, and handed back the rest. She reached for the basket and he handed it over as politely as a lord.

"Hurry on home. It's getting dark and I don't trust anyone on this street."

Meridee took a deep breath and stepped onto the sidewalk, wishing she had been smarter about venturing from her house in what everyone knew was a town with more rascals than paving stones.

She looked around and saw no women on the street, no friendly faces, just stares and leers. Eyes forward, she clutched her basket and told herself not to run.

"Hey, hey, missy. Whatever you're asking, I'll pay."

"Here's a handy close. What say we duck in for a fast one?"

"They must line up for you when the fleet's in."

Don't look around, she ordered herself. *Eyes forward and a prayer might be in order. The Lord might even bless you when you're stupid.*

She sighed with relief to see her house at the end of the street. She tried not to hear the footsteps coming closer. Maybe it was time to step livelier.

Meridee stopped in horror when an arm snaked around her waist and yanked her close. "I'm thinking you'd be good in bed."

She grabbed the stick of rye bread, ready for battle. The man pulled her closer. Why did he have to be tall?

"Death by rye bread?"

She looked up, desperate, then gasped and swatted him anyway, breaking the loaf in half over her husband's head.

Chapter Fourteen

❦

"**Y**OU ARE A SCOUNDREL!" she declared, and swatted Able again for good measure.

"And you shouldn't be out alone in Portsmouth," he replied. Able leaned against the wall and laughed, which meant she had to hit him again with barely more than the heel of the loaf.

"I'll summon the watch, miss!" she heard behind her. The baker lumbered in her direction, a baker's peel in his hand. "Let me at him."

"No, no, no!" she said, holding up her hands. "He's my husband."

The baker stopped and stared at him, then laughed. "I went into the street to watch you, lady," he said, still trying to catch his breath. He brandished the peel at Able. "I'll still thrash you if t'lady says I may. You shouldn't be scaring your little wife like that."

"On the contrary, yes I should," Able said. "You wouldn't want your wife out and about in Portsmouth, would you?"

"She outweighs me and has a fierce eye," the baker said. "But this one …"

"… is mine, and I'll see her home," Able finished. "If she's still speaking to me."

The rye bread was a lost cause, so Meridee dropped the rest of it in the gutter. "Maybe in a year or two," she muttered, which made the baker laugh. With a cheerful "G'nigh," he disappeared into the gloom.

Able picked up the basket and crooked out his arm. Meridee made a little show of ignoring him, but not too much. She put her arm through his. " 'Good in bed,' am I?" she whispered.

"The best," he replied, his voice low, too. "Confirmed. Ratified. Acknowledged."

Best to ignore the edgy feeling his words whispered low gave her. For heaven's sake, she was on the street. "I'm sorry I went out," she said. "I shouldn't have done that."

"No, you shouldn't have," he agreed, but she heard no anger in his voice. "I was looking out my classroom window when you and the maid left, and I followed you."

"You could have said something!" she declared.

"No. You were in no real danger, but maybe you needed to feel you were." He inclined his head toward hers. "I watched the baker step into the street after you left his shop. He had your best interest at heart, too. What say we give him all our business?"

"Aye, mister," she said, which made him hug her closer.

As they approached their house, he slowed down. "If you look through the gloom, you'll see someone waiting on the front step for us. I already said a word to her as I went after you."

"A cook?" she asked, squinting to see into the dark.

He turned to face her, his hands gentle on her shoulders. "You might not agree with me at first glance about our cook, but I know her, and I couldn't be more pleased."

She craned around for a look, and gulped to see a dark mound both massive and tall get to her feet. "I am already terrified," she whispered.

"I am never going to be frightened for you in the wicked streets of Portsmouth. Mrs. Perry will slam to the ground any jolly tar or miscreant who so much as looks at you."

As they came closer, the mound turned into precisely what her husband said she was, a most formidable woman.

"C-c-can she cook?" Meridee whispered.

"I neither know nor care," he replied. "You are now officially safe as houses. I don't give a rat's ass what her food tastes like."

Meridee stopped, unable to take her eyes from the woman still half a street-length away. She did notice that two men, sailors by their rolling gait, prudently crossed to the St. Brendan's side of the street when they passed her. "Hmm. Well," was the most intelligent thing she could think to say, which made her husband chuckle.

"Cat got your tongue?" he teased.

"I haven't met her and I'm already afraid of her."

"God's wounds, *I'm* terrified of her, too."

"You can't be serious," she replied, wondering where the bravest man she knew had suddenly vanished.

"Never more so, Meridee-licious," he said. "Handsomely now, my love. Ship to starboard. Her name is Daisy Perry."

And there she was, tall and black, blocking their path. To Meridee's relief, she turned her attention first to Master Durable Six.

"I wondered if anyone in the known universe would ever marry you, Master Six," she declared in round tones, by way of greeting. She whirled around to Meridee for a sudden appraisal. Meridee leaned closer to Able. "She's pretty, too. Wants feeding up some, though. Bright as you?"

"No one's as bright as me, Mrs. Perry," Able said. Meridee could tell he was enjoying this exchange. "She is kind and my keeper."

Mrs. Perry laughed and slapped Able's back, which made him stagger. Meridee put her hand to her mouth to cover her own mirth.

Meridee looked closer, amazed to see a ring though the woman's nose. The woman had a beautiful lilt to her voice. Where was she from, for goodness' sake?

When he recovered his balance, Able held out his hand, wincing when she grabbed it and pulled him close to her mountainous breast. "Daisy Perry, reporting as your cook, Mistress Six," she boomed out. "Introduce us properly, Master Six!"

"If you'll release my hand before you cut off all circulation …" he said.

Daisy Perry—what an incongruous name—released him and performed a surprisingly graceful bow in Meridee's direction. "Go on, laddie."

"Meri, this is Mrs. Perry, the … wife—"

"Widow, alas."

"I am sorry to hear such news," Able said, and Meridee heard precisely that in his voice. "Your husband was the best carpenter's mate in the fleet."

"Aye, he was," she said. "What's done is done."

"I was hoping to visit him soon, once we were settled," Able said. "When?"

"Two months. I miss the little man," she said quietly. She patted Able's hand. " 'Twas consumption what took him off, Master."

Meridee remembered she was mistress of the house. "Heavens, look at us," she scolded, but gently, because both her husband and the mountain of a woman were regarding each other with sadness in their eyes. "Come inside! I can't be the only cold person."

"You'll have me, then?" Mrs. Perry asked, her question straightforward, without a barnacle on it.

Had I met you a few weeks ago, I'd have been terrified, Meridee thought. *Not now.* She gestured to Able. "Don't just stand there, husband. Pick up Mrs. Perry's duffel. Certainly we will have you."

Head high, she opened the door and led the strange parade inside and down the hall to the kitchen. The Rumford itself deserved a grand gesture, so she gave a flourish with her hand. "Look at that bit of magnificence in this medieval building, Mrs. Perry! Did you ever?"

The Rumford was a substantial appliance, but her new cook towered over it. She nodded with approval.

"I'm no cook," Meridee confessed. "Mr. Croker kindly loaned me one of his housemaids today. We cleaned, and she brought over this wonderful pot of soup."

She smiled at her husband, who seemed to be enjoying himself hugely. "Dearest, put Mrs. Perry's duffel in that first room. I believe she is staying."

Grinning, he tugged at an imaginary forelock. "Aye, miss, aye!"

Her heart full, Meridee watched the two of them go to the first little bedroom off the kitchen. She followed, pleased to see Mrs. Perry nodding her approval. The cook dwarfed the room. Meridee wondered if the wife of a ship's carpenter knew another carpenter who could make her a longer bed.

"I'm afraid you'll be a bit cramped until we can find you a longer bed," Able said. "Maybe a wider one, too."

Mrs. Perry took Able by the back of his uniform and gave him a little shake. "Broad in the beam, am I, Master Six?" she chided. "Teach this cheeky boy some manners, missy."

"Aye, ma'am," Meridee said promptly.

Able shook his head as though to clear it. "Meri, this redoubtable female sailed with us at Camperdown. She treated me like this all the time."

"You probably deserved it, Durable Six," Meridee teased back. "Mrs. Perry, will you join us for some … some lobster cow? I'll serve ship's biscuits, too. Rye bread would have been better, but I brained the master with it for sneaking up on me."

Mrs. Perry roared with laughter. Meridee laughed again when the woman raised her hand to slap Able on the back, prompting her husband to move quickly out of her reach.

"Have I not one ally in this household?" he asked the world in general. "It's lobscouse," he said in an aside worthy of Shakespeare.

Mrs. Perry glowered at him. "Serves you right for sneaking up on a lady."

"I was trying to teach my lady a lesson about traveling abroad in this wicked city without an escort," he said.

"She has one now," Mrs. Perry declared.

"I know," he said quietly.

Supper took bare minutes to prepare. Meridee located plates, bowls and spoons, and Mrs. Perry went right to the Rumford to sniff suspiciously, then smile. "It's edible," she commented. "Hand me them bowls."

She placed the filled bowls on the table, but stood by the Rumford, her bowl in her hand. "I'm comfortable here," she said.

"You'll sit with us," Meridee said. "That's an order."

"'Tisn't proper," Mrs. Perry argued. "I'm your servant."

This is what it comes to? Meridee asked herself. *I can be as formidable as you.* "This is my house and we will eat together, until we get everything sorted out."

She said it quietly, spoon in hand but not dipping into her bowl until Mrs. Perry sat down.

She silently blessed her dear husband for starting a conversation to bridge the yawning chasm of servant and master sharing the same table. "Meri, let me tell you about that long, long day at Camperdown," he said. "A biscuit, Mrs. Perry?"

She took one, waited a moment, then dipped the biscuit in the soup. Meridee saw the emotion on the woman's face, not sure if it was from the fact of sitting at the same table, or from her own memories of that sea battle between the Royal Navy and an equally formidable Dutch Navy six years ago.

"I suppose this isn't dinner-table talk, but we are not likely to ever stand on much ceremony in this household," he said, after a few spoonfuls of lobscouse. "I jumped in after the surgeon died and amputated one arm and one leg, because someone had to. The pharmacist's mate recovered from his stupor enough to do a second arm, thank God. I was fair exhausted. Mrs. Perry tended all the men, not just her husband. I could not have been more grateful. She kept them alive. How in the world did you find out that we needed a cook here, Mrs. Perry?"

"It's an odd thing, master. I was sitting in my rooming house, wondering what was going to become of me, when who should knock on my door yesterday but the captain with all the names."

"Captain Sir Belvedere St. Anthony?" Able asked. "I wish I could say I'm surprised."

"He told me to report at the first dog watch, and here I am."

Meridee frowned and Able nudged her again. "Between four and six in the afternoon for you landlubbers," he said in a stage whisper that made her laugh.

He reached inside his uniform coat. "I sense the fine hand of Sir B in a related matter, ladies."

He took out a small sheet of paper folded several times and spread it out on the table. "We instructors each have a catch-all cubby by Headmaster Croker's office. I found this in mine."

Meridee picked it up. " 'To Whom It May Concern ...' " she read ahead. "He is a wit. Listen: 'Able, you had better not forget to give this to your keeper.' "

Mrs. Perry shook her finger at Able.

"Oh my! 'Since you will be providing room and board for four students of St. Brendan's, this entitles you to a two-pound per month victual allotment.' "

Meridee stared at the words in delight. "Mrs. Perry, we can feed them like royalty with two pounds a month! Surely this is an error, Able."

"I asked Thaddeus Croker that very thing. He said no. The boys are small and want feeding up. Two pounds a month. Don't argue."

"I've seen David Ten. Able, were you small for your age?" Meridee asked.

"Aye, lassie," he replied, a man with nothing small about him now. "I ran away from the workhouse before I starved to death. Only Irishmen and workhouse bastards grow tall on Navy food."

Meridee felt tears gather in her eyes at his calm statement of fact, which wouldn't do. "Here you are, this manly specimen," she joked.

"Are we in?" Her manly specimen asked with a laugh. "The three of us?"

Meridee and Mrs. Perry looked at each other and nodded at the same time.

Meridee gave her husband a triumphant glance. "Welcome aboard, Mrs. Perry." She knew it was an important moment, the three of them sitting in a kitchen, elbows on the table, eating ship's biscuit. "We are now officially a crew."

Chapter Fifteen

⁓

A s Meridee opened her lovely eyes the next morning and started on her nightgown buttons, Able reflected that his early-morning musings in more celibate days included thinking through Euclid's *Propositions*. All he wanted to do now was assist her with his own buttons. Had Euclid ever …? As his helpful wife tugged his nightshirt up and off, Able hoped the old Greek didn't spend *all* his time on geometry.

"Meri-delectable, I used to lie in bed and mentally run through all of Euclid's *Propositions*," he said as they cuddled again later. He smiled when her eyelashes fluttered a few times against his bare chest then closed. He felt her relax, enjoying the heaviness of her breasts against his side. "Ah, but you don't care about Euclid, my love."

"Only a very little," she managed, before he heard her deep breathing.

Amused and completely satisfied, he lay beside his wife, knowing he needed to get up and be about the business of the day. He savored her warmth and realized this glorious woman *was* the business of the day, too. There was no chance he would ever forget Euclid's *Propositions*.

As Meridee made little bubble noises against his chest, he thought through the day, certain he could cajole the younger students he already thought of as his own into mucking out the stone basin that used to be an inlet for barges or other small craft arriving at St. Brendan's. In its day, like other monasteries in Catholic England, it must have been a powerful place, with dignitaries coming and going. Now it was barely remembered on a forgotten street, perfect for their unusual scholarship.

He sniffed the cool air, relishing Meridee's personal fragrance, and then the smell of breakfast. Mrs. Perry obviously wasn't wasting a moment. Maybe she *could* even cook. Once her husband, a small man but a bold one, had bought her in Jamaica, Daisy had sailed with the fleet. Of children they had none, except that every young seaman, he among them, had felt her maternal interest.

He could see her continuing that benevolent dictatorship over the four boys soon to come into the house. She would likely love them as much as Meridee, but it would be a sterner love.

Love. He got up and gazed down at his sleeping wife, nearly overcome by the responsibility for her life that was his now. *I hope we have children*, he thought. He knew life held no guarantees, but the hope that had somehow not died during bleak workhouse days and burned still brighter in the fleet nourished him still.

He had spent his life as a stone-cold realist, and knew that would never entirely change; in truth he knew it must not change. But as he looked down in love and duty at his wife, he felt his heart soften. "Make me better," he whispered.

When he came into the kitchen, Mrs. Perry looked up from her contemplation of the pot on the Rumford. She gestured toward it with a flourish.

"Spotted Dick!" he exclaimed. "Won't that amaze Meri?"

"I found some rice, Master Six," she said. "The cook across the street gave me some milk and sultanas." She chuckled and pulled from her bodice the note he had left on the table last night. "I startled her, but she didn't argue when I told her I was cooking breakfast for you, and this letter was from Sir B."

"'Startle' has to be the understatement of the ages, Daisy," he said. "You probably well-nigh terrified her."

She took his gibe as he thought she would, with a middle finger pointed at him. He expected little deference from Daisy, who had known him from his youth. Sailing master now or able seaman then, it was all the same to her.

"Daisy, tell me true," he said, sitting down at the table. "Does anyone ever argue with you? I disremember Master Perry arguing much."

"He tried it once," she said. He heard her low, rumbling laugh that started somewhere deep inside her massive structure, like lava inside a volcano. "It's a good thing, don't you know, that I am invariably in the right."

They laughed together. "Take that letter with you, when you and my lady go out to hunt the wild victuals in evil, profane Portsmouth," he told her. "The headmaster said you can shop anywhere with it."

She nodded and dished him a bowl of rice and sultanas, sweetened with honey she must have coerced from the same source. He resolved to visit St. Brendan's kitchen to placate the staff, who were probably still wondering where the massive black woman had come from. He doubted they had ever seen a woman with a ring through her nose.

He ate until he was full, always a pleasant sensation no matter how many years removed from the workhouse he was, and stood up, ready for the day. He pointed overhead.

"She'll be down eventually."

"You don't have to wear her out so soon, Master Six," she said tartly.

"I appreciate your concern, but Meri and I seem to have a consensual arrangement," he said, and knew his face flamed. Surely no one in the Royal Navy over sixteen years old blushed, but here he was, blushing like a virgin.

Able reflected on that singular thought as he straightened his uniform coat, checked for rain, and slung his boat cloak around his shoulders, all for a short walk across the street.

He stood a moment on his own front steps. He was used to emotions crowding on top of one another in his overloaded brain, all of them clamoring for attention at once. He walked down the steps, went to the edge of the walkway, and looked up at his—their—bedroom. The high whine of all the emotions subsided, replaced by a single hum, low and sweet. He listened and heard, or remembered, or fancied—who knew what his brain was doing?— Meri's deep breathing as her head rested on his chest, and the beating of her heart.

The sweet moment became even sweeter when the latch on that upstairs window opened and Mistress Six herself leaned out, her hair still a mess, her shift at least on and buttoned now, but edging off one shoulder. She rested her elbows on the sill and simply looked at him. When she smiled, her eyes turned into little chips of blue.

He couldn't help himself. Once read, never forgotten. He cleared his throat. " 'But soft! what light through yonder window breaks? It is the east, and Juliet is the sun.' "

He could go on. He knew the entire play by heart, and all of Shakespeare's plays because he had read them one week when the *Theseus* was becalmed in the dog latitudes. He watched the glorious woman he had bedded no more than forty-seven minutes ago.

Gazing down at him, she asked, "Will you quote the entire thing for me sometime when you're bored, with nothing to do? I would love that."

"Aye, miss," he replied. He looked around, hopeful he was alone on the street. "Mrs. Perry thinks I am wearing you out."

Meri blew him a kiss. "I'll take a nap today. Go to work and earn enough to keep me in a shift, with sheets and blankets."

He blew her a kiss in return. "It's no hardship, Mistress Six." He walked across the street, chuckling to himself when he heard the window close. *Must remember to wipe this stupid grin off my face*, he thought, as he began his day at St. Brendan's.

He went first to the kitchen and did his best to explain Daisy Perry to the highly skeptical staff. "Trust me now: if you ever have need of a strong arm and boundless courage, just give a halloo and she will come running," he told them.

"That's what we're afraid of," the cook said. "You are certain she is entirely safe?"

"Never more so," he assured them, and beat a retreat.

St. Brendan's students were still in the mess hall, chatting with one another, in no hurry to go anywhere because they were at rare leisure. A few words with Headmaster Croker gave Able all the permission he needed to ruffle the serenity of their small vacation. They looked to him like lads in need of a challenge.

Tallyho, Able thought. *Let's see if I possess one iota of the persuasive skills of someone like Sir Belvedere, or that up-and-coming Arthur Wellesley of the Army.*

He held up his hand, gratified to see all eyes turn toward him. He already knew most of their names from his brief visit here before his wedding. He came closer to their tables, noticing what looked like the remains of cinnamon buns.

"Any of those left, lads?" he asked. "I don't know about you, but as far removed from the workhouse as I am now, I'm still a bastard who never minds a stray scrap."

Aye, lads, I'm workhouse scum, too. You need to remember that, he thought.

To his delight—the buns did smell heavenly—one of the older boys he remembered as Edward Monk stood up, half a bun on his plate. "I was going to save it for later, Master Six, but you may have it."

Able shook his head. "Thank you, Mr. Monk, but nay. I understand the urge to save something for later, as you are doing. We've all had that urge, haven't we? It's workhouse mindfulness."

He saw their nods. Only a few weeks ago, their acknowledgment of starvation might have broken his heart, but it didn't now. He had a wife and a job and a house and a cook, and they could too, someday, workhouse or not.

He patted his stomach. "Mrs. Six would scold me roundly if she found out I was trolling for food."

The boys chuckled. To his acutely observant eyes, they seemed to relax a little. That was all he wanted.

"I have a proposal for you," he began. "You can ignore it if you choose, because I know the next few days before the new Year of Our Lord 1803 are your only days of leisure, or so Headmaster Croker tells me."

More nods, but he saw their interest. "I aim to turn that grubby stone basin that curves beside St. Brendan's into a clean and tidy pool where you younger boys at least will learn to swim."

No nods this time, only frowns, which he interpreted easily. "Has someone told you the lie that good sailors never learn to swim because it tempts the devil?"

One or two hands went up and then came down, as if their owners were uncertain. Able held his hands out, palms up. "I've been in fleet actions where good men died because they went overboard and drowned. I call that a damned shame. I do not wish such a fate on any of you lads."

There wasn't a sound in the room. "Once we've cleaned out the basin, we'll ditch out the channel running to the harbor, so water can be carried in by the tides can carry in water. You'll learn to float first."

This time he saw nods. "I have official charge of you younger scholars, so I would like your help specifically," he told them. "In addition to mathematics, I'll be teaching something in the afternoon called seamanship, which can be anything we want." He took a deep breath. "By God, I want it to be swimming soon." He glanced at Headmaster Croker and took a bold step. "I will open *this* course to anyone."

Croker nodded. Able turned back to the boys. "That's all I have," he concluded. "Go about your morning business. After luncheon, if any of you wishes to help me, you'll find me in the basin with a shovel. Wear your oldest clothes because we're going to stink. As you were, men."

Chapter Sixteen

⌘

"WILL THE LADS COME?" he asked the headmaster as they walked upstairs.

"I predict they will." Thaddeus stopped on the stairs. "You're going to teach them to float in this cold?"

"Aye, sir. I'll watch for signs of desperation."

With a nod to the headmaster, Able went to his classroom, enjoying the silence, which meant he could let his brain run around for exercise like a leashed dog let loose to wander.

He had already told Meri that he could see everything he had ever read, experienced, sniffed, or swallowed, on a large scroll in his mind. He stood by the corner window and summoned a blank sheet. In no time he had mentally covered it with ideas for his math class. Everything was subject to change, of course, but he was ready for formal schooling to begin, all in a matter of seconds.

To say he had been looking out his window during this mental exercise was to overstate the matter. How could he ever explain that when his mind was unreeling, he saw nothing? Now that he had filed this new scroll, he looked and saw water and ships in ordinary. He looked out a different window and saw two women, both with a basket on an arm, leave and start up the street.

He smiled at the incongruity of the pair, one tall and black and capable, the other short and white and infinitely dear to his heart. He knew his wife was equally capable, which reassured him as nothing else could. She was not a woman to run shy if the going got difficult. For God's sake, only last night she had beaten her husband over the head with a loaf of rye bread. What further proof did a man need?

God protect the man who ran afoul of Meridee Six. He turned serious then, grateful down to his shoe leather that Daisy Perry would stick to her mistress like a barnacle when they reached the market. No one would dare leer and jostle little Meridee Six, not with her fearsome bodyguard present.

Lessons done, mind only thinking ten things at a time now, Able put on his boat cloak again and started down the stairs. He stopped a few treads down and took a long look at the wooden banister. After calculating the angle, he removed his cloak and set his rump on the banister. A little push with one foot and he zipped to the bottom, to amazed stares from two older students.

"Gentlemen, prepare for a lesson soon on velocity and the speed of moving objects." He hurried outdoors as they continued to stare.

The rain held off until he bounded up the front steps to Captain Sir Belvedere St. Anthony's house. A few cheerful words to the butler, a one-eyed veteran of some nameless fleet action, earned him a spot before a fire in the salon.

"How are you finding St. Brendan's, Master Six?" he heard from the open door minutes later.

"Intriguing, Sir B," Able replied. "Sorry to interrupt, but I wanted to thank you in person for sending Mrs. Perry to us."

Sir B was not an early riser, even though it was half ten in the morning. Able remembered the weary-looking brocade robe his former captain wore, in all its threadbare splendor. Who but Sir B would come on deck to fight an action with a French frigate west of the Azores in such a garment? For years after, wardroom talk claimed the Frogs were laughing so hard no one could defend the honor of revolutionary France.

"Sir B, you'd probably cut a more dashing figure if you had a wife with some fashion sense," Able said, knowing he had reached that level of friendship where humor wasn't out of the question.

"I daresay I would," Sir B agreed, as his valet wheeled him closer. "It appears you have found the only beauty on England's southern shores. Who wants a one-legged captain?"

"Only any number of gazetted fortune hunters! Seriously, sir, thank you for Mrs. Perry."

"Perhaps you should temper your gratitude until you've tasted her cooking," he said.

"I wouldn't care if she burns water and can't crack an egg," Able said frankly. "Mrs. Perry needs the work. More to the point, I am relieved to know she'll protect my darling from every lowlife scum, up to and including me, if I don't treat her right. She already thinks I'm wearing out Meri with my … attention."

Sir B laughed so loud and long that a maid stuck her head in the doorway, then hurried away. "Daisy Perry always was a woman of firm opinion," he said, wiping his eyes. "I gather Mistress Six hasn't started pleading headaches?"

"No, sir," Able said, wondering for the second time that morning why an experienced man such as he should blush so relentlessly. Sir B didn't need to know Meri had awakened him out of a sound sleep last night to play a bit. "We're in Portsmouth to stay."

"Have you sorted out your thoughts concerning St. Brendan's?" Sir B asked, more serious. "Most certainly you have. Your brain is relentless."

Able told his mentor of his plans for the stone-lined basin. Sir B nodded his approval over that bit of maritime innovation as well as the usual mathematics courses and a foray into the calculus with some hand-picked older students.

Sir B lounged in his ridiculous dressing gown, looking like the most bored dilettante on earth. Able knew better. Whatever the man said now would be worth remembering—not that Able Six had a problem remembering.

"Don't waste a minute," Able's former captain said. "I don't give this Peace—who in God's heaven names these things?—this *Peace* of Amiens much longer."

Able shivered as if a sudden blast of cold air shot down his neck and patted his backbone. No one could see into the future, but now and then ….

He fervently wished he were alone, but here he stood in an elegant sitting room, staring at a new scroll in his brain. He didn't like what he saw.

"What is it?" Sir B asked, no trace of indolence in his voice now, no casually studied indifference.

"I'm a fool," Able said simply.

"Impossible," Sir B told him. "What is going on in your head?"

"I can't tell you."

"It's an order, Master Six."

"No." He went to the window. Had he just disobeyed his superior?

Sir B's house had a most excellent view of the Solent, where ships passed, docked, revictualed, refitted, and returned to war. There was no more efficient seaport in all of England. He turned away because his brain saw many ships now, ready for endless war. Only an hour ago in his classroom he had seen five ships. Now there were twenty times that number, a phantom fleet from nowhere, ready to sail.

War was his business, but why hadn't he thought this through? Good God, his job now was to send boys to war.

"What, Able?" Sir B asked again. He whispered for his valet to roll him closer. "What are you seeing?"

"Ships with *my* St. Brendan's lads on them," he said, the words wrung out of him. "I haven't even begun my first term, and I'm training them for war where they might die. Why didn't I know that? Was I too busy thinking about Meridee?"

"Any new husband should be thinking about his bride," Sir B said. He leaned forward. "It's *entirely permissible,* Able."

"All I ever want to be is ordinary," Able said. "Tell me something to make me feel better, Captain," Able said finally, when he could not bear the burden.

"It's different when it's only *you* living—and thriving, I might add—in a dangerous career, isn't it?" Captain St. Anthony said, as the command seemed to leave his voice, replaced by something suspiciously close to tenderness.

"Aye, sir, aye," Able replied.

"We all live with uncertainty, Master Six," Sir B said. "I do, you do, King George does, and even Mrs. Six must be included." He shrugged. "I advise you not to seek counsel from your fears, else your life will be miserable."

Able mulled over the matter. By the time he felt himself wondering what Euclid would do, he knew he was on an even keel again. "I know good advice when I hear it, Sir B," he said, with equal measures of resignation and rue. "I fell into your lap like a trussed pigeon when Meridee Bonfort came here to find me a job teaching children. How did she *know*?"

"God's mystery." Sir B gave Able's arm a shake. "After she pleaded your cause so eloquently, I wondered why *I* had not thought of it. Man is ever vain, Able. Woman, at least *your* woman, not so much. She had an instinct that you would be good at what you face now."

"I can't guarantee I will not ..." Able stopped, well aware Sir B had seen him at his undeniable worst. Meri had not. "You know."

"I know," Captain St. Anthony said gently. "Still, there is no one better equipped than you to train young lads. My God, Master Six, to be able to put well-trained navigators to sea at such a time? They'll serve an apprentice under sailing masters, but think of the *time* you will save our fleet, our country, and our king. This war isn't going away."

Able looked out the window again, almost afraid what he would see, perhaps the Solent running red. He relaxed. The waterway was empty of ships, except for the distant prison hulks.

"Everything I teach will fit them for service," he said, more to himself than to the man standing beside him. "They'll not go unprepared."

"Teach them well, lad."

Able nodded, unable to speak.

"And when you can't bear another moment of it, turn to Meridee." Sir B chuckled. "I have my own premonition, laddie."

"Which is ...."

"You could not have picked a better keeper. Tell me, do you believe in God?"

Surprised, Able glared at the captain. "Why on earth should I?"

"I don't know. I do, and *I* see His hand in every minute of your life. You have a rare talent that a pretty lady in Devonshire noticed. England needs you. We all do."

"Nonsense."

"Don't scorn the idea, you heathen. Let me add that what you are doing is a special trust from God for king and country," Sir B added. "Do it well."

"What did the Almighty ever do for me?" Able asked, raising his voice because his vision of the blood-red sea was still too vivid. "You never heard a workhouse sermon, did you? You never knelt for hours on cold stone and writhed in shame as the minister thundered on about the worthlessness of the bastards. You never knew that people begrudged the very air you breathed because you wouldn't satisfy them and die!"

He hadn't meant to shout. "Forgive me, sir."

"I had no idea, Able."

They regarded each other, and then Sir B indicated the door. "Take your anger and use it against the French, you and your … your…." He chuckled. "You and your Gunwharf Rats."

Chapter Seventeen

DISTURBED, UNHAPPY, ABLE WALKED home to a still-empty house. He found the remains of the Spotted Dick, which he downed, not caring that it was cold. He had learned years ago that food was food and never to ignore it.

Upstairs, he dug through his slender wardrobe that Meri had either hung on pegs in the dressing room or folded neatly. There they were, cast into outer darkness, as ratty a pair of trousers as a man ever wore, and perfect for the afternoon's task. Maybe if he worked hard enough, his brain would leave him alone.

The damned things turned out to be a little tight. He thought a moment, and realized he hadn't worn them in six years since the Battle of Cape St. Vincent. Sure enough, the blood stains were faded now, and the rip was sewn. There was a corresponding rip in his thigh where a Spaniard had thought to emasculate him during an action in the Pacific, anything to stop Able's forward advance with cutlass in hand.

Any old shirt would do and he had plenty of those. He scrawled a quick note to Meri to let her know where he was going. He was setting it on the hall table downstairs when the door opened.

Merciful heaven, could his wife look any more beautiful than she did right now? The breeze had strengthened, and her cheeks were red. She looked right pleased with herself, so he knew the shopping expedition had gone as planned.

Taking Meri's basket from her, he kissed her cheek. "I don't even know where the markets are in Portsmouth," he said.

"Mrs. Perry does," Meri said. "She knows everything." She took Able's arm. "And when a sailor thought to get cheeky, she gave him *such* a backhand. Knocked him right into a turnip bin."

"He got the message," Mrs. Perry said as she came inside with two baskets. "Master Six, there is a man coming later today with a haunch of venison and a ham. We'll be eating well."

He surprised the cook by kissing her cheek, too. "I neither know nor care," he said quietly as Meri removed her bonnet and fluffed her hair. "All I ever want is for you to keep my wife safe."

"No fears, master. I'll take this to the kitchen."

"It's a rough town, Able, just as you said," Meri told him as she turned around. She stared at him, obviously not having paid much attention to what he wore when she came inside. "Husband, those trousers are so tight I don't know where to look," she said.

"Of course you do," he teased, which made her blush, his sole object. "Little boys don't care. We're starting the cleanup of the stone basin, and I'm not risking my one good uniform."

"It's too cold. They'll be uncomfortable," she said, ready to defend lads she didn't really know yet, which touched his heart.

"Dearest, you have no concept of uncomfortable," he told her as she gave him a fishy look. "I'll know when to stop."

He could tell she wasn't convinced. She had a way of raising her head and looking at him down the length of her nose that might have been intimidating, were she taller. The expression did call for compromise; he was no fool.

"You and Mrs. Perry show up in two hours with a monster pot of tea and mugs. If no one comes to help me, I'll drink it all. Ta, love."

"The boys will be there," she said.

"Will they?" he asked the closed door. He tried to convince himself he did not care how many showed up. His fraught conversation with Sir B— Good God, had he really shouted at his former captain?—made him wish for solitude to sort out his feelings. Physical labor was one way.

Soon he was staring down at the stone basin, with its full complement of leaves, twigs, papers, and God-knew-what-all. The depth was eight feet, maybe a little more. He had discarded measuring tapes years ago because his mind didn't need them. He went carefully down narrow, steep steps, slippery with matted vegetation.

The debris came about mid-calf, but his first order of business was removing the leaves from the steps. When Meri showed up in a few hours, the last thing he wanted was for her to fall.

Someone thoughtful, probably Headmaster Croker, had leaned six shovels and a smaller trowel inside the basin, plus two round bins. He took the trowel and scraped away at the steps until they were passable. The smell of rotten vegetation made him wrinkle his nose, but it was not unpleasant. With a smile, he recalled the Amazon where it flowed into the Atlantic at filthy old

Belém. *All I need are monkey sounds*, he thought. He waited; there they were, monkey sounds from his brain that never forgot a thing.

When the steps were cleared and the monkeys retreated, he looked up to see David Ten and Jamie MacGregor pushing a handcart close to the basin. Neither wore St. Brendan's neat and sober uniform, but ragged trousers and sweaters with holes.

"Come to lend a hand?" he asked. "I cleared the steps. Come on in, the water's fine."

Jamie laughed, but David looked as sober as ever.

"Aye, Master Six," Jamie said. "Headmaster Croker said to bring over this cart. We can dump the trash in the bay."

"Fair enough, Mr. MacGregor."

There was no mistaking Jamie's startled expression. "Lad?" Able asked.

"No one ever called me Mister anything, sir," the boy said.

"Get used to it then," Able said. "I've decided to call the lot of you mister."

"You can do that?" Jamie asked.

"I can do whatever I want in my classes, Mr. MacGregor," Able assured him. "Eventually you will be a sailing master, and the crew will address you as Master MacGregor."

"You believe that, don't you, sir?" Jamie asked as he shoveled.

"It is more than mere belief, Mr. MacGregor. It is utter conviction."

"Well then," Jamie said, and applied himself.

David Ten worked silently beside the older boy, giving Able darting glances and hunching one shoulder, as if wondering when the first blow would fall, and wanting to prepare. *You need time in my house*, Able thought. *You need Meridee Six's gentle ministry. We all do.*

Soon other lads showed up, quietly taking shovels and scooping great wads of gunk into the bins. Able noted that Jamie directed two of the younger boys to carry the first half-full bin up the steps to the cart.

Well done, Able thought. *You know a full bin would be too heavy for little fellows. I think we have a born leader here.*

Two more boys joined them, and then three. Able knew he could give orders, but he decided to see what Jamie would do. They had run out of shovels. He watched as Jamie MacGregor spoke to two lads, who ran up the stone steps and came back a few minutes later with pails. On his own initiative, one of the older boys left and came back with rakes. Some quiet words directed the younger boys to follow in the wake of the shovelers, and rake the remaining debris into small piles, while others filled the buckets with their bare hands.

After an hour's silent labor, trained in the workhouse to be seen but never heard, Able called a halt. He put his hand to his back, which felt fine. "I'm getting old," he said. "If I take a break and you do not, I'll feel guilty."

The lads grinned and stopped to lean on shovels and rakes. He squatted on his haunches and they did the same, forming a rough half circle around him.

"Aren't we a picturesque mob?" he said, and heard some laughter. "I know you sing, for I heard you at breakfast. Do you know 'Spanish Ladies'?"

The boys looked at each other, then back at him, as if singing was just for breakfast. "Aye, well, you can't sing at work on a Royal Navy vessel, but there are times when no one minds. I'll teach you."

He had a good voice. He sang, " 'Farewell and adieu to you, Spanish ladies, Farewell and adieu to you, ladies of Spain; for we have received orders for to sail to old England, but we hope in a short time to see you again.' "

He sang it once more, as his mind's picture of death ships sailing from Portsmouth retreated into a corner of his brain, to lie in wait.

"You try it," he said. "I'll give you the note and sing slowly."

He gave the note, started off alone, and soon heard his lads humming. They were all humming by the time the verse ended. He gave the note again, and they sang, to his heart's delight.

The next time was even better, almost good enough to overlook it when the rain, which had threatened all day, finally began to fall. He saw smiles this time, smiles through the rain, and the debris they shoveled, and the general stench of a stone basin neglected for years, much as these boys had been ignored.

"Wonderful!" he said when they ended with something approaching a flourish. "There's a chorus—I'll sing that tomorrow—and then lots of verses, some of them pretty vulgar. Should we stop for the day?"

He knew what they would do—look at each other as if wondering why anyone would let rain interfere with work. Right down to the stink, Able remembered workhouse sewers he had mucked out, paint he had scraped, and ground he had tilled, with never a suggestion from his task masters that he stop, no matter the weather.

"We'll do a little more then," he said and stood up. "I like 'Spanish ladies.' I barely know who my mother was, and I could be wrong about her, but I think my father might have been a Spanish sailor." He shrugged and fingered his sopping curls. "Or an Italian. Or a Portugee. You know, the blokes with curly hair and skin not quite as pasty-white as yours." He smiled at them. "You'll burn red on a quarterdeck, and I just get darker. Whoever my father was, maybe *that* was a kind blessing."

Some of the boys laughed. Others with skin the color of his seemed to turn inward. One of the lads raised his hand slowly.

"Aye, Mister ... Mister ... John Mark, is it?" He remembered the boy from the list of future lodgers at *chez* Six. His skin was a pleasant tan. "You're free to speak up. That's one of my classroom rules, by the way."

The boy hesitated. Able watched his mind turning and weighing consequences of asking a question, let alone giving voice to it. John Mark's chin went up then, and resolve took over. "Don't you wish you knew who your father was?"

All the boys were listening. "I thought it mattered once," Able said. "Thought if I were not a bastard, people would treat me fair."

Nods again. *Able, this is no time for tears*, he sternly reminded himself. "It doesn't matter now. I am who I am." He stood straighter, willing them to understand. "If you don't feel that is enough, you will by the time you are ready to go to sea."

"Will someone care about us?"

"Nick, is it?" Able asked, remembering the boy with no last name on the list.

"Aye, Master Six."

"Someone cares about you right now," he said quietly. "I do."

Nick smiled at him, a lovely smile, one any mother or father would give the world to see. "Thank'ee, master," he said with that peculiar dignity of workhouse children.

He looked at the others, solemn and wet now, but not minding it because they were used to adversity. "I care about all of you. I truly do."

Chapter Eighteen

❦

O N A TOP SHELF in the pantry, Mrs. Perry found a larger than average tea kettle. "We can make tea in this."

"Is there anything else on that shelf?" Meridee asked, knowing she could never see that shelf without a ladder. "Dead mice? Pirates?"

Mrs. Perry ran her hand over the shelf. She pulled out a tin box and handed it to Meridee. "Just a tin of Maltby's Finest."

Luncheon was dried sardines, ship's biscuits, and gunpowder tea. Mrs. Perry still objected when Meridee insisted on eating with her in the kitchen, but Meridee ignored her protests.

She ate and admired the tall, dark woman seated across from her, so black that her skin shone. Impressive in her girth, Mrs. Perry still had a delicacy to her face, with high cheekbones and a straight nose. Meridee knew she could search her own face forever and never locate any cheekbones.

Thank goodness Able appeared inclined to overlook her lack of classical beauty. Heaven knows he had enough classical beauty of his own, inclining her more and more to the belief that his *in absentia* father must have been a mariner from the Aegean. Whoever he was, mere minutes with a Scottish drab had produced someone remarkable to look at, of which she, Meridee Six, was the grateful beneficiary.

"My mother has been gone for years now. I wish she could have known Able Six," Meridee said.

"I wish *my* mother could have known Mr. Perry."

"Does she yet live?"

Mrs. Perry shrugged. "Who knows? I was captured by Portuguese slavers, put on a ship in chains, and taken to Jamaica."

"God forgive me, but I used to feel sorry for myself because I had no dowry and no man would marry me," Meridee said. "How did ... why did—"

"Mr. Perry happen along?"

The subject seemed to be too large for the cook. She returned to shelving the victuals.

"There I was in the Kingston slave auction, wearing not a stitch, tears running down my face because the buyers kept touching me between my legs, on my breasts …" she said when she could speak.

She turned away. Meridee leaped to her feet and grabbed the big woman around the waist. Mrs. Perry tucked her close.

"He was a little Welshman, not a great deal taller than you, but … I don't know …. How does a woman just *know*?"

Holding fast to Mrs. Perry, Meridee asked herself the same question. She had just *known* too, after a short time in Able's presence.

"I'll admit I was attracted to Master Six's undeniably handsome visage," Meridee said with a laugh. "Then I watched his eyes scanning book titles so rapidly in my brother-in-law's study, and I knew he was different. I kept looking at him, and then I couldn't look away. What did Mr. Perry do?"

"It's what *I* did," the cook said. She relaxed her grip on Meridee. "Mrs. Six, I was much thinner then, but certainly no shorter. I stepped forward, shook someone's hand off my thigh, looked that little man right in the eyes, and said, 'Buy me.' He did."

"My goodness. It sounds like he knew, too," Meridee said.

Mrs. Perry laughed, her melancholy either dismissed or shoved back into a recess in her mind. "He told me later he wanted me because I looked strong and could help him aboard ship."

"I didn't know women ever sailed on Royal Navy ships," Meridee said. She sat down, planting her elbows in the table and resting her chin in her hands.

"It happens. As a carpenter, Owen was a warranted officer. He made arrangements for me and I proved useful," Mrs. Perry said. "He never freed me and he never married me, but I was Mrs. Perry. I miss him to this day."

What can I say to that? Meridee asked herself, wondering deep in her heart and soul how any woman made her way in a world ruled by men. *I was lucky.* She looked at the kind lady across from her, the woman who had frightened her only yesterday evening. *So was Mrs. Perry lucky, each of us in our own way.*

"You frightened me at first, Mrs. Perry," she admitted.

"I could tell," Mrs. Perry said. "You practically tried to crawl inside Master Six."

They laughed together. "That was foolish of me," Meridee confessed. "I didn't know you yet. I know you now."

They decided on brown bread and jam sandwiches for, hopefully, the crowd of students who were helping Able Six. This meant a quick trip back to the baker's, who sold Meridee two more loaves of his crusty bread.

He scolded Meridee for coming without her powerful escort, but agreed reluctantly that the middle of the day was safe enough. Even then, he insisted on walking her back to the house, telling her about his two sons at sea and his daughter in Plymouth, married to her own sailor, a foretopman in the East India trade.

"No one wants to run a bakery?" she asked him, after thanking him prettily on her doorstep.

"It's too slow for lads seeking adventure," he said. He gave her a little bow, awkwardly done. Meridee suspected he seldom waited on ladies of quality in this corner of Pompey. "Ezekiel Bartleby, at your service, Mrs. Six."

"You'll have all of our business, Mr. Bartleby," she told him, and dipped her own small curtsy, because he was older, if not of her class.

When rain started to patter against the window, Meridee looked up from the loaf she was slicing. "They'll probably stop working," she said to Mrs. Perry, who was slathering the bread with plum jam. "Should we continue?"

"They won't stop, not workhouse lads," Mrs. Perry assured her. "Two hours, did the master tell you?"

"He did." Meridee looked around. A basket for the sandwiches would never do, not in this rain.

Still, she had her standards. She picked up the Maltby's Finest tin, lifted off the lid, and sniffed inside. "Smells like tobacco," she told Mrs. Perry.

The tin held all the sandwiches, with dried apple slices to pack the layers. Mrs. Perry pronounced the tea ready. She strung their six tin cups on twine, tied the ends together, and slung the rattling chorus over her shoulder. Meridee found several towels in the laundry room off the kitchen and added them to her own pile. Maltby's Finest sandwiches fit easily against her hip, so she had a hand free for the front door, while Mrs. Perry managed the teapot.

In the rain, they walked around St. Brendan's to the basin that faced the water. Mrs. Perry was right; the boys still shoveled and raked.

"My goodness, Mrs. Perry, only count them," she whispered. "We don't have enough sandwiches. I count fifteen lads and I made twelve sandwiches."

She stood at the edge of the basin, which had been half-cleared of leaves and whatever had lurked underneath. A cluster of small boys stood around a little mound. Able sat on his heels, staring down.

"What do you think they have uncovered?" she asked Mrs. Perry.

"Remains," the cook said, then chuckled. "Remains to be seen."

Able stood up, and gestured her toward a set of steep stone sets. He came to help her, trailed by little boys.

He was soaked to the skin, his curly hair plastered against his face. "We made quite a find," he told her as he helped her down the steps. He waved his arm. "Gentlemen, victuals! Mr. MacGregor, lend a hand to Mrs. Perry."

The boy she remembered as Jamie MacGregor took the teapot from the cook. David Ten took the cups, after a cautious approach. Meridee doubted he had ever seen anyone quite like the cook.

"Lads, we have a dilemma," Able said. "There are fifteen of you and twelve sandwiches. Three of you must go hungry, alas."

Her heart suffered a pang of startling proportions when the three smallest boys stepped aside. The littlest started back to the piles of leaves he had been raking and her heart broke.

"As you were, men," Able said in a loud voice. He cleared his throat. "That means, everyone back here." He looked around the circle. "Do Royal Navy men allow any of their number to go without?"

"They probably shouldn't," Jamie said, but he sounded uncertain.

"Correct, Mr. MacGregor. Everyone shares alike. But what do we do? How do we divide the sandwiches? Mister Ten, you look like a thinking man. How would you divide them? Can you see it in your mind?"

David Ten shook his head and hunched his shoulders, ready for a beating. Meridee put one of her towels to her face. Maybe no one would notice she was wiping her eyes.

"No matter." Able took a stick and David closed his eyes. "Let's draw this."

On his haunches again, Able drew the divisional problem in the mud and gestured to another of the older boys. He handed him the stick. "What say you, Mr. Poole?"

Mr. Poole knelt. "I would put an eight here."

"You would be correct, Mr. Poole. With the point there and the eight nestled as close as a barnacle to a keel, how much sandwich do you each get?"

"Eight tenths of a sandwich," Mr. Poole said, satisfaction writ large on his soaking-wet face. His expression changed. "We didn't figure *you* in, Master Six. And we didn't figure in the ladies."

"We already ate," Meridee said promptly.

"I feel deep in my bones that if I petition Mrs. Six, she will make me a sandwich later."

"She might," Meridee found herself saying, "if you didn't smell so abominable. What in the *world* have you found in this muck?"

To her delight, the boys shouted with laughter. When Able hung his head, they laughed louder.

"Very well, men," he said when the laughter subsided. "We had better divide these sandwiches again, since I am banished from my own hearth until I smell better."

Mr. Poole applied himself. "Point seven five, master," he announced.

"Which is also—"

"Three fourths or seventy five percent," piped up one of the smaller boys.

All heads turned his way and he shrank back. "I know I'm right," he said firmly, after a reassuring glance from Able.

"I know you are right too, Mr. Reynolds," Able said. "Who do we trust the most here?"

One boy pointed at Meridee. "I think, her, Master Six."

"You are wise beyond your years. Mrs. Six, do the honors while Mrs. Perry pours tea, will you?"

Meridee swallowed ridiculous, stupid tears that none of these boys with not one single advantage to their name would have understood. She divided the sandwiches in halves and then one half into half.

The boys stood in a circle—interested, hungry, muddy and wet. Soon everyone had a half and a fourth, including her husband.

"Begging your pardon, Master Six," Jamie MacGregor said when he polished off his sandwich. "We must decide what to do with ... you know."

"This may require considerable diplomacy, Mr. MacGregor," Able said.

"What have you done?" Meridee asked. "I have my limits."

"We've been warned. Should we show her?" Able asked. "Aye or nay, lads?"

"Aye!"

Able tugged her to the dark mound by the edge of the basin and whispered in her ear. "It's disgusting, but we have a plan."

"You always have a plan, husband," she replied.

The stink reminded her of the mouse found in an empty jar in the vicarage. The poor thing had obviously gone adventuring, with no concrete method of crawling out of a jar with straight sides. But this mound was larger.

"It's a wharf rat," he said, not even slightly surprised, drat him, when Meridee leaped back with a gasp. "Quite dead. In fact, we're not certain how long dead. Uh, we have a proposition."

"I am certain you do," Meridee replied in a tone most neutral, the one she had learned from her sister Amanda, in dealing with those sons of hers.

"Maybe if she sees it ..." one of the boys said, and carefully scooped away the leaves.

"Uh, I don't ..." he began, then stopped, because Meridee stopped him.

"Let me see it," she said, coming closer again. She knew this was another moment where she could not fail either her husband or his students. *But why a rat?*

Two boys moved aside the leaves. Meridee couldn't help her sudden intake of breath.

"It's ... it's *huge*," she managed.

"Twenty inches from snout to tail," her wretched husband said promptly.

"Durable Six, you are trying me," she declared.

"*Rattus norvegicus*," he said, more wary now, "commonly known as a wharf rat around here. Kingdom, Animalia; Phylum, Chordata; Class: Mammalia; Order, Rodentia. And, uh, so on."

She decided science was one thing, rats another. "Let us come to a right understanding, Husband," Meridee said, mincing no words. "No rat in my house."

She looked around the circle, aware of the disappointment on all faces, his included. Who knew it would be so hard to earn one pound a month? "Very well, someone tell me what the proposition is."

One lad, braver than most, stepped forward. "We want to boil down the carcass, remove the bones, and mount them on a board."

"You would, of course, label the bones?" she asked, finding that neutral tone again.

The boy nodded. "Master Able thinks it is a capital way to learn anatomy."

"He does?"

"Aye, ma'am."

Meridee glared at her unrepentant husband, marveling that anyone could find delight in a rotting corpse. Heaven help her if they ever found bats in St. Brendan's belfry.

Meridee avoided her husband's eyes. "Knowing Master Six well, I suspect there must be more."

Another boy stepped forward. "We're going to label it St. Brendan's Gunwharf Rat and hang it in our classroom." His head went up with pride visible to everyone in the circle, and probably nearby ships at sea. "You see, miss, *we're* the Gunwharf Rats. This old fellow is going to be our mascot. No one wants us, not really, but we'll show them."

Her eyes brimming, she looked at the boys, some of them newly sprung from workhouses, and others further along on their path of training for war. "One moment," she said.

Meridee joined Mrs. Perry. "Any opinion, Mrs. Perry? You know I have mine."

"I know, but these are good lads. There's an iron wash pot in a shed in the back," Mrs. Perry told her. "Use that."

I am outvoted, Meridee thought. She returned to the circle. "We have a pot you can boil him in, but *rattus norvegicus* stays outside. On this I remain firm."

"You're a soft-hearted female of the species," Able whispered, and laughed when she swatted him.

"You, sir, are England's most persuasive man. The wash house, all of you, after you start the rat boiling."

Chapter Nineteen

⤬

IT WAS BEST THAT Able knew Meridee's limits. The offhand suggestion over breakfast that he was short-crewed in the basin and maybe she could stir the rat around in his iron pot met with a menacing stare.

Captain Sir Belvedere St. Anthony laughed long and loud when Able paid him a visit later to report on his progress with the basin and mentioned the wharf rat.

"Master Six, I can only call this true love," he said, leaning back. "You must have amazing diplomacy to convince someone I know to be level-headed to go along with that scheme."

Able raised one finger for emphasis. "She won't stir the rat broth," he said, which set off Sir B again.

"The basin is clean and the channel dug out," Able said, when he could speak without laughing. "The tide changes in a few hours, at which point two of the older lads will stand the watch and put the wooden dam back in place when the water reaches a depth of one yard."

"Very good. The scholastic term begins tomorrow," Sir B said. "I am to say a few words. What should I tell the lads?"

"That England needs them," Able said with no hesitation. "So far, no one has *ever* needed them. If they hear it enough, they might begin to believe."

"For a nation that has produced the likes of William Shakespeare and Isaac Newton, we're more than a little prodigal how we treat the unfortunate among us," Sir B said. "No one ever gave you a hand up, did they?"

"Not many," Able agreed. He regarded his former captain, sitting there so complacently, but even now, after his injuries, with a coiled look of a man eager to leap into action, if only he could. "You did, sir, and so did Captain Hallowell."

"Once we winkled out your great secret, you became nearly impossible to ignore," Sir B said. "Think of the good you will do now."

"I am still training them for possible death," Able said, unable to forget his earlier vision of seas turned red.

"We have no choice, Master Six, as long as Napoleon is bent on conquest. What keeps him from our shores? The Royal Navy," his captain and mentor reminded him. "My words tomorrow? How about, do your job with a heart of oak."

ALL WAS QUIET WHEN he let himself into the house and locked the door behind him. He walked to the back of the house and peeked in the kitchen, where Mrs. Perry was taking a loaf of bread from the oven, the last one of the day. The four little fellows designated as St. Brendan boarders were coming home with him tomorrow after classes were done, and the ladies of the house had no notion of how much they would eat.

"Do you have a lonely little heel there?" he asked, as Mrs. Perry looked up.

She rolled her eyes at him and sliced off the heel. It crumpled because it was just from the oven, but Able saw no deficit in that. The butter dish was still on the table, so he grabbed a knife and slathered some on.

"This is manna," he said after the first bite. "I could sit here and finish the entire loaf."

"Go on! You have a wife upstairs," she retorted.

I do indeed have a wife, he thought, as he mounted the steps. At least he could report to her that the rat had been dumped from the iron pot, disintegrating entirely into a noxious snarl of hair, viscera, toenails and bones on the grass. A few buckets of water had sluiced away other questionable detritus, leaving mostly bones behind. He had set the pot on top of the bone pile, in case neighborhood cats and dogs on the prowl decided to have a go at the remains. Tomorrow they could retrieve the bones and dry them.

Meridee sat in a chair by the fireplace, book in her lap, head tipped forward, sound asleep. Able watched her a moment, knowing how busy she was during the day already, and how busy he kept her at night. Just the memory of her breath in his ear made him get ideas most unmathematical.

He touched her shoulder. He could have died with pleasure when, still asleep or nearly so, she turned her head to rest her cheek against his fingers. "I should wake you up so you can go to bed?" he asked, bending down to kiss her cheek.

"You're late," she murmured, "and you smell of … well now … I think it is rum. Were you leading Sir B astray or vice versa?"

"Just telling him about our Gunwharf rat and my plans for the students." He knelt beside her. "Meri, can you swim?"

"I never learned. Oh, now ...."

"You're going to be a pupil, too," he said, and tugged her to her feet. "I won't teach you when the boys are around."

"Husband, I am not going into your stone basin," she said.

"I intend to overrule you," he declared, in what he hoped was the kindest way. "No wife of mine will remain unable to float or swim. I must insist. Turn around. I'll unbutton you."

"Suppose I sink?" she asked, breathing a little deeper when he kissed her bare back.

"Nobody sinks, Meri," he told her, "especially not in three feet of water."

How easy it was to end up in bed, making love and cuddling afterward. Rather than succumb to the mattress, because they were both perfectly satisfied, he summoned that quirky spot in his odd brain that told him the time in exact increments.

"In twelve minutes, the tide should have filled the stone basin to the yard mark that I left for my crew," he said, sitting up. "Duty calls, my love. I'll be back."

He heard her murmur something, then roll over, taking his blankets with her. That was another matter they needed to discuss. His darling had a habit of snatching all the covers. He gave her a light smack on the rump and got out of bed. Debating clothing, he settled on his night shirt, moccasins acquired from a voyage to Canada, and his boat cloak.

He crossed the street to the bayside and St. Brendan's, coming up behind the school. His boys sat there, feet dangling over the side of the now-clean basin, talking. For the smallest moment, he envied them their coming years standing the watch, looking across the water, and maybe chatting with friends. In the South Pacific, such duty easily turned into a bit of heaven.

But Portsmouth was not Otaheite. He pulled his cloak tighter around his nightshirt, thinking trousers might have been a good idea. "Hailing the frigate HMS *Gunwharf Rat*," he said, which made his Rats laugh.

"At the marker now?" he asked as they stood up.

"Aye, Master Six," Jamie said.

"Put the gate back in, handsomely now, and hit your racks."

"Aye, sir," said Janus Yarmouth, the other student who had warily volunteered for the calculus.

"When will we start learning to swim, Master Six?" Yarmouth asked, when they finished.

"Let's give it some time, Mr. Yarmouth, and see how our studies settle out. I'll be working you two extra hard, with the calculus. As much as I would like all you older lads to learn to swim, I can't command in this. My duties are to the younger among you."

"I need to learn, sir," Jamie said. He nodded in the other boy's direction. "We both do."

"Very well. Go to bed now, before we all get in trouble."

Able walked beside them toward the back of the old monastery. "Mr. Yarmouth, satisfy my never-ending curiosity," he said. "Janus Yarmouth. Were you a January bastard, born in Yarmouth?"

"Aye, sir. Our workhouse master was devoted to the classics. Most people call me Jan, which I prefer to, uh, Anus."

"Who wouldn't? Goodnight, lads."

To Able's surprise, Meridee was sitting up in bed, quite alert, when he returned. The room was still lit with a glow from the fireplace, and she had lit the lamp closest to their bed.

"I was going to give this to you earlier," she said, eagerness in her voice, "but you distracted me."

"*You* are the distraction," he told her as he came closer to the bed and felt his heart perform an anatomically impossible leap. "My word, Meri."

"Pick it up. Better yet, try on the coat."

He did as she said after stroking the black wool of a cut far better than he was used to. From some source, she had procured a new sailing master's uniform, or what passed for a uniform, since Admiralty had never issued proper orders yet in the matter.

He came closer to the lamp and saw the patch on the left breast of St. Brendan the Navigator, cradling a medieval ship.

"Headmaster Croker had an extra patch," she said. Meridee stood before him now, patting the shoulders and then smoothing down the back with practiced fingers. "The first morning you were engaged across the street, I took your oldest uniform to Captain St. Anthony, who told me where to find a tailor. He took the measurements, made some drawings, and I put the old one back in the dressing room, with you none the wiser." She tugged on the front lapels. "It will look better with trousers and not a nightshirt."

"Let's see if I have enough stretching room," Able said as his arms went around her. "Excellent! Meri, you know we can't afford this."

"My sister gave me twenty pounds Mama told her I was to have, if I married," his darling explained. "There are two new shirts coming, as well, and a waistcoat. Mr. Berg said they would be ready in a week. I still have five pounds left over."

"Berg and Sons? Meri, that's where the fleet admirals and post captains go," he said. "I'm a bastard sailing master."

"Why not the best for you?" she said. "I hope your hat doesn't need immediate replacement, because I couldn't think of a way to steal it without your knowledge."

He kissed her and she folded into him in that boneless way that was Meridee Six's alone. He hoisted her up, and she wrapped her legs around him.

"Work all the magic on me you want," he whispered in her ear. "You still have to learn to swim."

She was laughing when he blew out the lamp.

Chapter Twenty

❦

ABLE INSISTED MERIDEE ACCOMPANY him across the street for the opening assembly of the new school term. She wouldn't let him out of the door until his neck cloth was just so. For all his brilliance, Able couldn't manage a simple neck cloth, at least not to her standards.

She fiddled with the thing a moment, happy to stand close to a handsome man whose eyes were bright with something, because heaven knows he didn't sleep much last night, not with checking the water in the basin, then coming home to general merriment over his new uniform. How he could function on practically no sleep was beyond Meridee.

"How do you manage, Master Six? You look ready to duel with dragons and I am about to perish from exhaustion."

"Every day is an adventure," he said. "I promise to sleep tonight, and let you sleep. The water is in the basin, my calculus students will be counting prematurely gray hair—"

"And I will be mothering four little boys," she reminded him, then rested her forehead against his chest. "Can I do this?"

"None better," he assured her. "They already admire you for the jam sandwiches each day while we worked in the basin, one whole sandwich per pupil and no arithmetic involved."

She remembered the only dark cloud to her existence. "Master Six, the unholy goo in the backyard must go."

"Oh, no! I am Master Six," he teased. "I have great faith in local gulls and dogs, who aren't too discriminating in a seaport with no gentility." Unbidden, he picked up her bonnet from the bed, set it on her head, and made a bow close to her left ear. "There. Matronly, but with a little sassiness."

"I am your wife," she said simply. "I love it."

Oh dear. She hadn't meant to make his lovely brown eyes fill with tears.

"Don't you dare cry," she scolded, and took a handkerchief from her sleeve, sniffing back her own emotions. "There now. We both look fine as five pence."

He touched his eyes and handed back the lacy square. Mrs. Perry was waiting for them as they came down the stairs, arm in arm. She nodded her approval and opened the front door, which reminded Meridee of something else.

"Mrs. Perry, I promise you I will find a maid of all work," she said.

"In due time," Mrs. Perry said. "We can assign our lodgers to various duties, you know." She glared at Able. "First of which will be to shift the mess in the backyard."

"You two are determined, aren't you?" Able asked the ceiling.

"We are," they both replied.

"I am overruled. Come, Meri, let us begin this term."

She tightened her grip on Able's arm. They crossed the street at the same time a carriage with a crest on the door pulled up to the entrance of the most unusual school in England.

Meridee waited as Able opened the door before the small African post-boy had time to climb down from his perch. Able pulled down the steps while the coachman took the wheeled chair from the boot and set the brake.

As she watched, Captain Sir Belvedere St. Anthony was carried in his valet's arms to the wheeled chair. Trust Sir B to give Meridee a gallant wave as Gervaise set him in the chair and straightened the blanket over his remaining leg and ruin of the other that ended halfway down his thigh.

For a moment, she hated the sea and ships and countries that felt a war would solve something. *Dear God, spare these men*, she thought. *Keep these boys of St. Brendan's from harm.*

She knew it was a foolish prayer, but she prayed anyway, her eyes closed. When she opened them, Sir B was smiling at her. She leaned close because she spoke to him alone. "Sir B, thank you from the bottom of my heart for finding something for Master Six to do on land."

"My pleasure." He patted her hand. "Come, come! We'll be late to the assembly. Master Six, get your lady inside."

"I love that man," Able said as he escorted her up the steps. He looked back, always the master on duty where his captain was concerned. They both watched as his valet and the post- boy lifted the chair up the steps. "We were on different ships at the Nile—I was with Captain Hallowell. I sometimes ask myself if I could have saved more of Sir B's leg, had I been there. By God, I would have pushed the surgeon away and tried."

"And landed yourself in the brig, more like," Meridee said.

"Doubtless. I was busy enough at the Nile, doing the job I was paid to do. We all were, maneuvering so close to a lee shore. Still …."

Headmaster Croker waited inside the door. Able shepherded her into the mess hall, with tables pushed aside and more chairs in place.

She saw David Ten and Nick and the others who had spent the last days mucking out the stone basin. "They'll make room for me," she said. "You're to sit in front, my love."

"I can't tell you how that terrifies me," he admitted.

"It's your place and you've earned it," she said. "In fact, I believe I am being summoned to a space on the bench beside Mr. Ten. I can't resist a man in uniform, no matter what his height. Go on, Master Six."

The students stood up respectfully as she made her way down the row of benches to sit between one boy who flinched only days ago in the basin when he could not answer a question, and Nick, the quiet lad who possessed only one name.

"Ready for the new school term?" she asked David Ten as she sat down.

"Aye, miss," he said, his voice faint. He touched her sleeve. "Do we come to your house this afternoon once classes are done?"

"You do, you and Nick here, and—let me think—Stephen Hoyt and John Mark."

"Stephen's a runner," David confided in a low voice. "He wants to escape to sea right now."

"We'll have to convince him that it is better to stay and learn something first," she whispered back.

"All rise!" sounded from the entrance. Meridee rose as Headmaster Croker made his dignified way to the front of the hall. He was followed by Captain Sir Belvedere St. Anthony, pushed by Master Able Six. They were followed by two other teachers she did not know, although one of them must have been the history and English instructor whose pointer Able had broken over his knee and thrown out the window. *I doubt you are a friend*, she thought.

It was a modest assembly, by anyone's reckoning, held on a quiet street in a city with Royal Marines and sailors, and all the scaff and raff that hang about such men used to violence and the worst sort of treatment. For one frightening moment, Meridee doubted her ability to do what was required of her, armed with no theories on mothering lads from workhouses.

Upset with herself, she looked at her husband, wanting to blubber out her misgivings and cowardice in the face of the strangeness of her life. He seemed to sense she was watching him, so he looked at her. It was almost as though he knew what she was thinking, which made her swallow and try not to show fear.

Her wedding was a blur, except for a quaint phrase that popped into her brain and seemed to settle there, plumping up the pillows and making itself at home—"I plight thee my troth."

She knew what it meant, because her brother-in-law had walked with her the night before her marriage and explained it. She remembered how he had laughed and assured her that most of what he said would go in one ear and out the other, because that was the nature of weddings, but she ought to pay attention to this.

She remembered what he had told her: *plight* meant a risk and also a pleading, *troth* nothing less than truth.

Standing there in the great hall of St. Brendan the Navigator School and looking at her husband, she felt the force of what she had committed to land on her shoulders, but lightly. "I promise you I will be true," she whispered. "There is risk, but I will be loyal and faithful."

She sat down with the others, committed, content, and in need of nothing more, or nothing that couldn't be made sweeter by quiet time later with the man into whose care she had committed herself.

Or so she thought. That was the moment when David Ten put his hand in hers. Startled, she looked down at his fingers, then into his eyes. She saw the pleading there, the plight. Her heart full to bursting, she curled her fingers around his.

Chapter Twenty-One

⁓⚬⚬⌇⚬⚬⁓

M ERIDEE PATTED DAVID'S HAND. Mindful of Nick on her other side, she tried to take his hand, too, but he would have none of that.

Every child is different, she thought, feeling no rejection because her heart told her that Nick intended no such thing. She contented herself with giving him a little nudge.

It wasn't her imagination that Nick began to lean against her. Some instinct informed her that she should take no notice. All she knew of Nick was that as a very small lad he had been found sobbing on the workhouse steps in the wilds of Northumberland, the solitary name of Nick pinned to his shirt, no coat, dead of winter.

The order in the room impressed her. She thought of her nephews, with their fidgets during their papa's Sunday sermons. These lads were silent and nearly motionless, reminding her of her husband's ability to sit still and silent, another hard workhouse lesson.

When Headmaster Croker introduced his teachers, starting with Master Blake, she heard a low murmur, barely audible, and felt Nick lean closer to her. *You are the man who strikes his pupils*, she thought, watching Master Blake narrow his eyes and look over the assemblage, as if daring anyone to breathe.

Master Fletcher was next, a stubby fellow with a peg leg who had the weathered, seagoing look that almost shouted massive capability. Able had already told her he had been drafted from the fleet to teach the older boys to use the sextant and plot courses. "He curses like an expert," Able also told her.

Next came her husband, introduced as Sailing Master Durable Six, which made him smile and return some whispered comment to Captain Sir B, who sat next to him.

She tried to observe him dispassionately, as though they had no acquaintance, and perhaps see him as others saw him. Glancing at the row of maids and kitchen workers by the back door whispering together, she smiled to herself, pleased he was hers and not theirs. The new uniform did look impressive, but more impressive was the man inside it.

She had reminded him over breakfast that he was due for a haircut. If he put off a haircut for another month, she had no objection; she liked twining his curls around her fingers. Not every man was destined to look like the hero in a Lord Byron poem, and she was happy to be married to one of those lucky few. In his uniform or out of it, Able Six was cap-able, ineff-able and of all things, most aff-able.

Meridee, behave yourself, she thought, then looked up in surprise when the headmaster called her name.

"Mrs. Six, stand you up, my dear."

Startled, she did as he said, still holding onto David Ten's hand. For one tiny, irrational moment, she hoped sincerely that she had not been obviously ogling the sailing master, or at least not caught at it.

"This kind lady has consented to lodge four of our newer lads, the better to smooth things over for them. We all know workhouse life has its … let's call them challenges," he said.

She watched the boys nod seriously. Headmaster Croker leaned on the podium, watching his charges, silent, but with expressions ranging from studied indifference, to neutral blankness, to outright fear. "She is to be obeyed every whit as much as these masters behind me. Have you a word for the pupils, Mrs. Six?"

A word? With a lump in her throat, she already knew she had many. She had watched these neglected, outcast bastard sons of England and Scotland clean out a rubbish-filled basin with no complaint, working cheerfully in the cold and rain. Able had taught them all the verses to "Lady of Spain," so they sang, too. What could she say that wouldn't involve childish tears on her part, she who was a wife and a woman grown, but miles and miles away from them across the great chasm of privilege?

It was easy, because she was Meridee Six, who had already decided there was room in her heart for each one. She pointed her finger at one boy and then another, trying and failing monumentally to maintain a stern visage. "You Wharf Rats know who you are. That *rattus norvegicus* had better be out of my backyard by tomorrow!"

The students whooped with laughter, whatever tension caused by Master Blake gone, whatever notion of inferiority at least tucked away for the time being. For a far-too-fleeting moment, they were boys much like her nephews.

"That is all," she said, and sat down, her own fear gone because she knew she had a roomful of allies.

David Ten tugged on her hand and leaned closer. "I'll see to the wee bones, Mrs. Six. I like that sort of thing."

Wee bones. Meridee swallowed, thinking of Able Six's comment about numbers One through Five in Dumfries Workhouse, who had not survived childhood. *No wee bones here*, she thought, then realized she was sitting in the midst of survivors. The wife of number Six, she said a silent prayer to the memory of One through Five.

"I have prevailed upon Captain St. Anthony to share with us some of his wisdom," Headmaster Croker said, as Able wheeled his former captain to the side of the podium. "He served king and country for years, and has taken a real interest in you lads. Give him your attention."

Sir B didn't speak for a long moment, but only leaned his elbows on his chair and looked into each face, hers included.

"Lads, you have inherited a troubled world," he began, his eyes serious. "I hardly need tell you that, because you have already endured more than most."

No one made a sound, but Meridee felt the boys relax. *You know you're safe here*, she thought, and gave David's hand a little squeeze.

"If you or I were wagering men, and I hope to heaven you are not," he continued, a brief smile crossing his face, "we could place bets on the probable duration of this Treaty of Amiens. Master Six here could probably come up with a magical percentage of time remaining on the treaty, down to the second. Could you, sir?"

Her darling man laughed and nodded, which gave the boys permission to laugh, too, since he was one of them. She would have to ask him sometime if cleaning out a nasty stone basin was more for utility or camaraderie.

"When the treaty ends, and it will, Boney will not stop his conquest of Europe until either he or we are bled dry. That we on our little island will prevent him, I have no doubt. You should never doubt it either. The effort will be monumental, however, and that is where you are needed."

Making no attempt to mask the concern on his face, Sir Belvedere looked over the students again, as if counting the cost already. Meridee swallowed down her tears. In her brief tenure as wife, she had already been wakened from sleep to hear her husband giving intense orders to phantoms in the middle of battle. A gentle stroke or two was enough to send him back to sleep; only she stayed awake, wondering how men could go to sea and fight.

" 'Needed,' you ask? When has England ever needed me?" Sir B said, his voice rising. " 'When has this little island ever given me a good goddamn,' you might be asking yourselves." He sighed, as though out of strength, except there was no lessening of the penetration of his gaze. Meridee watched him, aware he should have died at sea, except that he could not surrender the will or spirit or energy—call it what you choose—to let go.

"You will show England, you older lads sooner than I would wish, how well you can serve in the fleet and beat Napoleon back from our shores."

He held his hands out to the boys. "Cynical men have laughed in my face when I tell them about St. Brendan's. 'Workhouse lads, what do they know? What can they do?' they ask me, and I know it is not a question, but derision. I smile and change the subject. Why argue with fools?"

He seemed to speak to each boy individually. "You will not disappoint me, St. Brendan's, yourselves, or the fleet. You older lads will be headed to the fleet sooner than any of us would wish, not because you cannot do what will be asked of you, but because we care deeply for you and would keep you here longer, if we could."

Meridee glanced around at the boys he addressed. *You're sitting with warriors and survivors and you're married to one,* she thought.

"So I say to you one and all, study with diligence this term. You will soon be helming ships of battle, mixing potions as pharmacist's mates, serving the guns and keeping the ship on course as Brendan himself did, God praise the saint. Go to. Show England how much she needs you."

He made a gesture and Able wheeled him back to the space next to his chair. As Meridee watched, the boys stood up as one, silent, eyes forward, completely still. Her eyes on her husband, Meridee rose, too, her hand to her heart. Putting his hand to his heart as well, Able looked at her and into her.

At a nod from the headmaster, the students filed out in silence, heading to their classrooms. Meridee watched them, struck with the reality that when they left the school and joined the fleet, some might never return.

How will you bear that, my love? she asked Able silently. *How will I?*

Chapter Twenty-Two

cɔ∽

Mrs. Perry was not pleased when Meridee waved away even the notion of luncheon and took herself upstairs for a nap. She pulled Able's pillow close so she could breathe in the fragrance of his hair and slept.

When she woke, shadows were beginning to slide across the bed. She lay on her back, staring at the ceiling, thinking how well she already knew this ceiling, seen mostly over her husband's shoulder. She listened to the rain, then sat up, alarmed and more concerned than she would have thought possible about a pile of *rattus norvegicus* outside and perhaps in peril of washing away.

If she did not get up right away and do something about it, she would lose her nerve. The mere thought of touching rat bones was already sending little marching feet down her spine. Still, St. Brendan's was going to pay her one pound a month to become a mother to little boys. Maybe she could call this stifling of her fear and loathing of rats her tariff to pay for the time when her own children might be curious in ways she wasn't and never would be.

"I'll do it for my unborn babies," she told herself out loud as she changed into a fading work dress and hurried downstairs.

She dashed back upstairs to hunt through her possessions for a square of dark fabric and found just the thing. It was wrapped around her mother's prized china cup and saucer, one of a set that constituted the rest of her dowry, after the twenty pounds that mostly went into Able's uniform.

The moment of truth. In the lightly falling rain, she stood looking down at a moldering stew of fur and … parts that constituted the remains of a tenacious little beast. No wonder the lads were styling themselves after wharf rats. Not even scavenging birds or other critters who might have wandered through the backyard last night seemed interested in the mess. She couldn't blame them.

She stared down, steeling herself. "Meridee Louisa Bonfort Six, this mess is not going to separate itself," she said out loud.

Kneeling on the wet grass, Meridee set the black square beside her. She took a deep breath, regretted it instantly, and leaned back for her stomach to settle. She readied herself to stick her hand into the nasty brew, but was sitting back again when Mrs. Perry loomed over her, holding two forks.

Her own cheery temperament resurfaced. "Mrs. Perry, we look for all the world like two Bedlamites getting ready to eat."

With some effort, Mrs. Perry knelt next to Meridee and handed her a fork. Meridee jabbed her fork at what remained of the carcass, barely maintaining her composure when the whole thing slid open in a slimy gush.

"Mercy," she muttered and retched, grateful she had passed over luncheon.

The cook set down her fork and hurried to the back steps.

"Mrs. Six, you are made of sterner stuff than I am," the woman declared. "I cannot."

Meridee gave her a jaunty salute that belied every single one of her real emotions and picked up the other fork. She gritted her teeth and prodded in the bundle, relieved when the slime parted and exposed tiny bones.

She decided to do the worst first. Mr. Wharf Rat still had enough face left to reveal melancholy eyes, one drooping from its socket, the other in place. She soon exposed the skull, which separated from its neck with no preamble. She didn't even want to think about the gray goo inside the skull, so she forked the disgusting thing onto the black cloth.

Braver now, Meridee observed the tiniest bones, perhaps toe bones, which were already free of their muscle and tissue and in danger of being lost in the muck as the rain poured down. They were too small for the fork, so she used her fingers, reminding herself there wasn't anything she couldn't wash off her hands.

Meridee was fishing out the other leg when someone tapped her on the shoulder. She jumped and put her hand to her throat, not a wise move. To her relief it was David Ten. He knelt beside her and picked up the extra fork.

"Master Six thought you might do something like this," he said. "He told me to come ahead while he finishes the calculation, um, calcification."

"Calculus. I was afraid the bones would wash away," she said. "It appeared that Mr. Wharf Rat is made of sterner stuff."

"Like us," he told her as he scraped away with some skill.

Meridee sat back on her heels and watched how meticulously he separated the tiniest bones from what remained of the viscera. She marveled at his interest; he seemed to forget she was there as he devoted himself to the rat that she had to admit wasn't as huge and menacing as it had seemed when she came outside armed with only a square of dark fabric and multiple good intentions.

He dissected the creature with some flair, even, and surprising skill. "How do you know so much about rats?" she asked finally.

He chuckled at that, as if she were a slightly slow child. "Mrs. Six, when you're hungry enough to eat a rat, you want to get all the good parts."

Meridee decided right then to complain less. "I'll take your word for it."

He continued his slow progress through the rat. "That's the tibia and fibula," he said, pointing to tiny bones. "You know, that part between your knee and your ankle." David whistled. "Wow. This must be the tail. Look at those tiny little bones."

Meridee looked, and hoped no one at St. Brendan's would ever see the need for another set of rat bones on the premises.

"There's the femur," he told her. "It's the meatiest part and tastes fine with salt."

"David, you amaze me," she said.

He shrugged. "I'm not really much good at numbers, and I hope Master Six isn't too disappointed." She saw the worry on his face. "You don't think the master will send me back to St. Pancras if I don't like numbers as much as he does, do you?"

"There is not the slightest chance," she said firmly. "I'm no expert at numbers, and he's not sending *me* back."

"But he picked you especially," David argued. "It's not the same."

He did, didn't he? she thought, delighted at the little fellow's observation. "No, it isn't the same," she agreed. She made herself look down at the rat stew. "I think you're an expert at bones. There will be a place in the fleet for someone who likes bones and has a strong stomach."

"Do you really think so?"

"I am convinced."

She heard the door open behind her and turned to see Nick coming down the steps. "Did Master Six send you to help David and relieve me?" she asked.

He nodded, and hunched down, because the rain was both constant and getting colder. "He said he didn't think David would be persuasive enough, think on." He stood with a frown, then shook his head. "I don't know about this."

"Join me, then, because I don't either," she said, moving over and a little farther from the rat. "I am leaving all major rat decisions to David Ten. I will do what he tells me to."

He looked at her in disbelief. "You *listen* to him? He's a workhouse boy, same's me."

"He knows bones, and I never argue with experts," she said, only half joking. "Nick, what is your particular talent? I have observed already that St. Brendan's boys seem to excel at something or other. Do you like numbers?"

"Well enough. I like books better," he conceded as he took the fork from her fingers. "I will help Davey now."

He said it with finality, and had no qualms about taking the fork from her. She wasn't being dismissed, because there was nothing in his voice that sounded arbitrary. He had been sent to relieve her, and he obeyed. She sensed no dismay at their obvious differences or her evident superiority. He obeyed.

"So you like to read?"

"I love to," Nick said, his eyes on the task at hand as David pointed to a tangle of fur. "This, not so much."

Meridee was cold, but so were they. She knew Able intended for her to go inside, but she wanted to stay in the orbit of these interesting children.

"Davey, how would you display these bones?"

"I'd find a board and sand it down," he said with no hesitation. "I'd put the rat in the middle of the board. I'd splay out the arms and legs, and label each bone."

"I can see that," she said, and she could. "Mrs. Perry knows wood. Her late husband was a carpenter's mate."

"She scares me," Davey said. "Maybe you should ask her."

"We'll ask her together," Meridee said. "Strength in numbers."

"My penmanship is good," Nick volunteered. "We would need a pen with a small nib for the lettering by the bones." He moved his hand as if seeing bigger words march across the board. "And then really big at the top, ST. BRENDAN'S WHARF RATS." He smiled for the first time, a shy smile that told Meridee he didn't do it often. "We'll hang it in our classroom because *we're* the rats."

Impressive, she thought. Nick had ideas.

"We could find a way to attach little strips of wood hanging down, with our names on them," he said. "P'raps our names and the years we spent at St. Brendan's before we go to the fleet."

"You only have one name," Davey pointed out.

"I know. It's a problem," Nick said.

"Nick, you have the amazing good fortune to be able to choose your own last name," she said. "How many of us can say that?"

She could tell from his wide-eyed expression that he had never considered the possibility. "You mean, I could *do* that?" he asked. "Is it legal?"

"Why not?" Meridee replied, praying with all her heart that it was legal because it suddenly mattered to her. "My name is Meridee, and I always thought that was a little silly. I'm stuck with it, howsoever."

"Not as silly as Ten," Davey said.

"Sillier," she insisted. "My five sisters have good solid names like Louisa and Amanda, and Augusta, Jane, and Mary. And Bonfort? What could I do with that," she laughed out loud, "except marry a man named Six?"

They laughed and the rain poured down.

Chapter Twenty-Three

∞

"**D**O YOU KNOW WHAT I will find when I go home today, gentlemen?" Able asked Jamie MacGregor and Jan Yarmouth, who looked stunned after an hour of merely starting to think about the calculus. "I will find my wife still out in the backyard, trying to save rat bones."

"Master, you sent two of the younger boys ahead to do that, didn't you?" Jamie asked.

"I did. I know my wife, though."

Back to the matter at hand—the stunned looks. "Remember this about the calculus: it's the study of how things change. When you know how things change, you will be able to predict how other things change."

Jamie's hand went up slowly, as if he feared ridicule. Able remembered times he had raised his hand like that and been beaten. At the time, he couldn't understand why. He did now. His workhouse teachers, overworked and underpaid and probably hating their teaching assignment, knew less than he did.

"Aye, Jamie? Let me assure you that there will be no ridicule for any question."

"Maybe it is silly, but why is the calculus important?" Jamie asked.

"It's a sound question, Mr. MacGregor. What if we could change an atom, something so small you cannot see it with your eyes? That was a question the philosopher Leucippus asked in 370 BC. He said the universe is composed of two elements, atoms and the void in which they move."

"If we can change an atom—and I don't understand how we even know they exist—everything is possible then," Jan blurted out. "Beg pardon, I should have raised my hand."

"It's just the three of us. Leap in whenever you wish," Able said. "You're correct, Mr. Yarmouth. Everything is possible."

He eyed his students, pleased to see more understanding. "Here is your assignment for tomorrow. Think of a machine you believe people need. Write a paragraph about it." He held up his hands for emphasis and stood up. "Nothing is beyond the realm of possibility. Think large. And now I must go home and pry my wife from rat bones."

The boys laughed and left the room. He stood in the doorway and watched them chat with each other down the hall. Headmaster Croker told Able that one of the first rules he instituted at St. Brandon's was the abolition of workhouse silence in the halls and dining room. He smiled to see Jan gesturing large and Jamie laughing about it, imposed silence a memory to them now.

As he stood there thinking, Able entertained a new idea, something he had never considered: as harsh as the workhouse had been, it had given him the strength for the Royal Navy, and the knowledge that there wasn't anything he couldn't manage. He knew himself to be tough and resourceful. Maybe he should give some of the credit to bleak, cruel, and dreadful Dumfries Workhouse.

He swung his boat cloak around his shoulders and closed the classroom door. A few steps took him toward the classroom of Master Blake, who had already glared at him today, pointedly ignored him during luncheon, and demanded of his students loud enough for Able to hear that in *his* classroom that there be no talking.

Master Blake, don't punish your students to get back at me, he thought, and wondered what Meri would do if confronted with such outright loathing. He swallowed his pride and knocked on Master Blake's door.

"Enter."

Able walked in and closed the door behind him. Master Blake stood there, black-robed because he had walked the rarified halls of Cambridge and earned a Bachelor of Letters. He might have been a handsome man, but his face was set and disagreeable, as if he had breathed in too much shoreline at low tide. Everything about him reeked of privilege and condescension.

"You've come to reimburse me for a new pointer?" Master Blake asked.

"Never," Able replied. "St. Brendan's boys don't need to be beaten. They've been abused for years, and I can tell you personally it is no pleasant thing."

"You teach your way, and I will teach mine," Master Blake said and turned his back on Able, dismissing him.

Not so fast, Able thought. "I wanted to thank you for teaching these lads history and law," Able said. "Heaven knows they—"

"Need it?" Master Blake interrupted. He turned around, and there was no mistaking the hostility in his eyes. "I never saw such ignorance."

"That is why they need what you can give them," Able said, forcing down his own dislike. "We're training leaders, sir."

Master Blake laughed. "This, *Master* Able, is a farce." He turned his back to Able again.

Then why in God's name are you here? Able wanted to ask, but allowed prudence to reign instead. "Could I ask … could you possibly teach them to write in a fair hand? Some of them will be keeping ship's logs, and they will need that instruction. No? Ah, well, it was a mere suggestion. Good day, Master Blake."

"Don't ask for anything else, bastard," Master Blake said.

Able flinched. He itched to wrap his fingers around the insufferable man's throat and watch his eyes fill with blood and pop from their moorings, as he had seen a thief killed in Morocco once. Better to *think* about the pleasure of murdering Master Blake and leave it at that.

He invoked a passage from his favorite Euclid, which calmed him. When Able started down the stairs, he was met this time by Master Fletcher, the old salt hired to teach the upper class navigational techniques. Able had spent some time under Master Fletcher's tutelage in the Mediterranean, and knew him to be competent and thorough. For a moment he felt like a pup again, sitting cross-legged on the deck behind Fletcher's actual students, taking in what the master taught because Captain St. Anthony had ordered him to learn.

Master Fletcher motioned him closer and they walked down the stairs together.

"I couldn't help overhearing that bit of bombast from Blake," Fletcher remarked. "I also heard how you broke the whiny fellow's pointer."

"For my sins," Able said. "I couldn't help myself."

"He's a strange one, is Master Blake," Fletcher said, after a glance back up the stairs. He lowered his voice. "I know scuttlebutt is worth what you pay for it, but I've heard that Headmaster Croker was forced to take him on as a favor to one of the uppity ups in the gov'mint who controls the purse strings here at St. Brendan's."

"Blake has high crimes and misdemeanors he is atoning for?" Able said, striving for a light tone. As much as he admired Fletcher's skills, he shied from gossip.

"Gambling debts, I hear," Fletcher confided. "Maybe a touch of fraud. Blake comes from a good family. Maybe someone at Whitehall or Admiralty wanted to spare an illustrious name unused to the tar brush."

"And we get him," Able said, with a shrug. He remembered the boys waiting for him below. "Maybe he'll improve, Master Fletcher. Meanwhile, I have little boys to escort to their new posh digs across the street."

Fletcher laughed at that, but his troubled expression betrayed him. "Go then, young master," he said. Then, taking his arm, he added, "Come with me some night to the Bare Bones for a drink."

"Now that brings back a memory or two," Able said, well-acquainted with the worst grog shop and brothel in Portsmouth and unwilling to return. "Meri would kill me and no jury would convict her."

"I have my reasons for inviting you," Fletcher said. "A time or two, I've seen Master Blake in there, which I do not understand. I wonder what you might make of it."

Master Blake in a sty that some of the captains in the fleet had declared off limits to their men? "That does surprise me," he said. "Why would a gentry cove take himself there?"

"He's up to something, sure as the world," Fletcher said. "What, I could not say. Well, here are your lads. When you have time and can sneak away from your pretty ball and chain, I'll shout you a snootful at the Bones."

They had stopped in front of the statue of St. Brendan. Able nodded at the sailing master, his eyes on the boys. "You have aroused my curiosity, Master Fletcher," he said. "Seems a strange place for a superior sort of fellow like Blake. We'll see about that grog."

Clothing bundles in hand, their eyes betraying their uncertainty, Stephen Hoyt and John Mark stood close together, two lads against the unknown. Thaddeus Croker had told them earlier that Stephen was a runner. They were also new to St. Brendan's, cried in their beds at night, and needed a kind touch, even though they likely had no idea what a kind touch meant. How to begin?

"Are you hungry?" he asked.

Both boys lowered their gaze to the stone floor and shook their heads.

"I am fair gut-foundered," Able said. "I am not certain what Mrs. Perry and Mrs. Six have prepared, but I can guarantee it will be tasty."

He shepherded the silent children across the street. The rain had stopped, but the gray day was about to surrender to darkness.

"I don't know what state of affairs we'll find inside," he told his quiet charges. "Mistress Six has been cleaning rat bones. Remember that stone basin?"

"Aye, master," he heard from John Mark. His voice was scarcely audible, but at least he spoke.

"I hope David Ten and Nick have relieved her of that duty," he said as he opened the front door. "Come in, please." He sniffed the air. "I smell meat pie."

Telling the boys to set down their bundles by the stairs, he motioned them to follow him out the back door, where three people knelt in the wet grass, heads together.

Able put his hand lightly on Stephen Hoyt's shoulder. "Just what I thought. What should we do, Stephen?"

He didn't expect an answer; he didn't know what he expected, which was a novel enough sensation.

"You could beat her, Master Six," the boy said softly.

God above, why? Able asked the sky. He knelt beside the boy who ran. "We don't do that. Not her, not you. Here's what we do."

He walked down the back steps and cleared his throat with a loud and entirely theatrical harrumph. "Aren't you the wife who abhors rats?"

"Guilty," she said, sounding anything but. "We're nearly done. Could you bring out a lamp, Master Six?"

He squatted beside her, unwilling to muddy his new uniform. "Master Six stays across the street," he whispered in her ear.

"Able then," she said. "A few more minutes?"

He stood up, then flicked his finger against her head, which made David Ten laugh.

"David and Nick, how about this?" he said. "You two finish up in the next five minutes. Mrs. Six will come inside with me and dry off."

"Aye, sir, that's fair," Nick said. "I'll fetch a lamp."

"Thank you. Up you get, Mrs. Six. You're sopping wet."

Nick hurried back with a lamp. There was a final consultation between the three bone pickers, after which Meri carefully wrapped the square of cloth into itself and carried it up the steps.

"What miracle is this?" Able joked. "Is this the same lady who swore never to have rat bones in her house, let alone hold them?"

"The very one," Meri said. "They won't take up much space." She looked over her shoulder. "Take one more look around, Davey and Nick. We need to dry off."

What a dear woman she was, this wife of his. Once inside the house, she set the bones on the hall table and put her hands on each new boy's shoulder. "You'll get used to us, I promise," she said. "Master Six will show you to your room, while I dry off. Lead on, husband. Mrs. Perry will be unhappy if supper gets cold. Doesn't it smell divine?"

He led Stephen and John upstairs and into their room directly across from the chamber he shared with Meri. She slogged behind him and stood in the hall as he ushered them in.

"It's a trifle cozy," she said, apologetic, the perfect hostess even as she dripped on the carpet. "I know the mattresses are comfortable and there are plenty of blankets."

With a wave of her hand, she went into their chamber and shut the door. Able watched the boys turn toward the closed door like flowers following the sun.

"You're in good hands, lads," he said quietly. "This is what it feels like when Dame Fortune smiles."

Chapter Twenty-Four

◊

D INNER WAS AN UNALLOYED pleasure: meat pie with steam rising out of a hole in the top crust, potatoes boiled in their jackets and mashed with a great dollop of butter that had Nick's full attention, crusty bread, stewed dried apples, and rice pudding with sultanas moist and plump.

To Able's eternal delight, Meridee—hair damp, eyes lively—presided with all the panache of a woman who took in strays every day and fed them almost to the point of pain.

At first they had not known what to do when Mrs. Perry set the empty plates on the table and left them there. At St. Brendan's, they were used to being served filled plates, with a bowl or two going around once. The idea of dishes allowed to roam free on the table seemed to frighten them. Stephen shrank back when Meridee passed him the mashed potatoes.

"You can put as much as you like on your plate," she told him. "Take what you know you will eat. There is more in the kitchen."

Able could tell Stephen didn't believe her. He excused himself, went to the kitchen, and asked Mrs. Perry to bring out the entire pot of potatoes. "They need to see there is more in here," he told her.

He sat down again, and Mrs. Perry carried in the pot, tipping it to make sure they could see that more remained. Only then did the anxious look leave Stephen's eyes. When Meridee handed him the bowl again, he served himself a tentative spoonful, then another.

"What you do now is hand the bowl to Nick," Meridee said.

Nick took his turn, then handed it on to John Mark. Touched, Able watched how Stephen's eyes followed the bowl all around the table, until his wife set it in front of him again.

"We do that with each dish," she explained. "If you want more of something and it is out of your reach, you ask, 'Please pass the whatever-it-is.'"

"Suppose he won't pass it?" Stephen asked.

"I can think of a time, becalmed in the doldrums and hungry, when I didn't want to pass the food," Able said. He ducked when Meridee took a swing at his head. Stephen even smiled.

"That is precisely what my sailing master was ready to do to me," Able said. He looked at each boy in turn, seeing years of hardship ahead for them, but also a certain camaraderie he doubted his wife would understand. "I wish I could tell you that life at sea is all grog and pasties, but it isn't. You'll be hungry, frightened, and uncertain, at times."

"It's still sounds better than St. Pancras," Davey said, ever-hopeful David Ten.

"Aye, lad. Nothing is quite as lovely as seeing the Southern Cross in the night sky near the tip of South America. By the time you join the fleet, you will each possess skills the Navy needs. You will have useful work to do, in this time of national emergency." He looked down at Mrs. Perry's wonderful meat pie and his own mound of potatoes. "Eat and talk, lads, but don't talk with your mouth full or Mrs. Six will probably give you her evil stare."

To his delight, Meri opened her mouth to protest, then shut it and glared at him. "It looks mostly like that," she said serenely.

He blessed his wife again and again through that first meal with their young lodgers, as she kept up a steady, mundane conversation, asking him about his day, telling him the tailor had delivered those two promised shirts, and reminding him that a haircut wouldn't be a bad idea. It was married-couple conversation, in its own way gently reassuring the boys that their lives were different now.

When the meal ended, Meridee asked the boys to help her carry the dishes to the kitchen. "We don't have a maid of all work yet, so you'll be helping Mrs. Perry with the dishes," she said. "Pass me your plates and follow me with the bowls."

Without a word, they did as she said. Able smiled to see Nick pocket one of the remaining meat pies, which gave Stephen silent permission to do the same. Studiously unmindful, Meridee led her gaggle of lodgers into the kitchen while Able went into the sitting room and stood by the window, wondering how he had become the luckiest man in the realm.

Meridee joined him at the window, putting her arms around him and resting her head against his back. "Mrs. Perry is ordering them about and they are doing exactly as she demands," she said. "We must recommend some house rules to them."

"First one, Meri: no one bothers us once lights are doused," he said.

"Unless I hear them crying," his wife amended. "No one cries in the Six home without attention."

Only last night, he would have carried her up the stairs after dinner and plopped her on their bed. Now they had a houseful of boys to consider. "What are *our* rules?" he teased, taking her by the hand. "You know, general merriment and all that."

"We might have to become more creative," his practical wife told him. "Earlier rising, perhaps? Middle of the night frivolity?"

"We already do that," he reminded her.

"Then we'll continue."

He looked toward the open door. "Dishes done, lads? Kitchen clean?"

"Aye, sir," Nick told him.

They stood close together at the door, uncertain, wondering what was next. He gestured them inside. "Find a chair or sit on the deck, if you'd rather. We don't stand on much ceremony in the Six household."

The floor suited them, so it suited him too, as he sat on the carpet with them and leaned his head against Meridee's knees. "We need rules," he began, "same as on a ship." He looked up at his wife. "What say you, Meri? Should *we* make the rules? It's our house."

"I think John, Stephen, Nick, and Davey should," she said. "I might have one or two rules, but no more."

"Let's start with yours."

Able stood up and took a sheet of paper and a pencil from the desk. "Who of you has the best hand?" he asked.

"I'll do it, Master Six," Nick said, reaching up.

"Good. Meri?"

He sat cross-legged again and her hand went to his head this time. "Clean up after yourselves," she said. "Yes, write that, Nick."

The boy did as she asked, then looked at her.

"Do as Mrs. Perry asks," she said, then patted the boy closest to her, which turned out to be Stephen. In fact, he was almost, but not quite, leaning against her other knee. "I know she is intimidating, but Mrs. Perry has your best interests at heart." She laughed. "Don't look so doubtful! She watches out for me, too. That's all the rules I have."

Able didn't know if the boys would say anything. He knew no one in the Dumfries Workhouse had ever wanted *his* opinion on any subject. "Your turn, lads," he said gently. "You'll be abiding by the rules, so you should set them."

"We shouldn't fight," Davey said finally. "Aye, that's it. No fighting."

"How will you solve your difficulties, if you do not fight?" Able asked, remembering desperate struggles over food in his dormitory, twenty-five boys tussling over scraps.

"Maybe we could talk about it with you, and let you decide?" John suggested.

Able nearly answered, then he realized John was looking at Meridee. "Meri?" he asked.

"I would listen to both sides, but I would expect the warring parties to solve it themselves," she said. She turned her attention to Nick, who had sprawled on his stomach now, pencil poised. "How should we say that?"

" 'Come to Mrs. Six and discuss hard feelings,' " John said. He looked over Nick's shoulder. "There's one more E in feelings."

Nick wrote as directed, then looked at his fellow lodgers. "How about 'Obey all orders?' "

The others nodded, so he wrote it. "That's four."

Able regarded Stephen, the fellow Headmaster Croker said was a runner. "I have one," he said. "No running away."

Stephen lowered his eyes and traced the carpet pattern with one finger.

Meri watched him too, and put her hand gently on Stephen's head. "Mrs. Perry tells me Portsmouth isn't a safe town. I doubt she would let me go in search of a runaway, because she would worry about me, too. I daren't cross Mrs. Perry."

Nick wrote, *No running away* on the paper, his expression troubled. "I wanted to run away in Northumberland," he said. "I hated it." He sat up. "Master Six, did *you* ever run away?"

"You have me," Able said, knowing better than to lie to these boys. "I ran away three times, was brought back and beaten soundly. Ask Mrs. Six. She has seen the marks on my back."

His dear one nodded, and sniffed back tears.

"The fourth time I ran away, I crossed the Scottish border in a wagonload of potatoes," he said, looking at Stephen, whose face wore an old man's expression. "I ate those potatoes all the way to Plymouth, dirt and all. I hid under bushes at night and hopped on the wagon before it started to roll at dawn. I snuck aboard a captain's barge under a pile of canvas. When it tied up to a frigate in the harbor, I climbed the chains and said I wanted to join the Navy."

"How old were you?" Davey asked.

"Nine. They took me into the service and I rose in the ranks the usual way." No need to tell them that he read every book he could find, learned to tie knots by one observation, had no fear of climbing the sheets and furling sails, and learned to use a sextant by watching the sailing master teach the midshipmen while he was supposed to be scrubbing the deck.

"Couldn't we do that, too?" Stephen asked, his voice soft. "Work up the usual way?"

"No need. The purpose of St. Brendan's is to provide you with nautical training," Able said. "You'll know enough to be a rated seaman, and not a lubber with nothing to recommend him. No running away," he repeated.

There were a few more rules, but the point was made, at least he hoped it was. Who knew? Stephen's expression was unreadable, not unusual in a workhouse lad. "Nick, make another copy and we'll hang one in each of your rooms," he said.

He looked up to see Mrs. Perry standing in the doorway, filling it as only she could. "Aye, Mrs. Perry? You look like a woman with a question."

"I want to know what to do with the rat bones in my kitchen."

Able couldn't help laughing at the guilty expressions Davey and Nick exchanged with his wife.

"Davey? You're the one who seems to like the bones the most," Meridee prompted. "Stand up."

Davey did as she said. To Able's gratification, Nick did too. *Bravo, lad. Stand by your mate*, Able thought. *You never know when you might be required to keep each other alive.*

"We cleaned them pretty well, Mrs. Perry," Davey said. "If we can boil them one last time in clean water tomorrow, we can dry them off and … and …."

"Yes?" she prompted, looking none too pleased.

"Uh, maybe find someone who knows wood to make us a proper plaque to hang them on," Davey finished in a rush. "If we knew someone like that."

Mrs. Perry shook her finger at the boys, but he could tell her heart wasn't in it. She took her time looking at each child rendered old by hardship. "We will see," she said. "No promises, mind."

"No one promises us anything," Davey piped up cheerfully.

Mrs. Perry muttered something and left the room. Able saw her shoulders shaking. Whether he knew it or not, Davey had conquered.

"Time for bed," Meridee said. "You'll breakfast at eight o'clock and—"

"How many bells is that, John Mark?" Able interrupted.

"Eight, Master Six," he sang out, as though he already inhabited a quarterdeck. "Eight bells and all's well!"

It was the traditional call at the end of each watch. Oddly enough, all *was* well; he felt it in his bones. He stood up. "To bed, lads, and handsomely now."

He stood by while Meridee supervised them below deck in the washroom, acquainting them with the wash basin, soap, and towels, and the need to use the necessary, and not just let fly in the yard, even though it was dark out. He went to his room first and stood in his open door as they followed her upstairs like goslings after mama goose.

"Get into your nightshirts and I will come back and tuck you in."

He had to hide his smile when that statement, which might have originated on Mars, left them frowning and puzzled.

"Beg pardon, miss?" Nick asked.

"You know, wish you goodnight," Meridee said. "Don't you … perhaps not."

He had to give his woman credit. She squared her shoulders when he knew she wanted to weep.

"Make that another rule, Nick," Able said. "Every night Mrs. Six will wish you goodnight, because she wants to."

"Five minutes! You had better be in bed," she told them.

He gathered her close in their room. "At one pound a month, St. Brendan's isn't paying you enough," he said.

"Silly husband," she whispered back. "I would do it for nothing."

Chapter Twenty-Five

❦

IN THE MORNING MERIDEE saw her little charges off. They trooped along beside her husband, who looked back from the other side of the street and blew her a kiss. To her amusement, Davey did the same, and then Nick.

"They're already behaving like sailors," Mrs. Perry said. "Cheeky boys."

Better express contrition now. "Mrs. Perry, I apologize for the bones."

"If that is the worst thing that happens, we will be numbered among the fortunate," her cook told her. "The bones are simmering. I will say no more."

"What have we gotten ourselves into?" Meridee asked.

"You should have thought of that before you married a crazy man," Mrs. Perry said. She looked down at Meridee from her great height. "Take a nap! Don't you two sleep?"

Not really, Meridee thought, as she went upstairs to make her bed, not sleep in it, because she had work to do. To be honest, she had wakened him out of a sound sleep once. Then they both lay awake, listening to someone cry across the hall.

Able got up and wrapped his robe around him. She lay in the warm spot he left, as he opened one door across the hall, stood there listening, closed it, then opened the other and went inside.

Her eyes were closing when he came back to bed and nudged her out of his spot. Pulling her close, he said, "Of all people, it was Nick. He seems so assured. He said he was sorry but sometimes he can't help himself."

"We can take turns," she told Able. "Is he the one found with just one name pinned to his shirt?"

"Aye. Maybe it's better to have no memory of a family at all. How can you miss a family if you never had one?"

So much for her resolution to get a great deal done that morning. When she woke up near noon, weak sunlight had wrestled its way through the gloom of

Portsmouth's winter sky. Rubbing sleep from her eyes, she went to the window and looked across the street to St. Brendan's. Two floors up and two windows over, she saw her husband gesturing. She watched in appreciation as he threw back his head and laughed.

Gadfreys, but the man was in his element in the classroom.

"And he married you, Mrs. Six," she told the mirror's reflection as she brushed her hair and wound it into a bun low on the nape of her neck. "All that brilliance and amazing good looks married you. Heavens."

Probably long since back from the baker's, considering that the sun was overhead now, Mrs. Perry stirred a pot in her kitchen, accompanying herself with a tuneless whistle. Meridee gasped when the cook took a sip using the long-handled spoon. The small sound made Mrs. Perry turn around, start in surprise, then laugh.

"Mrs. Six, this is not rat bone broth!" she said, pointing to the dry sink. "Of course, you might not wish to ever use that strainer again. I think the bones are clean enough to satisfy any barbarian, for such are little boys."

Meridee looked into the wire strainer, dreading the sight of the bones, then struck again by how small they actually were. She poked them this way and that, thinking how much they would please Davey Ten.

"Davey wants to adhere them to a plaque," she said and tested the waters. "Who might have a really fine piece of wood on which to mount this ... this specimen?"

"I have one," Mrs. Perry said. "I spirited away Mr. Perry's carpenter satchel before the Navy thought they needed it more than I did."

In for a penny, in for a pound, Meridee thought. "We'll need glue. I wonder ...."

Mrs. Perry saw right through her. "I have that, too."

Meridee knew when to stop fishing. "Mrs. Perry, are you the best thing that ever happened to Able and me?"

Mrs. Perry's African dignity was impressive in its depth. "Let us say we are all fortunate. Care to try a rout cake?"

"I thought you would never offer," Meridee said simply. "I would love a rout cake."

Meridee spent a lengthy time deciding which petite cake she wanted. "This one has more sugar on the sides," the cook suggested.

"I want more icing," Meridee declared. Mrs. Perry finally handed her two.

Meridee closed her eyes in bliss as the more sugar-sided morsel dissolved in her mouth. She followed it up with the tang of lemon icing on the other rout cake, and shook her head over another of the moist offerings. "I daren't," she said, but reluctantly. "Master Six might not care for rotundity in a wife."

"You could add another stone or two, and he would never complain," Mrs. Perry said, as she selected a cake of her own. "He admires you."

Not half as much as I admire him, Meridee thought. She eyed the cakes with another purpose in mind. "Do you think … is it possible there might be enough of these to give the boys some extras to take to their rooms at night? Able tells me they might sleep better if they know there is food close by."

"I think it entirely possible," Mrs. Perry assured her. She sighed and sat down. "I didn't want to tell you this earlier, but I caught Stephen trying to open the front door last night and run away."

"I didn't … we didn't hear him!" Meridee exclaimed. "He's already been warned. What will we do if he does scarper off?"

"We will find him," Mrs. Perry said, her voice firm.

"Have I bitten off more than I can chew?" Meridee asked, as she reached for another rout cake.

"You will surprise yourself with what you can do," Mrs. Perry replied. "Did I hear the master mention to you this morning that Captain Sir What's His Name wanted you to pay an afternoon visit? That's one reason I made rout cakes. Take him some."

"Able did, didn't he?" Meridee said. "I confess I am a little afraid of someone with a title."

"That is a poor excuse to avoid a visit," Mrs. Perry said, again sounding remarkably like Meridee's mother. She pointed to the square box on the counter. "Here are the cakes. I am going to shoo you out the door and watch until you get at far as the baker's, where Mr. Bartleby will hail a hackney for you."

"You are a tyrant, Mrs. Perry, and apparently in league with the baker," Meridee said.

All that comment earned was folded arms and a set expression from the woman who could make delicate rout cakes and would probably follow little Stephen Hoyt into a nest of vipers, if he thought to run away on her watch.

"Life was simpler in the Devon countryside," she countered. It wasn't exactly a whine, but maybe a close cousin.

"You know you wouldn't wish yourself back there," the cook parried back.

True to her word, Mrs. Perry watched Meridee until she reached the baker, where some silent, cosmic, preordained signal handed her off. Ezekiel Bartleby wiped his hands on his apron, presented her an almond biscuit with a little flourish, and stepped from the curb on this busier street to hail her a hackney.

"Number Twenty-Five Jasper Road, if you please," Meridee told the jarvey, who appeared reluctant to let the baker hand her into his hackney.

"Mind you don't jostle this lady," Ezekiel said, and it was no suggestion.

Meridee leaned back in the hackney, secretly pleased with all the attention, and even more delighted that she was a dignified matron now, someone not requiring a chaperone. She also reminded herself that she had some years left to acquire dignity, and she still didn't mind protection in this rough city full of seafarers. For some reason, she had been summoned to Number Twenty-five, so to Number Twenty-five she would go.

The jarvey must have taken the baker's threat to heart because the ride was smooth. They left the narrow streets behind, and also the accompanying odors of tar, rope, and tidal flats. Looking back at the harbor, she imagined it in high summer, with blue skies and gulls wheeling gracefully about. There was the Isle of Wight, trees bare now. Always in the distance was the row of prison hulks moored to each other bow to stern, a wooden necklace of misery of the acutest kind. Able doubted the prisoners had been freed by the Treaty of Amiens. She hoped he was wrong.

Number Twenty-five was far grander than any house she had ever visited, even in those distant days before dear Papa's business failures had sent them quietly into genteel poverty. Chez St. Anthony was a pale-blue three-story house on the end of a row of brick houses curving back from the street.

Able had told her Sir B came from wealth and had added upon it with prize money from captured enemy ships sold as salvage or to the Navy, to be renamed and used against the enemy. *Gentlemanly piracy pays*, she thought, amused.

She paid the jarvey, tipped him enough to elicit a smile and a tug on his hat, then stood in the quiet street. Capable, wealthy, and admired, Sir B had sailed into battle at the Nile and become one more statistic on the lengthening roster of wounded men struck down by Napoleon Bonaparte.

And here she stood, holding a pasteboard carton of rout cakes, done up in a bow. What good could sweets possibly do this man she barely knew? Able had told her over breakfast that Sir B wanted the pleasure of her company. Why did such a comment make her feel like she had thumbs on all her fingers, a shabby dress, and hair obviously not touched by a lady's maid? Fearful, she took off her glove and sniffed her hand, hoping she did not smell like *rattus norvegicus*.

She reminded herself that the rout cakes weren't getting a minute younger, which furnished the fortitude to march up the shallow steps and give the door knocker a respectable bang somewhere between gentility and audacity.

The footman who opened the door looked at her for a long moment, as if not certain he should let her in, ask her to go around to the servants' entrance, or simply tell her to go away.

"My husband, Master Able Six, told me this morning that Captain Sir Belvedere St. Anthony requested a visit," she said, drawing on all the matronly dignity she wished she possessed and knew she didn't. "I am Mrs. Six."

To her surprise, he ushered her inside and almost but not quite smiled. She thought she detected relief in his expression, but that couldn't be. She had nothing to offer this top-of-the-trees household.

"Mrs. Six, if you would follow me into the sitting roo—"

They both started at the sound of a high-pitched wail that sent prickles racing up and down Meridee's spine so fast they probably bumped into each other.

"I … I … could come back another day," she said.

He left her in the foyer and took the stairs two at a time, as the screaming grew louder. Meridee clutched the box, wishing for her husband because he always knew what to do.

Suddenly, so did she.

Chapter Twenty-Six

∽

MERIDEE GATHERED HER SKIRTS and hurried up the stairs too. The footman tried to motion her back, but she ignored him. Another servant stood by an open door and waved her away. Brushing past the startled man, she threw herself into what had to be Sir Belvedere's bedchamber.

Sir B lay there, eyes closed, hands knotted into fists and twisting his sheet about. Sweat poured off him, and no wonder; the room felt close and humid.

She could have backed out and fled the house with no one the wiser, because the servants had never seen her before. She discarded such cowardice as unworthy of the wife of Master Durable Six. Instead, she opened a window, then approached the bed, her footsteps firm, and grasped his hand.

Sir B opened his eyes, then blinked, as though he did not know who she was.

"Sir B, you wanted me to visit," she said calmly. "Able said."

"Aye, I did, but not like this," he managed to gasp out. "The pain!"

"Where is it worst?" she asked. She sat down and removed her bonnet as calmly as if she had been invited to tea at a neighboring manor.

"Right above the amputation," he said. "Sometimes it feels as if the whole mangled … *thing* is still there, throbbing and spurting blood." He wailed again. "You should leave," he managed when the terrible moment passed.

"On the contrary, Sir B," she said, wondering where her courage came from. "What can I do to make it better?"

"Too much to ask," he replied. "Nothing you can do."

Those were his words, but that wasn't what she heard. Somewhere in the middle of the sentence spoken between nearly clenched teeth, she heard uncertainty, as if he knew a remedy but wouldn't subject her to it.

"Tell me," she insisted.

She noted how his skin was finely drawn across his already thin face, every crevice in sharp relief. It dawned on Meridee that Sir B's face bore the look of war. It wasn't highly fleshed like those one associated with bankers, solicitors, vicars, and teachers. Did war do something to men's visages? After waking early a few mornings just to watch her husband sleep, she thought so.

"Tell me, Sir B," she repeated softly.

He let out his breath in a rush. "God forgive me, but I am desperate. Hold my leg firmly above the amputation. My damned servants are afraid to touch me."

"I'm not," she lied. She pulled back the light blanket that covered him and averted her eyes. Scolding herself for being so missish, Meridee pulled down his nightshirt to make him private. She rested her hand on the scarred abomination that formed what was left of his leg and felt the heat. She put her hands around what remained of his thigh and squeezed.

He started at first, then she felt the tension leave his leg. "Is this what you want?" she asked. Her voice quavered, but there was nothing she could do about that.

"Tighter, if you can," he gasped. "Squeeze my leg as long as you can."

Unflinching, she did as he said. Because sitting in the chair didn't get her close enough, she begged Sir B's pardon and sat on his bed. She turned her back to him and strengthened her grip as she looked down his stump.

"Please, please tell me if I am causing you pain," she begged. "I am squeezing as tight as I can."

"My dear Mrs. Six, you cannot imagine the relief," he said after a few minutes. There was nothing calm in his voice yet, but the desperation had vanished. His breathing gradually slowed. As she leaned against his hip, she noted the moment when he relaxed completely. His good knee splayed out slightly and she knew she could lessen her grip.

She heard Sir B sigh. "You can let go now," he said, "but please don't leave me. I have no one."

He said it simply, without an ounce of self-pity that Meridee could hear. "I wouldn't care to be alone at a time like this, either," she said, and meant it.

Though she turned around to face him, she didn't return to the chair. She felt no embarrassment, even though a married woman should only see such sights on her husband. She dabbed at Sir B's dripping face with the end of the sheet, wiping down to his neck. While she patted him as gently as she could, his breathing slowed even more and he slept.

He woke up only a few minutes later. "Now, where was I?" he asked, his eyes still closed. Meridee laughed, relieved that he could joke.

She took his hand and he opened his eyes, or tried to. Finally he gave up the effort and settled for half-open and a lazy, dreamy expression. "Have you ever met anyone with such ragged manners?" he asked.

"No, not actually," she teased gently. "Sir B, I have to ask. What just happened? Why this? Did it not heal?"

"It healed, except that every now and then, my vanished leg feels as though it is still attached, mangled to bloody bits, and hanging on by mere tradition, habit, and great force of will. It's as though I feel every screaming nerve."

"My goodness," she said, and put her other hand on his. He returned her squeeze with one of his own. "How you must loathe and despise the French!"

He shrugged. "We are at war. The difficulty comes in the realization that war plays no favorites. Neither fame, fortune, rank, or a title exempts a man from carnage. My regret is that the ball didn't strike me lower. If I still had a knee, Mrs. Perry's husband could have whittled me a peg leg. I could still be on a quarterdeck." He patted her hand in turn. "That is my regret."

She hadn't intended to cry, but there she sat, shoulders shaking, tears on her cheeks, trying not to make a spectacle of herself and failing.

"No, no, Mrs. Six. Save your tears," he said. "This is a risk we all run."

She took a handkerchief from her reticule and blew her nose vigorously. The situation demanded a massive change of subject, and she was equal to it. "Sir B, can I interest you in a rout cake? Mrs. Perry is the most amazing cook."

"I believe you can," he said, and raised himself up on one elbow, looking about with interest. "I'll warn you now: I like the sugary sides best."

"This is most fortuitous, because I prefer the lemon icing," she said. "Now where …."

The pasteboard box rested on its side by the door, where she must have flung it when she ran into the room like a crazy woman. She stared down at the ruin of perfect little cakes. "I meant well," she said, picking them up.

"What's a bit of a jostle?" the captain said. "Bring them over here."

He *did* prefer the sugary ones. As if on cue, the butler brought in tea and left it to her to pour. The niceties of even modest society were not lost on Meridee as she poured for a man lying there in his nightshirt. Her mother would have been aghast, but these were no ordinary times.

"Captain St. Anthony, what have I gotten myself into?" she asked, only slightly in jest. "Stephen has already tried to run away. I am uncertain what to do there. Nick wants a last name; I just know it. Davey Ten practically salivates over disgusting rat bones. And John Mark barely speaks. There is a black woman from some African country ruling my kitchen," she laughed, "and I already cannot manage without her."

"How is Durable Six coping in the uncharted sea of matrimony?" he asked, waving away another rout cake, then changing his mind. "Good God, these are delicious."

"He seems to take it all in stride, and he is wonderfully good to me," she said frankly. "He insists I learn how to swim, too, in that abominable stone basin."

"You will do quite well, because he can teach anything or anyone. Is there some tea left?"

She poured him a half cup. "No advice for me?" she asked. "I hate to sound pathetic, but there you are."

Sir B drank his tea and returned the cup to her. With only a small expression of discomfort, he tucked his hands behind his head. "Your real task is to tend this extraordinary chap. We—Headmaster Croker and I— saw a need for a housemother for some of the newest lads, and presto! You materialized alongside our genius. I call that serendipity. You seem capable of both tasks."

"I call it a flagrant abuse of power," Meridee teased, grateful when the man laughed, he who had so recently screamed in pain. She couldn't help herself then, because she was Meridee Six and amazingly in love. "Able is no burden to me. Quite the contrary."

"There now. I knew two old bachelors such as Croker and I could not be wrong," he told her. "You can thank me later. People of Able's rare ability are different. I had never met such a person before Master Six. *He* didn't even know what he was, but I daresay he is reconciled to the reality by now."

"How did you meet?"

"He was just one of several new able seamen who came aboard when I captained the *Dissuade*." Sir B's eyes grew dreamy. "She was the sweetest frigate."

"You and Able speak of ships as though they are living, breathing entities," she said.

"I suppose they are to us. Where was I? Able. Every task the bosun gave him, he learned instantly, but the sailing master brought him to my attention first. 'Watch his eyes, Captain,' said he. I did. Seaman Six was supposed to be scrubbing the deck while the master taught the midshipmen the care and feeding of a sextant."

Meridee laughed at that. "I watched his eyes scan the bookshelves in my brother-in-law's study. I've never seen anything like it."

"Then you know. I positioned myself close by and spied out of the corner of my eye as Able scrubbed away, a dutiful lad. When he thought no one was watching, he sort of popped his head up for mere seconds and seemed to simply *absorb* everything on the blackboard that the master had propped against the mast." He reached for the final rout cake. "My stars, Mrs. Six, did you eat *all* those cakes?"

"You know I did not," she scolded.

"When the master dismissed his *real* pupils, I collared Able Six. Scared him! I ordered him to stand by the mast, handed him the sextant, and told him to tell me the ship's position. I've never seen it done so fast and correctly, and all in his head. So it began, and here we are now."

"Able can't arrange a neck cloth to save his soul," Meridee said softly. "I've noticed that he sometimes puts his shoelaces in the wrong holes. How strange is genius."

"That is why I asked you here, Mrs. Six," the captain said most formally. "I want to warn you."

"Warn *me*? Warn me about what?"

"There is a darker side to his brilliance, one I hardly can explain," he began, seeming to pick and choose his words with inordinate care.

"Don't mince words with me, Sir B," she said quietly. "I have some questions, myself."

"I know Ben Hallowell told you about the time Able stepped in for the surgeon and saved his nephew's life."

She nodded.

"There was an earlier time aboard the *Dissuade* when a similar incident occurred," Sir B said. "Some water, please."

She poured him a glass from the bedside carafe and put her arm under his neck as he drank.

"Thank you, my dear. We were under fire, and in this instance, my surgeon panicked. He ran on deck and threw himself overboard."

Meridee gasped and he took her hands.

"I cannot describe war to you, other than to say it is the supreme equalizer. No man knows what he will do in his particular realm. The surgeon was new and untried. The pharmacist's mate was a solid fellow and he worked steadily. When matters righted themselves and we sank the Spanish ship, I ran down to the orlop deck to see for myself what my men had been telling me."

"Able was operating," Meridee said.

"Aye, he was. I think he was fifteen, if that. For hours he worked alongside the mate, amputating and stitching. I marveled at the intensity of his concentration. He didn't make a single wrong move, and men are alive today because of his work. However ...."

He brought her hand to his lips and kissed it. "Meridee, when the entire ordeal was over, I feared he was going to do himself damage." He sighed, remembering. "He shook like a leaf for hours. I seriously thought he was going to die."

Meridee didn't try to stop the tears that ran down her face, met under her chin, and dropped onto Sir B's coverlet. It was his turn to dab at her face, and he did it so gently.

"It was then that I realized the price of genius. At least in Able's case, it seems to allow no leisure, no relief from mental exhaustion." He looked away, as if thinking over what he wanted to say, then faced her again, not a man to flinch from a hard subject, apparently. She knew what he was going to say before he said it, and nearly stopped him.

"Your—what shall I say?—your personal comfort provides him some relief," the captain said, and it was his turn to blush. "Look at us. A pair of red faces! Seriously, Meridee, you are a blessing."

They were both silent. She hesitated to speak, then took a page from the captain's book. "Even w-when we are together in bed, sometimes I hear him murmuring Euclid's *Propositions*. It's as though he has many conversations going on inside his prodigious brain."

"Poor you," Sir B said, "sharing your bed with Euclid."

Expressed aloud, the idea was absurd and made her smile. "Truly, Euclid doesn't take up much space."

The captain stared at her then burst into laughter. "Meridee, you're a wit!" he exclaimed, when he could speak.

"Since you are plagued with geometry in your marriage bed, let me throw in physics," the irrepressible captain said. "What holds up an arch? Hand me that tablet."

She did as he directed, including a pencil, from his nightstand. He drew an arch.

"It's stress, isn't it?" she said, after a thoughtful perusal. "One force pushing against another."

"Most certainly. The stress of that awful afternoon and evening in the sickbay kept your man going. When it ended, he collapsed. The stress was gone." He sighed heavily. "This is what I fear for Able Six."

Silence again, with just the tick of the clock on the nightstand. "I will watch him closely," Meridee said, and then sucked in her breath. "He won't even see this coming, will he?"

"Unlikely. I think he has a blind spot that prevents him from evaluating certain events or emotions. We can blame that on the workhouse, too. I can only imagine what it must feel like to be unwanted."

"He's wanted now," Meridee said quietly. "I want him. You want him. The school wants him. The Royal Navy wants him." She couldn't help herself as her voice rose higher and higher. "Sir B, will it prove too much?"

"Who can say?" he asked in turn, holding out his arms as she fell into them, weeping.

He patted her back until she sat up, appalled at her rag manners. "Meridee, don't worry about propriety," he soothed. "We are living in difficult times and we are adults."

Meridee blew her nose on the handkerchief Sir B had at the ready. "What can I do?"

"Watch him closely. There isn't much time before either we or the French will break this Treaty of Amiens," he said. "Some of his lads will be ordered to warships."

Meridee knew what he was going to say. "Some might die."

"It is inevitable," he replied. "We at St. Brendan's will feel the full measure of devastation, but no one will feel it more than your good man."

"Why is this his burden?" Meridee demanded to know.

"Because if you peel away the sheer genius, talent, and charm of your remarkable husband, he still has his humanity."

"Not even the workhouse could destroy that, but it tried," she said. "I worry."

"You're not alone in your fears," Sir B assured her.

Chapter Twenty-Seven

❧

CAPTAIN SIR BELVEDERE ST. Anthony insisted upon sending her home in his own carriage, her protests notwithstanding.

"If you need me to sit with you again, only ask," she said quietly.

"What will I do if your outraged husband calls me out and challenges me to a duel?" he teased.

"For heaven's sake! I doubt either of you know anything about dueling," she declared, wondering if she was destined to be the only practical human in Portsmouth. "I will visit you whether you ask for my company or not." No sense in making a proud man pawn his dignity. She kept it light. "My mother warned me about sailors. I didn't listen. Good day."

It eased her heart to walk down the stairs followed by the sound of laughter, rather than the screams of pain that had propelled her up them hours earlier.

Since it did no good to protest Sir B's kindness in sending her home in a carriage with a crest on the door, Meridee leaned back, wishing she could enjoy the drive through the gentrified side of Portsmouth, where captains and admirals lived. Instead, she worried, arguing with herself about her ability to be and do what her amazing husband needed.

Sir B, you seem to think I can manage four troubled boys and one genius, she thought. As the carriage returned her to the less genteel part of Pompey, she fought back a sudden urge to demand that John Coachman take her back to the vicarage in Devon, instead of to her house on Saint's Way. They had received a brief note yesterday from her brother-in-law, announcing that Amanda had been brought to bed with another daughter. Meridee had assured Able it wasn't necessary for her to return now to visit, but as she rode home, she suddenly wanted to run away from the trouble she sensed was coming. She could call it a visit to a beloved sister and her newest niece, but Meridee knew better.

The terrible moment passed and she saw the absurdity of her childish plea. "Grow up, Meridee," she said out loud. "Grow up. Others need you more."

She waved goodbye to the coachman from the top of her steps and let herself into the house. An appreciative whiff told her that Mrs. Perry's pease porridge was ready. She followed her nose down the hall to the kitchen, where two boys, heads together, leaned over a table and stared at tiny bones. Mrs. Perry loomed over them both, a hand on each shoulder. Meridee smiled to watch Davey Ten leaning into the African cook the same way he leaned into her.

She hung her bonnet on a convenient nail and came closer. Nick made room for her.

"Mrs. Six, what do you think?" he asked, and she heard all his enthusiasm.

A rat it will ever be to me, she thought. "I think it is marvelous, they way you are laying him out." There. That was ambiguous enough.

"Master Six copied the skeleton on this paper," Davey offered. "Said he saw it in an anatomy book once. How does he do that?"

"He just does, Davey," she said. "You can be certain it is correct."

Mrs. Perry must have found a piece of black fabric from somewhere. "It's a side view," Davey explained. "Some of the tiny leg bones are missing, so Mrs. Perry said we should just show half the rat."

"That way, we have enough parts," Nick added. "Mrs. Perry has some carpenter's glue, so here we are."

"You would think Mrs. Perry dealt in rat bones every day," Meridee said.

She heard her cook's rumbling laugh. "I even found this wonderful board to mount it on. Nick says John Mark has the best hand to write 'St. Brendan's Wharf Rats' across the top."

"And John Mark and Stephen Hoyt?" Meridee asked her cook.

"In the dining room, studying. It seems their instructor, who will remain nameless, mentioned something about potential greatness for lads who know their numbers. Dinner's at six, Mrs. Six."

Meridee went into the dining room, where John Mark, elbows on the table, chin in hands, applied himself to fractions. Stephen stood at the window, rocking back and forth on his heels. Nodding to John, she went to the window and stood beside him. To touch him or not to touch him? She rested her hand lightly on his shoulder and took it away when he flinched.

"What do you think of the rat?" she asked.

He was silent. She looked at his face and saw his tears. Wordless, she handed him the still-damp handkerchief she kept up her sleeve. He wiped his eyes and continued staring out the window at something she could not see.

"Will you talk to me sometime?" Meridee asked. "I want to know how I can help you."

"No one's ever helped me," he whispered.

"Then it's time someone did," she whispered back.

Meridee made her way next to the sitting room, where she thought she might find the master. He sat in a wing-backed chair, long legs out in front of him, head back, eyes closed. He wasn't asleep because his eyes moved behind their lids. No doubt he saw something no one else did. With a small sigh, she knew whatever raced through her husband's brain was oceans kinder than what Stephen Hoyt saw. All she saw when she looked out the window was the street below and the backyard.

"My darling," she said, and Able opened his eyes and held out his arms. She slipped onto his lap and into his embrace, her head against his chest.

"Isn't this where a good wife asks her husband how his day went?" Meri asked.

"I suppose it is, whereupon that good husband replies, 'My dear, you would be amazed how rapidly these lads are taking to fractions.' "

"I have no skill whatsoever with fractions," Meridee admitted.

"I never required it from you," the good husband said. "And my calculus students: yesterday I asked them to imagine something useful of a mechanical nature that we need."

"And ...?"

"Jan Yarmouth wants to land a man on the moon, which led to an animated introduction—mine—to Newton's various and sundry laws. Jamie MacGregor wants something to transmit information from place to place using Benjamin Franklin's electricity." He kissed her cheek. "Meri, such students! I have been sitting here imagining travel through space and instant messages, and then you sit on my lap. I am in transports of delight."

"Knothead," she said with feeling.

"You've been all this time with Sir B?" he asked. "He was adamant a few days ago that you visit. I trust you found him well enough."

She shook her head, and he tightened his grip. "Able, he was in dire pain. None of his servants were brave enough to do what he wanted, so I—"

"You marched in there and helped him," he said, a statement of fact. He couldn't help himself then. "I doubt you gave him a black eye."

"Wretched man," she murmured. "Am I never to live down one weak moment when I could not suffer one more twang to my nerves?"

"Probably not. We all enjoy a good story, especially when the protagonist looks so lovely and incapable of violence." He turned serious. "It was his leg, wasn't it?"

"He was in mortal agony from pain that ... that ... I can't explain it. A ghost pain from a mangled leg no longer there."

"I've seen this, even in amputations not as grievous as his. What did he ask of you?"

"That I hold his leg and squeeze it," she told him. "I was embarrassed at first, but it did give him some relief." She rested her forehead against his chest. "When he felt better, Mrs. Perry's rout cakes worked their wonder."

He spoke into her hair. "What did he really want with you?"

"He wanted me to take good care of you, especially after the treaty ends and some of the boys must go to sea," she said in a rush.

"And serve and run the risk of death at sea," he finished, agitation in his voice. "Meri, I came so close to not accepting this position for that very reason. It's one thing to risk my own life, but quite another to train lads for war. And these lads! They've known suffering enough already."

"He fears for your peace of mind, and I am to watch you closely," she said, preferring frankness to a dodge. She rested her head against his chest, took a good whiff of his shirt, and sat up.

"Where have you been, Durable Six?" she demanded.

He laughed, but she saw little humor in his eyes. "This is where the good husband says, 'Why, tender Meri, whatever are you referring to?'"

"You are still a knothead." She sniffed his shirt again. "I know you don't smoke."

He glanced at the clock. "I'd better make this fast, or Mrs. Perry will give us what for. Get comfortable."

That was simple. She put her hand inside his smoky shirt, and he pulled her close.

"I told you that Master Fletcher wanted me to tip a glass with him at the Bare Bones," he began with no preamble—not that any well-bred words she knew could ever dress up *that* stinky pig.

"And you succumbed," she said.

"I did, and it was disturbing," he replied. "Well, not the grog. I came back here first and dug through my duffel until I found sailor's trousers. Where did you put that shirt you want to burn?"

"I burned it," she said, which made him chuckle.

"Which is why this new one smells. I didn't want to run into a drunk who dislikes sailing masters, now, did I?"

"You're much too smart for that," she agreed. "Very well, you're dressed rough like a sailor and …."

"We found a quiet table and Master Fletcher shouted for the grog," Able said. "I must admit it tasted fine and took me back a few years."

"I gather you have been to the Bare Bones a time or two when you were young and impressionable and in port?" Meridee teased.

"Indeed I have. Didn't lose my virginity there, though."

She punched his chest and he laughed. "I saved that for Spain. Ow! Meri, you know I didn't come to you a saint."

"Oh, be quiet and tell your story," she said, wondering what all her sisters would make of such a conversation. Better they never knew.

He gave her a little shake, then tightened his grip on her. "I wondered why Fletcher asked me there, and then I saw him."

"Who?"

"Master Blake, of all people. He sat across the room from us, talking with a true hard case. Blake was dressed pretty rough, too, and he didn't see us, thank God. I asked Master Fletcher what in hell was going on and who was that man?"

He stopped and stroked her cheek, as if seeking immediate comfort, and Meridee thought of Captain St. Anthony's worries about her husband. "You can tell me anything, Able," she whispered into his neck.

He nodded. "Master Fletcher said he didn't know why Blake was there, but he had heard scuttlebutt that Blake had been 'sentenced,' if you will, to St. Brendan's for gambling debts."

"Then who was the other man?" she asked.

"My very question to Fletcher," Able said. "All he knew was he thought the fellow was an ugly customer who—I should cover your ears—is a well-known pimp."

"I don't even know what that is," she said. He whispered in her ear and Meridee gasped.

"I still don't understand," she said, her face flaming. "Master *Blake*?"

"I don't either," Able said. "I came back here, but Master Fletcher said he was going to wait a bit and see if he could follow Blake when he left." He spread out his hands. "That's all I know."

"Should you ... should you say something to Headmaster Croker?" she asked, as she heard the bell for dinner ring. Mrs. Perry had given that prized task to the boys, and whoever had the duty today was ringing for all he was worth.

"Our summons," Able said. "I don't know what I would tell Thaddeus yet. I'll wait and see what Master Fletcher learns. I admit to some confusion."

"That's a rare confession for you," Meridee said.

"I don't much like it," he replied. "Let's go to dinner before one of our lodgers wears out that bell."

They did what they had done the night before, Meridee beginning with ordinary conversation and an additional reminder for Master Six to get a haircut, which made serious John Mark giggle this time. To her distress and Able's, Nick told her that Master Blake nearly beat one of the boys because he could not recall who ruled England when the Magna Carta was signed. Fortunately, the schoolmaster changed his mind.

"Who was the ruler?" Able asked.

"King John, and he wasn't a good'un," Davey said, then turned to Stephen. "Please pass the bread."

A discussion of English kings followed the boiled potatoes, with no consensus reached on the current trials of poor George the Third. The rout cakes satisfied everyone, and Nick yawned out loud, to his embarrassment. Meridee helped the boys and Mrs. Perry in the kitchen, leaving Able to stand by the window, staring out at the rain sluicing the panes and probably thinking about Master Blake and a pimp. Meridee wondered at her own odd education.

God bless Mrs. Perry. When the chores were done and Nick and John both yawned, the cook handed each student two rout cakes bundled into a square of cloth, saying, in an offhand manner, "In case you need something in the middle of the night."

Able watched his students troop upstairs, cakes in hand. Meridee nudged him. "Do you need a little something if you wake up at night?" she teased.

"I have a little something, name of Meri Six," he teased back, and she blushed.

The newly established bedtime ritual followed. Indeed, from the way they sat up so expectantly in their beds, Davey Ten and Nick were waiting for her. Sitting on each bed, she wished them goodnight, then tucked the blankets about them when they slid down. She debated a moment, then kissed each forehead.

Stephen Hoyt was already lying down, his blankets high and his body turned toward the window. *Oh, no you don't,* Meridee thought. She touched his shoulder and wished him goodnight anyway.

John Mark had a smile for her. "Is this what real people do when they go to bed?" he asked as she tucked him in.

"I believe it is," she said. "See you in the morning."

Her bed had never looked better, especially with Able lying in it, flipping rapidly through what looked like Greek writing. All she wanted was to curl into a little ball and wish away, if only for a brief time, what she had learned today. She knew her burden would come crashing back in the morning.

But what was that? Able tossed aside his book, listening intently.

She heard it, too, someone banging on the door, and, "Please help us!"

Meridee moved aside as Able leaped out of bed. He darted into their dressing room and came out with a knife. "Don't leave this floor."

Meridee threw on her robe and ran into the hall, determined to keep whatever ill fortune this was between her and the boys' rooms. She listened, and held her breath when she heard the front door creak open. Voices and then, "Meri, come down here, handsomely now. No fears."

She ran down the stairs, and stood still in surprise to see Jamie MacGregor, his hair wet and plastered to his head, his face set and frightened at the same time.

His arm was tight around a girl equally wet, and shivering visibly, even from a distance. Jamie looked to Able, and Meridee saw all the pleading, along with that ineffable dignity of the workhouse child that Meridee had first noticed in her husband.

"Master Six, help me! We don't know where to turn except to you."

"Come," he ordered in that voice of command Meridee seldom heard in their home. "We'll sort it out, won't we, Meri?"

"I expect we will," she said. "Come inside. Close the door."

Chapter Twenty-Eight

⚮

A BLE KNEW MERI WOULD never fail him. If he had a watch with a second hand, something he never needed, he would have given his wife four seconds to know what to do. She bettered his estimation by two seconds and held out her arms.

"My dears, come here," she said. "My word, are you twins?"

Jamie nodded. With the barest glance at Able, he gave his sister a little push into Meri's open arms. She grabbed the girl, who began to sob, and held out her arms again for Jamie, too.

He watched the three of them, knowing without seeing her face that Meri was in tears. She turned to look at him, and damned if he didn't feel tears coming on too. Standing there, seeing this reunion of desperate children, he knew he would have given the earth for a sibling.

"Ma'am, I have lice," said the girl, pulling away. "Maybe you shouldn't ...."

Any sane woman would have leaped back. The unexpected reunion must have unhinged his wife, who pulled her close again. "I have a fine-toothed comb, and it works well. Don't you worry," Meri said.

Jamie was made of sterner stuff, but Able already knew that. "Let's be kind to the good lady," he said as he gently pulled his sister away. He kept his arm around her, obviously unconcerned for himself about wee beasties.

"Some introductions, Mr. MacGregor," Able ordered.

The girl stared from Able to her brother. "Jamie," she whispered, "he called you *mister*."

"Master Six does that all the time," Jamie said. "He says that if you want to be treated as a person of worth, you have to act like one."

"This is my twin sister, Betty MacGregor," Jamie told them. "Miss Betty MacGregor."

He sent a silent plea toward Able, reminding the sailing master that the workhouse would always loom in the background. He wished he could assure Jamie that eventually he would forget all the misery of the place, but he couldn't.

"Master, please don't be angry."

"That your sister found you? I couldn't be more delighted."

Meridee seemed to have regained her sanity, and probably not a moment too soon, because Mrs. Perry opened her door and glowered at all of them. "What in the world is going on?" she asked, evidently not a woman who thrived on commotion.

"Only the best thing you can imagine, Mrs. Perry," Meridee said, which made Able wonder if the redoubtable cook realized how firmly she was wrapped around his wife's little finger. "Consider this: Jamie MacGregor has found his twin sister."

"I trust she's not in trouble with a magistrate," Mrs. Perry said, injecting a note of reason.

The girl shook her head, but the fear returned to her eyes. "I couldn't stay at the workhouse," she said. More tears made tracks down her dirty face.

"It will keep until we get you washed and dressed, and put some food in your stomach," Meridee said firmly. "Mrs. Perry, you organize a bath, and I will fetch one of my nightgowns and some pine tar soap. Able, you and Jamie may retire to the sitting room."

After pointing Jamie toward a comfortable chair and advising him to add some coal to the grate, Able followed his wife upstairs. He found her in their dressing room, pulling out a clean but faded dress and a petticoat. A nightgown came next. He knew she had plenty of those, most of them unworn lately. He put his arms around her.

"I have the distinct impression that you just found your maid of all work," he said. He gave her a smack on the rump and walked downstairs, hand in hand with her.

"That may follow, Master Six," she said, and waved him off to the sitting room. "Sort out this matter with Mr. MacGregor."

He could have told her why Betty MacGregor had probably run away, but he hadn't the heart; Meri would learn soon enough. Under Betty's grime and fear, he saw a pretty lass with red hair like Jamie's and the same snapping green eyes. He remembered other young girls from Dumfries Workhouse, shy and winsome in their Celtic way, who turned wan and listless after reaching a certain age. Able trusted that someday there would be a fearful reckoning for evil men who preyed on the defenseless and ruined all hope.

Jamie sat in the chair closest to the fireplace, staring down at his hands. He got to his feet at once.

"Master, I didn't know what to do, except bring Betty here," he said.

"You did right," Able said, happy to reassure his calculus student. "You are both from the Carlisle Workhouse, eh?"

"Aye, sir. Me mam and da drifted south from Glasgow for work, couldn't find any, and left us in Carlisle." He lowered his gaze and Able felt the boy's shame. "Said they'd return for us, but that was six years ago."

Able thought again that he had an easier time of it because he never had a single expectation of family. In his lively mind's eye, he saw two little children waiting, their faces pressed to a barred window.

"Why did Betty run away?" he asked gently. "Or can I guess?"

Old eyes looked into Able's equally old eyes. "You can guess, sir. She said the teacher started hanging around the girls' dormitory. Claimed he was looking for stolen goods, but he was sniffing out the lassies."

"Damn him. Too bad we cannot flog such men around the fleet."

Jamie nodded. "He trapped Betty in a closet and she bit him, which meant he howled to the workhouse master, who put her in the Hole." He looked up. "Sir, did you have a Hole in your workhouse?"

"Aye, lad. After two beatings for the same offense, down we went. Shared it with *rattus norvegicus*."

That brought a slight smile to Jamie's face that vanished quickly. "Ours had rats, too." He leaned back, thought better of it, and straightened up.

"Go ahead and relax, laddie," Able said. "I'm sitting here in my nightshirt, advertising my hairy legs, so I don't think we're standing on much ceremony."

James leaned back and sighed. Able heard all the unhappiness in that small sound.

"She got lucky, did Betty. The grating was loose and she wiggled out." Again that sigh. "She started walking south to Portsmouth in November. From Carlisle! She knew I was at Saint Something in Portsmouth and that was all. Not a penny to her name. Walking and hiding and walking."

Able nodded at that bit of news, knowing that if Meri were to come into the room and hear the discussion of twelve-year-old Betty running away without a copper and probably no cloak, she would burst into tears. *Meri, you have no idea how resourceful we workhouse rats truly are*, he thought, and felt an odd sort of pride she never would have understood.

"I came south in a potato cart," Able said. "Took me a few years before I wanted another potato in any form."

"Betty stole food. Said her best night's work was in a village where the residents left puddings on their doorsteps for Father Christmas. She hid in barns. Probably what you did, Master Six."

"Aye, except I wasn't smart enough to run away at Christmas," Able joked.

"Needs must, when the Devil drives, sir," Jamie quoted. "I, um, imagine you were the smartest runaway in England, even at nine years old."

"I managed, same as your sister did," Able replied, amused at such an odd conversation. Meridee wouldn't know what to make of it. He applied himself for a few seconds to the problem, then asked, "Does anyone know she is here besides us?"

Jamie made a face. "Of all people, Master Blake found her trying to eat out of the kitchen ash cans. He grabbed her and tried to drag her to … to Master Croker, I suppose, after she kicked him good and gave him what for." He looked down at his hands again. "He called after her and said something strange."

"Which was …."

" 'I can help you find a good place with food. Trust me.' " Jamie gave a snort of derision. "Hah! As if old Blake would ever help any of us, think on."

Able's mind plunked him right back in the Bare Bones, where all over again he saw Master Blake whispering with a pimp. He knew it was physically impossible, but his blood seemed to run in chunks. He forced himself to listen to the boy.

"She gave him a kick for his pains and he changed his tune pretty fast," Jamie said grimly. "He grabbed his leg and said he was summoning the watch."

"That's unfortunate," Able said.

"She ran inside screaming my name and I heard her." He didn't try to stop his tears. "I didn't want to leave her alone in the Carlisle Workhouse, but she insisted I go to St. Brendan's and make my fortune." He sobbed into his hands. "Was I wrong?"

Able knelt by his chair, his hand on Jamie's back, wishing for Meridee to magically materialize and supply her special comfort. He reached toward the pocket where he carried a handkerchief, then remembered he was still in his nightshirt.

"Nay, lad, you were not wrong," Able said. "Sounds as though Betty knew it."

"She's all I have, sir," the boy said as he sniffed back more tears and tried to compose himself. "Sorry, sir."

"No need to apologize to me, of all persons," Able told him. "We workhouse scum don't survive by hanging back. You didn't, and from what I see now, she didn't either."

It sounded feeble to Able's ears, but Jamie looked up. He pulled out his shirttails and wiped his nose. "Sorry, sir."

"I'll find you a handkerchief. I'm remarkably ill-equipped at the moment."

"I'd rather you let me see Betty, sir," he said quietly.

"Wait here. I'll consult with the ladies."

He knocked on the kitchen door, which Meridee opened. "She's washed and I'm combing her hair while Mrs. Perry warms up the pease porridge,"

Meridee said. Able saw all the compassion on her face. "Betty is so frightened. Could you bring in Jamie MacGregor?"

"He's feeling the need, too. I'll be right back."

Telling Jamie to wait a moment more, Able ran upstairs, threw on his clothes and found a handkerchief. He commanded Jamie to make a hearty blow, and then shepherded the boy to the kitchen, where Betty, clean now, her hair wet, pulled him close with a sob.

He looked down when he felt Meri's hand in his. "I'll wager you didn't suspect this might be part of our wedding vows: 'Thou shalt render aid at all hours,' " he whispered.

Her grin told him more about the woman he thought he already knew inside and out. He clapped his arm around her shoulder, bumped her hip with his, and told her she ought to get dressed. He expected a visit from the magistrate at any moment, Mr. Blake being a heartless man. Whatever else he wanted to say about Blake could keep.

While Meridee hurried upstairs, Mrs. Perry sat Betty down in front of that evening's warmed-up pease pudding. Betty stared at the bowl, and her lips started to quiver.

God bless Mrs. Perry. The cook gave the child's shoulder a little shake and a pat, which seemed to give Betty permission to nearly fall on the food, shoveling down the thick stew as if it were her last meal on earth. As the level dropped in the bowl, Betty turned anxious eyes toward the stove. Mrs. Perry ladled in more food until Betty sat back, full for perhaps the first time in her life.

With a shy smile, she took the bread Mrs. Perry handed her, stared at the butter in amazement, and wiped the bowl clean.

Meridee came into the kitchen then, neat as a pin as usual, except that she hadn't bothered to tie back her hair, which fell prettily past her shoulders. She held out a shawl to Betty, then draped it around her. "I don't need two," she said.

Betty tried to shrink into her chair at a knock that sounded like a peremptory summons. Jamie stepped in front of her, feet planted firmly.

"I'd better let him in," Able said. "In fact, Jamie and Betty, let's adjourn to the sitting room. Meridee, you and Mrs. Perry remain here."

He led the twins into the sitting room, but Meridee wouldn't stay in the kitchen. She took his hand. "Master Six, this is my house, too."

"This might not be a pleasant interview," he warned her.

"We're in this together."

Chapter Twenty-Nine

❧

MERI'S HAND IN HIS, as if they always welcomed visitors at midnight, Able opened the door on a sour-looking fellow who had likely been ordered to leave the warmth of the magistrate's office near Landport Gate to sort out some nonsense involving a runaway.

"I have a complaint from Master Leonidas Blake of St. Brendan the Navigator School," he said, holding out a document. "A runaway snooping around ash cans in the alley. Why this couldn't wait until morning I could not tell you, but the man insisted. Vehemently."

"Please come in," Able said. "We've gathered in the sitting room, and you are welcome to join us there. Meri, could you ask our cook to provide Mister … Mister …."

"Walter Cornwall. Now look here, I don't need—"

"—Mister Cornwall with something to warm him?"

"We have tea, but I think such a cold night demands something a little more rigorous," Meridee said, just as Mrs. Perry barreled out of the kitchen.

Mrs. Perry's glower bordered on a snarl that made the magistrate take an involuntary step back. Meri and Mrs. Perry returned to the kitchen while Able led a more subdued Walter Cornwall into his sitting room. Cornwall looked over his shoulder, which made Able silently cheer Mrs. Perry's ability to terrify bullies.

Eyes determined, the twins sat close together. Betty shook visibly, no matter how tight her brother's arm around her shoulder. Able wished he could tell the terrified girl that she was never going to fight another battle alone, not with her brother there, and what Able already knew was a formidable pair in the kitchen.

And one person more. Without knocking, Headmaster Croker strode in, dressed in his black academic robes. His impressive rig-out included a stunning gold collar around his neck bearing a pendant of St. Brendan, whose enamel glower almost equaled Mrs. Perry's. Able had to bite the inside of his lip to keep from laughing. All the scene lacked was Captain Sir Belvedere St. Anthony to demand entrance.

Good God, he had underestimated the headmaster, who stood back deferentially while Sir B rolled in, clad in *his* best uniform, complete with the distinctive star signifying the wearer as a Knight Commander of the Order of the Bath.

With what he personally considered masterful aplomb, considering how much he wanted to laugh until he hurt himself, Able ushered the two men into his sitting room. Sir B's valet pushed the chair close to the fireplace. Headmaster Croker sat beside the twins, who stared, mouths open, eyes wide.

"Gentlemen, what a delight to have you in my sitting room," Able said. His wish that Meridee would quickly materialize to help weave him through this labyrinth was answered. He felt a soft hand against his back and then her arm twined through his.

"What an honor, gentlemen," she said. "Make yourselves at home." She turned kindly eyes on the constable. "Mr. Cornwall, Mrs. Perry has a fine mug of grog that should keep you warm, once you resume your … your … beat, is it called?"

The stunned man nodded and took the tankard from Mrs. Perry. Cornwall drank his grog in what sounded like one gulp. He set the tankard on the end table, which made Mrs. Perry mutter something about rings on good furniture. Snatching up the offending mug, he moved it from hand to hand until Mrs. Perry relieved him of it and stomped out of the room.

"Mr. Cornwall, what business have you with St. Brendan's?" Captain Sir Belvedere St. Anthony said. His timing was exquisite and well-remembered by Able, who had watched Sir B haul a seaman up short on the deck and threaten him with what sounded like kindness at first, until it modulated into menace. He began to feel sorry for Walter Cornwall, and for Master Blake, too, even though he was nowhere in sight, thank the Lord. Able didn't think his sitting room large enough for one more bully.

And here came the lodgers, clad in their nightshirts. Led by the redoubtable Nick, they found a space along one wall and sat there, interested.

"Lads, you needn't be here," Able said.

Nick stood up. "Master, we considered the issue and decided you might need our support. Mates stick together, as you have told us," he said, in a voice that oozed leadership. He ruined the effect with a grin. "Besides which, this looks more interesting than sleeping."

Meridee chuckled at that artless rejoinder. "I agree," she said. She gave Able her sweetest smile. "Please let them stay, dearest."

His face warm, Able glanced at Sir B, who was trying to suppress his smile. Headmaster Croker didn't even try. He gave Mrs. Six a courtly bow. "I hope Dearest listens to you."

"He does now and then," Able's incorrigible wife replied.

Sir B cleared his throat. An ordinary mortal doing that would attract little attention, but Able knew his former captain had taken the art of throat clearing to its highest level. Silence reigned.

"Constable, Master Blake's threats aside, what reason do you have in coming here to disrupt this man's household?" Sir B asked.

Looking more than a little dazed, Cornwall pulled himself together. He pointed his cudgel at Betty MacGregor, who tried to burrow into the sofa cushions to hide herself. "Master Blake said she was nosing around the ash cans across the street at *your* school, Master Croker."

"She might be hungry," the headmaster said mildly.

"Sir, all due respects to you, but we get regular warnings to look out for runaways from workhouses," Cornwall replied, his voice less menacing. He lowered his cudgel and looked at it, as if wondering who it belonged to.

"Mr. Cornwall, may I ease your mind? The terms of my recent contract at this fine institution plainly state I am promised a maid of all work," Able said. "We intend to hire Betty MacGregor, who is the twin of one of my more promising students. I trust we may follow through on that lawful contract."

"I dunno," Cornwall said. "Where'd you come from, missy? You still look like a runaway to me."

God bless his wife. Meridee sat next to Betty, who inched slowly away from the sofa cushions. She stroked the girl's cheek, a gesture Able personally knew to be most satisfactory, in his case, in soothing his overactive brain.

"Betty, you'll have a room of your own, plenty to eat, and good wages," Meridee said.

"I still say she's a runaway," Cornwall declared, but less strenuously. He took another look at his cudgel and set it on the floor.

And God bless Jamie MacGregor, who if not the smartest pupil among the older class was certainly the shrewdest. "Mr. Cornwall, will you satisfy my curiosity about something?"

The constable grunted, which could have meant anything.

"With a name like Cornwall, did you come from a workhouse, too?" He gestured toward the wall. "Davey Ten there is the tenth bastard of the year. Nick doesn't have a last name yet." He took a deep breath. "And my calculus instructor standing by you is Master Durable Six. We seek a chance, sir. Nothing more. Possibly someone gave you a chance? Give my sister one, please."

The constable looked at the floor for a long moment. Able watched Sir

B eye Jamie, evidently impressed with the lad's courage and cleverness, two qualities essential to a successful Royal Navy career. *Well done,* he thought.

Cornwall didn't speak. As Able returned his attention to the constable, he realized that the man couldn't speak. He swallowed over and over and dabbed at his eyes. Without a word, he picked up his cudgel and quietly left the room, and moments later, the house.

Since her brother and refuge was on his feet, Betty leaned against Meridee, whose arm went around her shoulders as naturally as if she hired maids of all work at midnight all the time.

"Impressive, Mr. MacGregor. To bed now, you scamps," Able said to his lodgers.

They filed out obediently. Sir B turned his attention to the headmaster. "Master Croker, I don't think our august presence was even necessary, do you?"

"No, sir, I do not," the headmaster replied, with the smallest twitch of his lips. "It appears that Mr. MacGregor had the matter well in hand. Goodnight all."

"One thought," the captain said, as he stopped the headmaster. "What plans do you have for Master Blake? He seemed to be taking an odd interest in hungry folk nosing about the ash cans."

"I have a monumental rebuke in mind," Croker said. "Just short of termination, mind you, because teachers are hard to find. I'll put him on notice. Will that do?"

It's not enough, Able thought, as his uneasiness returned. He glanced at Meridee, whose thoughts seemed to mirror his. He opened his mouth to speak, and say what, he was not certain, but Sir B spoke first.

"A stout warning should suffice, Thaddeus," the captain said. "Goodness but the hour is late. Gervaise, roll me away, if you please."

"It is late, indeed," the headmaster said. "I'll call Blake to account tomorrow. Hopefully, that will be enough. Goodnight, my dears."

"Here we are, alone at last," Able joked when their remaining guests left. "Jamie, tell your sister goodnight and hurry back to your dormitory. She's in good hands now."

James gave his twin a quick peck on the cheek, told her not to worry, and hurried after the headmaster. Meridee tightened her arm around Betty and spoke quiet words of reassurance. In another moment, his wife and Portsmouth's newest maid of all work walked arm in arm toward the kitchen.

Able watched them go, certain Betty MacGregor had no idea that she had stumbled upon a good pasture. She would learn. He saw the boys to bed again, after they ate the remaining rout cakes and settled down.

Uneasy and wishing he could have put voice to his fears, he returned to the sitting room and took a sheet of paper from the desk. Meridee found him there a few minutes later. He relaxed at the touch of her hands as she peered over his shoulder.

"What are you doing, my love?" she asked.

"I can't forget that man's face," he said, and held up the drawing to the one remaining lamp in the room. "The man from the Bare Bones."

"He looks like the devil incarnate," Meri said, and tightened her grip on his shoulders.

"An ugly customer, to be sure," Able said. He put the sketch in the drawer. "It's a good likeness. If I see him again, I'll know him."

"You would anyway," his practical wife said, as she let him lead her upstairs.

He allowed himself to sink into the mattress and delve into the serene luxury of thinking about nothing except his wife, his students, and only a little about force and acceleration, with some Euclid on the side. When Meri came to bed with a sigh of her own, he cuddled her close, a happy man.

"How did we fare, Meri?" he asked.

She put her leg over him, which, since he was not a slow man by any means, he knew was her favorite position for sleep. "Betty will do. She's afraid of Mrs. Perry, but weren't we all?"

"Aye, miss. How do you think my esteemed colleague Master Leonidas Blake will take a well-deserved scorching? Meri …?"

Silence. Meri was such a dear to start blowing bubbles against his chest. At least she didn't snore too often.

Chapter Thirty

❦

THE CURIOUS HIRING OF Betty MacGregor felt to Meridee like an answer to a prayer and a welcome addition to the Six household. Able informed her the following day of Master Blake's monumental scold, delivered by an irate headmaster.

"Master Croker told me that our dear student beater felt supremely put upon," he told her, "when all he was doing was righteously announcing to the Portsmouth constabulary a poor girl nosing about the ash cans." He had grabbed Meridee rushing about from afternoon duties to pull her onto his lap in the sitting room.

"Sir B told me that Master Croker had instituted a policy of never turning away a beggar. Why didn't Master Blake just let her alone?" she asked.

Able grimaced. "I may be gloating about the verbal Dutch rub Thaddeus gave Master Blake, but I am still wondering what Blake's game is."

Meridee caressed his cheek. "I remember some ladies from my brother-in-law's parish who could never wait to spread rumor and innuendo about, and generally ruffle the calm waters of St. Matthews Parish." She shook her head. "There are some who seem to delight in muddying their nest."

"Calm parish waters and muddy nests?" Able joked. "Dearest, when it comes to metaphors, you don't precisely shine."

"Is this my reward for marrying such a man?" Meridee asked the ceiling, which made her husband laugh, and at least try to shake off the introspection he had fallen into.

"I feel a little sorry for Blake," he said. "If I had been tongue-lashed that way, I'd be skulking around and avoiding people."

"He deserved it."

"True, but I cannot trust a man who will sneak into a grogshop like the Bare Bones and chat with a pimp. He worries me."

Meridee hugged him, then reminded him that dinner might come faster if she wasn't cuddled on his lap.

"I'm in no hurry," he said. "I don't worry about my next meal anymore."

She had no objection to her current position, but there were others in the household to consider. "There are still five—I'm adding Betty—who do worry about that next meal."

"True. I'll sit here and think."

Always amazed at his capacity to withdraw inside his fine brain, Meridee remained in the doorway a moment. Soon his head tipped to one side and he started to breathe in a slow rhythm that wasn't sleep. She knew his eyes moved under their closed lids. He had explained to her that he saw scroll after scroll reel through his brain with writing on it, or merely numbers. He assured her it all made perfect sense.

It does if you're brilliant beyond imagining, Meridee thought.

Her husband opened his eyes and craned his neck around to see her at the door. "I'm thinking about liquids, solids, and gasses," he told her, and closed his eyes again.

"What? No Euclid? He might become jealous of liquids and gasses," she teased.

"Since you asked nicely enough, Prop. Three this time: 'Given two unequal straight lines, to cut off from the greater a straight line equal to the less.' "

She ran back to his chair and gave his head a shake. "Take that, Euclid!" she said and kissed the top of Able's head. "Now he's all mixed in with the solids and gasses."

"Meri, are you getting tired of Euclid?"

"I'd rather he stayed here in the sitting room and not in our bed." She looked around to make certain no one overheard and spoke into his ear. "You're all the lover I need."

"Aha! You prefer physics under the sheets to geometry," he exclaimed.

"If you drag in Sir Isaac Newton, you will all three be on the sofa down here," she warned. "And anyone else roaming around in your head."

He grinned, then resumed his dream-breathing, as she called it.

The atmosphere around the dinner table was almost jolly that evening. Meridee wasn't confident the boys would say anything about Master Blake's scolding, which Able had assured her was common knowledge throughout St. Brendan's. Apparently scuttlebutt traveled as fast in a maritime academy as aboard the smallest jolly boat in the fleet.

Trust forthright Nick to make the comment all of them must have felt. Still under the influence of life in a vicar's household, Meridee had instituted a nightly blessing on that evening meal. In rotation, it was Nick's turn. He clasped his hands together, looking around until everyone seemed suitably reverent.

He bowed his head. "For what Master Blake received today, may the Lord make us truly thankful, and bless the food, too. Amen."

His fellow students giggled, then cast little glances her way. Meridee knew she should give Nick what Able dubbed her fishy-eyed stare, but she didn't, especially when Able opened his eyes and usurped her own patented glare with one of his own.

"Nick, all of you, remember this: when you are in positions of power, be firm, but do not strike someone for a wrong answer or even a hesitation," he said. "And there is no need to make fun of Master Blake. He must have troubles of his own we know nothing about."

"Aye, sir," Nick replied in a small voice. His contrition lasted only a moment; the child was blooming into an everlasting optimist, despite his workhouse toil. "Master, what did *you* do when an instructor hit you?"

"I bore it because I had to, and resolved never to treat anyone that way," Able said promptly. "So should you. Mr. Hoyt, please pass the turnips."

DAME ROUTINE REIGNED SUPREME as Meridee continued to learn her duties, limits, and obligations to her household and her remarkable husband. The most pressing issue she thankfully left in the hands of her lodgers, who spent several evenings in the kitchen, grouped around the handsome wooden plaque Mrs. Perry had produced out of nowhere and which everyone dubbed the perfect place for the wharf rat's bones.

She observed how quickly Betty MacGregor had folded herself into the calm waters of the Six household. However dreadful her workhouse experience, there were no marks against her domestic abilities, and so Mrs. Perry informed Meridee.

"She's a quick one, make no mistake, and can lay a fire as well as I can," Mrs. Perry said. "Her workhouse matron knew her duties."

"Does Betty need extra food at night?" Meridee asked, as Davey Ten supervised the correct positioning of the rat's lengthy tail.

"Aye, miss," the cook said. "I remember hungry days, myself."

"You're welcome to anything from the larder too," Meridee told her, which earned her a pat on the cheek that left her feeling not much older than Betty.

Jamie MacGregor, with Headmaster Croker's permission, spent part of his evenings visiting with his twin in the kitchen. Sometimes they talked; sometimes they simply sat close together, no words needed.

"There is a telepathy between twins," Able told Meridee one evening after they sent Jamie back across the street. "Some of the early Royal Society members—they were a strange lot—experimented with twins by putting them in separate rooms and asking each to record what the other twin was thinking."

"That sounds absurd."

Able shrugged. "Seventy-eight percent of the time, they knew."

There was general rejoicing throughout the kitchen the night *rattus norvegicus*, glued to his plaque, received Nick's carefully painted title of Gunwharf Rats, in big letters. Underneath, Mrs. Perry herself had placed eyehole screws, from which hung small wooden strips bearing the names of everyone in the younger class.

"It's a masterpiece," Able agreed. "Gentlemen, take it to my classroom tomorrow." He looked closer at the plaque. "You forgot one name—mine."

To Meridee's surprise, John Mark, quiet John Mark, spoke up. "Master, you feel like a Gunwharf rat?"

"Now and then," their instructor replied. He reached for Meridee's hand and squeezed it. "Just remember to not let what happened turn you bitter."

Meridee wished the matter could have rested there, resolved, but there was no avoiding the tension she soon felt from her "boys," as she increasingly thought of them. In the weeks after Master Blake's chastisement, genuine camaraderie seemed to dribble away. She tried to get them to chat again at the dinner table, but no one had anything to say.

She took the matter to Able one night, after tucking in four boys who were now reluctant to meet her eyes. She almost hated to bother her husband. He seemed to have preoccupations of his own, having mentioned rumors to her of ships in Plymouth and Torquay being refitted for duty. Even she, no nautical observer, had noticed more ships in the Solent.

She thought of Sir B's warnings and watched him as closely as she watched her workhouse children, until she realized they were *all* masters of evasion.

Able lay in bed, frowning, a book in his lap. She was accustomed to him ruffling through pages at unimagined speed, but he just sat there. *This won't do*, Meridee thought. She took the book from his slack hands and sat on him.

He flashed her a look of real irritation, which startled her with its intensity. Putting up her hands, she said, "One moment, Able. It is I. Remember me?"

His face changed, but there was no overlooking his discomfort. "Able, please," she whispered. "What is the matter?"

"You won't understand."

"Of course I won't," she exclaimed with some spirit. "There is one thing you must never overlook: I love you to utter distraction. Tell me, please."

He gently pulled her off his stomach, tucking her close to his side. Calmly, with no emphasis, he told her about his earlier dream of staring at the Solent from Sir B's sitting room and watching it fill up with frigates and ships of the line, all under full sail for Europe.

"It's coming, Meri," he said. He turned away and couldn't look at her.

"What else, Able? Please don't shut me out."

"I looked out my classroom window today and the Solent was red," he said, his voice barely above a whisper.

She held him tight until he slept, then tried to compose herself for slumber.

It wouldn't come, so she lay next to her husband, her heart aching to help, with no knowledge of how.

She heard sobbing from the room across the hall and knew she could help someone, if not her lovely man. At Davey and Stephen's door, she listened and heard nothing. Quietly she put her ear against John Mark and Nick's door and went inside.

What she saw startled her and she gasped out loud. All four boys were cuddled close to each other on one bed, in tears.

"Dear God, whatever is the matter?" she asked as she knelt on the floor by the bed. "How can I help?"

Four tear-stained faces looked back at her. She held out her arms, felt her heart ache at their hesitation. Nick was the first to move, nearly leaping into her arms. The others followed, weeping.

Stunned, she held them close—as close as she wanted Able to hold her. *What is the matter with their world?* she asked herself as she rocked back and forth.

This would never do. She sat back and looked into Davey Ten's swollen eyes, then cupped her hands around his face.

"Tell me what is the matter," she said firmly. "I won't leave this room until you do. David Ten, you and I have knelt in the mud and the rain and picked through rat bones together. I deserve an answer."

Slowly, he nodded. He looked at the others, then back at her.

"It's Master Blake," he whispered, as though the teacher stood in the hallway listening. "If we have a wrong answer, he twists the skin on our arms and dares us to cry out."

He sobbed out loud, then took her hand and put it on his head. She felt one bump and then another. Alarmed, Meridee touched the other boys' heads and felt the same—wicked injuries no one could see.

"Roll up your sleeve, Nick," she insisted. "Do it now."

By the light of the lamp she had brought into the room, she saw cruel red marks. She touched the bruise and Nick flinched.

"We weren't supposed to say anything, we four," Stephen Hoyt whispered.

"It's just you four, my lodgers, that he is punishing?" she asked, appalled.

All four boys nodded. She took a deep breath, and another, unable to speak.

"Master Blake is getting even with me, with you, for his reprimand. I'll kill the man."

Startled, Meridee turned to the door and saw her husband standing there, his face like thunder. She stood up, took his hand, and pulled him into the room.

"No, love," she said, taking in the ferocity of his expression as she quailed inside. "What we will do, *we six*, is cross the street right now and wake up Headmaster Croker."

She held his hand until his expression changed, mellowed, even. His lips were moving, as he no doubt recited Euclid's Propositions. She watched his shoulders relax and his eyes regain their usual benign gaze.

If that's what it takes, she thought, *so be it. Have at him, Euclid.* She turned to her children, for so she considered them.

"Dress yourselves. We're going to see the headmaster right now."

"He'll be angry," Nick said, suddenly fearful.

"No, my dears. He will be sorrowful and he will right this wrong. Hurry now."

Chapter Thirty-One

❦

"I'LL DEAL WITH MASTER Blake first thing in the morning," Headmaster Croker said.

Dressed as casually as his late-night visitors in his nightshirt and robe, the headmaster took a serious survey of his students. "Lads, look me in the eye," he said quietly. "You've done nothing to be ashamed of. Master Blake used you poorly, and it was not your fault."

Her heart tender, Meridee watched the boys slowly raise their eyes from the carpet, which had consumed their entire attention. She thought of the few moments in her life where she had been hauled up short for some infraction or other, usually on the order of pouting or talking back to her older sisters. Papa or Mama would assign some punishment of the weed-pulling, book-dusting variety, which once accomplished was forgotten, along with the initial misdemeanor.

She watched these sad children who had wormed their way right into her heart and realized no one commanding a workhouse ever let them forget their crimes, probably amplified as proof that their illegitimate, unfortunate beginnings were somehow their fault. The injustice of it made angry tears run down her face.

Embarrassed, Meridee lowered her eyes to the carpet this time, only to have her husband put his arm around her.

"There is one thing in life we all learned, didn't we, lads?" Able asked. "The unfairness."

They nodded, solemn.

"There were times I knew I was punished because I deserved it," he continued, looking around with a half smile. "I'm certain you know how that felt too." He touched Meridee's face. "You, as well, dearest? I doubt you were an angel when you were seven or eight."

Heaven bless you for your light touch, she thought, as she watched their little boarders smile shyly at her.

"But this was not one of those times," Headmaster Croker reminded them. "If something of this nature ever happens again, and I mean that with all my heart, tell me. Tell Master Six. Tell Mrs. Six. We are disciplined and rigorous here at St. Brendan's, but we are not cruel. That is all. Goodnight to you. Wait in the hall for a moment, please. I would speak to the Sixes."

As one, the boys rose and filed out. The headmaster's expression hardened as he closed the door and turned to Able and Meridee.

"What happened was abominable. Master Blake will be dismissed tomorrow morning, and I will chance the consequences. I will take the class until I find another instructor." He passed his hand in front of his face as though swatting flies. "I regret I cannot do anything more than that, because Leonidas Blake is the nephew of the Chancellor of the Exchequer, who controls this nation's purse strings."

"My goodness," Meridee said.

"We all dance to *that* man's tune," her husband said. "Can you at least lean on his family enough to get him far from Portsmouth?"

"I wish I could. The Blake estate is a mere thirty miles away..." his voice trailed off. "I can try."

"Here's something else to chew on, sir," Able said. "You told me earlier that Blake was—how did you say it?—foisted on you as punishment for his gaming habits."

"Aye, he was," Croker said, his voice full of a fair measure of rue, to Meridee's ears. "This position was to—ahem—rehabilitate him."

"Master Fletcher told me he followed Blake one afternoon right up to the doors of the Pot of Gold," Able said.

Able must have noticed her puzzled expression. "It's a gaming hell," he told her, his lips practically on her ear. "Don't ever let me catch you playing faro in there, dearest."

"You are absurd," she said, trying to maintain her composure.

"I wonder where he got the ready to gamble?" Croker asked. "I know his family cut him off from any cash, barring enough to live on."

"P'raps he pimps," Meridee said calmly, which made Able burst into laughter and the headmaster gasp and stare at her.

"I've been giving my sweet innocent a bit of Pompey education," Able said, when he could talk. "I didn't expect that, either, Headmaster."

"It's a thought," she said.

"And a crazy one," her husband retorted. "Pimps are usually charming fellows, at least with clients. We could never call Master Blake charming, could we?"

"No," Meridee said, "we could not."

"Take her home, Master Six," Croker said. To Meridee's relief, the gloom had left his face. "And keep her away from gaming hells, for the Lord's sake!"

Four little boys waited for them in the hall. They looked at each other and nudged Nick, who stepped forward and cleared his throat. "Me mates and I were wondering what was so funny in there," he said.

"Mrs. Six," Able said promptly. "I won't tell you what she said though, because you're too tender."

"Gor, Master Six, no one ever called us tender before," Nick said with a grin.

"Oh, you men!" Meridee exclaimed. "I am outnumbered."

"Aye, Mam," silent Stephen Hoyt said.

Meridee turned away so he could not see her tears. "He called me Mam," she whispered to Able.

"Smart lad," her husband replied, and she noticed his own struggle.

She clapped her hands. "Gentlemen, it is past the bewitching hour of midnight, and we will still rise at seven," she said, while her soft-hearted man composed himself. "Mam says."

They crossed the street more cheerful than when they came this way earlier. "I'm too old for this much drama," Able said.

"You are twenty-six," Meridee said, ever practical.

"And you can step back from your Pompey education," he teased.

"You started it," she teased back.

"I did. I'm happy this whole nasty business is over." He opened the front door and ushered in the lodgers.

"Upstairs to bed," Meridee said.

"Aye, Mam," John Mark said, as if trying out the word. He stopped on the first tread. "Mam, don't you think we're due for some good fortune, now that Master Blake will be gone tomorrow?"

"I could not agree more," she said, and tugged at her husband's hand. "We've all earned it."

Master Blake was gone before the first classes convened on the morrow. Meridee stood at her front window and watched him leave, carrying a pasteboard box with what must have been his teaching supplies, and his pointer in one hand.

She stepped back when he turned to stare directly at her and mouth something she could not interpret. Stepping back farther, she bumped into Mrs. Perry.

"Beg pardon," she said, startled. "I didn't know you were in the room."

She looked down at the serving spoon in her cook's hand. "I don't think it will come to death by cutlery," Meridee said, trying to joke, but finding her mouth almost too dry to speak.

"I don't trust the man," Mrs. Perry said. She went to the window. "And there he is, cheeky man, still staring! And look, he pointed a finger at me."

"It's just a finger," Meridee said.

"It's the wrong one," Mrs. Perry replied.

Mrs. Perry ran into the hall and yanked open the front door. As Meridee watched, open-mouthed, the woman ran down the front steps, brandishing the spoon. She watched what appeared to be a spirited exchange of words, with Mrs. Perry jabbing Master Blake with the spoon most recently used to stir that morning's porridge. Little blobs of oats flew about and stuck to the black robe Master Blake wore so proudly.

When Mrs. Perry raised the spoon to bat at his head, Master Blake abandoned all dignity and ran, dropping papers and pencils on the street. Meridee looked up at her husband's classroom windows across the street, not surprised to see a row of little fellows watching. No one smiled.

"Good riddance to rubbish," Mrs. Perry said when she came back inside and closed the door with a flourish. "And that is that."

Chapter Thirty-Two

❧

"I'M A PROPHET," ABLE announced a week later when he came home from afternoon class. He grabbed Meri and hauled her away from the Rumford while Betty MacGregor watched. "You won't believe what just happened!"

Good Lord, it wasn't fair for someone to look so dee-lectable and dee-licious while stirring rice pudding. Heaven knows she needed a little jollying. Mrs. Perry had told him a week ago about Master Blake staring so long and hard at his wife and frightening her. The matter with Blake had turned her quiet. How nice that he had good news to share—the best news, really.

"This is probably sitting-down sort of news, but I suppose it is hard to stir dinner from a chair," he told her. "Who should appear today in Headmaster Croker's office but one Mabel Thomas, a butcher's widow from Cardiff."

"And …?"

"She produced legal documents to prove she is Nick's great aunt on her husband's side," he said. "In the space of a fifteen-minute interview, Nick has come away with a home and the last name of Thomas."

That got his wife's attention. She gasped, took the pot off the stove, sat down, and burst into tears. Able stared at her, uncertain as he rarely was, and wondering if he should laugh at her—inadvisable—sit down and cry with her—also inadvisable—or simply gape at her sudden bout of tears as husbands since time immemorial had probably done when confronted with a weeping female.

He chose to sit beside her, handkerchief ready, and wait until she reached for it.

"It's good news," he said softly, after she blew her nose. "Meri, if I could somehow express with words how every workhouse child wishes and wishes for such good fortune."

"But I will miss Nick most awfully!" she wailed, and retreated into the handkerchief.

She blew her nose again, and he watched her face as she mastered her emotions and became once more the woman he adored, and not some mercurial flibbertigibbet.

She put her hands in her lap. "Better tell me the whole story, Able."

Relieved, he started from the beginning, seeing the matter clearly through his eyes as he saw everything. "Her name is Mrs. Mary Thomas," he said. "She is the widow of a butcher from Cardiff, Wales. It seems her late sister-in-law had a daughter who went far astray to Northumberland."

He thought of his own mother, wondering if anyone had ever looked for her in dingy back alleys and places like the Bare Bones. Street women lived at the mercy of pimps, and their customers could number in the dozens, one after another, on the first night when the fleet was in. He remembered his own urges after months at sea. Like other men of the fleet, he never had to look too hard for such women; they were thick as fleas on a cur. He had stood in lines he wasn't proud of.

"Able?"

"Oh? Oh, aye. With tears, she told Headmaster Croker how she had followed up every rumor and searched for her niece. It was a deathbed promise extracted from her by her sister-in-law."

"She found Nick," he said simply, shortening the lengthy session with Headmaster Croker and Mrs. Thomas's many tears, rendering her incoherent, at times, except that she patted Nick on the head until he started to dodge her.

"You're satisfied?" she said finally.

"Aye, Mam," he said, which he regretted instantly, as tears welled in her eyes again.

"I'll miss him," she said simply, and left the room.

Wise woman, Meri knew better than to show a sad face to Nick, who came to the supper table with a light in his eyes that Able envied. He thought of the times he had joined other workhouse lads, to stand in rows and watch as couples came through the bleak halls, looking anxiously at each face until the master pointed out the lucky boy or girl in question. He had never asked, but he doubted there was a single child among that number who did not hope, even after hope had left with the closing of the workhouse door.

"So soon?" Meri asked when he told them Nick was leaving tomorrow.

Even Mrs. Perry, ordinarily so neutral of expression while serving the food, frowned and looked away as she set down circles of cinnamon and sugar pie crust, created on the fly because it was Nick's favorite. She chose not to linger in the dining room to hear oohs and aahs of appreciation, but left the room as soon as she could.

"Mrs. Thomas wants to get Nick home to Cardiff, and it is a long journey," he said.

"She promised me my own room and a pony," Nick told the others. "Well, she did!" he repeated, when his friends looked away.

Bless Meri. She put her hand on Nick's arm. "It's hard to be left behind," she told him, her voice soft. "We will miss you more than we can say."

Who would have thought packing his few garments, a handful of pebbles taken from the stone basin when he was cleaning it, and an extra knit cap would create such melancholy? Able would have given the world to erase the sorrow in Meri's eyes as she did her best to put on a cheerful face.

"I can help him pack," Able offered, to spare her further pain.

A spark of her good humor returned when she poked his chest. "Husband, you are perfectly wretched at folding anything. I hate to wound you, but it is so."

He handed her the small case Mrs. Thomas had pressed into his hands when she left Headmaster Croker's office, barely controlling her emotions when she told both men it had belonged to Nick Thomas's poor, frail mother, dead of consumption.

Meri had accepted it with a sigh. She managed a smile that went no farther than her lips. "Able, there are times when I know this is the easiest pound a month a body could earn," she said. "This is not one of them."

He stayed with her as she tucked in the boys for bed that night, watching as she pulled up the covers, swept back hair from eyes, and kissed each forehead. She held Nick's hand a little longer, then squeezed his fingers.

"Nick Thomas," she said. "I like that. You have a surname now."

Able held her close all night.

Chapter Thirty-Three

❧

SEE HERE, MERIDEE SIX, you are behaving like the worst sort of female, she told herself, after a night of tossing and turning, and stifling her tears because her eyes were beginning to ache from so much weeping. She finally gave up and dragged herself downstairs, to stare out the window—it *would* be raining—and remind herself that she was a woman grown, a wife, and not a baby.

She had extracted a promise from her husband that Mrs. Thomas would come to the house to fetch Nick. "If our own lads"—heavens, she had almost called them sons—"our own lads are so downcast at Nick's good fortune, why should we torture other boys across the street who want to be happy for him, but wish it were them?"

Able had agreed with her reasoning, or maybe he was just weary of her emotions. She could make it up to him in spades when she felt better.

When Meridee heard Mrs. Perry banging around in the kitchen, she dragged herself in there to plump down at the table and stare moodily into space until the cook, looking no happier, joined her with two cups of tea.

"We are obviously not looking at this situation in a sanguine manner," Meridee said, after tea had begun its restorative work. "Why are we not delighted?"

"Because we love the little boy too," Mrs. Perry said promptly. "We've been tested and tried with rat bones, and food in the middle of the night, and tears from young'uns with old eyes."

"And now it's Mrs. Thomas's turn," Meridee said quietly, after long thought. "Let's see how excellent a Sarah Siddons I am when she comes to fetch him."

If some cosmic observer had watched the Sixes with their boarders that morning at breakfast, he would have come away puzzled by how people trying to look happy could make such a muddle of it, and for so many reasons.

Davey Ten didn't even attempt joy. He shook his head over Nick's favorite rye bread, butter, and jam, complained of a belly ache, and stated he could not go to school this morning.

Able opened his mouth to object, but Meridee put her hand on his arm. "Let him be, dearest," she said softly. "We all agree this is hard."

"I don't," he declared. "Finding a family member is the dearest wish of every workhouse boy." He sighed. "Perhaps I cannot help some melancholy, either. This is too complicated, even for my brain."

She leaned across the toast and whispered into his ear, "Tell Euclid to move over and leave a little space in your head for the everyday commotion we both live in."

Her reward was a weak smile, but that would have to suffice. She sent the lot of them off to school across the street with a fake show of good cheer, when she really wanted to join Davey upstairs, because her stomach ached, too.

But there was no time to mourn, not with Nick right there, anticipation writ large on his face. She stationed him in the sitting room to watch for Mrs. Thomas, had herself a quiet cry in the kitchen, and came out like a champion when the doorbell jangled.

And there stood Mrs. Mary Thomas, all smiles. Meridee smiled back and looked beyond her for a conveyance. Had the woman come on foot?

"Do come in, Mrs. Thomas," Meridee said, wondering. "I am Mrs. Six, and here is .... I believe you met Nick yesterday at St. Brendan's."

Mrs. Thomas nodded to Nick, bustled in, and looked around. "Pretty sparse in here, Mrs. Six," she said, sounding jollier than three Father Christmases and somewhat ruder.

"Master Six and I have only just married, and barely set up housekeeping," Meridee replied. She turned to Nick, who was practically jumping up and down in his excitement. "My dear, ask our guest if you can take her coat."

" 'My dear,' is it?" Mrs. Thomas said. "How long have you known my dear dead niece's boy?"

"Not long, Mrs. Thomas," Meridee said, putting her hand on Nick's shoulder, gratified how he leaned in to her, and sorrowful at the same time because soon he would be transferring his affections to others.

Bowing, Nick did as he was bid and invited Mrs. Thomas to take a cup, which made the woman laugh, showing her mouth to be shy of several teeth. "Lord luv you, boy, we're not staying that long. Time to be off."

But here was Mrs. Perry with a tray bearing tea and cups and what looked to Meridee like significant umbrage. She stalked ahead to the sitting room, and Meridee gestured, so Mrs. Thomas followed.

"I hear you are the widow of a butcher," Meridee said, as she poured.

"Aye, Mrs. Six, a grand old fellow. We had a fine store in Shrewsbury. Thank'ee," Mrs. Thomas said as she took the cup.

"I had thought you were from Cardiff," Meridee said, wondering if she had misheard Able. She knew the error hadn't been Able's; he never made conversational mistakes.

"Shrewsbury, Cardiff," Mrs. Thomas said. "It's as near as."

No, it isn't, Meridee thought, dismayed. She took a good look at her guest and wondered why she wore a wig, and not a good one, at that. Peeking out from under the more respectable gray hair was a curl or two of red in a color not found in nature.

Still, one should be polite whilst drinking tea. Meridee knew that. She tried again. "You have gone to considerable trouble to locate the child of your unfortunate daughter," she said.

"Aye, miss. Blood is thicker than water, ain't it?" the woman said. She gave her attention to Mrs. Perry's rout cake, seemed to reconsider, and reached for her handkerchief. She cried.

"Do excuse me, Mrs. Thomas. I believe Nick is actually the daughter of your sister-in-law, isn't she?" Meridee asked.

Her reward was a blank look, followed by another sniffle. "Sometimes young people get in trouble, don't they? It's our duty to make things right." Mrs. Thomas stood up and motioned to Nick. "Come along, laddie. We need to procure a conveyance to take us to the mail coach."

"Yes, Mrs. Thomas," Nick said.

The full weight of the change in his life must have settled on young Nick's shoulders right then. His expression turned serious, even melancholy. "Mrs. Thomas, may I return to St. Brendan's now and then to see Mrs. Six and my friends? I would like that even more than a pony."

"You'll get used to your new life soon enough," Mrs. Thomas said with an airy wave of her hand.

There was no overlooking the sadness in Nick's eyes. *We can't have this,* Meridee thought. She hugged him, then reached for a tablet and pencil with fractions scribbled on it, left by one or the other of her little boarders.

"Do give me your direction, Mrs. Thomas, so the boys can write to Nick," she said. She poised the pencil over the tablet.

"It's ah ... well." Mrs. Thomas thought a moment, narrowing her eyes as if wondering why it was her lot in life to deal with plaguey people. She huffed and sighed. "It's 123 Fourth Street, Shrews ... Cardiff."

Meridee wrote down the address, curious why it took the woman who had lived there so long to recall what was probably the simplest direction in England. *Able would find you slow, indeed,* she thought. *And who confuses Shrewsbury with Cardiff?*

By now Mrs. Thomas had edged Nick close to the door. Davey stood in the hallway, his face solemn. He held out his hand to Nick, shook it, then turned and ran upstairs, slamming the door to his room behind him. Meridee winced.

"Cheeky bastard," Mrs. Thomas said.

"He will miss his friend," Meridee said, shocked at the woman's language with Nick standing right there.

"You'll have your own room where we're going, laddie," the woman said. "Come on now. Time's a-wasting."

"You can easily hail a hackney if you stand by the baker's shop two blocks that way," Meridee said. Steeling herself, she held out her arms for Nick, who threw himself into her embrace. She hugged him close, cried with him, wiped his face with the tail of her apron, and gently moved him toward the door.

"We'll write to you, my dear," she said, and closed the door, only to lean against it until she felt strong enough to stand upright.

Her eyes suspiciously swollen, Mrs. Perry came out of the kitchen and silently retrieved the tea tray from the sitting room. She frowned at the tray, then looked at Meridee.

"Mrs. Six, I have never heard a Welsh accent like that one," she said.

"How would you know?" Meridee asked, feeling her doubts return about Nick's odd aunt.

Mrs. Perry gave her an indulgent look, the kind a mother might give a not-so-bright child. "Perry is Welsh. My man was from Merthyr Tydfil. He joined the Navy to avoid the colliery."

"Did you notice she was wearing a wig? I distinctly saw bright red hair," Meridee said. "And do you know what else? Not a tear, for all her noise."

"I wasn't going to say nothing, but I noticed. I …."

They looked around as Davey came dragging down the stairs, his face more tragical than any character Edmund Keane ever played on Drury Lane. "I miss him already."

Meridee looked down at the address in her hand. "Then I believe you should write him a letter immediately, Davey. That way when he gets to Cardiff, it will be waiting for him."

Davey clutched his stomach, and she laughed. "Don't you try to pull wool over my eyes, Mr. Ten! You are *not* sick."

He smiled. "Mam, you have never called me Mr. Ten before."

"See here, I am being emphatic," she said. "You'll find some paper in the desk."

He went into the sitting room, not dragging so much. She shook her head over little boys in general and trailed Mrs. Perry into the kitchen, where Betty McGregor was already chopping carrots for dinner.

Meridee put her hand to her forehead in a gesture worthy of Sarah Siddons. "Give me an onion to chop, Mrs. Perry. That way I can cry and you'll nev—"

She stopped, startled, when Davey, his face white, threw himself into the room and grabbed her around the waist.

"Mam! Mam! Look!"

His hand shook as he held up the sketch Able had drawn several weeks ago of the ugly customer talking to Master Blake in the Bare Bones, and put in the drawer.

"Yes? He's an evil man, but …. What, Davey?"

Davey clung tighter to her until she pulled him away, alarmed.

"Tell me!"

Davey swallowed a few times, his eyes huge in his face. "Mam, I was looking out the window when Mrs. Thomas and Nick walked away. That … that same man joined them when they were almost to the baker's. He looked scary, but what was I to do? And now I see this picture. Mam! Something is really wrong!"

Meridee put her hands to her face, using the small moment as time to gather her tangled thoughts. She reached for Mrs. Perry, who had already opened the door to her room and pulled out a cudgel.

"I always keep this handy," she said, and there was no mistaking the menace in the cook's voice.

Meridee wore her house slippers, but what did it matter? She grabbed Betty. "Stay here, lock the doors, and don't leave the house. Chop carrots. Mrs. Perry and Davey, come with me. Bring the drawing."

"Are we going to find Nick?" Davey asked, fearful, but with a look of determination that gave Meridee strength.

"We'll tell those who will do the most good," Meridee said. "Hurry."

"Master Six?" Davey asked, running beside her as she threw open the door and bounded down the steps, holding her skirts up so she would not trip.

"And me," Mrs. Perry said, keeping up with surprising grace.

Oh please dear God, don't let us be too late, Meridee thought as she ran up the stairs to Able's classroom and threw open the door so wide that it banged against the wall.

"Mrs. Perry, find the headmaster," she called over her shoulder as she ran to Able, who stared at her.

"Good God, Meri!" he exclaimed, tossing aside his book.

Breathing hard, she pulled Davey in front of her and pointed to the drawing he held in shaking hands. "Tell him!"

"Master, I saw this man meet up with Mrs. Thomas and Nick," Davey said. "He grabbed him by the back of his coat and gave him a shake." He started to cry. "She's no aunt, is she? What are they going to do with Nick?"

Bless Able Six right down to the soles of his shoes. Without a word, he sat Meridee down at his desk and plunked Davey into her lap.

"You're certain?" he asked calmly.

As Meridee watched her husband's face, she saw the same look of determination Davey wore. She glanced at the other boys in the room—the workhouse bastards, the Gunwharf Rats—all of them tensed to rise from their desks at the smallest indication from Master Six.

With no more preamble than her own indelicate entrance, Headmaster Croker burst into the room, followed by Mrs. Perry, who was starting to puff from all the stairs. She held her cudgel at the ready, and Meridee wondered how many times she had used it during *her* naval career.

Able took Meridee by the arm and steered her and Thaddeus Croker into the hall with Davey, who explained again what he had seen.

When he finished, Thaddeus shook his head in sorrow. "We were all fooled. I think now we know how Master Blake earned his money to gamble." He let out a deep breath. "Dear God, what of the other three boys who went to families before you came here?"

Meridee gasped at that further horror and saw Davey's puzzled expression. She gently turned him around and sent him back into the classroom. When he protested, she kissed his head. "Do it for me."

"Aye, Mam," he said.

"We weren't all fooled," Able said slowly.

Meridee flinched to see how old his eyes looked, those same eyes that could gleam with pleasure and joy when the two of them were making merry. "What do you mean?" she asked.

"*You* knew," he said.

"No, I—"

"I'm muddling this. You didn't *know*, but it's what you said when I told you about Blake and the man ... this man." He stabbed at the sketch he had taken from Davey.

"I don't remember," she said, mystified.

"I do. Every word." He closed his eyes, and she knew he was looking at one of those cosmic scrolls where his brain recorded all works, facts, sentences ... everything. "Thaddeus, you said, 'I wonder where he gets the ready to gamble? I know his family cut him off from any cash, barring enough to live on.' "

"I did. Word for word," Thaddeus said. "My God, Able."

"My love, you replied, 'Maybe he pimps,' " Able told her.

"I did. I did," she whispered, horrified.

"And I said, 'I've been giving my sweet innocent a bit of Pompey education.' I laughed! Meri, how did I miss it? Where did I go wrong?"

She grabbed both his arms. "Able, you can't know everything!"

"But I can. I should. What's my excuse?"

She pulled him close, thinking of her conversation with Sir B about Able's brain. There wasn't time to discuss it now, not with Nick's future in a precarious state. She swallowed down her panic and put her hands on either side of Able's face.

"What are we going to do now?" she asked, her voice firm, even as she quailed inside. "Right *now*. We'll sort out other matters later."

That was all he needed. "We will summon the watch," he said, speaking with the voice of command again. "Headmaster, send one of the older boys with a note to Landport Gate. Tell the watch to meet us at the Bare Bones and to send others to the Pot of Gold."

"Consider it done," Thaddeus said as he started down the stairs.

"Take some money for a hackney," Able called after him. "Send ... send Jamie MacGregor and Jan Yarmouth to Sir B with a similar note. I don't know how he'll do it, but there will be Marines on the streets soon."

"And you?" Meridee asked.

He smiled, but there was not an ounce of mirth in his eyes. "Mrs. Perry, what do you say to joining me on a visit to the Bare Bones? I imagine we can enlist the baker, too."

"Do you have a knife, sir?"

"Aye, plus a cutlass across the street, Mrs. Perry."

"And me?" Meridee asked. Don't you dare leave me behind, Durable."

He rolled his eyes. "Durable, is it?" he asked, and gave her a whacking great kiss on her forehead. "Then Durable it is." He shook his finger in her face, and when he spoke, it was in the voice of the sailing master. "If you or *anyone* in this school so much as steps outside these doors until this matter is settled, I will send you back to Devonshire on the first mail coach. Do I make myself clear?"

Meridee nodded, because she wasn't stupid. "We'll gather in the dining hall and read ... something. Maybe not Euclid."

He smiled then and some of the despair left his eyes. "I'll see you soon, and I'll have Nick, too. I promise I will."

Chapter Thirty-Four

✣

Thirty minutes later, Gervaise rolled Captain Belvedere St. Anthony into the dining hall, followed by Jamie MacGregor and Jan Yarmouth. Meridee had been reading *The Children of the New Forest* to St. Brendan's future navigators, all of whom wanted to be anywhere but sitting there inactive. But they knew an order when they heard one, same as she did.

Sir B wasted not a moment. "Meridee, I have summoned the Marines from their barracks," he said. "They are in the streets now. We'll find Nick."

She bowed her head over the book. "I'm worried about more than Nick, Sir B."

"Able? What was his state of mind when he left?" Sir B asked.

"Calm enough. In control. It was what he said," Meridee told him. " 'I should have known,' he said, and 'How did I miss it? Where did I go wrong?' Oh, Sir B."

"I knew it was bound to happen," he said. "After that awful afternoon and night of battle when he was forced to operate and amputate, some of the patients died." If possible, his expression grew more grim. "No one can help death at sea, no one." He stopped, unable to go on.

She knew, and felt the chill. "He takes it personally, doesn't he?"

"Aye," he said simply. "I told you earlier he shook like a leaf. He did, but there was more. He collapsed. Dropped like a stone."

"What did you do?" she asked, horrified.

"Since the surgeon was gone, I put him in the surgeon's quarters. I sat with him for hours. He was barely breathing."

"Can I help him if … when this happens again?" Meridee asked, wishing her responsibility to the boys was in someone else's hands so she could find a quiet place to be alone with terrible thoughts.

"Aye, you can, Mrs. Six," the captain said. "That's the beauty of you."

"How did … what did …."

"I'll tell you in a few minutes," he said. "Right now, we have some lads to mind. Wheel me closer to the boys, Gervaise," he told his valet. "Meridee, you go to the kitchen and find some tea or biscuits for all of us."

Nodding, she started for the kitchen. She turned around to see what the august captain, the hero who was a Knight Commander of the Order of the Bath was doing for the scum of England's workhouses whom other men of his class and social sphere ignored.

She laughed softly. Bless the man's generous heart, he was teaching knots to the fleet's future sailors.

She returned with macaroons and tea, carried to the dining hall by the cook and kitchen help. Sir B held them off from serving until he was satisfied with the knots.

"Fall to, men," he said finally. "When you're done, test each other on what I have taught you."

He made Gervaise wheel him to a more secluded corner of the hall and then excused him. Meridee had followed with tea.

"Whatever would England do without tea," he said. "My dear, there is a crank on the back of this chair." He chuckled. "Some would say there is a crank sitting in it. Ha! High time you laughed a little. Could you put the crank through two revolutions so I can recline a bit? Ah, yes. Now, where were we?"

"You know perfectly well where we were," she said. "Tell me straight up, with no bark on the words. What happened?"

"Even now, after some eleven years, I am not certain what I was hearing," the captain said, when he was more comfortable. "Hand me a macaroon or two, if you haven't eaten them all, Mrs. Six."

"You know I have not!"

"I know," he said, and she heard all the sympathy in his voice. "He was talking non-stop to someone, no, to many people, almost as though he saw them."

"Dear God," Meridee said.

"He sounded almost conversational, at times. He mentioned Euclid—your best friend—and some chap named Keppler, Nicolaus Copernicus, if you can believe me, and the great man himself, Isaac Newton." He held out his hand to her and she grasped it. "Not so tight, my dear. I am a delicate being, these days."

"Beg pardon."

"I think he saw them. How, I could not tell you. He argued. He seemed to listen. Several times he seemed to be on the verge of—this is odd to say— *joining* them somehow. That was when I grabbed his hand and held it. He resisted, and then it was over. He slept until morning, then sat up and went about his business."

Meridee could think of nothing to say. She sat close to Sir B until she calmly returned to her chair and continued reading aloud to St. Brendan's boys and hers.

Throughout the long afternoon and into dusk, she read, alternating the book with Sir B and his knots. When the servants returned to light the lamps, she heard a commotion in the hall. One of the older lads ran out and returned to announce that Master Six, Mrs. Perry, the baker and a remarkable number of Marines were coming up the steps.

"Nick?" Meridee asked, alert. "Oh, please."

The boy nodded. "One of the Marines is carrying him, and Nick doesn't look too happy about it."

Meridee leaped up and ran to the entrance, Davey Ten beside her. Her hand to her heart, she watched as the Marine set Nick down. She knelt and held out her arms, and he threw himself into them. She rocked him back and forth until the little boy with no last name and the beginnings of a black eye said he was fine, and could they please go home?

"I'll take you home, Nick," Meridee said. She stood up and held out her hand for him to grasp. "Davey, Stephen, and John Mark, too." She turned to look at her husband, who had stood so quiet, almost as if he was observing from a great distance. The sight chilled her heart. "You as well, Able."

"I should stay here and explain ..." he said. He shook his head, and she saw his dazed look. "Headmaster Croker can tell the story."

"And you can tell me," she said, quailing inside because she did not know what to expect, not after Sir B's narrative.

"I'll come, too, if you'll have me," Sir B said.

Her look of relief must have been visible to ships at sea, so happy was she with this kindness. "I cannot express my gratitude to you," Meridee whispered. "I feel remarkably inadequate to the task at hand."

"You're not," Sir B told her, "but you will learn that for yourself."

They left St. Brendan's accompanied by the baker, who gave Meridee a funny little bow. "Nick's fine," he said. "We got there in time before anything happened." His expression turned grim. "It was a close-run thing. Mrs. Six, that master who used to teach here was in the process of selling t'little fellow to an old satyr who arrived in a carriage with a crest on the door. What is the matter with some people?"

Meridee patted his arm. "I hardly know. Thank you for your help, Mr. Bartleby."

The baker rubbed his hands together. "Took me back to me own Navy days. A man should knock a few heads together now and then. It's good for the soul." He gave her a cheerful wave. "Send Betty down tomorrow for some brown bread."

"Wait. Tell me please: Master Blake ...?" Meridee felt a shiver down her back, just saying his name. She prayed silently that no matter what, Nick wouldn't be required to testify in any court convened.

"Master Blake?" The baker took a liberty and patted her shoulder, which bothered Meridee not a bit. "Let's say no one is ever going to find *him* again. There may be bits and pieces floating by, but that's enough of the story from me."

I am loose in a town full of madmen, she thought, even as she felt amazing relief. Surprised, she looked around, wondering when day had turned into dusk. Practical matters resurfaced and she wondered just how many carrots Betty had chopped, since that was the only command she had given before she dashed across the street.

Meridee should have known better than to discount Betty's resourceful nature, close kin to the reliable lads around her. She followed Able up the steps and breathed deep of beef stew.

The boys hurried inside while Able stood still in the foyer, Davey remarking that he was gut-foundered. She watched her husband as he lowered his head, as though he couldn't move another step. Silent, she put her arms around him and rested her head against his back.

He turned around in her arms and held her close, pressing her head to his chest now and trying to cover her eyes, almost as if he didn't want her to see what she knew *he* was seeing.

"After dinner, you are going to lie down and I am going to sit with you," she told the gilt buttons on his uniform.

"Meri, why couldn't I see what was about to happen?" he asked, as if he hadn't heard a word.

In truth, she doubted anything she said would register in a unique mind filled with pictures, thoughts, and commands, and who knew what else, all leaping about for attention. What did her words count, against so many? She would try, though. She leaned back in his arms and looked up at him.

"No one can know everything," she said, speaking distinctly and slowly. "Not even you, Able."

He looked down at her, almost as if he were seeing her for the first time since she burst into his classroom hours ago.

"You knew, didn't you?" he asked, searching her face for what, she knew not. "Mrs. Thomas didn't fool you."

"Maybe it's an instinct women have." She spoke with great care. "I was suspicious. I was wary, simply because I did not want to give up Nick." She pressed her hand against his chest with some force, trying to hang onto him, because his eyes were starting to look past her. "You wanted so badly for Nick to have something you did not—a family."

"Aye, Mam," he said, with the vestige of a smile and the pale cousin of his usual good humor. "I let it override what should have been my caution, too. I have my own blind spots that I am learning about, Meri. Am I always going to be a workhouse boy?"

He leaned heavily against her suddenly, and she staggered to hold up his weight. She was saved from a tumble to the floor by Gervaise, who grabbed Able and lowered him carefully to the floor.

"It is happening, my dear," she heard behind her. "Corporal, help my valet carry Master Six upstairs. Show them where to go, Meridee."

She nodded her thanks to Sir B, whose wheeled chair was half and half out of the front door. Running upstairs, she motioned for the men to follow. Her little lodgers looked on in real fear, so she leaned over the railing and put on her best face.

"My dears, he is exhausted from this very trying day," she said, grateful to see Mrs. Perry in the front hall now. "Mrs. Perry, settle them with dinner, will you? I'll be down when—"

"You'll stay right beside your man, if I am not speaking out of turn. I will take charge of the boys," the cook said. "Come on, lads, you can help Betty and me put the finishing touches on dinner, and Nick can tell us about his adventure."

Meridee opened the door to her room and pulled back the coverlets on the bed. "Put him there," she said. "I'll manage him now." She pressed her hand to her heart and failed miserably at a smile to Gervaise and the Marine.

"It was our pleasure, Mrs. Six," the corporal said. "Master Six is formidable in a fight."

After the door closed, she set about making her husband comfortable, removing his shoes, tugging him out of his coat, unbuttoning his trousers and pulling them off. He lay there with his eyes partly open, unnerving her because even in this state of near unconsciousness, he seemed to follow her with his eyes.

When he was reduced to his smallclothes, she shifted him as best she could and covered him. She sat next to him on the bed and lay against his chest, aware of his beating heart, which seemed to move slower and slower. Alarmed, she sat up and shook him.

"Don't you dare desert me now!" she said.

In response, he opened his eyes wide, which alarmed her even more than his half-aware state, because he seemed to see someone over her shoulder. She turned around and saw nothing, to her immense relief.

But *he* saw something; she knew he did. She patted Able's cheek, then forced herself to stand and turn around, facing his demon, too.

"Go away," she said in a loud voice. "I don't care who you are, or what you think you need, but we need Able Six more. Go away. Leave him in peace."

Well, that felt remarkably stupid, she thought, as she turned around and sat down again. "Able, I …."

His eyes were closed all the way this time. For one terrifying moment, she thought him dead. Sick at heart, she rested her head against his chest again, and after a few moments that seemed like hours, felt his heart beating more regularly.

He put his hand on her head and rubbed his thumb against that spot behind her ear that she liked so well. "Meri, you were awfully rude to my mental guests just now," he said, slurring the words as though he had drunk too much grog at the Bare Bones.

She remembered what Sir B had told her. "I care not a fig if I was curt to Sir Isaac Newton," she replied. "I'm not too pleased with your great friend Euclid, either. You've had a trying time, Nick is safe, and I am here."

"I cannot argue that," he said. "He won't bother any more workhouse boys, will Leonidas Blake."

"So you are safe, too," she said. "Go to sleep."

He slept through the night. Sir B joined her for a few hours, once the boys were asleep. The captain's pallor distressed her, but she understood as never before that captains—the good ones, at least—were never free of responsibility for the lives of every crew on every ship. He told her the rest of the story.

"That corporal who helped Gervaise said that when he arrived with his patrol, Mrs. Perry had just administered a whack to the back of Master Blake's head and he lay bleeding on the floor."

"Where was Nick in all this?" Meridee asked. "Pray God he did not see such a spectacle."

"Alas, he was already in the carriage of as foul a member of the peerage as I can imagine, but I will spare you his name, because he has some power," Sir B said. "He had gone no farther than removing Nick's coat, and the boy was resisting with all his might." He paused and gave her a look of great kindness. "Calling for Mam, too, and he didn't mean that wretched woman who turned him over to the man in Able's sketch."

"I failed Nick, too," she said, hard put to hold back her tears.

"On the contrary. Nick knows who loves him best," Sir B said. "He'll have some nightmares, I don't doubt. Hug him close, just the same as you hug this man close."

"Aye, mister," she said, in imitation of her boys, which made the captain smile.

"The woman?"

Sir B chuckled, his merriment genuine. "I wish you could have seen Mrs. Perry yank off that wig and grab that harridan by red hair that my corporal said fair blinded him. Held her by her hair and lifted her quite off her feet." He laughed. "The corporal said Mrs. Perry held her out so she couldn't even hit her, no matter how hard she tried. I'd like to have seen that."

"Not I," Meridee said with a shudder.

"No, not you, my dear Mrs. Six. You are a gentlewoman and I know Able intends you to remain so," Sir B told her. "Anyway, the watch hauled her away, kicking and screaming. A repairing lease in Australia should remedy her inclination to associate with low company. I will so stipulate that in a letter to the Navy Board tomorrow morning."

"Thank goodness," Meridee said. She put her hand on Able's chest when he started to move. "No worries, dearest. I'm here and Nick is safe."

"Good," he replied, sounding almost himself, except that his eyes behind their closed lids were moving at a fantastic rate. She covered his eyes until he relaxed.

"There now, my love, I wish you would sleep," she whispered and kissed his cheek. Able pursed his lips and made kissing noises, then did as she asked.

"You're far better for him than any sea captain sitting beside his hammock in the South Pacific," Sir B told her, his shoulders shaking with silent laughter. He turned serious soon enough. "The pimp is gone, too. Someone in the Bare Bones—Mrs. Perry has no idea who—grabbed up the man and gave him a good shake, like a terrier with a rat. He will bother no one else."

"My stars! I certainly hope whoever killed him doesn't get into trouble for it," Meridee said, even as she wondered, probably for the final time, what her sisters would think of such a comment from their well-mannered little sister.

"Trouble in the Bare Bones? Ha! Mrs. Perry said the watch made a feeble stab at questioning the, um, patrons in that distinguished grog shop, but apparently no one shook the man to death. I will draw a curtain over that lamentable episode in Portsmouth's lively history, and you should, too."

"With pleasure. And Blake is dead?"

"As dead as a man can be. On that score, the watch wisely did not question Mrs. Perry or the baker too closely, either." He put a hand on her arm. "And you shouldn't."

"Not a word, although Mr. Bartleby did make some remark about 'bits and pieces.' "

"The Bare Bones is next to a butcher's shop," Sir B said. "And now let us draw an even heavier curtain over *that* matter. I do not believe even Blake's family will mourn overmuch."

"We are back to Blake again," Meridee said, wishing her next thought would vanish, because it disturbed her greatly. "Those three other lads from the younger class who went to homes," she began, and couldn't finish. "Did Blake—"

"Did Blake play a role there, too?" There was no mistaking Sir B's shudder. "Meridee, I do not know."

"Is there some way to find out?" she asked. "Is it too late for them?"

He couldn't meet her eyes, and she had his sad answer.

They sat in silence, holding hands, until Mrs. Perry tapped on the door and said that the boys were ready to be tucked into bed. Letting go of Sir B's hand, she went across the hall to Davey and Stephen Hoyt's room. She wished Stephen a good night and was rewarded with a hug, the first she had ever received from the silent lad, who would probably mourn the loss of his parents until he died.

In the next room, she hugged John Mark, and then Nick for a long time. "I still want a last name, but not that badly," he said finally. "Mayhap it's not so important."

"Maybe it is not, Nick," she said, and kissed his forehead. "Sleep now. If you need me, I am merely across the hall."

"Thank'ee, Mam," he said, as his eyes closed. "Beg pardon, but Master Six needs you, too, and my mates are here."

Grateful, troubled, she returned to the first room. "Davey, you're my hero," she said. "If you had not watched out the window, then found that sketch, where would we be?"

A few more words with both boys, and she closed the door and returned to her own room, where Captain Sir Belvedere St. Anthony was wrapped in his cloak again and preparing to depart, the redoubtable Gervaise behind to push.

"Madam, I will take my leave," he said. "Gervaise tells me the corporal waits below to help him get my feeble carcass down the stairs and out the door."

"Any advice?" she asked, feeling more alone than ever.

"Only this, and I hate to bring it up." He was silent a moment, marshaling his forces. "When his students go to war, where some might die, I do not know what will happen."

Meridee saw her guests from the house, hugged Mrs. Perry and Betty in the kitchen, then returned to her room. She curled up next to her husband, her hand on his eyes, her head on his shoulder until he woke in the morning, looking around, declaring he was hungry, and why hadn't she got under the covers last night?

"We had company, and it was late," she told him.

"Company? Who?"

"Sir Isaac Newton, Euclid—your friend and mine—Galileo, plus several other gentlemen I cannot recall," she told him calmly.

"Meridee, do you wish you had never met me?" he asked.

"Don't be absurd," she told him. "Your friends are always welcome, as long as they do not wear out their stay."

"And if they do?"

"I'll sort them out and send them home, Able Six."

Chapter Thirty-Five

❦

IMPERVIOUS TO STRIFE AND terror, apparently, the good ship St. Brendan the Navigator School for the Misbegotten and Mostly Forgotten righted itself and sailed on into spring.

Was there telepathy in the very air of Portsmouth? That evening when the boys were busy with extra pages of fractions at the kitchen table, her husband announced it was time to try out the water of the stone-lined basin.

She knew the boys had been taking turns skimming leaves and other detritus from the calm waters of the basin, everyone waiting for spring to warm the water a little. Surely Able wouldn't have time to teach her, too, and how could he do it so she remained modest?

She had to give him credit for sheer nerve.

"Dearest, the time has come," he announced after she had tucked her charges in bed. "You and I are going to the basin."

"Able, really," she tried.

"Aye, really." She heard the firmness he seldom used in her presence that reminded her he was not merely a husband, but a sailing master. "You need to know how to swim. I also want to test my ability to teach someone how."

"It's cold. I'll die."

"You won't," he assured her. "I'll haul you out before your lips turn blue."

"It's dark out. You won't be able to tell," she argued, even though he was already moving her toward their dressing room.

"Strip down to your shimmy," he said. "I'll get bare, too. We'll wrap up in our cloaks and take along blankets. Handsomely now."

"How did I get myself into this position?" she grumbled as they crossed the street and walked around St. Brendan's toward the stone pool.

"You married a man not easily discouraged."

It was easy enough to put on a brave front, but more difficult as she stood on the steps leading down to the water. "You first," she insisted.

He took off his boat cloak, sidled past her and into the pool with no hesitation, drat the man. He looked down. "Gracious, but my testes just crawled into my abdominal cavity, begging for sanctuary."

Meridee laughed out loud, unable to help herself. "When in Rome," she muttered under her breath, threw off her cloak, and followed him into the water. The shock of sudden cold made her gasp. She grabbed Able's bare arm as he towed her into the pool.

"I can see I'm going to want to anchor a taut rope against the basin wall at this three-foot level," he told her. "Until then, hang onto the waistband of my smalls."

Her teeth already chattering, she did as he said. "I should have my head examined," she grumbled, getting a grip on his drawers.

"Too late for that. You said aye to the vicar."

Why did the man have to be so disgustingly cheerful? She knew there was no danger of her drowning in three feet of water, and no one would stroll around the stone basin at this hour and chance upon nearly naked lunatics.

"Do this," he directed. "Splay out your knees, you know, as if, well, you know."

She did. Maybe blushing would warm up the water.

"Good. Lean back as though I'm tugging you up by your belly button. And breathe. Fill those marvelous lungs. They'll make you more buoyant."

"You are certifiable."

"And you have lovely … lungs."

She gave him a filthy look, probably unnoticed in the gloom of near midnight. Ready to scream from the cold, she splayed out her knees cautiously and leaned back, all the while keeping a death grip on Able's waistband. "I can't lean back," she whimpered. "It's too cold."

"If you are ever thrown overboard, you might wish you had learned to float and tread water until another ship picked you up."

"I doubt that will ever happen," she assured him.

"Lean back! Show me your tits."

The man was unstoppable. She leaned back, raised her chest and stomach, and felt herself begin to float.

"Success!" her husband exclaimed. "Heavenly days, can your nipples ever stand at attention."

"Don't make me laugh, you wretch! Now what?"

"Pretend you're a starfish. Keep your head back, and angle out your legs and arms. Big breaths. Let go of me. Remember: belly button up."

She did as he said and floated, her hair loose around her head, her teeth chattering. "I'd rather be thrown overboard in Australian waters," she told the man of her dreams. "It must be warmer."

"Sharks love warmer water, too."

That did it. Meridee planted her feet on the stone basin and whipped her head around. Able laughed. She splashed him and he splashed her back.

"Not a shark in the pool. One more time. Do you need to hang on or can you flop back on your own?"

She splayed her knees, tipped her head and stretched out, ready to die from the cold. Wouldn't her husband be upset then?

"One thing more, my bountiful, adorable woman," he said, incorrigible to the end. "Turn over onto your stomach."

"That will never work," she argued.

"I could quote you any number of sources that would dispute your prejudice against floating on your stomach," he said, teeth chattering, but so unflappable as to be nearly insufferable, if she hadn't loved him amazingly. "It's how you learn to s-sw-swim."

She flopped over, shrieked when she started to sink, then remembered to spread out her arms and legs and breathe. Able put his hand under her stomach until she stabilized herself, then took his hand away. She floated stomach down, face turned to the side to breathe.

"Are you satisfied?" she gasped. "I'm going to die and you will be alone in this cruel world."

"Oh, the drama. Put your feet down. Let's get out of here."

She needed no coaxing to leave the frigid pool. Able bound her up in a blanket, helped her scuff into her slippers, and wrapped her cloak around her before he took care of himself. She took a good look at him, standing there shivering in his drawers.

"You weren't teasing me about your testes," she commented. "Will they ever return, or are they fated to become a distant, fond memory?"

"There are some things I never joke about," he said with some dignity, even as he struggled not to laugh. "Give them a little while, oh lusty female."

They hurried across the street, into their house, and up the stairs double time, where Meridee sat down in front of the fireplace in their bedroom. Able pushed her chair as close to the flames as he could, then sat down beside her, still wrapped up. In a few minutes he convinced her to strip off while he found a dry blanket. Wrapped up, she crawled into bed.

He joined her in a few minutes. "We'll do this again tomorrow night, and the night after," he informed her. He nudged her. "Don't you pretend to be asleep! You heard me."

"Was ever a new bride so put upon?" she asked the ceiling.

"The drama continues," he replied, addressing the same ceiling.

She felt him begin to shake with silent laughter.

"If I die from the ill effects, you're to blame."

"You won't. I'd never put you in harm's way, Meri-deelerious. Go to sleep now. You'll feel more cheerful in the morning."

She didn't. They woke before daylight to Davey Ten pounding on their door, announcing that Stephen Hoyt had run away during the night.

Chapter Thirty-Six

❦

A BLE LEAPED OUT OF bed and grabbed him. He let go when Meridee, blanket tight around her, pulled the little boy close.

"Davey, it's not your fault," she whispered, her arms around him as he sobbed. "How were you to know?"

"He woke me up around midnight," Davey said, when he could draw a breath without tears. "He was standing there at the window." He peered over her shoulder at Able. "Master, he said he saw you and Mistress Six walking toward St. Brendan's."

"Aye, he did," Able said, calmer now. "I'm teaching your mam how to float, so I can teach you. Did Stephen go back to bed?"

"I … I … think so. I know I went back to sleep." The fright returned to his eyes. "I'm sorry. I should have done … something …."

"What?" Meridee asked gently. "He's not your responsibility, and you didn't think anything was amiss, did you?"

Davey's confidence started to return. "Nay, Mam. He cries sometimes— we all do—and sometimes we eat our 'midnight biscuits' together, as Nick calls them." He shook his head. "Where's he going?"

"To Australia," Able said.

"He doesn't know enough to get there," Davey said, ever practical.

"No, he doesn't," Able replied. He touched Davey's head. "Get dressed. We'll have breakfast as usual." Meridee held her breath as her husband kissed the boy's head. "Don't fret. We'll sort it out."

Davey patted his head where Able had kissed him and left the room.

"He needed that kiss," Meridee said. "I need one, too."

Able folded her close and kissed her. "What do you know: my testes have returned," he announced in her ear. "That's better, Meri. Laugh, don't cry.

We'll find the little scoundrel. I'd better go disrupt the headmaster's baked eggs and toast."

"Stephen must have heard us leave and thought he could get away," Meridee said as she followed him to their dressing room. "Able, can we find him?"

"I hope so. He's too young to be roving Pompey's docks," her husband replied, as he pulled on his clothes in record time. "We have ample evidence in Nick's experience to know it's a rough town for children."

He was out the door and across the street by the time she dressed and made their bed. While Betty buttered toast, Mrs. Perry stirred oats into boiling water in the kitchen. She looked up with a frown.

"Is something wrong, Mistress Six?" she asked. "You don't usually let the master escape without his neck cloth tied properly."

Meridee sat the two of them down. Between her own tears, she told them Stephen Hoyt was missing.

"Poor lad. All he wants is his parents, even if they are thieves and rascals," Mrs. Perry said, shaking her head. "I was thrown into a slave ship when I was thirteen or thereabout. I know what it feels like to want what you cannot have."

"At thirteen I was wondering which ribbon to wear with my day dress," Meridee said. "My hardships in no way equaled yours."

"Don't chide yourself," Mrs. Perry said. "Not everyone has the good sense to survive the Middle Passage in chains, or … or … live in a workhouse."

Both her cook and maid of all work looked at each other, bound in a sisterhood she did not share.

No wonder I am naïve. "I'm learning," Meridee said simply.

Meridee already knew Mrs. Perry to be the soul of generosity, even though she had the height and girth to intimidate little Admiral Nelson himself. Still, the woman could surprise her. "I imagine you worried when no one wanted to marry you without a dowry. That's a bleak life too."

Meridee had no argument for her. "Thank God a poverty-stricken bastard of unknown origin rescued me from such a fate," she joked.

Mrs. Perry whooped with laughter. Betty was still too new to the Six household to understand self-deprecating humor. *You'll learn too,* Meridee thought. "Let's get breakfast—handsomely now!" she said. "You know that's what my curly-haired fellow would say."

They didn't require her help fixing breakfast, but seemed to understand her need to keep busy. With a nudge from Mrs. Perry, Betty kindly turned over to Meridee the task of buttering the toast, while she set the table and poured milk in each glass.

Three sober boys came downstairs at the usual time. Davey had obviously acquainted them with Stephen Hoyt's disappearance, and they looked as long of face as he did.

Meridee sat them down at the table. "Here is another rule for all lodgers: no one is to blame for the actions of another. You mustn't chastise yourselves over a situation out of your control."

"Can we help find him?" Nick asked. The others nodded, too.

"Your duty is to attend classes across the street," Meridee said. "Master Six is at St. Brendan's already, talking with the headmaster. They will think of something." She clasped her hands together. "Let us pray and then we will eat."

The long faces staring back at her suggested that no one was up to taking his turn for morning prayer. She bowed her head. "Please Lord, bless this food. Please help Stephen find his way back to us. Amen."

Backs bent, eyes down, the boys crossed the street after breakfast. Her own heart breaking, Meridee watched them, wishing she could keep them with her for the day. She thought of times when she had felt low, or ill, and Mama took the time to make sugary cinnamon toast and let her wrap up in a blanket on the sofa, with a hot water bottle at her feet. It certainly wasn't a specific for any known ailment, but it always cheered her.

"They say you don't miss what you never knew," she said to the window. It fogged with her words, but she could still see her little charges trudging to class. "Where are you, Stephen?"

She had a lapful of mending—how did one fairly new husband could go through stockings so fast?—but she paced in front of the sitting room window instead, her eyes on the street as if wishing Stephen to appear.

An hour later she was rewarded to see Able at the door to St. Brendan's. She opened their door as he came across the street, his boat cloak tight around him against the chill of a brisk wind.

"What? Do you know anything?" she asked.

"Nothing yet," he said. "No, I can't stay. I'm here between classes. You can imagine the gloom across the street."

"Then why—"

"Am I here?" He walked her to the door of the sitting room and nodded to Mrs. Perry, who had come out of the kitchen when the door opened. "Master Croker wanted you two to *not* attempt to find Stephen on the docks."

"It crossed my mind," Meridee admitted. "Mrs. Perry and I could—"

"Absolutely not," Able said, in a tone of voice that gave her no room to maneuver. "I feel confident enough for the two of you to roam our few streets here, but *not* down at the docks. Never, in fact." He turned his attention to Mrs. Perry. "You and I and the baker were lucky in the Bare Bones."

"You needn't raise your voice," the cook said with some spirit.

"Did I? I apologize," he said, and put his arm around Meridee, drawing her within his cloak in that way she liked so well. "The docks are more dangerous than the Bare Bones and I won't risk anything happening to either of you."

She heard all his worry and forgave him at once. "Master Fletcher has sent out an alert to his friends on the docks, for all the good that will do."

The three of them stood there in silence for a moment, then Mrs. Perry went quietly back into the kitchen.

"Poor lad. He wants to go to Australia to find his family, and I for one don't blame him," he said.

He pulled away after another too-brief embrace. "I must return to my classroom, put on a good face, and explain the care and feeding of fractions to lads who are worried about one of the Gunwharf Rats."

Meridee kissed him and stepped out from the protection of his cloak. "I have a pile of mending that isn't exactly calling my name, but there it is."

He smiled at that and tugged a curl that had escaped from her cap. "Meridee, I really came here because I knew you would stuff the heart back in my chest, since you are my keeper. Thank you."

Standing in the open doorway, she watched him until he crossed the street and the cold defeated her. She remembered a time she had run away from home over some infraction soon forgotten. Running away had consisted merely of sitting in the neighbor's apple tree, grumpy and put upon, until she started to miss luncheon. When she came trudging home—looking much like the little boys she had sent across the street that morning—Meridee remembered how Mama had paddled her backside, then pulled her close, murmuring admonitions and love at the same time.

"Stephen Hoyt, I would do the same to you," she said, picking up her darning egg and pulling one of Able's socks over it.

She finished two stockings and was starting on a third when someone knocked on the door. Meridee threw down the darning egg and ran to the front door.

Dignity, dignity, she lectured herself and then yanked open the door anyway, and stared, open-mouthed, at the sight before her. Ezekiel Bartleby, the baker at the head of the street, pushed Stephen Hoyt forward. He was trying to hide behind the big man's legs.

"T'lost is found, madam," Ezekiel said. "C'mon, lad, face the music."

Chapter Thirty-Seven

❧

I T WAS ONE THING to remember how her mother had reacted to her own childish misdemeanor, but there Stephen stood, looking penitent and defiant in turn. His lips trembled as he tried to sidle closer to the baker and make himself invisible.

Meridee snatched him and paddled his backside, then pulled him close, her arms tight around him. "Stephen, what were you thinking?" she exclaimed.

She held him off, looking at the obvious tracks of tears on his face. Gathering him to her more gently, she murmured, "I am so relieved, Stephen, so relieved."

Her heart turned into a puddle when his arms went around her and he cried into her neck. She carried him inside, indicating that Ezekiel should follow her.

"Mrs. Six, I shouldn't … flour everywhere …."

"Certainly you should," Meridee said over her shoulder. "We're going in the kitchen, so no fears about flour."

As Mrs. Perry looked on in amazement, she sat down at the kitchen table and held Stephen as he melted into her arms and sobbed. She closed her eyes in relief and something singularly close to love.

Meridee saw Betty with a dishcloth in her hand, drying the same plate over and over. "Betty, hurry across the street and tell Headmaster Croker that Stephen has returned. In the front door, up the steps, and first door on the right," she added, to forestall any questions.

Betty ran out the door. Meridee returned her attention to Ezekiel, who sat there looking monumentally uncomfortable as he tried to brush little pills of flour from his hairy arms.

"What happened?" she asked him.

"My wife and I, we was working as usual, early-like," the baker said. "Thou knowest, miss: bakers get up early. Heard a noise out back and there he was, sitting on the steps." He touched the little boy's back. "Thought he was one of yours, but he didn't want to go back."

"Stephen wants to find his parents in Australia," Meridee said. "I know he does." She put Stephen off her lap. "I'll be back, Stephen," she told him. "I need to walk this good man to the door. It's polite."

Mrs. Perry took her place. Meridee nodded to Ezekiel and he followed her from the kitchen.

"Do you think you could locate his parents?" Ezekiel asked as they stood together at the front door.

"I don't know how, but there are those who do," she said, and looked across the street where Headmaster Croker and Able were hurrying from St. Brendan's. "Perhaps these two. Thank you again, Mr. Bartleby."

The baker ducked his head, evidently a man unused to even the most rudimentary praise. "Just so you know, all the merchants on my street keep a watch out for St. Brendan's."

"We're grateful to you, Mr. Bartleby."

"Ezekiel to you, Ma'am," he said shyly.

"And Meridee to you," she told him.

"Ma'am, I could never presume," he stated.

"You're not presuming, Ezekiel."

She remained in the doorway as the three men met on the sidewalk, knowing that the straightforward, plain as a pikestaff baker was rehearsing again his role in Stephen Hoyt's sad little saga.

She put her hand on Able's arm when he greeted her at the door. "He's terrified of what you or Headmaster Croker will do."

"Mostly we're giving thanks, Meri," Able said. "What did you do?"

"I swatted his bottom then embraced him," she said. "Exactly what my mother did to me, the one time I ran away."

"You ran away?" Able asked with a grin. "How far?"

"Our neighbor's apple tree," Meridee said with some dignity. "I received a swat and a hug, and don't you laugh, you reprobate."

"Then that's all the punishment Stephen requires," Able told her. "You've seen the welts on my back for running away," he said seriously, speaking into her ear so no one else could hear. "We don't do that in *our* house."

She grabbed her husband, and he held her close, much as Stephen had held onto her. "He wants to find his family."

Headmaster Croker spoke to her next. "We'll have to find them, won't we? Go inside, you two sillies. St. Brendan's doesn't pay you enough to heat a March morning."

They adjourned to the parlor, where Stephen sat. Mrs. Perry brought in biscuits and tea, then stalled so long that Able told her to sit down, too.

"We are all involved in this," he said. "Headmaster?"

Thaddeus Croker gave Stephen a long, measured look. "We can't countenance running away, lad," he said, his tone firm but kind.

"My parents—"

"Are on the other side of the world," Thaddeus finished. "Will you get there someday? I don't doubt it, with your determination, but you must be better prepared for such a journey. Will you at least agree to that?"

Stephen sat in silence. He put his hand in Meridee's, finally. "Aye, sir," he said softly. "Mayhap I realized that when I went no farther than the baker's shop."

"Mayhap you did," the headmaster agreed. "P'raps we can at least find where they are and send a letter."

Stephen gasped. "You would *do* that for me?"

"Aye, lad," the headmaster said. "It will take some time, and you must practice patience."

"Aye again, sir," Stephen said.

Meridee heard something different in his voice. Gone was the uncertainty she had noticed from his first day in her care. He sat a little taller, too. *Hope is a useful tool,* she thought, touched to see its application before her eyes. She squeezed his hand and he squeezed back.

The headmaster rose and so did the others, deferring to his evident leadership. "I want you and Master Six to return to your classroom."

"Fractions await us, lad," Able said. "Let's leave Mistress Six and the headmaster to plot our next course."

Stephen nodded and let go of Meridee's hand. "I'm sorry I frightened you."

"You have to trust us to help you," Able said.

"I don't trust anyone."

"I didn't either, for a long time," Able told him. "I assure you Mrs. Six is deserving of all your trust. Come. We have work to do."

"Mrs. Six, I have a plan," Thaddeus Croker said after the front door closed, and Mrs. Perry had returned to the kitchen. "Are you game for a visit to London?"

Meridee shook her head, feeling not at all game. She had been to London once in her life, and the visit had satisfied all her curiosity on the subject of large cities: noise, filth, fog, and confusion. "My goodness, alone?"

"Heavens, no. Able would never agree to such a thing, nor would I ask it," Croker said. "I have contracted with my sister, Miss Grace Croker, to finish this school term while we search for a permanent replacement for the unlamented Master Blake. She is in London at our townhouse. I will send a message by post this afternoon. You and Stephen will travel to London in a post chaise, and you will stay in my townhouse while you three visit the Board of Prisoners."

"Oh, I don't—"

"Nothing to it. With my sister along, there is not a government door that would dare remain shut to you. I will send a note around within the half hour to Captain Sir Belvedere St. Anthony. He will prepare a letter to Admiralty House, and we will see what happens."

"But London …" Meridee said, irritated with her lack of courage.

"When you and Grace have accomplished your purpose, she will return to Pompey with you and teach Master Blake's class."

"No stick to beat the boys?"

"Grace needs no weapons to exact obedience," he said. "Will you do this for one little boy?"

"Aye, Headmaster Croker," Meridee said, shoving aside her fears as another of her duties made itself plain. "I will be his advocate."

"He will have none better," was the headmaster's quiet reply.

Mrs. Perry frowned over the news after the headmaster left. "You'll be safe from Portsmouth to London?" she asked, her tone decidedly militant.

"Master Croker said Stephen and I will be taking a post chaise," Meridee said. She sat down at the kitchen table and made no objection when Mrs. Perry slid the plate of biscuits her way. "Why is he being so kind to this little fellow?"

Mrs. Perry looked around and noticed Betty polishing silver by the window. She moved closer. "I've heard rumors from the kitchen staff across the street. He seems to be atoning for some misdeed, but no one knows what, poor man."

"How could this be part of that?"

Mrs. Perry shrugged.

Meridee spent the afternoon fretting over a bolt to London. She had almost convinced herself that it wouldn't happen, until a post rider stopped by her house, removed his hat and bowed, and declared he would be by tomorrow morning at five o'clock to pick her up, along with one small boy.

Supper was a quiet affair, with the other boys sneaking glances at Stephen Hoyt, who ate everything on his plate as he always did and kept his eyes directed at the mashed turnips in the bowl in front of him.

Able pushed his plate away first. "Lads, Mrs. Six and Stephen are going to London tomorrow to the Board of Prisoners." He raised both hands against their shocked expressions. "Nay, lads. Excuse my clumsy diction. He's going to *learn* which ship his parents sailed on, and we'll try to track them down."

He leaned forward then, eyes intense. "No one must run away to Pompey's docks ever again. There are too many evil men willing to prey upon young boys. Nick knows that."

"Aye, sir," Nick replied.

"I had my troubles, too," Able said softly. He directed his attention to Stephen. "What were your parents sentenced for? How old were you?"

"I was five, I think," he said. His eyes went to his plate. "Da was nabbed for poaching. We were hungry. And me mam was nabbed because she did not turn'm in."

English justice. Meridee could see it: a man wrenched from his family because he trapped a hare or trolled for fish in a stream belonging to some lord who never visited the property and who, if asked, would have been hard-pressed to explain why a hare or a string of trout even mattered to him. Sentenced to another hemisphere for hunger.

"Do you know the length of their sentences?" Able asked.

The boy shook his head. "A long time, is all I know."

Stephen seemed inclined to talk, and the conversation continued as they adjourned to the sitting room, usually the place for jackstraws and simple card games she was teaching them. Stephen could have sat anywhere, but he stayed by her side this night.

"Did you see them again after that court appearance?" Able asked.

"Nay, sir. They whisked us away," Stephen replied. "Mam cried and held back, but she was shackled to Da. What could we do?"

Meridee bowed her head against such a picture in her mind, and wished she had no imagination. Able's hand was warm against her back and it calmed her. What had Stephen just said?

"Us?"

"Me and me little brother. He was four and cried and cried." Another sigh. "He died of the damp. Couldn't stop coughing. My folks need to know. The matron told me Willy was better off. How can that be?"

"I don't even want to think about such scenes," Meridee declared frankly, after the boys were tucked in bed and she crossed the hall to their room, where Able sat staring into the fire. He held out his arms automatically and she sat on his lap.

"No floating tonight," he said, speaking into her hair. "I'd rather keep my man parts where they belong, considering that you'll be gone for a few days."

"Oh, you," she said softly and started on his trouser buttons.

"Suppose we don't learn anything in London?" she asked him later, after the room had quit throbbing. Funny thing about old houses.

"You'll learn enough, if the records are good. Stephen *needs* to send a letter to Australia. No telling if it will be answered, or what has happened in the past few years, but he needs to send it."

Meridee composed herself for sleep. "I'm probably going to dream about a little boy dropping a letter into a great ocean and expecting it to somehow arrive on the shores of Australia. I'll be awake all night."

"Not after that massive bit of pleasantry we just enjoyed," he said. "Before we married, had you any concept of the soporific effects of coitus?"

She poked him in a tender spot. "I also had no concept of a man who could go from lover to scientist while he's still breathing heavily. Soporific effects?"

"I'll give you one minute before you are blowing bubbles against my chest."

"I don't do that!" she declared. She would have to ask him someday if she was a scientific experiment.

"Aye, you do, and I love it. And *you*. Go to sleep."

Chapter Thirty-Eight

⸙

M ERIDEE AND STEPHEN ARRIVED in London at the end of a long day. Trust Captain Sir Belvedere St. Anthony to smooth their way. Just before the post chaise arrived on their doorstep, Sir B's man brought around an official-looking letter, as well as a note tucked inside an envelope containing money, telling her not to argue and try to send it back. *A little luxury never hurt a body*, he had written. *Besides, you're on St. Brendan's business, and St. Brendan is my business, too. B.*

"I never argue," Able said, enjoying her distress, or so it seemed to Meridee.

Strange how sitting in a comfortable post chaise could be so exhausting. As much as London with its noise and size frightened her, Meridee felt only relief when the post chaise pulled up in front of a three-story row house on Half Moon Street.

The front door opened and Stephen couldn't help staring. He backed up to Meridee and whispered, "Gor, but the Crokers are a tall lot, Mam. She's a reg'lar Long Meg."

Tall lot, indeed. Miss Grace Croker came down the steps, owning every single tread with a dignity that made Meridee want to back up, too, except she was the adult. She came forward instead and they met in the middle of the sidewalk.

A curtsy from each was proper, then Meridee held out her hand. She saw a starchy sort of kindness in the lady's eyes.

"I am Meridee Six," she said, breezing right past the more formal Mrs. Six, because it didn't seem necessary. Able had already remarked on her ability to see right into a person, a trait he thought he lacked, and Meridee understood what he meant.

"Grace Croker," the woman said, and clasped Meridee's extended hand in hers. "We have a little boy to assist." She laughed, which made even the sober

Stephen smile. "I owe *you* the thanks. Life was getting slow here."

Tea revived Meridee. Stephen needed no reviving. Like her brother, Grace Croker seemed to have an instinct about little boys. Meridee listened with delight as the tall woman prompted the ordinarily quiet boy to describe the rat they had cleaned and mounted on a plaque in their classroom.

"All nine of us are the Gunwharf Rats," he told her proudly as he polished off the last of the petits fours and shook his head over another plate of them, offered by the maid who just happened to be standing by with reinforcements.

"I am eager to meet all the Rats," Grace said. She turned her head when a personage of near-majesty who must be the butler cleared his throat. "Nash, please escort our young guest upstairs to his room. Dinner will be at six."

Alarmed, Stephen looked at Meridee as though she were his lifeline. Grace noticed immediately. "You will be in the room right next to Mrs. Six." She touched his shoulder. "If that proves not close enough, I strongly suspect Mrs. Six would have no objection to a cot in her room."

"None whatsoever," Meridee said. "I'll be upstairs in a few minutes, Stephen. This is a good moment for you to write in your log about what we saw today."

Equanimity restored, he followed the butler from the sitting room, after one glance back.

"He is keeping a log already?" Grace asked.

"Able—Master Six—requires that of all his students," Meridee explained. " 'Ye shood stay-airt yoong to lay-ern yer dooties,' " she said, in perfect imitation of her husband's Dumfries accent.

Grace laughed again, that hearty sound going right to Meridee's heart, because after only ten hours away from him, she missed her man. "My brother tells me that Master Six is a complete and utter Genuine Article."

"He is," Meridee agreed, feeling as at home here as with one of her own sisters. "There isn't anyone quite like him." She considered a moment. "Now that I think on it, no one at St. Brendan's is like anyone I have ever met before." She took a chance. "You will fit right in."

"I could not be more delighted with my new calling in life than if King George himself had summoned me to duty," Grace said. "Er, dootie. You cannot imagine the boredom of life here." She clasped her hands in her lap, which Meridee already sensed was less a ladylike mannerism than a need to contain the exuberance bottled up inside this tall woman.

"Portsmouth and St. Brendan's are never dull," Meridee assured her.

Not one to waste a moment, she described the situation and why they were here. "Able and your brother feel Stephen will never function to his potential if he cannot know more about his parents and where they are. We're to learn what we can."

"So we shall." Grace picked up a sheet of paper from the end table and handed it to Meridee. "I received this from someone rejoicing in the name of Captain Sir Belvedere St. Anthony, giving us carte blanche to roam the Admiralty itself, once we have established which ship the Hoyts sailed on."

"That man!" Meridee exclaimed after she read the letter. "He seems to know precisely what we will need. 'In the bowels of that building, perhaps we should call it a catacomb where misdeeds and triumphs go to perish, you will find the Royal Navy logs of each convict convey,' " she read. "He does have a way with words."

"Thaddeus has mentioned Sir B, as he calls him," Grace said. "Will I like him?"

"More than you know," Meridee said.

"Thaddeus assures me I will only be at St. Brendan's to teach until the end of the term," Grace said. "He promises I will return soon enough to Half Moon Street to continue my boring life."

"He never said that," Meridee chided gently.

"No, but it is a boring life," Grace assured her. "I intend to make myself so valuable at St. Brendan the Navigator School that I will be able to put the furniture under Holland covers here and take the knocker off the door." She looked kindly at Meridee. "You have purpose and I need purpose, too."

After they spent a pleasant evening in Grace's company—Stephen serious and close to her side—Meridee quietly arranged for that cot in her room, plus a small snack for the middle of the night. She sat beside Stephen's cot for his nightly cry, then tucked the extra pillow on her own bed close to her side. Missing her husband, she went to sleep.

They headed for the Office of Criminal Business as soon as the earliest morning traffic died down. *If this is calm, I am grateful I live in raffy-scaffy Portsmouth*, she thought as their carriage moved slowly through streets with strange smells and shouting people.

"I lived in little Pomfrey in a vicarage with my sister and her family," she told Grace. "Then it was Portsmouth. I doubt I could manage London."

"Then thank the Lord you are with me," Grace said. She sat calm and above all tall, which seemed to Meridee to be almost a character trait of its own. "Here we are. Brave faces, everyone."

"Please, Mam, what is this place?" Stephen asked as the coachman deposited them on the sidewalk in front of a magnificent building.

"Someone in the last century decreed that London didn't have enough imposing structures, hence Somerset House," Grace said. "Even the Royal Society is housed here." She took in Stephen's puzzled look. "That's where the brilliant men of our age hold forth with experiments and treatises."

"Master Six should be there," he said, then frowned. "But he is a bastard wharf rat, too, and these are probably proper gentlemen."

Meridee was used to plain language, but she saw Grace was startled. "H'mm," the lady said, but she recovered quickly. "Some rules in our stuffy society need to change."

"As for now, we'll find the Office of Criminal Records and then the Navy Board," Meridee said. She took a deep breath, frightened nearly out of her shoes, except that Stephen Hoyt was looking at her as if she did this every day.

A porter directed them to a high desk where they faced their first hurdle, a clerk. "Gatekeepers are sometimes annoying little fellows," Grace said under her breath.

This gatekeeper surprised them. "We've been expecting you," he said, peering down at them from his great height. "Follow me, please."

Meridee exchanged a startled glance with Grace Croker, and Stephen Hoyt took her hand. At the end of the corridor, the clerk ushered them into an office full of ledgers and occupied by one small man, who stood and bowed.

Will wonders never cease? Meridee asked herself, as she curtsied. "I am Mrs. Six, and this is Miss Croker and Stephen Hoyt," she said. "We have come to—"

"I know why you are here, madam," the man said. He indicated a letter on his desk with a familiar crest. "Captain Sir Belvedere St. Anthony directed me to locate ship's manifests and whatever else you might need." He bowed again. "I am Edmund Guillory, chief of the Office of Criminal Records."

"Heavens, Captain St. Anthony is everywhere," Grace murmured, as Mr. Guillory gestured toward a long table and pulled out a chair. "You first, Meridee."

Meridee sat and removed her bonnet. When the three of them were seated, Mr. Guillory sat opposite Stephen Hoyt. "Lad, we are to find your parents?" he asked kindly, which further startled Meridee. She had expected a long face from someone searching for criminals, but Mr. Guillory seemed above that pettiness.

"Aye, sir," Stephen said in a soft voice. "Me mam and da were transported." He looked down at the table, shame coming off him in waves. Meridee took his hand.

"Can you recall what year, young fellow?" Mr. Guillory asked, pencil in hand now and poised over paper. "And their names."

"I was just turned five and now I am ten," he said. "It was autumn because the leaves were yellow. Lester and Mary Hoyt, sir."

"Five years ago," Mr. Guillory said. "That would be 1798. Let us see what we see. Lester Hoyt. Mary Hoyt."

The chief of Criminal Records turned to one ledger and flipped only a few pages. He ran his finger down one column. "That means they likely sailed on the *Hillsborough*, because that sailed in … let me see … mid October. Here we are: two hundred ninety-nine passengers, one hundred with life sentences." He ran his finger down the column and stopped. "Lester Holt, convicted of poaching. Here he is."

"Two rabbits. We was hungry."

"Two rabbits!" Grace Croker exclaimed. Mr. Guillory held up his hand with a warning look.

"A seven-year sentence."

"Thank goodness it wasn't three rabbits," Grace said, and Meridee heard all the venom one tall spinster was capable of. "Might have been ten years!"

"Miss Croker, we live in a society with rules," Mr. Guillory warned.

Alarmed, Meridee looked sideways at the tall woman who nearly seethed with indignation. *He's being so kind, Grace. Don't muddle it*, she thought, wishing the woman was susceptible to the process of thought telepathically rendered.

Perhaps she was. Grace sat back and tightened her lips into a thin line.

Mr. Guillory returned his attention to the ledger. He flipped a few more pages. "Sometimes the women sailed on separate ships, but this time … no, men and women." He ran his finger down a different column and stopped. "Here she is. My, my, battery of an officer of the crown." He looked up. "Ten years. What did she do, lad?"

Stephen leaned against Meridee. "A man came to take away Da and Mam hit him with a crockery bowl."

All they wanted was a meal, Meridee thought in misery, seeing in her mind's eye the crying, the shouting, the ferocity of a woman taken from her children, and an officer of the crown, perhaps bleeding. *Mary Hoyt, you shouldn't have struck the man*, she thought. *Ten years.*

"What … what happens after they have fulfilled their sentences?" Meridee asked into the deep silence of the room. "Somehow I thought anyone—"

"Any *convict*—"

"Yes, yes! Any convict must stay his whole life in New South Wales."

Back on firmer ground, now that Miss Croker remained silent and Meridee had asked a reasonable question, Mr. Guillory managed a tight smile.

"The crown is not entirely heartless," he said. "Once their sentence is completed, the former convicts are free to return. Of course, they must pay their own way back to England." He stopped. Maybe the crown *was* heartless, might have been on his mind.

"The world is not a fair place," Grace Croker said.

Mr. Guillory folded his hands together across the ledger that contained so much sadness. "It is not," he agreed. He turned his attention to Stephen Hoyt, who was sitting up straight and alert. "Lad, I see the emblem on your … is that a uniform?"

"St. Brendan the Navigator School in Portsmouth," he said. "When I get older and learn more, I'm joining the fleet. I'll find me mam and da."

"I wish you all success, lad," the chief said. He sat in silence a moment, then pulled out what looked like a memorandum tablet. He thought a moment more before he dipped a pen in his ink well. After blowing on the paper to dry it and dusting it with sand, he handed it to Meridee.

"Take this to the Navy Board," he said, all business again. "The *Hillsborough* was a ship contracted to the Royal Navy, with a civilian crew required to keep a log to turn over to the Board when the voyage ended."

"What will that tell us?" Meridee asked.

Mr. Guillory glanced at Stephen, and hesitated before he spoke. "It will list any deaths at sea or other misadventure. Let's provide this St. Brendan's lad with as much information as we can, if he is going to look for his parents."

Meridee folded the paper and slipped it into her reticule. "Will you direct us to the Navy Board?"

"Nothing simpler," he said, describing a few corridors to travel, and a descent into that underground cavern Sir B had called a catacomb.

He walked them to the door of his office. "Good luck to you, lad," he said. "Rumor swears the Treaty of Amiens is showing some fearful cracks. You may be at sea sooner, rather than later."

Chapter Thirty-Nine

⬦

A BLE SIX KNEW HE was too old to be moping over Meridee's absence. Trust Sir B to take a good look at him. "You are dragging around like a stallion with no mare in sight," he exclaimed, when Able plunked himself down at the dinner table in the St. Anthony residence. "My God, man! She'll return."

Sir B peered closer. "Your neck cloth is crooked, and did Mrs. Six abscond with the only comb when she went to London?"

"I'm a poor excuse for a master of *anything* right now," he admitted, running fingers through his hair.

Sir B gestured for more Madeira in Able's glass. "I have to tell you: Captain Hallowell and I once drank our way to the bottom of a bottle about this size in Plymouth, wondering if there was a woman anywhere who would succumb to your undeniable oddness." He raised his glass in salute. "You did extraordinarily well. She'll be home in a day or two."

Late as usual, Thaddeus Croker arrived when they were well into the first course. "I hope my sister is proving useful to Mrs. Six," he said. "She has a propensity to speak before she thinks, and I cannot imagine her holding her tongue in a department rejoicing in the name of Office of Criminal Records."

"Good," Sir B said. "No one should ever be complacent in such a place. I wonder what your student will learn, Able."

"Probably that the world remains unfair," Able said.

That sobering thought kept them silent through a handsome pheasant dish, removed with a figgy pudding and followed by fruit and nuts and smuggler's sherry.

Thaddeus had been silent, anyway, looking to Able like a man with bad news. Maybe he thought it would go down better with sherry.

"Out with it, Thaddeus," Sir B said finally, with an ease of command that

Able knew would never be his. From the look on Headmaster Croker's face, Able could tell which way the wind blew.

"Master Fletcher announced to me just as I was leaving for your house that he has been recalled to the fleet, effective at the end of the week," the headmaster said. "War is coming sooner than we reckoned."

"Are any of us surprised? I'll wager the issue is Malta," Sir B said.

"Yes, Malta," Thaddeus replied. "Haven't we suspected that? Only a fool would surrender Malta, our stationary frigate in the Mediterranean."

"Who d'ye think will strike first, Able?" Sir B asked.

"We will, because we must," he said promptly, as he felt dread grow inside for the boys he was teaching. "This will be a war without end."

"I must ask you for further sacrifice," Thaddeus said.

Able needed no hints. "Aye, sir, I will be happy to assume control of Master Fletcher's navigation classes."

"You read my mind," Thaddeus said. "Well and good, but how will you manage the older class with your younger lads each afternoon?"

"Would your sister be inclined to focus her time on rudimentary English and something as mundane as penmanship?" Able asked in turn. "I have my lads keeping their own logs, but they could use some improvement. She could take them for that part of the afternoon I teach navigation, after which *all* the boys will be learning to swim. Not just my class, if I may."

"Of course you may, Able. I can almost guarantee Grace will agree, to further the aims of the Royal Navy," Thaddeus assured him.

"Ah-ha! The truth comes out," Sir B joked. "You will probably tell me your blue-stocking sister once rejoiced in a lover in the Royal Navy."

"She did," the headmaster said, "a promising man who succumbed to yellow fever in Jamaica, two months before they were to marry." He gazed beyond the dining room wall. "My parents feared for her reason."

"I didn't mean …" Sir B began.

"I know you didn't. Grace Croker once had a gentler side," the headmaster said. "The war has wounded us all."

"And soon the conflict returns."

"We live in interesting times," Thaddeus said. He turned his attention to Able. "My apologies to your wife, but we need you more than she does. There will be an increase in salary." He peered closely at Able. "You might even be able to afford a comb soon, lad."

Able laughed, happy to banish a melancholy moment. "I *have* a comb, both of you. What I lack is my keeper, who reminds me to use it."

Thaddeus Croker elaborately turned his attention to Sir B, as though Able weren't there. "Captain, you and I know precisely what Durable Six will never give up for Lent."

"Indeed. It's lower down than his hair," Sir B said, equally serious.

"Gentlemen, it is no crime to miss my wife," Able protested.

"It's been only one day, Master Six," Thaddeus reminded him. "Go invent a theorem or something. Discover a new galaxy."

Sir B insisted on furnishing his carriage for the return to St. Brendan's. Thaddeus asked the coachman to drop them off at Gunwharf so they could walk the remainder of the way. They sauntered along slowly, until the headmaster stopped and looked up at the stars.

"Spring is here," he said. "My father used to tease me when I told him I could smell spring. 'M'boy, you possess an anticipatory nature,' he said, as though it were a crime. Spring's in the air, though. So is war. Any boys ready for the fleet?"

How long have I been dreading this question? Able asked himself. "Jan Yarmouth and Jamie MacGregor come immediately to mind," he replied, hating himself for speaking their names. He mentioned a few other lads, and then his voice trailed off. "I fear they will never know enough. Pray God we won't be ordered to reach down into the lower grade."

"Not yet, but I fear for them as well," the headmaster said.

Speak of the devil, his two calculus students sat on Able's front steps, arguing with each other. "Send them over here as soon as you can," the headmaster said. "It's late."

Able sat below them on the front steps. "What in the world have we here?"

"Jan swears he understands the calculus, and I remain lost," Jamie said honestly.

There they sat, two thirteen-year-olds, stewing over something most ordinary mortals would never comprehend. He invited them inside, where Betty scolded her twin for not knocking sooner. He glanced at Jan Yarmouth, who appeared as mystified as Able had been at that age, having no relatives who cared what became of him.

"Give us a lamp in the dining room, Betty," Able said. "There must be petits fours or treacle pudding in some cubby or dark corner, because this is a well-run establishment. Find them, please."

Smiling, she ran into the kitchen. Jamie followed her with his eyes. "Thank you for letting her join this household," the boy said.

"Thank Mrs. Six," Able said. "Betty is becoming precisely the maid of all work my wife needed."

"And if Betty had not been so proficient, sir?" Jamie asked, not a lad to shy away from hard questions.

"Mrs. Six would have kept her anyway," Able said promptly.

"Either way, I am in your debt, Master Six," the boy said. He was also not a lad to waste a moment. "We will be going to sea soon, won't we?"

"Did Master Fletcher say something?" Able asked.

"He didn't have to, sir. Master Fletcher has been timing us to see how long we take to climb that mast he set up next to the basin," Jamie said. "At the top, we can see activity in the Solent—little boats darting about, and masts going up on two of the frigates."

"You're observant," Able said.

"Jan saw them first, master," James told him. "Then Master Fletcher said we would have a new teacher of navigation starting next week."

"You will have me."

Jan had already seated himself at the table and was spreading out his proof. He flashed a rare smile at this news, which warmed Able as a fire never could.

"We will still have time for calc?" Jan asked.

"We'll make time."

Betty arrived with the lamp and Mrs. Perry followed with a tray of treacle pudding in large bowls. Meridee had remarked only last week that their cook seemed determined everyone should weigh as much as she did.

Betty set the bowls around and Jamie dug into his. Jan pointed to the paper. "Sir, I think I did it," he said.

Able picked up the paper, smiling at earlier crossed-out symbols, letters, and numbers, and then nodding as disorder coalesced into order and yielded the marvelous result, written plainly. Yes, Jan Yarmouth, bastard boy from a workhouse, understood Isaac Newton's masterpiece.

"Bravo, lad," Able said simply.

"Will you send me to sea with more problems?" he asked. "I need to keep my hand in this."

"I will."

He sat back as Jan explained his proof to Jamie, who shook his head. "Master Six, am I a dunderhead?" the boy asked in exasperation.

"Not at all, Jamie. The calculus is a mystery to many. Don't be hard on yourself. Master Fletcher tells me you are developing competence with the sextant."

Jamie was a stubborn Scot, a race Able recognized because whoever his father was, he knew his mother was from that damp, inhospitable region. "Then what is the purpose of calculus?"

Able turned to Jan. "Well, lad?"

"It is opening my mind to the universe of motion," he said simply.

Able stood on the front step until Jamie and Jan were inside St. Brendan's. After locking the front door, he went upstairs to look in on the boys, who—not to his surprise—had decided to sleep three in a room, now that Stephen Hoyt was in London.

In bed, he stared at the ceiling that Meri told him in a moment of sass had become her view, seen over his shoulder. He slept finally, but woke too soon, caught in a nightmare unlike any other.

His classroom was full of blood. He watched as if from a distance as his students struggled to stay afloat. The room turned into a drain swirling them around and then sucking them down, faster and faster.

Eyes open or eyes closed, it made no difference. He leaped out of bed, wide awake, but the dream did not abate until every one of his students had drowned in nightmare blood so authentic he could smell the iron in it.

Why did the dream feel so real? He darted across the hall and opened the room where the three lads slept. Turning back to his own room, he felt his relief turn to terror as he watched blood seep across the hall, moving directly toward his students. Soon the blood pooled around his ankles as he stared down in disbelief.

The blood began to pulse and he heard the beat of a superhuman heart. The door to one of the empty rooms opened and there stood curly-haired William Harvey holding up a copy of *De Motu Cordis*, his treatise on the circulation of blood, written in 1628. Able had read it in Latin during a slow afternoon in the Mediterranean.

He gasped when Harvey vanished into the circling drain too, pointing at his book and expressing indignation that someone with so much knowledge about blood should be treated so shabbily.

The vision mercifully passed. Able pressed his hand to his racing heart. *I am turning into a murderer*, he thought. He leaned against the wall, wondering how Meri would feel if he resigned from St. Brendan's and dragged her to a noisome rooming house while he sailed with the fleet into uncertainty, danger, and death.

Climbing into bed, he flopped onto his back, after absurdly checking his feet to make sure there was no blood on them. He knew Meridee would remind him that he had signed a contract to teach, and he could not go to the fleet unless he was summoned.

"I must see this through, Euclid," he said out loud to his friend who always waited to keep him company. "Hurry home, Meri."

Chapter Forty

⌘

To Able's relief, Meri arrived just before dinner the following night, full of good cheer and conversation. He took in her dear beauty, then smiled at Stephen, wondering what had happened and how soon he could have his wife to himself, because he needed her beyond words.

But setting an example for his students was important, even for a desperate man. Able took another look at Stephen and saw something in his eyes that appeared remarkably like hope. "Was it good news, lad?"

"Some good, some bad," Stephen replied. He glanced at Meridee, who gave an encouraging nod. "I can manage now."

When the boys trooped in to the dining room at Mrs. Perry's command, Able stole a moment with his wife while she removed her bonnet and fluffed her hair. And then she took a good look at him, and the light went out of her eyes.

"Able, what is the matter?" she asked … no, demanded.

"It will keep until the lads are in bed," he said, even though he wanted to blubber out his misery there by the coat closet.

"It's war, isn't it?" she asked, holding him off to better search his face.

"Aye, lass, and more," he said. "Dinner now. You know Mrs. Perry is a dragon when we dawdle."

The dragon didn't roar too loud, considering that she had been watching his drawn and melancholy mug for three days. He pretended not to notice the worried glance that passed between the two women and took his place at the head of the table, the man who had everything under control, except when he didn't.

Bless Stephen, who commanded conversation, telling his mates about the wonders of London, including Astley's Royal Amphitheatre their final evening in the great city, with tickets provided by Captain Sir Belvedere St. Anthony.

"There were horses," Stephen said between bites of pease pudding and brown bread. "One man even controlled four at the same time."

"Were you close enough to see well?" Nick asked.

"Close enough to smell horse shit," Stephen declared.

"I stayed at the Croker's townhouse," Meri told Able, leaning close. He breathed in the fragrance of lavender and knew he could survive until bedtime.

"A townhouse? Is our headmaster a far grander man than I suspected?"

"I believe he is," she whispered back. "And Grace Croker is a force to be reckoned with." She tapped the side of her glass with her fork and the boys turned to her, expectant.

"We also brought along your new British history and English instructor, Miss Croker," Meri announced. "She will be staying across the street at St. Brendan's."

Silence met this news. David Ten raised his hand tentatively. "Please, Mam, does she have a pointer?"

"Emphatically not," Meri said. "What she will do is fix you with an awful glare if you have not studied your books." She smiled at Stephen. "You may ask Stephen about her later."

"May I tell them what we learned?" Stephen asked.

"In the sitting room," Meri said. "You need to eat now."

Into the sitting room they went, with Mrs. Perry and Betty invited too, which meant that somehow Jamie MacGregor knew when to knock on the door, followed by Jan Yarmouth.

"I would say we have a true sitting room, wouldn't you, Husband?" Meri asked, as the younger boys ranged themselves cross-legged on the floor.

He said something, happy to let Meri direct the flow of conversation. Her arm went around his waist and she hooked her thumb into the waistband of his trousers, not really caring if anyone in the room noticed.

"Out with it, Stephen," John Mark said when everyone was seated. "Talk!"

The others chuckled. John Mark had the patience of a gnat.

"You first, Mam," Stephen said.

"We went to the Office of Criminal Business in a marvelous building called Somerset House," she said, then turned her lovely eyes on Able. "The Royal Society meets there, and you should belong to it."

"When pigs fly," he said, feeling amused for the first time since she went away. "Earthworms have more exalted pedigrees than mine."

"I suppose. I must thank Sir B personally for greasing our way. Mr. Guillory had the ledgers with their manifests right there on his desk and ready for us."

Stephen nodded. "We found my parents' names in the manifest for the *Hillsborough*, which sailed in October, five years ago."

"Once we found the names and the ship, Mr. Guillory directed us to the cellar of Somerset House, where ships' logs are kept," Meri said. "I don't precisely understand why the Royal Navy keeps those logs. Aren't those commercial ships the convicts sail on?"

"Aye, but they are contracted by the Navy Board," Able said. He felt himself relax as Meri leaned against him. "Mr. Hoyt, I'll wager you saw some pretty gruesome penmanship in those logs, did you not?"

"Aye, sir," Stephen said. "Gruesome."

"What did that tell you?"

"That maybe we need to improve our own penmanship in the logs we're keeping."

"Excellent, lad. Do continue."

"Miss Croker and Mam—uh, Mrs. Six—"

"Mam will do," Meri said.

Able watched the others in the room smile at that. He knew his darling was going to be Mam from now on, no matter how many little Gunwharf Rats eventually passed into their home. *Better and better*, he thought.

"The ladies looked through nine months of entries," Stephen explained. "I couldn't read the writing too well, so the porter set me to work putting memoran ... memo—"

"Memoranda," Meri inserted. "They are little orders and comments that get batted from office to office, I daresay."

"I put memoranda in order by date," he said. "I had me own desk too."

"He did," Meri told the others, quashing any disbelief. "He had a little date stamp too, to indicate when they were alphabetized."

Stephen took a deep breath. "Mam found the entry about me da." He looked down at his hands, as if gathering himself together.

Don't let it be something awful, Able thought.

When Stephen spoke, Able heard the pride. "Me father broke up a fight among the convicts when one of them tried to knife the other over some ship's biscuit," he said. "He died saving the victim."

The whole room seemed to sigh. "Gor, a hero," Nick whispered. "I'm sorry he died, Steph, but a hero!"

"I know," Stephen said. "The log entry stated it was the most noble act ever seen on a convict ship."

"And your mother?" Meri prompted.

Stephen's face brightened. "Nuffink in the daily logs about her death, but she did save a lady ... well, you explain it, Mam," he said, his face red.

"Apparently Mrs. Hoyt is a midwife," Meri said, and Stephen nodded. "Stephen remembers that about her from north of the River Thames, where they used to live. One of the convict women was brought to bed and had difficulty delivering the baby. Mrs. Hoyt saved her life and the infant boy's life."

Dear Meri. Her face was rosy telling something so intimate to lads. And now Australia had a future settler, plus Stephen's convict mother.

"Excellent," Able said. "Mr. Hoyt, your mother possesses a valuable skill that will serve her well in a new colony. I think you need not worry too much about her future there."

"That's what Mam said, too. She and Miss Croker had me write a letter to her, which will be sent with the next convict ship." His face fell and his shoulders drooped. "It'll be seven months getting there, then they have to find her, and then seven months getting back to me. That's a long time to wait for a letter."

Everyone in the room nodded. Jamie MacGregor patted the boy's shoulder. "But you *know*, and that's worth almost gold. When you have trained here for two or three more years, you'll be ready to sail to Australia."

The boys nodded again. *God bless Jamie MacGregor, leader in the making.* Able already knew the Gunwharf Rats looked up to the older lad who had found his twin sister.

"You won't be tempted to fly the coop again?" Jamie asked, and again Able applauded silently. Better the admonition come from one of their own.

"I might be tempted, but I won't," Stephen promised. He yawned, and Able glanced at the mantelpiece clock, a gift from that same Sir B who seemed to be greasing everyone's wheels.

"Lads, morning comes early," Able said. "Steel yourselves. Tomorrow afternoon, it's into the stone basin with all of you. Mr. MacGregor and Mr. Yarmouth, you are requested and required to attend as well. Inform the others your age. We're going to float and we're going to swim." He clapped his hands. "Bedtime." He looked at them expectantly.

"Handsomely now!" his Gunwharf Rats shouted and raced double time for their rooms, after snatching up the biscuits twisted into wax paper that Mrs. Perry always set by the stairs.

"Enough for us, sir?" Jan asked. "We like the goodies too."

"Aye. Goodnight. And we *will* have time for the calculus tomorrow," Able said.

Go away, go away, he thought, as Meri took her time saying goodnight to Mrs. Perry and Betty. In their room, he shucked his clothing into an untidy pile and threw on his nightshirt. Perhaps he could close his eyes tonight after general merrymaking and not see that damnable river of blood again.

His wife seemed to take her own sweet time saying goodnight to the lads across the hall. He heard their laughter and begrudged them every second with his darling, even as he cursed himself for being a fool of magisterial proportions.

Ah, there she was, her face stark and serious because no matter how vaunted *his* mind, Meridee Six had a special knack for knowing when all was not well.

She went right to the bed where he lay and sat down beside him. "My love, what is wrong?"

"I don't even know how to tell you," he began, and then the words tumbled out. By the time he finished his narration of bloody drains, his little students swirling down to their deaths, and the Treaty of Amiens in tatters, she lay next to him, her hand over his eyes. Were his eyes closed and moving? He had been unaware.

He prepared to let her cry, not that he could have stopped her, and then Meri surprised him.

She sat up. "Husband, you have just told me about a room of blood and your students drowning, and the Treaty nearly gone. Then you told me about a Pythagorean theorem, and something about Euclid and isosceles triangles. With scarcely time to draw a breath, you were back on the steps of that church in Dumfries, newly born, and then it was something about 'For every action there is an equal and positive—' "

"Opposite—"

"Reaction."

She grabbed him by the shoulders and shook him, her face close to his. Was she trying to stop the flow? "I have to know something. When you are just … just going about your business on an average day, how many thoughts go through your mind at the same time?"

Thank God. She was going to save him because she understood, as much as any sane person could understand. "At least three major conversations or events—battles, beatings, amputations," he said, "plus little scenes jumbled in somehow, depending on how tired I am or discouraged or overworked. Or missing you."

She rested her head on his chest. "I had no idea it was such a quantity," she said finally. "Able, how do you manage a mind like yours?"

He had no answer. He had never known anyone like himself either. He lifted her from his chest and looked at her closer. "There is only one time I have close to a single thought in my head. Is there any wonder I crave such times?"

The terror left her eyes, and she understood. Was ever a genius so fortunate?

She turned around. "Unbutton me." When he finished, she looked him in the eyes and took off every stitch of clothing as he watched. Naked, she carried her dress, stockings, and shimmy into their dressing room and laughed when she saw the disordered mound of clothing already there. She threw hers on top, which made him smile.

"I won't go away again," she said as she pulled back the covers. "Able, get rid of that nightshirt. Handsomely, now."

Chapter Forty-One

⚬⚭⚬

"**H**USBAND, IT IS A good thing I am also fond of general merrymaking," Meridee said. "A more skeptical wife might think you are making up all this and preying on my good nature just for more … um … you know."

That earned her a pat on the fanny. The pat turned into a caress, followed by his hand growing more heavy. In another moment, he slept.

She nudged him awake a few hours later, ready to confess, because her lively conscience would not let her sleep. He reached for her, and she held him off. "You need to know something first, Romeo," she said. "I must confess to a lie of massive proportions."

"How bad can it be?" he asked, sitting up and folding his hands primly in his bare lap, sort of but not quite covering his private parts.

She pulled the blanket over him. "I don't need any added distractions," she scolded, which made him chuckle and relieved her heart, because he appeared to be focusing on her alone. But how could she know?

"I lied about that entry in the *Hillsborough* log, describing the incident with Stephen's father," she said, too embarrassed to look her husband in the eye. What must he think of her? "Lester Hoyt was the perpetrator, not the hero."

There. She had confessed. "I should have known better, but Able, did Stephen need *more* bad news? How much becomes too much?"

She held her breath as Able leaned toward her and kissed her forehead. "You aren't too disappointed in me?" she asked, after he did it again.

"You rendered a kind service to a child."

Her husband's quiet assessment was balm to her soul. Still, she knew better. "I can't imagine the Lord is pleased, but thank you," she said.

"*Au contraire*," Able said. "The Lord has probably already directed one of his angels to place an entire row of gold medallions in your book of life. Come closer."

Meridee moved closer, her back to the headboard, and rested her cheek against his shoulder. "Certainly Stephen was sad to learn of his father's death—I daren't alter that—but his face turned calm when I ... after I told my lie."

"I suggest you dismiss the matter from your mind," he advised. "This is what he needed to hear now. Leave it at that." He rubbed her bare shoulder. "Goodness, you're cold. We can either light a fire, or we can economize on fuel by taking advantage of the dark and quiet."

"I vote for the latter," she said, and slid down in the bed again. "You're thinking only of me?" she whispered in his ear as he kissed her throat this time.

"Only you."

PERHAPS ABLE WAS RIGHT about her book of life. After Stephen's errand to London, Meridee knew she would never look at her little charges the same way again. Where she had been silent about their earlier lives, fearing to open barely healing wounds, she asked questions and learned more than she wanted to know, except it was exactly what she needed to know. To her further surprise, they seemed almost eager to talk about their trials.

After strategizing with Mrs. Perry to keep the others busy, Meridee spent a delightful evening with Nick, alone at first, then joined by the others. They all ended up with a fit of giggles as he auditioned last names, ranging from Haydn, because she liked *The Surprise Symphony*, to Kedgeree, because the homely dish Anglicized with fish and cream instead of lentils and Indian spices had become his favorite meal.

Able contributed Cosine as a possible surname, because Nick had a right understanding of geometry before the others in his class, while David Ten suggested Nick consider numbers. "Six and Ten are taken in this household, but think of the variety," Davey had said.

"And you're short, so p'raps Eight and a Half will do," John Mark said. "Just run it together like one word." He wrote Eightandahalf on a spare scrap of paper. "And look, you can pronounce it however you choose. I like Atandehalf, with the accent on *tan*."

It was monumental silliness, but nothing made Meridee happier than to hear the solemn boys ribbing each other. Able, not so dignified, slapped his forehead and flopped back on the sofa, carrying her with him. The boys laughed harder, and her heart was at peace.

There wasn't much else she could do for her husband, except make sure he was tidy every morning and love him at night, provided she wasn't half dead from household duties and doing battle in the market with grocers and butchers who were devious in the extreme.

"I ask you, Able, do those men train before mirrors to pull long faces and bring tears to their eyes when I suggest in my politest fashion that they are overcharging me?" she asked one night while he brushed her hair. It was a pastime she adored, and which she noticed relaxed him.

"Have you tried batting your eyelashes at them and swaying your behind a bit?" he suggested. "I know it inspires *me* to pay attention."

"That is a perfectly wretched idea and you know it, Husband," she said. "I suppose it is impossible to expect fair play in a Navy town where victuallers tell me that if I do not cough up their prices, there are many ships preparing for long voyages who will."

He put his hands on her shoulders at that. "Have they said as much?"

"One or two. It seemed to slip out." She looked up, met his gaze in the mirror, and understood. "Able, are they outfitting ships for war?"

"I fear so, but keeping it reasonably quiet. I suppose there are French spies everywhere." He set the hairbrush on the dresser. "Life is going to change soon and I dread it."

"You're doing everything in your power to make lads like Jamie MacGregor and Jan Yarmouth prepared and useful," she reminded him later, comfortable in bed, as her eyes started to close.

"It will never be enough."

"Able, you would say that if you had been teaching them for years, and not mere months," she countered. "This is your Keeper, ordering you to go to sleep. You, too, Euclid."

"Aye, Mam," he said, and she felt his chuckle.

THE MORNING BROUGHT A handwritten note from Sir B, informing her that his carriage would be in Saint's Way at ten o'clock to take her to his house.

"He's getting peremptory," Able remarked, as he stood still while Meridee gave his neck cloth one more twitch. "I often wonder how much he knows about the current state of affairs in the fleet."

"Should I ask him point blank?" she said.

"He will never tell you. Stay out of trouble and send Mrs. Perry to joust with the butchers and greengrocers today, will you?"

"Aye, sir," she said.

Sir B's carriage was there at ten precisely. She made John Coachman stop at the bakery and picked up macaroons from Ezekiel, who asked about Stephen Hoyt. She told him about their experience in London and he nodded.

"It's tough to be a workhouse lad, I would imagine," he said, giving a little pat to the pasteboard box before he handed it to her.

"I'm grateful it was never my lot," she said and tried to pay him.

He waved away her coins. "Sometimes I am overcome with a generous nature," he whispered. "Just don't tell me ball and chain in the back room."

"My lips are sealed. These are going to a bona fide hero, a man with one leg. He'll be grateful, too."

I wish all shopkeepers were as kind as our baker, she thought, as they rolled from their rough streets to the more genteel heights. She looked down at St. Brendan's, small in the distance, and her own home across the street, more dear to her with each passing day.

Each visit to Captain St. Anthony's mansion started with a wary knock on the door, but none of them had reproduced her first frightening experience. Sir Belvedere reclined on a chaise longue, wearing an eye-popping paisley robe that an Oriental potentate would envy. He waved a hand at her and pointed to a chair pulled close.

"I'm standing on no ceremony this morning," he told her. "I hardly stand at all, do I? And what have you brought me?"

"Macaroons from my favorite baker," she said and undid the ribbon on the box. "Save me one."

He popped one in his mouth and rolled his eyes. "Magnificent."

"Bartleby swears that he gives us the day's leftovers. Between you and me, I believe he bakes us fresh goods and thinks I won't know the difference."

"My dear Meridee Six, I do believe you gather admirers like a magnet attracts metal filings. I have some news for you."

"Say on, sir, and stop filling your face with macaroons," she teased.

"You brought them, remember," he teased back. "I have a friend from earlier days, one Bradford Quaiffe, who is sailing to New South Wales with his wife and hopeful family."

"On purpose?" she asked, dubious, which meant it was her turn to reach for a macaroon. Hours of reading depressing log entries from the *Hillsborough* convinced her that any passage to Australia was unhealthy in the extreme.

"Yes, Mrs. Six, on purpose! He has accepted a position as chief clerk in the colonial government offices, and sails next week from Plymouth."

"I'm happy for him," she said politely.

"Quaiffe and his wife belong to the Society of Friends," Sir B said. "They've suffered their share of indignities for their religion, and now children at school have started bullying their little ones. A change is in order."

She knew Sir B well enough now to at least suspect he had something to do with the events at hand. "And you found him employment in Australia," she said, knowing it was more fact than question.

"I happen to know a lot of people in more exalted circles than St. Brendan's," he replied, vague as usual when she tried to press him for details. "He was grateful for my help, and I asked for his." He leaned forward. "Meridee, he is perfectly willing to take Stephen Hoyt along with him."

Speechless, she reached for another macaroon, and he slapped her hand. "Mine," he said. "What do you think?"

Could it be more obvious what she thought, especially when she started fumbling in her reticule for a handkerchief? She swallowed, she sniffed, then she boohooed into a handkerchief that Sir B generously provided, since she couldn't find hers.

"I am going to assume that is a yes, you noisy baggage," he teased.

She nodded. After a vigorous blowing of her nose that made her laugh because Sir B put his hands to his face in mock horror, she managed, "Yes!"

"What a relief, since I already told Mr. Quaiffe that I would have one little boy ready to sail from Plymouth within the week," Sir B told her.

"You are nearly the best man I know," Meridee said, and she never meant anything more. "Stephen has agreed to wait months and months for a letter back, and promises to never run away again, but his heart is already in New South Wales."

"Then we should put the rest of him there," Sir B concluded. "I've already discussed the matter with Thaddeus, and he agrees. Will Able be disappointed?"

"No. I believe he will be relieved," she told him, uncertain how much of their intimate conversations she should share. She decided the captain needed to know. "Sir B, my dear husband will see this turn of events as saving one student from possible death in the fleet."

She opened her heart to Sir B, telling him of Able's awful nightmare of his students drowning in blood. "I do everything I can to distract him from the way his mind turns at times, but I defy even the best keeper in the world to distract him from death. He's far too intelligent to be tricked."

"Without question."

Meridee stood and paced the room. How much to tell this man? She stopped and regarded him, and knew she could tell him anything. What's more, she had to. "When this war resumes and his lads are in danger, I fear it will go beyond the collapse I witnessed after Nick's recovery. Sir Belvedere, I love him! What can we do?"

No answer. Meridee went to the door. "I'll have Stephen ready to travel."

More silence. She opened the door and looked back when Sir B cleared his throat. *What am I doing here?* she asked herself. *I am treading in deep water.*

"I would fear more for Able, except for one thing, madam."

"Which is?"

"He has a worthy keeper."

Chapter Forty-Two

❦

ESPITE MRS. PERRY'S CONCERN, Meridee said she needed to rest and supplied no further commentary on her visit. She took off her shoes and lay down, long past questioning her decision to marry Sailing Master Durable Six.

Without a qualm, she had brushed past the forest of red flags warning her away from such a decision. Life had been simpler when she was a spinster with not an expectation in the world, but she never wanted to retreat to that state again.

What had changed in recent weeks, when she became even more aware of her husband's startling intelligence, was that such a gift was more curse than blessing. She never doubted his ability to teach anything to anyone. This skill was evident to all who spent any time in his orbit as he instructed so casually in his classroom, shivered with his students in the stone basin, or sat on the floor playing jackstraws, where he turned sticks into geometry. He could forge the simplest game or comment into purpose, research, hypothesis, experiment, and analysis as his students learned almost without knowing they were learning. What was evident to no one but her was the toll it took on his heart.

Only someone sharing intimate moments with Able Six could ever understand how his brain raced, caught in a remorseless cycle of thought. Coupled with the disturbing images of destruction to come, her man was trapped by a superabundance of emotions mingled with blinding knowledge that no ordinary person could even fathom. His genius ruled his life, and hers, too, whether she wished it so or not.

She cherished moments when his thoughts turned only, or nearly only, to her. No matter what lay ahead, she wanted to be nowhere but in her husband's arms, chatting through the day as normal people did, then drifting to sleep after general merrymaking that seemed to intensify as the threat of war came closer.

With the departure of Master Fletcher to the fleet, Able had assumed the entire mathematical and navigational instruction at St. Brendan's, much to Thaddeus Croker's relief and approbation. "My God, but the man has amazing facility to bring a classroom of ordinary lads to unexpected potential," the headmaster had told her one evening when she visited with Grace Croker while Able taught his two calculus students in their dining room.

The cost is high, she wanted to tell the headmaster, but doubted he would hear her. Although nothing specific had reached them, all thoughts in Portsmouth focused on war, and soon. Ever the observer, Meridee had noticed how little the matter was spoken of, but how activity had increased along Gunwharf, as newly refitted ships loaded their cannons back on board. More seamen seemed to arrive daily, and more ships sailed. Silent for months, the ropewalk not far from St. Brendan's announced its renewal with screeches and groans.

She had extracted permission to take the younger class to visit the ropewalk. They had all come away fair amazed at the noisy work in the stone building some quarter mile in length, and suitably impressed with the fact that nearly four miles of rope found its way on board the average frigate.

The smell of hot tar bothered her stomach, but that was nothing to the thrill of walking alongside the rope maker as he directed the twisting of thick strands into even more stout rope destined to support the sails that put wings to His Majesty's fleet.

Under Mrs. Perry's direction, her little lodgers applied themselves to making wooden platforms to support ballast. When at dawn she asked him why, Able took a moment, her head pillowed against his shoulder, to explain the importance of proper arrangement of ballast to correct sailing.

"Husband, you realize this is odd conversation, both of us naked," she teased, which made him laugh and tug her closer. He was still smiling when he drifted back to sleep, his eyes calm this time under closed lids.

Master Six taught his lads how to distribute ballast on their simulated ships to keep them afloat. Meridee's fingers grew scratchy from making small burlap bags for varying weights of miniature cargo.

Stephen Hoyt's last official duty as a St. Brendan the Navigator student was to stuff the bags with varying amounts of wood chips, soil, and iron filings. He had always worked quietly and soberly, but there was a difference now. Meridee saw it in the way he held himself. When she looked in his eyes, hope looked back at her. He was going to find his mother.

Able had stressed the "might be" part of the equation that last night, as

Meridee counted and packed stockings, smallclothes, and shirts into her husband's extra duffel.

"It held my gear through many a voyage, but it still won't pack itself," Able said, as he sat on Stephen's bed and folded the clothing even tighter. When most of Stephen's clothing and four books, courtesy of Grace Croker, were stowed away shipshape, there was still room for more.

"Are we forgetting anything?" Meridee asked, looking around at the spartan room.

"Nay, Mam. I didn't come with much, think on," Stephen reminded her.

"Just with what was between your ears, my dear," she said with a smile and a look at Able. "That's all you really need."

"Know this, too, Mr. Hoyt," Able said seriously. "You might not find your mother right away. You might not find her at all. That's the risk you run."

Stephen nodded, but the hope never left his eyes.

"One thing more." Able left the room and returned with a collapsing telescope. He held it out to Stephen. "Every lad on a lengthy voyage should spend some time in observation. Use your log to record something every day, including fish sighted, whales blowing, and squalls approaching. Keep a record, Mr. Hoyt."

It was almost too much for the workhouse boy. He stared at the telescope in his hands. "Sir, no one has ever given me anything," he managed to say.

"Mr. Bartleby sneaks you the occasional pasty from the bakery," she said.

"Then looks at me as if daring me to say no, Mam," Stephen said. "I expect he'll find another excuse, once I leave."

"I expect he will, my dear," Meridee said, then held out her arms to him. "We'll miss you, but it's a good kind of missing, isn't it, Able?"

Silent, he gathered the two of them close. "Remember what you've learned, boy, and find your mother."

Sober in his black uniform with the St. Brendan's crest, Stephen Hoyt climbed aboard Sir B's carriage, where the captain's valet waited to accompany the boy to Plymouth and the HMS *Dauntless*, frigate, sailing to the Antipodes. To Meridee's relief, there was also a plainly dressed lady in the carriage. She stepped down long enough to introduce herself as Mrs. Bradford Quaiffe.

"Rest assured that Stephen will be well-tended in my household," Mrs. Quaiffe said, as she patted Meridee's hand. "The captain says we can mail letters home when we reach Rio de Janeiro to take on supplies. I'll make certain Stephen writes to thee."

And then he was gone. Meridee held Able's hand close to her body as they watched the carriage travel to the end of the street. Her heart tender, Meridee saw the baker and his wife wave to the carriage as it passed.

"Back to work, my love," Able said as he put his arm around her shoulder and turned her toward their front steps, where their other lodgers stood. "Plenty of us still have need of you—me more than most," he whispered in her ear. "I spy three melancholy lads. Should we move Davey permanently into the room with Nick and John Mark?"

"I'll ask them."

"You'll stay with me, won't you, Mrs. Six?" he teased.

"Even if I blow bubbles on your chest?" she asked, joking in turn, even though his eyes were serious. Perhaps he would always wonder a little if someone was going to come for him; workhouse ways seemed to die hard, if at all.

"Aye, Mam. Even then."

Chapter Forty-Three

⌒⌒∞⌒⌒

W AR CAME, NOT WITH a bang or tumult, but with a tap on the front door, and the whisper of a late-night meeting in Thaddeus Croker's chambers.

The boys were in bed and Meri was putting the finishing touches on what had become the nightly ritual of reading, prayers, and a final hug. Able had returned to the sitting room, craving a moment of as much solitude as his noisy brain ever permitted him to think through tomorrow's lessons.

Was he a creature of ritual, too? He blamed Mrs. Perry for a nightly baking of bread that always drew him into the kitchen for the buttered heel of a loaf of brown bread. He had never known white bread in the workhouse, and certainly not butter, but the fragrance, texture, and odor of too much butter meeting with the coarser brown bread invariably sent him upstairs to bed with a smile.

He had explained to Meri with some dignity that his only purpose in the kitchen was to make certain all was shipshape below before he relinquished the HMS *Six* to the night watch, but she saw right through him. "Call it a ritual or whatever you wish, but you had better bring me a piece of that bread, too, if you know what's good for you," she warned.

David Ten had begun his own ritual in Able's classroom. No math scholar he, Davey began what Able mentally assigned the name of Gunwharf Rat Ritual.

After a particularly grueling written examination involving dread fractions and decimals, Davey survived to fight another day. As his fellow students filed out for their next class, Davey had walked over to the wall where the Gunwharf Rat hung. He touched the rat's tail, then left the room. Soon the others did the same after each test, touching *rattus norvegicus's* tail.

His own heel eaten and buttered bread in hand for Meri, Able bid the kitchen ladies goodnight. From the hallway, he heard the soft tap on the already locked front door. He knew what it meant. He stood there a moment as his brain raced, then opened the door.

Thaddeus Croker's valet had merely to look at Able and with solemnity, declare, "Master Croker's chamber, as soon as ever possible."

He had been waiting for the summons, dreading it, and trying to avoid it, although every corner of his brain had mocked him with the word *war*, repeated ten times a second over the past month. Not even Meri's lovemaking had entirely blocked that drone, though he never told her.

He walked upstairs slowly, bread in hand. She sat in bed already, hair brushed, waiting for the bread. Looking down, he noticed he had eaten half of it on the way. "I suppose I was hungrier than usual," he said, and handed it to her.

She took it, her eyes on his face. "What now?" she asked, and got out of bed.

"I'm been summoned to Master Croker's chambers," he said, and turned away to find his shoes.

"War," she said. It was not a question.

He nodded, unable to reply.

"I'm coming."

"No, love, it's my summons," he reminded her.

"And you are bone of my bone and flesh of my flesh," she told him. "I will sit with Grace in her room, but I am coming with you."

He knew better than to extend an argument he had already lost. Truth to tell, her hand in his as they crossed the street buoyed him up. Magnanimous in victory, Meri had already given him the remaining bread and butter; she was never one to chortle over success.

Headmaster Croker seemed not at all surprised to see them both. "You'll sit with Grace," he told Meri. "She knew you were coming too."

Master Fletcher and Sir B waited in Thaddeus's office. "You first, Master Fletcher," Croker said with no preamble.

"I'm sailing tomorrow with the fleet," the former instructor said. "I wanted you to know."

"Where away?" Able asked.

"Malta."

Of course. Sir B had assured them that Henry Addison's ministry had stalled for fourteen months, unwilling to return that strategic real estate to the Knights of St. John, Malta's legal owners. Sure as the world, the French would seize it, if the Royal Navy was not there to stop them.

Silence ruled, broken finally by Sir B. "Are any of us surprised?" he asked. "I thought not." To the headmaster, he held out a sheet of paper that had been folded twice and sealed in that manner employed by Admiralty. The seal was broken. "This came my way by special messenger this evening."

Thaddeus read it to himself, then out loud. " 'With the consent of all parties concerned, you, Thaddeus Croker, are requested and required to furnish to the fleet four lads of St. Brendan the Navigator School to serve as apprentice sailing masters to the four captains listed below.' "

Thaddeus named them, and Able felt his heart relax a little. He knew the men as sober, reliable, and of utmost courage. They would never shy away from a fight.

" 'Prepare them for the fleet,' " Thaddeus continued. " 'They sail with the tide on or about the tenth of April, Year of our Lord 1803.' Signed John Jervis, Earl of St. Vincent, First Lord of the Admiralty. There you have it, gentlemen."

He looked around the small circle and stopped at Able. "Render me the names of your four best students, Master Six. We are at war."

"This is a hard decision," Able said, even though he knew it was anything but.

So, apparently, did Sir B. "Come, come, Able. You know precisely whom to select. I daresay you have known for weeks." He smiled at Able, and Able hated him for a moment, but only just. "That is your dilemma, my friend. We know you know and you cannot deceive us."

Certainly, I know, Able thought. *I wish I could say otherwise, but then I would be a worse liar than Meri Six. She is dreadful, except when it comes to not breaking a little boy's heart.*

"Janus Yarmouth, without question," he said promptly, hating every word that came from his mouth as he sent his boys to the fleet and possible death. "Jamie MacGregor. He is proficient enough, but his greater skill lies in leadership. Eventually he will command men, I do not doubt." He named the two other students in his upper class equally worthy and sat back, exhausted and sore of heart.

He had to know more. "Sir B, does your information state where away these specific frigates?"

"Two to the renewed blockade, and two to Malta. Beyond that, I know not."

The meeting got worse then, if that were possible. The headmaster picked up another sheet of paper, stared at it a long moment as if he had only seen it for the first time, and handed it silently to Able.

I've been recalled to the fleet, was Able's first thought. Last year, when he was starving ashore in Plymouth on half pay, he would have welcomed such news. Now with Meridee Bonfort Six in his life, he wasn't so certain.

Could it be worse than this? Good God, no. He read the words in a blink. "The Navy Board wishes to know if there are any lads in my lower class who might be suited for duty, as well." He rested his overworked head in the palm of his hand then looked up. "I will ask them, sir, but it must be voluntary. They are so young."

"You went to sea at nine," Croker reminded him, damn the man.

"Aye, sir. It was that or die of beatings," he snapped.

They stared each other down. Thaddeus Croker looked away first. "Very well, Able. They must volunteer."

There was nothing more to ask or say. Able turned his attention to the headmaster, and noted with some small satisfaction that he was not the only man to suffer with such news. The headmaster's eyes had filled with tears. He swallowed several times, then mastered his emotions.

"To bed, gentlemen. It is late, and I am certain we all wish to toss and turn tonight and get up bleary-eyed and cross. I will make the announcement at breakfast. Master Six, your lodgers will break their fasts across the street tomorrow."

"Aye, sir."

Not trusting himself to bid either man a civil goodnight, Able fetched Meri from Grace Croker's private sitting room, a tiny nook tucked in the corner of the headmaster's rooms.

He didn't walk his wife directly home, but circled around behind the school to stare down at the water level in the stone basin. "We'll raise it to eight feet tomorrow with the tide and practice nautical rescue."

Meri cried when he told her the news of Jan and Jamie joining the fleet. He held her close, or maybe she held him close. It was hard to tell.

Chapter Forty~Four

❧

ABLE GAVE UP ATTEMPTING sleep after hours of lying awake and twisting himself into the blankets. Getting up as quietly as he could, he tiptoed downstairs and sat in the dining room to create page after page of geometry questions and solve them. He had moved on to the calculus when Meri joined him.

"I tried not to wake you," he said, speaking to her even as he continued his relentless diagrams.

"Who was asleep?" she asked. "I'll sit here and mend stockings. Able, you really need to trim your toenails now and then. You are not an orangutan."

Gadfreys, but she was hilarious. Able shoved away the papers and laughed. In a moment she was smiling too. She pulled out her darning egg and he returned to his calculations. By the time dawn made its way to the forgotten street in scabrous Pompey, she announced her morning plan.

"I'm coming with you to breakfast."

"I wouldn't recommend it."

"Then thank goodness it isn't your decision," she said firmly.

The six of them crossed the street an hour later, Mrs. Perry having inserted herself in the equation. No, seven. After dodging a grocer's cart, Betty joined them at the steps of St. Brendan's, her expression allowing no denial.

Able surveyed his entourage. "I used to think I had some power of command," he said to no one in particular, which made Meri jab him in the ribs. "Ow! The women in my life ignore me. Let this be a lesson to you boys. Ladies rule."

Funny how the very air could change in the venerable old refectory where monks had once eaten more sparing meals as they listened to St. Benedict's Order read aloud. After the prayer, Headmaster Croker slowly rose, almost as if he had aged a century since last night's meeting.

"What I say here is secret. Divulge it on pain of immediate return to your respective workhouses," Thaddeus said. "War will be declared soon and the fleet at Portsmouth will sail within the next week."

He paused for a deep breath. Able knew what such a declaration cost the man who had started this school on his own, before the idea took hold in Navy circles. "Janus Yarmouth, Jamie MacGregor, William Five, and Arthur Trevithick will report in a week to the HMS *Terror, Albemarle, Arundel,* and *Speedwell,* there to serve as apprentice sailing masters."

Able looked at Jan and Jamie, who whooped with delight at the news that was causing him nothing but grief and misgivings of a profound nature. Betty burst into tears and ended up folded in Mrs. Perry's embrace. Meri pressed her lips tight together.

"Master Six, I believe you have an announcement, too."

Meri looked at him in surprise. Last night he had lacked the courage to tell her the rest of Headmaster Croker's order. He walked to the front of the dining hall to stand beside Thaddeus. He decided it would be better not to look at Meri while he delivered his news.

"The Navy Board is also soliciting the service of younger lads."

Meri's sudden intake of breath went into his heart like a cutlass and lodged there.

"For the present, such a commitment must be on a voluntary basis. I, for one, have much to teach you younger men to prepare you for successful service in the fleet. I would prefer that you remain with me, but this is your choice. See me in class."

He sat down next to Meri and did not imagine that she slid away from him. "No, Meri," he whispered. "Never do that to me. I follow orders."

Silently, she moved close to him again. He put his arm around her and kept it there through breakfast, which neither of them could swallow. He listened to the excited chatter of the boys in the upper class and understood the emotion of going to sea for the first time. It had never grown old for him, and for a small moment, he envied their chance to pit themselves against the French and Spanish navies. He knew Meri would never understand.

"There you have it, my love," he told Meri when the meal was over and he walked her to the main door. "I'll see you this evening. We'll be practicing nautical rescue and showing up wet for dinner."

She nodded, not looking at him, but burrowing close as if she did not want to ever let go. "This is too hard," she said finally.

"Would you believe me if I tell you I hate war?" he asked.

"I am not certain I would," she said. She hurried across the street.

Pray God I have not ruined the one person who keeps me alive, he thought, as he prepared to join his younger students. Miss Croker was taking the older lads for morning classes and so walked beside him up the stairs.

"Meridee has a soft heart," Grace remarked in her spare way. "I do not. Your younger boys are going to practice more penmanship and composition until either I am satisfied, or Napoleon himself appears in my classroom."

"Miss Croker, you are certifiable," he said, happy to tease and lift the gloom that had settled around his heart. So she thought only Meri was soft? He must be a better actor than he knew.

In his classroom, Able handed back test results, which made Davey Ten sigh and rest his forehead on his desk.

"Mr. Ten, I recommend more earnest delving into the wonderful world of decimals," he said. "The dining room. Tonight." He looked up. "The rest of you may attend, if you choose."

The morning passed quickly enough. When the boys filed downstairs for the noon meal, Davey stayed behind and Able's heart dipped lower.

"Aye, Davey?" he asked, knowing what was coming and dreading it.

"I'm no great shakes with mathematics," Davey said. "Master Six, I would go into the fleet now."

"You will greatly disappoint Mam," he said.

"I know, sir, but I have an idea," the little boy said, looking at Able with those old eyes all the workhouse boys possessed—he, as well.

"Speak."

"Sir, you know I like bones, and I didn't flinch when John Mark rammed that splinter up his fingernail."

"No, you didn't. In fact, I told you precisely what to do to remove it and you followed every direction," Able replied, feeling hopeful because he suddenly had a plan. At times his cursed brain did him a real favor.

"Master, I will go to sea as a loblolly boy," Davey said. "I'd rather do that than mathematics, and shooting the sun and plotting courses."

"Possibly," Able agreed. "I hate to bring up another sore subject, but you're not precisely proficient at swimming yet."

Davey's face fell. "I could try harder," he mumbled.

"You could. We'll practice again today, once the afternoon classes are finished."

"Aye, sir. But what do you think?"

Far too much to ever explain to you, he told himself. "I think it is a good idea, Davey. Mam won't."

"I know, sir." Davey brightened. "Can you sweeten her up?"

"I'll try," he said, wondering what the boys thought about Able and Meridee Six behind their bedroom door.

He wrote a quick letter and made certain it went with the day's mail.

Lunch in the dining hall was gall and wormwood again, but he knew he had to eat, so he did.

He sat at the table with his upper class boys, watching the animation on the faces of the ones headed to the fleet. No matter how many facts he stuffed into their heads, it wouldn't be enough. Now they would learn from others, and from the hard school of fleet action.

Headmaster Croker had wrangled a jolly boat from Gunwharf, and it was bobbing in the basin when they adjourned for nautical rescue. The boys wore their oldest clothes, sparing their class uniforms as they tossed each other into the basin and swam to the boat, to be hauled aboard by a firm hand on their waistband. They practiced over and over until the sun began to sink in the west and everyone was shivering. Able wasn't certain how Meri would receive him and three soaked lodgers, but he told himself he was a man and not a mouse.

"That's it, lads. You four there take turns practicing your cleat knot to fix the boat to the basin," he ordered. "We'll practice again tomorrow."

He had to smile at their high spirits. He understood their air of expectation, their awareness that the arrival of war meant they were soon to graduate four of their number, but that their time was coming, too. He looked toward his home, also aware that women wanted to nurture. Please to God that Meri wouldn't slide away from him again.

Their lodgers trooped inside first, to be met at the door with towels and Mrs. Perry's stern injunction to strip and wrap in a towel.

They did as commanded, which made Betty turn away and laugh. Mrs. Perry ordered them upstairs, then faced him.

"Master Able, your wife said you are to come upstairs as-is."

"Am I in the brig?" he asked. "She was unhappy with me this morning."

Mrs. Perry rolled her eyes and pointed to the stairs. Able knew as well as the next man when to take orders.

Meri sat on their bed, holding out a towel. He stripped and let her wrap him up, listening to her mild scold as she wondered how he kept from coming down with his death by a cold, or putrid throat, or pneumonia, and what would she do then? Bury him in at sea and be forced to earn her bread in a grog shop?

He listened to her, dried off, then folded her in his arms. She whispered into his chest, "I heard Davey volunteered for the fleet."

"Aye, he did. He wants to be a loblolly boy and work in a sickbay," Able said. No sense in trying to fool the unfoolable. "I have some thoughts on the matter, so do not despair yet, Mrs. Six."

"I do not like this part of your job," she said, helping him into dry small clothes, even though they both knew he needed no assistance.

"I don't, either, if it's any consolation," he told her. "Blame Boney for wanting to rule the world."

"Hurry up, Durable. Mrs. Perry has no patience with dawdlers." She left the room.

"How long am I going to be Durable?" he called after her.

"Until I decide you are not."

He was Durable only until a knock on the door later that night, after he gave up attempting to insinuate more calculus into heads far too excited about going to the fleet to pit themselves against one of Sir Isaac Newton's embarrassment of riches. A pity, that. He had been about to introduce Gottfried Leibniz's easier approach to the calc, too.

He opened the door, and could have fallen down in relief to see a man bearing a twice-folded document, the corner of which had a single word: Haslar.

He sent the fellow away with a coin, closed the door, and leaned against it, prying off the seal of the Sick and Hurt Board. He read the reply in the usual burst of words, then made himself read it again the way ordinary people did. Occasionally there was a certain pleasure in savoring something, and this was one of those times.

He took the stairs two at a time, then reminded himself that he was twenty-six years old and not a child ready to pluck at some kind lady's sleeve until he had her attention. He knew plenty of ways to get his wife's attention, but this one required some dignity, since he didn't relish being Durable.

He stood in the doorway as she patted the last child, tugged up the blanket on another, and answered a question concerning breakfast from John Mark, who still seemed to worry about food more than the other two. She blew a final kiss into the room, then closed the door.

He couldn't help that he grinned like a fool as he handed over the letter right there in the hall.

"I can't take much more today, Durable," she said.

As she read the letter, she sagged against the wall. He picked her up and her arms went around his neck.

"Will this do?" he asked, and she nodded. "I'm Able?" She nodded again.

Carrying her into their room, he deposited her gently on their bed. She clung to him, and he felt her relief flow right into his own body. He lay down beside her, because it was always the best place to be.

"I couldn't say anything until I knew for certain that the superintendent would see it my way, but he owed me a favor," Able said. "Are you all right? You're not one to faint."

"It's been quite a day of emotions," she said simply. "You truly have arranged for him to be a loblolly boy at Haslar?"

"He'll be one mile away from you. Hospitals on dry land need loblolly boys, too. Davey has the wit to become a pharmacist's mate, and we'll see what else."

"Why does the superintendent owe you a favor?"

"A simple thing."

"For you, maybe ..." she began.

"I was laid up for a few weeks .... You know that scar on my thigh which you like to kiss, before moving on to adjacent attractions?"

She nodded, and he saw her blush.

"He needed a particular tool to delve deeper into an abdominal wound. I designed him one and supervised its construction. I told you it was a simple thing."

"Are you always going to amaze me?" Meri asked.

"I'd rather astound you with my prowess in bed and my blinding good looks," he teased.

"Able! For heaven's sake."

He pointed to the letter. "In two days, *you'll* take David Ten to Haslar. That is an order."

Chapter Forty~Five

cᴏ⌒⌒ᴏ

MERIDEE TOOK DAVID TEN, the Royal Navy's newest loblolly boy, to Haslar Hospital two days later and left him in the care of Superintendent Welby, who assured her Davey could return to Saint's Way occasionally for meals.

"It won't be easy here, Davey," she said, as Surgeon Welby and her boy walked her back to the entrance.

"I know, Mam," he said, "and I know I'll be afraid now and then. I want to do my part for king and country."

She held him close and breathed in his fragrance of wool and little boy, and that odor of brine she also noticed about her husband. Where it came from, she wasn't certain. Maybe she smelled that way, too. The ocean had a way of seeping into a person's heart, so why not the pores, as well?

"What would Master Six say at a time like this?" she asked as she nodded to Surgeon Welby, who held open the door.

"Probably, 'Go oon naow, Mizdress Six, and tayk heersilf hoome,' " Davey said, so she was still laughing as she climbed into the waiting conveyance Master Six had insisted upon.

"Able, I felt like Hannah in the Bible, taking her son Samuel to that old Levite in the temple," she told her husband that night. "Dear me. Maybe I shouldn't be a house mam to these waifs and strays, if I am going to get so teary-eyed every time one of them moves on in the world."

"Headmaster Croker discussed that with me this very morning," he said. "He already has two new lads in mind for your extra-special care."

She put her hand on his arm. "Let me have a few weeks to get used to the idea that Stephen and Davey …." She couldn't go on, still wondering over how quickly little boys could worm their way into her heart.

"We'll see," he told her. "You might need to bear me up in a week when my older students go to the fleet."

He closed his eyes and she automatically put her hand over them, well aware they would soon be racing behind their lids. "You've trained them all you can," she soothed, as her practical nature surfaced. "Able, not everyone dies, who goes to sea." She nudged him. "And you accuse me of high drama!"

"I do, don't I?" he said, cuddling her close. "You're right; there are quite a few of us who live to fight another day. I shouldn't worry so much, should I?"

He sighed and she heard all the uncertainty.

Words were easy, reality harder. The entire school turned out to send the four lads to the fleet as sworn servants of the Royal Navy. They wore their uniforms with the distinctive patch of St. Brendan the Navigator. Meridee pronounced them tidy, but Able called them squared away.

She had some idea how hard to maintain was his cheerful demeanor with the four boys singled out, at ages twelve and thirteen, for a taxing apprenticeship. Now their training would take on new meaning as they sailed to revolutionary Europe.

Even her eagerly given heart and body had not been enough to entirely force back the demons that tried to worm their way into an already over-crowded brain. These last few nights, she had done nothing more than hold him close as he recited all of Euclid's *Elements* out loud in what passed for sleep.

Euclid, dear Euclid. Meridee had to turn away to preserve her composure as Able gave his beloved, battered copy of *The Elements* to Janus Yarmouth, a most promising student of calculus and now an apprentice sailing master.

"You'll find time to look through Euclid when you're standing a dull midnight watch," Able told the boy. "I know I did."

"Aye, sir, but we all know how fast you read," Jan reminded him.

"I read Euclid more slowly," Able said in humorous protest.

Jan must have felt the loosening tie of student to master, now that he was a duly sworn member of the Royal Navy, too. "Sir, did it take you forty minutes more than your usual thirty to memorize it?"

"More like thirty to twenty," he said. "I cannot lie, Jan."

And so they were laughing as all four young men—how was it they looked older than mere boys now?—gave smart salutes to Headmaster Croker and Master Six and turned their faces toward the Channel.

"We'll have time for more calculus later," Able called, and Jan waved back.

Meridee kept her arm tight around Betty after she ran to give her twin a final kiss, then watched him climb into the jolly boat taking him and Jan to the HMS *Terror* and HMS *Albemarle* anchored in the Solent. Another jolly boat waited to take the other classmates to frigates anchored farther out.

"He's a brother to be proud of," she said to her maid of all work.

"He could die tomorrow, Mam," Betty whispered.

"We could all die tomorrow, my dear," Meridee whispered back. "I daresay your twin would remind you that a well-trained sailor has odds in his favor."

Her maid nodded, then gave her a searching glance out of workhouse eyes. "As bad as the workhouse is, it sometimes feels safer than the world, think on."

It was. Trust a workhouse miss to know the difference.

"This life is better, my dear, as onerous as it feels right now," she said. "Let's stop at our favorite bakery and see what Mr. Bartleby has of a spectacular nature to drive away our megrims."

"My lower boys number seven, and my upper grade stands at eight, all of whom can swim. We are fifteen to our original twenty-four," Able announced a week later, after another session in the stone basin. "Tomorrow we are arranging ballast in that jolly boat I think I will not return, if no one seems to miss it." He put a casual arm around Meridee as she set the table in the dining room, since Betty was lying down with cramps from her monthly.

He stopped her and took the plates from her hands. "Here and here and here," he said, placing them, then shrugged. "For the life of me, I can never remember whether the forks belong on the left side or the right side."

"You're also not very good at simple adding and subtracting," she said as she edged past him to set the knives and forks. "The butcher came to me hat in hand this morning to say that someone in this household, who put the initials A.S. on a bill along with the funds, had underpaid him."

"Did I foul that?" he asked, tugging at her apron strings until they came undone.

"Royally." Meridee poked his chest. "I paid him the correct amount and sent him on his way rejoicing, after promising you will have no more hand in the matter."

"Why do you tolerate me, Meri-deelectable?" he asked.

"Heaven only knows," she said, although she could have given him any number of reasons. "You stick to the calculus and I will somehow manage adding and subtracting. What is it about genius? Sometimes you are not so smart, Unendurable Six."

"Since I do not know anyone like me, I cannot even hazard a guess," he said cheerfully.

Even now, weeks after the sailing of the frigates, followed by more and more ships leaving their Portsmouth anchorage, Meridee wasn't certain her husband had reconciled himself to his students in the fleet. Grace Croker assured her that Able taught in the classroom next to hers with his usual flair.

"I hear them laughing. I peeked in once to see them balancing chairs on top of each other," she said over tea. "When I asked what they were doing, he said something about Newton and gravity."

"I would like to sit in his classroom someday," Meridee said. She took another sip, grateful how easily tea went down. *I wish he still did not mutter about Euclid*, she thought. *I am getting tired of Greeks.*

Grace Croker took her leave then, after reminding her they were coming to dinner tonight in her brother's private quarters. "I tell my brother I want to entertain now and then," she said, kissing Meridee on both cheeks. "I also said it would be something besides everlasting pickled herring and spotted dick!"

Meridee was putting the finishing touches on Able's neck cloth when Mrs. Perry called upstairs to say there was a messenger at the door. When he did not return, she finished buttoning up the back of her dress, except for the one button she could never reach, and went to the top of the landing.

Meridee shrieked and ran down the stairs, horrified to see her dear man prostrate on the floor, gasping as though there wasn't enough air finding its way into his lungs.

She recognized the astounded messenger as one of Sir B's servants. She knelt beside Able and tugged at his shoulders, trying to turn him toward her, while Mrs. Perry paid the messenger and slammed the door.

"Able, oh please!" Meridee said. "Mrs. Perry, do you see a note?"

The cook forcibly moved Able into Meridee's arms, where he tried to breathe. Mrs. Perry moved his leg and found a crumpled note. Smoothing it out, she handed it to Meridee. Her hand shook as she read the note, cried out, and pulled her husband closer.

"I cannot manage you alone," she said, speaking as distinctly as she could into Able's ear. "Who should I send for? Please tell me, my love. Please!"

Nothing. She looked up to see her lodgers on the stairs, fear on their faces. "Master Able has had a setback." She looked over her shoulder. "Mrs. Perry, please take them into the kitchen."

The cook gestured and the boys came down the stairs, filing past her and Able, who now lay in her arms, breathing again, his eyes closed.

"Please, Mam, was it something we did?" Nick asked.

"Heavens, no," she managed, as her own heart shattered into tiny pieces. "I'll tell you later."

"It's as I saw in my dream," Able told her, his eyes still closed, his voice ragged. "They're dying one by one."

They were still crouched together in the hall when Headmaster Croker ran inside without knocking. His face its own Greek tragedy mask, he knelt beside them as Meridee gently rocked her husband and stroked his face.

"Sir B warned me this might kill him," she whispered. "It is Jan Yarmouth."

Chapter Forty-Six

⌒∞⌒

Don't console me, Able thought. *Don't question me. Don't tell me it was just an accident. Don't tell me we are all called upon to make sacrifices in wartime.*

He sensed that he lay in his own bed, a nightshirt on, but with only the vaguest memory—unusual for him—of Meri removing his clothing and snapping at someone else in the room who tried to help—unusual for her. He heard voices that were mere mumbles, and then, oddest of all, nothing— no thoughts of any kind. He seemed to be drifting through space and even beyond the planets, into an empty part of the universe inhabited by men wearing clothing of earlier times.

He recognized Galileo first, with his droopy eyes and high cheekbones. And there was Johannes Kepler, with a high ruff around his neck and intense brown eyes. Beyond him sat René Descartes, distinct with his long nose and supercilious expression. He smiled to see Isaac Newton and Gottfried Leibniz sitting far, far away from each other and darting angry glances back and forth.

"Gentlemen, gentlemen," he murmured. "Have some patience. There is fame enough to go around."

Then he felt his wife rest her head against his chest. He breathed deep of her familiar lavender fragrance, even as he sniffed the salt of her tears. He wanted to say her name, but there were more scientists and philosophers piling into the room in his mind's universe. Artists, too. Michelangelo lay on his back painting the Sistine Chapel, while Leonardo gnawed his lip over a curious flying contraption with a rotor on top.

Dear God above, you terrible, omnipotent, unfeeling deity, he thought. *I told Jan Yarmouth to imagine any kind of machine he thought the world needed. He said something about a glorified ship of the air that could travel to the moon*

*and back. Did we tempt your domain? Are you angry with us? With me? Why
Jan? Why not me?*

He must have spoken out loud, because Meridee sobbed into his nightshirt
that was already wet, either with his sweat or her tears.

"Able, God is not angry with you. Please believe me," she said.

He tried to speak, but the lure of the scientists assembling distracted him.
He smiled to see Aristotle chatting with Nicolaus Copernicus, and there
was Galen in Greek robes, talking to Antonie van Leeuwenhoek, chubby
Dutchman with a flowing wig. Van Leeuwenhoek had observed his own
sperm under a microscope he built. Able chuckled. Meridee would probably
laugh if he told her that, but she would also blush.

Why were these men gesturing toward him, a workhouse bastard who
couldn't even cope when his prize pupil died in a stupid accident at sea? He
didn't belong in this exalted group of men, each of them as dead as Janus
Yarmouth. He was nothing and nobody.

As much as Meri tugged on him, he couldn't resist the urge to pull away.
He sighed with pleasure. Seated beside an empty chair sat Euclid, his old
companion through years of loneliness and self doubt. Euclid smiled and Able
smiled back. "I know you," Able said out loud.

Euclid nodded, pointed to the empty chair and patted it. Able stood where
he was, his attention captured by a sign high above them all. It was in Greek,
but that was no obstacle. " 'Polymaths,' " he read. "I belong with you. You are
my friends. How kind of you to make room for me."

He took another step closer to the empty chair, then turned around,
startled, when Meridee called his name.

"Don't you dare leave me!" she said most distinctly. He knew a command
when he heard one, no fool he.

Still, he looked back at the assembly of giants, his friends, his mentors.
Euclid no longer beseeched him, however. Able frowned to see someone else
sit down in the chair he wanted. Something told him it was a man from the
future, a fellow wearing felt slippers, with a moustache sorely in need of a
trim, and wispy, white, wild hair.

"I have lost my place to an interloper from the future," Able said. Someone
cleared his throat and he glanced at Newton, who gestured him closer. "Yes,
sir? What would you like from me?" he asked.

"We're a lonely lot, boy," the exalted, amazing Sir Isaac told him. "Go back
where you were. Teach those lads like yourself. We'll keep for another fifty or
sixty years."

He wanted to argue with them, but someone else was arguing louder. He
heard, "Leave me alone with him," countered by "But you need help," and "Let
me summon a physician." He heard, "Leave us alone!" and knew deep in his

heart and soul that Meridee was fighting for him. "Get out, the whole pack of you!" *Really, Meri*, he thought. *I didn't know you were so ferocious.*

He heard a great whooshing sound, as a monstrous figure carrying a cross and an astrolabe sucked in all the polymaths, geniuses, philosophers, artists, and musicians in his odd universe. Immensely grateful, he realized Meri had not been shouting at someone in the room, but at his spectral colleagues.

Able grabbed Meridee, the only anchor in his peculiar life, and she clung to him. The others tumbled away, leaving him alone in an empty, distant room.

As he felt a familiar hand stroke his forehead, he relaxed. He saw Meri's dear face without opening his eyes. She was beautiful and kind, and apparently quite willing to banish a roomful of well-meaning people, as well as the brilliant specters crowding in his brain. He had no idea she could be so fierce.

He probably deserved a good scold. He had behaved in a most unmanly fashion, dropping like a rock over the death of a student with abundant potential, gone forever. *Blame Napoleon*, a quiet voice told him. *Defeat Boney by providing the best navigators for the Royal Navy.*

Wait. Did he hear that from his cosmic friends? Or did someone more infinitely precious just whisper in his ear?

He knew sound advice, especially when his dear one lay across his chest, inhaling and exhaling with him, as though compelling him to breathe on his own.

He had his doubts. What if those awful, blood-drenched dreams returned? Could he dismiss them? Had he the power? Might as well decide if Meridee Six really wanted him, with all his quirks and weirdness.

"Very well, Meri," he said. His voice sounded distinct, and he knew he spoke out loud this time. "If you want me, you must give me some good news. It has to be something grand enough to give me reason to keep going, because I need it in the worst way. If you have nothing, I cannot stay."

He opened his eyes as Meri sat up, her hair wild around her face, tears on her cheeks, worry in those eyes he loved so well. She gulped and turned rosy. He also saw two men against the wall by the door, one standing and one in a wheeled chair, so he understood her reticence.

"Good news," he repeated. "Handsomely now," he added, which made her smile.

"I have some." She took his hand and placed his palm against her belly. "You're going to be a father," she whispered. "Is that good enough news? We need you *here*—your students, me, and this baby of ours."

He knew he was having trouble breathing again because Meri breathed along with him until he righted himself in the HMS *Six*.

"How long have you known?" he asked.

"About seven weeks."

"Why didn't you tell me?"

"Your mind is so busy," she said, and his heart broke a little. "I ... I wasn't certain you had time for two of us. Prove me wrong, my love."

"I will," he replied. "I pledge you my troth on it."

Her eyes filled with tears at his mention of their marriage vows. She smiled, and became his keeper again.

"Tomorrow you are marching to a barber shop, because your hair is in serious want of cutting. You will not, repeat *not*, ever attempt to manage household funds again. You will teach the calculus and how to work a sextant, and introduce a generation of navigators to sines, cosines, tangents, and ... and isos ... isocentric? Eccentric triangles."

He laughed at that and patted her belly gently. "I promise, Mrs. Six."

She whispered in his ear, "No more Euclid when we are in bed together, just you and me. Banish him. I know you can. You can do anything."

You just raised me from the dead, he thought. No sense in telling her, though. She might get a swelled head.

Chapter Forty-Seven

❧

"DURABLE, YOU KNOW I would follow you to the ends of the galaxy, but my current condition would suggest I not go swimming with you," Meridee said later on in the day, after Able had eaten and actually slept a little.

Blushing appropriately, his darling sat on the edge of their bed while he lounged most comfortably against both pillows, hands behind his head. Sir B watched them, his eyes filled with something close to glee.

"We will agree that you need more diversions, something to take your mind to a better, calmer place," Sir B said. "Move me closer, Gervaise. Either that or push me up and down so I can pace."

Meri laughed at that, perhaps banishing any embarrassment she felt about speaking of what was going on inside her. She may not have been more than seven weeks pregnant, but already she was proprietary of their baby.

"Anything not to be Durable," he joked, and she squeezed his leg. "Very well, Mrs. Six, I will concede the necessity of not continuing our swimming lessons."

He closed his eyes and started to think about his recent brush with infinity and the friends waiting for him in that weird cosmic anteroom. His betraying eyes! Meri's hand covered them and she told him to relax.

"Able," was all she said, but it was enough. He willed himself to only one or two thoughts pinging around, which felt like his brain was on holiday. One thought concerned their unborn child, which soothed him remarkably.

He opened his eyes, and she took her hand away, resting it on his chest over his heart. "That's better," he said, "but Sir B is right."

To his amusement, Gervaise did begin to push his former captain here and there, until Sir B stopped his valet.

"I think I have it. Wheel me closer, Gervaise."

Sir B came as close to the bed as he could. The smile in his eyes was contagious, at least to Meri, who smiled back. *My God, the woman was beautiful.* He had read somewhere about the glow of pregnancy, but Able had no idea it came so soon, even when their child couldn't be larger than her little finger yet.

"I sense a conspiracy," he said.

Meri turned innocent eyes on him. "Not at all, dearest. Don't you see that Sir B has an infectious enthusiasm?"

He didn't. "This must be added to my blind spot, you two. I don't seem to pick up those cues as rapidly as you do. But say on, sir. I know I need at least one release that doesn't involve my wife. Meri, will you always blush?"

"You are almost Durable again," she said, her face flaming. "Don't press me."

Sir B laughed out loud. "Gervaise, find yourself something to do in another room."

After the door closed, the captain in Sir Belvedere St. Anthony came to the forefront again. *Once a captain, always a captain,* Able supposed. It was certainly true of sailing masters.

"What was it you used to do in the South Pacific when we were becalmed?" he asked. "Remember? Well, damn my eyes, certainly you remember."

Able did. "We all did that, sir," he said. "We found the fishing tackle, lowered a jolly boat or two, and cast in a line. Why was that remarkable?"

"The others were fishing," Sir B said. "I watched you. What were you doing? Sometimes you never even baited a hook."

What was he doing? Did this captain-mentor-friend know him almost as well as Meri? The whole experience expanded to Able's mental view: the endless water, the desultory wave here and there, the sun bright and hot, the creak of the frigate, the odor of heated tar, and the ever-present tang of brine. He knew.

"Captain, I was not thinking of anything in particular."

"Well, lad?" Captain B asked. "How did you feel afterward?"

"I was at peace."

Sir B nodded and addressed himself to Meri. "Madam Six, what say you I take this man off your hands at least once weekly and go fishing?"

"My life will be simpler," she joked. "How will you manage?"

His captain turned his attention to Able. "Master Six, are you aware that I own a little yacht that has seen no action since, well, since my own misfortune?"

Able knew better than to pity the one-legged, weary man sitting so close to his bed, the man who was probably never out of pain. *We all bear a burden,* he thought. *Who am I to imagine for even a moment that mine is the heaviest?*

"Summer is nearly upon us," Able said. "I have no ..." he paused as a wave of pain washed over him. Meri saw it and took his hand. "I have no calculus students right now, so my late afternoons are open. Aye, sir, let us fish. I can easily commandeer some lads to crew such a vessel."

"Bring them 'round this Saturday to that wharf below Gunwharf," Sir B said. "I have the tackle."

"Aye, aye, sir. Meri, summon Gervaise, will you?"

After she left the room, Able touched his captain's hand, noting how bird-bone thin it was, with every vein in high relief. "Thank you," he said simply. "I will never be out of your debt."

He knew Sir B was not a man who enjoyed compliments, but his former captain surprised him. "Master Six, I have never known anyone like you. Whether what we do with you is a blessing or not, England needs you." He looked toward the door. "Meridee needs you more."

THEY TOOK OUT THE incongruously named *Jolly Roger* on Saturday. The water and waves beyond the Isle of Wight had more chop to them. Able did his best to ignore Nick's sudden turn of head as he vomited into the ocean.

"Sorry, sir," he muttered.

"You're in good company, Nick," Sir B said as he lounged in his chair lashed to the railing. "I believe Admiral Nelson himself suffers from *mal de mer*."

Able turned the tiller over to one of his older students and let down an anchor, and another. The movement slowed, then stopped, and Nick sighed with relief. "You'll accustom yourself, lad," Able said.

Able rolled up the legs on the rough seaman's trousers he wore. The sun was warm on his back as his mind flashed to those calm days in the South Pacific at latitude .... *Stop it*, he ordered his brain. *You know the latitude and longitude, but let it go.*

He put his long legs in the gap in the railing and felt water on his ankles. The yacht listed because Sir B sat in his heavy wheeled chair close by. The water reached Able's calves, and he smiled inside, completely at home in his watery world. In went his line, without benefit of bait.

Amazing how quickly his thoughts slowed to one or two complexities, and then one, the ineffable image of his wife, his keeper, his lover, his lodestone. That was all he needed. Fish might be nice, but they weren't necessary. He hadn't come to fish. Even in those days in the South Pacific when everyone welcomed some change to their dreary diet of ship's biscuit and kegged meat, he had never fished to catch fish.

He knew he would not burn from the sun, thanks to whoever his father was. His skin would darken, but he would not suffer. He glanced at Nick, with his light complexion, and resolved to cajole a ship's surgeon out of some zinc oxide for his lads.

He observed the water, at peace. After an hour and twenty-three minutes, he took his line out and stood up. Two of his older students had caught a few fish, and Sir B's eyes were closed.

"We had better start back," Able said to the boy at the tiller, who was dozing, too. "Anchors aweigh, lads."

He stood by the gap, his stance wide because a sailor never forgets. Sir B opened his eyes, and Able saw all the understanding. *I have two keepers*, he thought, and the idea warmed his workhouse heart, the one that might always search for his father.

"Able, I have a brilliant notion," Sir B said. "Call it a veritable epiphany. Suppose your lovely wife is brought to bed with twins, one boy and one girl? You can name them Polly and Matt."

Able laughed at the same moment that Sir B pushed him into the ocean with his remaining good leg. He gasped and thrashed, then treaded water, loving the feel of his second home.

Above the amusement of his students and the unrepentant Captain Sir Belvedere St. Anthony, Able heard the faraway laughter of his spectral mentors, biding their time. He hoped it was distant thunder instead.

Epilogue

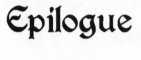

SUMMER CAME, AND WITH it the return to port of Jamie MacGregor and the HMS *Terror*, battered and in need of a dry dock to fix a puzzling rudder shimmy. His twin close to his side, Jamie ate dinner with them, telling them of Mediterranean fleet actions from Malta to Egypt. Nick and John Mark, their eyes wide, took it all in. Betty piled more and more dessert on her brother's plate until Nick kindly reminded her that younger boys like excessive amounts of dessert, too. He had a way with words, did Nick.

Jamie requested a moment alone with Able after dinner, before he had to return to his ship. "We're still waiting our turn for the dry dock. Captain Baldwin said he will give me permission to board here with you during repairs, if you'll have me."

"Without question. I'll drop him a note too," Able said. "You might also want to accompany me on fishing trips beyond the Isle."

"Captain Baldwin is a bit of a stickler, sir," James said. "He might consider that too much fun."

"Not the way I'll word it," Able said. "And if that's not good enough, I'll sic Sir B on him."

Jamie shuddered elaborately and they both laughed.

They walked together by the stone basin, which in addition to the jolly boat now boasted floating platforms where the lads in both divisions were learning to arrange ballast to keep it afloat, even when the boys tasked to be the current created waves that could swamp an unbalanced ship. No one wanted to take a turn treading water and being the current, until Meri promised biscuits to the best waves crew. She had a way with little boys.

"They're learning, and they all swim like porpoises," Able said. "I'd like to get Mrs. Six back in the water, but she reminds me that someone is already swimming around inside her and that is enough at present."

"Congratulations, sir," Jamie said. "You'll be an excellent father."

"I never knew my own," he replied. "I sometimes wonder if he is yet alive."

While they walked, Jamie told Able of Jan's death, a freak accident when a damaged yardarm under a jury rig suddenly dropped to the deck as Able's best pupil passed below.

"We met up with Jan's ship at Malta, and the sailing master told me what happened," Jamie said. "The crash paralyzed him from the chest down. The surgeon said he wasn't in any particular pain, but Jan only lived another two hours. The paralysis moved higher and his lungs ceased to function."

Able let the healing balm of tears slide down his face. "I wish matters had been different—we all do—but sadly, such is life at sea."

Jamie nodded. He reached into his uniform jacket and took out good old Euclid. "The captain told me Jan asked the surgeon to lean it against his neck so he could feel it, and get it back to you somehow. Here it is, sir."

Able took the book, thinking of the years of comfort it had given him, grateful Euclid had not failed Janus Yarmouth at the end. *Let him join you in that polymath circle, Euclid*, he thought. *He's a fast learner.*

He returned his attention to Jamie, pleased to see that he had added several inches in the three months since their farewell. He noticed confidence in his eyes and a firmness to his jaw. Jamie MacGregor was growing up.

"Would you like to keep Euclid?" Able asked. "If you are superstitious, feel free to tell me nay."

"I would like to keep him, sir," Jamie said quickly, "but I didn't want to say anything. I know Euclid is special to you."

"He's yours."

He saw Jamie off and ambled back to Saint's Way, in no particular hurry. There in the door stood his keeper, gently rounded now. Last night she had taken his hand while they sat close together as he thought and she knitted, and placed it against her belly. "Feel that?" she asked, her face glowing.

"Bit of a traveler," he had said, nearly overwhelmed. He poked back gently and felt a returning kick. "He'll wear you out, Meri-deependable."

Here she was now, beckoning him in. He told the usual cacophony in his brain to cease for the night, and it did. He had promised his wife there wouldn't be anyone in their bed except the two of them, and Euclid had to go.

"Is our baby entertaining you?"

"Certainly," she said, and put her arm around his middle, drawing him into their home. "I've started talking to him, but only when no one else is around." She gave Able a bump with her hip. "I wouldn't for the world usurp your role as mutterer-in-chief, you and Euclid."

"Wretched female," he teased.

Arm in arm, they walked into the dining room, where their two remaining lodgers waited impatiently.

"I told you Master Six would be along soon," she said as Able pulled her chair out for her. "Nick has something to tell us that will not wait."

"Then accept my apology for dawdling," Able said. "Out with it, lad."

Nick pushed back his chair and stood up, shoulders back, eyes front, hands so tight together that his knuckles showed white. He looked directly at Meridee.

"Mam, I've decided on a surname, if it pleases you."

"You hardly need *my* permission, Nick," she said. "Will we like it?"

"I hope so." He took a deep breath. "How does Nick Bonfort sound to you, Mrs. Six?"

Meridee's gasp told Able what he needed to know.

"I … I mean, you're not precisely using it now, are you?" Nick asked, uncertain. "Y-you said it could be the name of some I admire and I …."

He never finished his sentence. Meri rose so quickly that her chair fell backward. She grabbed Nick and they clung together.

"She likes it, sir," John Mark told Able. "Last night, Nick asked me what I thought. I wasn't certain."

"Mrs. Six has a soft heart," Able said.

"I love it, Nick," she said finally, holding the boy off to see him better. "We'll go to Headmaster Croker and see what we have to do to legalize everything."

"You really don't mind?" he asked, and Able heard all the workhouse uncertainty.

"Nick, I have four sisters and no brothers," she said and drew him close again. "This means *you* can carry on the Bonfort name. Thank *you.*"

The sheer loveliness of her words sank into Able's very bone marrow. He thought of lonely Isaac Newton, England's greatest genius, who was probably still sniping away at Gottfried Leibniz over who had devised the calculus first. That cosmic anteroom of legendary minds he had nearly joined seemed to fade with every day in his wife's presence.

He was a man most fortunate.

A WELL-KNOWN VETERAN OF the romance writing field, **Carla Kelly** is the author of forty-two novels and three non-fiction works, as well as numerous short stories and articles for various publications. She is the recipient of two RITA Awards from Romance Writers of America for Best Regency of the Year, two Spur Awards from Western Writers of America, three Whitney Awards, and a Lifetime Achievement Award from **Romantic Times**.

Carla's interest in historical fiction is a byproduct of her lifelong study of history. She's held a variety of jobs, including public relations work for major hospitals and hospices, feature writer and columnist for a North Dakota daily newspaper, and ranger in the National Park Service (her favorite job) at Fort Laramie National Historic Site and Fort Union Trading Post National Historic Site. She has worked for the North Dakota Historical Society as a contract researcher.

Interest in the Napoleonic Wars at sea led to numerous novels about the British Channel Fleet during that conflict. Of late, Carla has written three novels set in southeast Wyoming in the frontier era that focus on her Mormon background and her interest in ranching.

You can find Carla on the Web at www.CarlaKellyAuthor.com.